A LARK'S FLIGHT
VERITY LARK MYSTERIES
BOOK II

LYNN MESSINA

potatoworks press • greenwich village

Title Production by The Book Whisperer

Never miss a new release! Join Lynn's mailing list.

Prologue

✦✦✦

Thursday, June 5
 12:52 p.m.

Of the small assortment of things Damien Matlock remembered with absolute clarity about his mother, her appearance was the sharpest. Harboring little fondness for either the country or her child, the duchess spent the vast majority of her days in London, receiving visitors in the extravagant mansion in Berkeley Square. On the rare occasions when she deigned to visit the family seat in far-off Cambridgeshire, it was in the company of a large coterie of admirers as well as a paramour or two, and she would smile with a sort of jaded familiarity as they gawked at the splendor of Haverill Hall.

The stately home was truly magnificent, and the duchess would stand in the middle of the soaring entry hall, her graceful arms held aloft as she gestured to the painted ceiling teeming with beauty as Cybele crossed the sky in her golden chariot drawn by lions.

Although the country did not suit his mother, the mural did, for there were few things she enjoyed more than showing off. There was a particular glow in her eye that ignited only when she knew she was the source of envy or discontent in others, and she would laugh with a restrained coquettishness, as if she could not help being charming *and* amused.

Damien recalled that laughter well, for it seemed to follow her everywhere.

Her laughter and the cloud of lavender that lingered in every room and the brusque cruelty with which she treated her hateful husband—these were all fixed in his mind.

And yet it was her face that was most indelibly pressed in his memory: those sharp cheekbones, that sculpted jawline, beguiling hazel eyes that sparkled from every direction. Reynolds had replicated each stunning detail in his portrait of her, which hung now on the first-floor landing of the primary staircase in Kesgrave House. Every time one climbed the steps, there she was, her beauty growing finer the closer one drew.

His father, the fifth duke, objected to the placement, for he had loathed the obligation of having to look at his hated spouse when she was not present to bedevil him, and had the canvas removed to the portrait gallery. Tucked in the far-left corner, it was all but hidden by Thomas Hudson's towering depiction of the first Duke of Kesgrave. His mother, who had not overcome her humble beginnings as a cobbler's daughter to be obscured by a long-dead courtier with an excess of chins, returned the work to the top of the stairs. In response, his grace hung it in the blue parlor, a room notable only for its lack of use. Three hours later, it was back on the landing. Furious, the duke relocated it to a third-floor guestroom, then the servants' hall, then the stables.

Every time he moved it, she moved it back.

La Reina, whose illustrious career as the most celebrated courtesan in all of England had been built on tenacity and mulishness, was content to play the game for months, if not years, should that be what was required to emerge as victor over her husband.

The duke, however, did not have the temperament for a long campaign.

Brief and brutal—that was his mantra.

Acting rashly, usually out of anger or annoyance, he rarely thought more than one step ahead. Having no end point in mind meant he seldom reached it, which was why his wife often outmaneuvered him. In this battle, as in all others, he lost interest after a few days and consequently had to endure the placid smugness of La Reina's Mona Lisa smile every time he mounted his own staircase.

Damien, lacking affection for either parent, made no effort to move the portrait after they died. Merely the thought of mentioning it to the housekeeper felt complicit, as if he were allowing the deceased pair to draw him into their petty squabble. Leaving it where it was—within his sights but beneath his notice—struck him as the only rational response, and if he paid attention to the work at all, it was only to appreciate the artist's expert hand. The silk on the duchess's silver dress shimmered with depth and dimension.

All that was true, yes, and yet it remained a startlingly faithful reproduction of his mother's face. Intimately familiar with its lines and contours, he knew what it meant when he saw her double in the doorway of Fortescue's Asylum for Pauper Children.

To be clear: He did not know what it meant, not in any specific sense.

Her actual identity was a mystery, but he knew he was looking at a relative of his mother's. The woman was someone in the Price family line—presumably a younger sister, given the remarkable resemblance.

The problem with that conjecture was his mother did not have any sisters, let alone one who was a full generation younger. The baby of the family and inordinately beautiful even in leading strings, she was pampered by her father, a respectable tradesman who did the best he could with limited means. He could provide security and a kind of comfort but not excitement, opulence, or ease, and she craved excitement, opulence, and ease.

Lorraine Price wanted to stand on the top step of a grand staircase and peer down on everyone with a glimmer of amused superiority, and when a cit offered her a reasonable alternative to her mundane present and dreary future, she accepted his improper proposal as if it were precisely the opportunity for which she had been waiting.

Damien knew these details about his mother because it was in the report he had compiled a few years after her death from scarlet fever. The file went into great depth about her early life, and although he had never met his grandfather, he could recite his address, per annum income of his shop, and the name of the tailor who fitted his waistcoats. According to the report, Mr. Price was a respectable man who took great sadness in his daughter's decision to trade her virtue for status and firmly believed she would have chosen a different path if her mother had lived long enough to guide her. Unfortunately, Mrs. Price died in childbirth a mere eighteen months after Lorraine was born, leaving the widower to fend as best he could with four children.

Mr. Price hired a series of governesses to raise them but never remarried.

Based on what he knew about his maternal grandfather, Damien rather suspected he would like the man well enough but made no attempt to establish contact because the gulf that yawned between a duke and a cobbler seemed unbridgeable to him. Every attempt to picture the meeting ended in awkward silence, and he knew Mr. Price would feel no more at ease in a Berkeley Square drawing room than he would in a Cheapside parlor.

Aware that the woman he had spotted at Fortescue's could not be a younger sister required him to consider another explanation. He toyed briefly with the notion that she might be a cousin or a niece, as there were plenty of Price relatives to justify the supposition, but it did not wash. The similarity was simply too great for the connection not to be closer.

She could only be a daughter.

It was not an outlandish deduction.

His mother was a courtesan, and as such was constantly at risk of increasing.

An unexpected pregnancy was the reason she had married the duke, who had seen an opportunity to thwart his brother, appall his mother, offend society, and secure an heir all in one vicious stroke.

Having arrived at this conclusion, Damien assured himself it bore no consequence. It was not as though he would track the woman down and introduce himself. Even if they did share a mother, they were naught to each other, and he refused to be so maudlin in his sensibility as to think of her as his sister. Imagining his mother's by-blow at Kesgrave House was as impossible as imagining his grandfather, and he knew there was nothing to be gained from it but awkwardness and discomfort.

He pushed the idea from his mind, and when it nudged its way back in, he pushed it out again. He would not allow curiosity to overcome his good sense, and even as he mounted his gig to return to the asylum, he told himself he was not returning to the asylum.

It had been exactly the same with Bea.

In his head he refused to do the very thing he was doing, such as climbing the tree outside her room in the Lake District or paying a condolence call when he read that absurd death notice for Mr. Davies in the *London Daily Gazette.* He could not fathom why he would bestow the pleasure of his attention on an impertinent busybody who displayed no respect for his authority.

Only a hoyden would flaunt his command—and grin with utter delight while doing so. He had never been so astonished in his entire life as when she openly questioned him in the drawing room at Lakeview Hall. He knew blaming Otley for his own death was ridiculous given the placement of the wound, and he knew the entire company knew that too. But recasting a readily apparent murder as suicide and having the company nod in docile agreement was what it meant to be the Duke of Kesgrave.

His standing ensured he could say whatever preposterous thing he desired and receive unwavering agreement. He could announce that the sky was green, and Wellington himself would note that it was an appealing chartreuse. It was an easy power to abuse, and Damien, mindful of the responsibility, deployed it sparingly. He had no interest in altering the reality of others unless it furthered a higher goal, such as figuring out who murdered the swindling spice trader without enduring the helpful support of a half dozen toadies.

And there was Bea, withholding her compliance.

Thank God, he thought now as he crossed the Thames into Lambeth.

He had noticed her among the party, a dour little thing with a frown etched permanently between her brows. Her discontent was not surprising, given both the quality of her relations—the silly aunt, the fawning cousins—and the multitude of services she was obliged to perform for them. It was quite obvious to even the most uninterested observer that she was nothing but an unpaid servant.

A workhorse, he determined, dismissing her as irrelevant.

And irrelevant she would have remained had she not wandered into the library a few seconds after he had stumbled across the freshly murdered corpse of Thomas Otley. He could have gone his entire life without seeing Beatrice Hyde-Clare's impish grin.

The notion terrified him.

All that he possessed—land, money, breeding, status—and he was still just as vulnerable to the capriciousness of fate as the humblest resident of St. Giles. He thought often of their late-night exchange in her room at Lakeview Hall, conducted after he had climbed the tree, and the amused disdain that lit her whole face as she asked him if he was now boasting about not boasting.

He was, yes, very much so, because he was driven by an inexplicable compulsion to earn her approval. He had recognized even then that there was something worthwhile in her judgment, and in seeking it he comprehended a revelation both startling and profound: For all his puffed-up consequence, for all his reality-altering significance, he had never liked himself so much as in that moment.

Bea enjoyed teasing him about the woman he should have married: a paragon of beauty and grace who smoothed feathers instead of ruffling them and never asked impertinent questions of her suspects (who did not even *have* suspects). She was only tweaking his nose, and yet he had to acknowledge the accuracy of the description. If not for her interference, he would have wed an Incomparable of impeccable taste and breeding and counted himself fortunate.

And it was that prospect that truly made his knees weak

with terror, for he could have so easily been that other man: the preening peacock satisfied with a dull union and convinced that his wife should be a credit to him rather than the other way around. It was bewildering for a man who had always considered his worth unassailable to realize he would have lost out on himself as much as Bea.

Turning onto Lambeth Road, he saw the gloomy towers of Fortescue's Asylum for Pauper Children come into view. It really was a grim building, all dark and brooding, with its gray stone and climbing vines, and it did not seem strange at all that something in its Gothic desolation brought Bea's child-hood fears to the fore.

Any orphan facing an uncertain future would be petrified at the thought of being consigned to such a desolate place.

And yet for all its grim dreariness, he could not help but feel a jolt of happiness as he contemplated the green expanse where Bea had revealed his impending fatherhood. He could not say it was the last place he had expected her to impart the news because he had never given the matter any thought. Scarcely married two months, he had not raised his head from the delights of the marital bed long enough to consider its fruits.

But as strange as the location was, it struck him yet again as the only appropriate setting. If Bea had made the announcement in a more conventional manner—while they were eating supper, for example, or reading quietly in the library—he would have immediately worried about her frame of mind. The prospect of childbirth was extremely daunting, and he did not want her to approach it without anything less than her usual confidence and equanimity.

Damien wished the same thing for himself and sought to quell his own fear by reminding himself he was accustomed to experiencing it. With her investigations, Bea frequently threw herself into dangerous situations, and if there was any consolation to be had in having a murderous earl try to suffocate the life out of one's spouse in her sitting room, it was that childbirth felt like a stroll through Hyde Park in comparison.

Bea fended off deadly assaults with dismaying regularity.

She would be fine.

But as he strode across the lawn to the building, he allowed that perhaps his parents had gone about it the right way, never caring about anyone but themselves. Selfishness spared them a tremendous amount of grief and anxiety. Their hearts were still broken, but in a defective way like a scale that no longer measured weight, not in a cripplingly sad way.

In that respect, the duke and courtesan had been very well suited.

He arrived at the door, and as he waited for someone to answer his knock, he assured himself again that the woman whom he had seen on this very threshold a few days before was not his sister. The resemblance was only a coincidence or —and he considered this prospect to be the more likely one —a mistake on his part. He had been standing a dozen feet away from her, and the shadow cast by the building made the light dim. She probably looked nothing like his mother.

It would serve him right to make this absurd effort to locate her only to discover her cheeks were broad flat plains and her chin was wide. Already, her height was wrong, for La Reina was famously petite—a pocket Venus, as an item in *Parker's General Advertiser and Morning Intelligencer* once described her—and the woman he spotted had been tall and willowy.

No, she was not his sister.

Impatient to be done with the whole business, he wrapped his knuckles against the door again. He felt foolish for even being there, and his foolishness made him cross. It was not as though he had heaps of time to waste, what with the weight of a vast estate on his shoulders as well as a burgeoning steam engine concern and manifold social obligations. Too embarrassed to admit he was chasing a phantom, he had told Bea he was interviewing new physicians with his dowager grandmother. It was the first time he had lied to her, and to make it slightly less of a falsehood, he intended to follow through on the meetings at some point—when precisely, he did not know. It would depend, he supposed, on how long this wild-goose chase lasted.

The door was answered by a giggling boy whose laughter suddenly ceased when he took note of the visitor. "You're not Pickle," he said accusingly.

Amused, Damien admitted he was not, no, just as a woman with a harried expression trotted to the door to apologize for her charge's impudence. "Matty is supposed to be in the dining room having a treat with the rest of the children. Do return there at once!"

"But there is no milk!" he protested. "Pickle is late with his delivery, and I can't eat a hot cross bun without milk."

The woman, unimpressed with this argument, pointed meaningfully down the hallway, and Matty, his lips pressed together sullenly, scampered away. As soon as he turned the corner, she smiled at the caller and apologized for the unruly greeting. Although she would not go so far as to say the children were usually docile, they were especially excitable on treat days. "We do it only once a month, so they look forward to it with uncontained excitement. But I am sure you do not care about that!" she added with a self-conscious titter as she stepped aside to allow him to enter. "You will want to speak with our head matron, your grace. Please let me take you to the front parlor, where you can wait for her."

Damien was not surprised she recognized him from his

previous visit. The head matron, Mrs. Chaffey, had led Bea and him on an exhaustive tour of the establishment to engage their interest and encourage a generous donation. They were shown every single leak in the roofs and had to evade drops of water like soldiers dodging bullets. Naturally, he could not blame her, for he was a very ripe fruit for the plucking.

Having led him to the front parlor, a square room with white walls and simple furnishings in which he and Bea had waited during their prior visit, she paused in the doorway and asked if she could get him anything. "Tea or coffee or a hot cross bun? They are fresh from the oven."

"Thank you, no," he said, clasping his hands behind his back. "I require only Mrs. Chaffey's attention."

"Then I will get her for you immediately, your grace," she said, ducking into a curtsey. Then she stepped sedately out of the room before breaking into an undignified run through the corridor to fetch the head matron.

Damien did not doubt that his visit would be the subject of much speculation and hope among the staff. Although the asylum seemed to be well funded, another wealthy patron would not go amiss, and he had no intention of disappointing. His steward had investigated the institution and found nothing untoward in either its bookkeeping or the treatment of its charges. There had been some terrible abuses under its previous governorship, but the bad actors had been rooted out several years ago and their replacements were by all accounts devoted and decent.

Mrs. Chaffey, a sturdy woman in a plain gray dress and well-worn shoes, greeted him warmly and owned herself pleasantly surprised to see him again. "I had assumed after my lengthy conversation with Mr. Stephens that all business going forward—if there *was* business—would be conducted either by him or via messenger. We are humbled that you would take such personal interest in us as to call again. Please, do sit down."

Despite his impatience, he took the seat across from her, one of a quartet of exceedingly hard chairs, and said that his steward had been impressed by her management. "He appreciates a well-organized ledger, but he also admires your understanding of the details. He said your plans for the asylum were at once extensive and attainable."

Lowering her eyes demurely, the matron said, "You are going to make me blush, your grace, which is not an easy thing to do. But I found Mr. Stephens impressive as well. He asked all the right questions and did not waste my time with irrelevant queries. Most potential patrons want to know how much money we spend on laundry detergent each month and then chastise us for coddling the children with clean sheets."

"I am relieved to hear it," he said firmly before explaining that his bank had been instructed to allow Fortescue's to draw three hundred pounds from his account. "I am certain that will solve your leaky roof problem with enough left over for a few months' worth of laundry detergent."

"You underestimate me, your grace, if you do not realize I will get years of laundry detergent from that amount," Mrs. Chaffey replied with a wide grin. "On behalf of all the children here, I thank you for your generosity. Now please tell me how I can help you. I remain convinced that you would not have trudged across the river simply to see a middle-aged woman smile with gratitude."

"Ah, but it is a lovely smile," he said sincerely. "And it is my pleasure to give a deserving cause exactly what it requires. That said, I am hoping you can provide me with some information. When my wife and I called earlier this week to discuss the Dugmore matter—"

"Such a tragedy that," she murmured, shaking her head.

Damien paused for a moment to acknowledge the truth

of her statement. The murder of Roger Dugmore was indeed a sad waste. Then he continued. "I saw a woman leaving the building who looked familiar to me, and I would be grateful if you could supply me with her name and direction. She was tall and thin with brown hair."

"Wearing a poke bonnet?" Mrs. Chaffey asked thoughtfully.

"Precisely, yes."

"That was Miss Lark," she explained. "She is the sister of Robert Lark, who wrote a series of stories for the *London Daily Gazette* exposing the corruption of my predecessor here at Fortescue's. I trust you are familiar with the articles because your Mr. Stephens is too efficient not to have found them."

"I know of them, yes," he replied, for his steward had included a detailed summation of the fracas in his report on the asylum. The revelation that the institution's wealthy patron was selling children to further enrich himself had caused quite a scandal, and although Lord Condon did not suffer any legal consequences for his actions, he had been unequivocally rejected by polite society. The last Damien had heard, his lordship had returned to his country seat in Ireland to wait for the outrage to pass.

"Miss Lark has taken a kindly interest in us since her brother published his exposé," Mrs. Chaffey continued. "She visits once a month or so and spends time with the children. And she always brings toys they can play with. This time it was an assortment of pewter soldiers and a jump rope. And playing cards! She gave them several decks because they do so love to play snip-snap-snorum. We appreciate her interest."

If she was curious to know where someone of his stature might have come into contact with Miss Lark previously, she was too well mannered to inquire.

"That is very helpful, thank you," Damien said, before asking again if she knew of the woman's direction.

Mrs. Chaffey fluttered her eyes blankly, as if taken aback by the query, and confessed she did not have the least idea. "Where Miss Lark resides has never come up in any of our interactions. But I am sure the resourceful Mr. Stephens will be able to find out quickly enough."

Damien, rising smoothly, granted the accuracy of her assessment even as he silently acknowledged that he would not assign him the task. He had no intention of sharing his mortifying quest with the steward.

Nor was it necessary.

He was perfectly capable of calling on the *Gazette*'s offices himself.

"I really cannot thank you enough for your generosity," Mrs. Chaffey said as she darted to her feet to escort him to the door. "I was worried that the wretched business with the Dugmore family might turn you against us. As an organization charged with instilling morality in vulnerable children, all of us must be above reproach."

"I do not hold myself to an unreasonable standard, nor anyone else," he replied, stepping outside into the dim sunlight, the large building blocking whatever weak rays managed to penetrate the thin layer of clouds. "Everything should be in order, but feel free to contact Stephens if you encounter any problems with the bank."

Murmuring gratefully, the head matron promised to provide Mr. Stephens with regular updates of their progress, and Damien bid her good day.

It was a short but frustrating drive to the *London Daily Gazette,* the route beset with traffic, and he arrived to the Strand a good twenty minutes later than he expected. Annoyed, he stopped his gig, climbed down, and gave a shilling to a young boy to watch his vehicle. Striding to the door, he realized he had not been in the vicinity since the attack on Bea. Kneeling on the pavement in front of the building, desperately clutching at the pages of a manuscript before they blew away, she was knocked onto her back and pummeled several times in the face by a jealous suitor who mistook her for a rival for a young lady's attention because of the masculine costume she had donned.

He remembered the rage he had felt, seeing her lying there, bloodied and dazed, an impediment to other pedestrians, who had the unimaginable temerity to grumble about the trouble of having to step around her—as if she had thrown herself onto the pavement simply to inconvenience them. He recalled, too, the need to restrain his fury, to keep it in check, because releasing it would have made the situation worse. As satisfying as it would have been to punch the fellow who dared to kick her thigh while calling her a drunken layabout, the reprisal would have only drawn more unwanted attention.

Gently cradling her shoulders as she haltingly shifted into sitting position was among the most difficult things he had ever done.

A smarter man would have realized in that moment the depths of his feelings.

Instead, the supposedly clever Duke of Kesgrave remained confounded by his compulsion to spend time with the vexing creature.

It would be *weeks* before he understood.

In retrospect it seemed almost impossible that he had been so dimwitted.

Entering the building now, he noted the room buzzed with activity as workers hurried across the floor and called out questions to each other. As he stepped further into the office, the hum grew dimmer and dimmer until every single occupant had stopped what they were doing to watch his progress.

They recognized either his consequence or his identity.

It appeared to be the latter when a tall man in a dark suit took a half step forward and announced that they did not know who Mr. Twaddle-Thum was. He said it firmly, almost combatively, but then his courage faltered and he stammered an apology for failing to be more helpful.

"But he is anonymous even to us," he rushed to explain as the color in his cheeks deepened to fuchsia. "It is the way he and Mr. Reade set up the arrangement. You can browbeat us or issue threats, but it won't make a difference. We cannot tell you what we do not know. Mr. Reade will say the same if you choose to wait for him to return. That is the God honest truth, I swear! Now you may do your worst to us, your grace."

The man stiffened his shoulders as if expecting to suffer a punishing blow, and Damien wondered what in his history would lead the reporter to believe he would respond to banal information with brute force. He did not, as far as he knew, possess a reputation for indiscriminate violence. If anything, he was famous for his moderation. Not since his salad days, when he ardently pursued an opera singer who considered him too callow for her attentions, had he vented his spleen in public. The few times he had responded to an injury with his fists had been in retaliation to a harm done to Bea, but those acts of reprisal were known only to the parties involved. No word of them had been published.

It was possible, Damien supposed, that the man's concern was more general in nature. Given how gleefully the newspaper's gossip tormented his victims, the reporter might find it difficult to imagine anyone responding to Twaddle's taunts calmly and the treatment of the new duchess had been particularly harsh. In the months since her marriage to him, Bea had been unable to take a step outside Kesgrave House without a description of her gait appearing in the *London Daily Gazette*.

And inside as well.

One especially sneering item described her fondness for rout cakes with such malevolent wonder it was as though she were consuming the bones of a beloved hound rather than a confection made of flour, butter, and sugar.

That column had infuriated Bea, with its loving description of each granule of sugar dusted generously on top of the pastry, and if she'd believed it would have yielded anything other than more derision, she would have marched down to these very offices and issued a challenge to the contemptuous writer.

Damien, however, found it easy to dismiss all the prattle. It was obviously the nonsensical blather of an aggrieved magpie, and although he could not conceive what injury the small-minded gossip imagined Bea had done him, Twaddle made only himself look ridiculous by publicly nursing his wound.

Bea emerged from the reports more or less unscathed, for she was too clever and capable to appear as anything less than coolly proficient. But even if the opposite were true and Twaddle had managed to portray her as an empty-headed miss with an overweening pretension of competence, he still would not have paid him any notice.

It was his privilege to ignore all the aggrieved magpies that flocked around London and every other type of person he found tiresome or insipid or even just a little bit annoying.

But his opinion of Twaddle was neither here nor there, for his visit to the Strand had nothing to do with the notorious scribbler. Correcting the misapprehension, he explained that he was hoping to speak with Robert Lark. Then he swept his eyes over the crowd to see if any of the men present matched that description and noted with wry humor the visible relief that passed among them.

The tension drained from the tall man's shoulders as he

introduced himself as Mr. Banks. As the deputy editor of the newspaper, he had the pleasure of working with Mr. Lark, who was not in the office. "He rarely comes in. He prefers to work from the study of his home, and since he scrupulously submits his articles on time, Mr. Reade—he is our employer —does not protest. I am sure we can give you his direction," he added, calling to a younger member of the staff, who dashed eagerly across the floor. "Lester is Mr. Reade's clerk. He will find Mr. Lark's address for you, your grace. It won't take a minute."

In fact, it took five.

As Lester, who had disappeared into a closed-off space in the back of the room, remained stubbornly out of view, Banks sought to fill the increasingly awkward silence with effusive praise for Mr. Lark. "He is an excellent reporter—concise and accurate and, as I mentioned previously, always prompt and timely. We have never had a complaint against him, not a single one in the eight years he has worked here. Well, it did happen once, but I think it is a sign that you are doing something correct when the villain of your harrowing exposé on abused orphans comes pounding on your door to protest the accurate description of her crimes. All of which is to say that Mr. Lark is a credit to the newspaper, and I hope you will find him agreeable when you meet with him. If Lester would just return with his—"

He broke off abruptly as the young clerk emerged from the office, a scrap of paper held triumphantly in his grip. "Ah, there he is."

Lester, muttering about having to look in several places to find the information, apologized for keeping his grace waiting. Then he handed him the slip of paper and dashed away to resume his duties. Damien glanced at the address as he slid it into his pocket, thanked the men for their assistance, and took his leave. Although struck by a sharp pang of hunger, he continued directly to Bethel Street. He did not have the patience to extend the investigation into a second day.

He would find out the identity of the woman now and put the matter to rest.

Drawing to a stop in front of number twenty-six, Damien noted it was a tidy house of three stories with a graceful stone arch over the doorway. He tried to picture his mother occupying such a modest residence, and although it should have been easy because her own father was a cobbler, he found it impossible. Lorraine Price left all remnants of her previous existence behind when she agreed to be a wealthy man's mistress.

Damien did not blame her for accepting the cit's proposal and did not even judge her on moral grounds. Having been handed every possible advantage on a silver tray, he was not so sanctimonious as to begrudge a woman for seeking more for herself. It was human nature to desire comfort and ease.

What he did resent, however, was being ruthlessly exploited in the pursuit of power and revenge. If his mother had just done it kindly, if she had made the smallest bit of effort to at least feign affection for him, he would not have minded being regarded solely as a cudgel to be wielded against his sire and society.

Irritated by the maudlin turn his thoughts had taken, Damien dismounted his gig and decided he already disliked Miss Lark for making him think of his mother so much. Despite the portrait on the staircase, he rarely gave her the time of day, and as he approached the front door, he decided he would have the painting removed. He could not explain to Bea why it was there without feeling stupid and callow.

Indeed, he felt stupid and callow just knocking on Robert Lark's door.

Seeking out a woman whom he had glanced at from a distance of a dozen or so feet because she might have borne a vague resemblance to his long-dead mother was a fool's errand. If he had any sense at all, he would turn on his heels and leave before he embarrassed himself further.

And yet he remained rooted to the spot.

Calling himself a lackwit, he raised his fist and knocked.

Chapter One

❧

Saturday, May 23
10:39 a.m.

Verity could not pretend to know what sort of tasks were typically assigned to astoundingly competent females. As a reporter for the *London Daily Gazette* as well as its inimitable gossip, Mr. Twaddle-Thum, she was accustomed to choosing her own assignments. Freddie—that was, Frederick Somerset Reade, the editor of the newspaper and her oldest friend—frequently made suggestions but ultimately left the decision to her.

Furthermore, nobody had ever described her in that particular way.

Freddie, she knew, had the utmost respect for her proficiency, and Delphine, another dear friend who served as her companion, frequently wrung her hands over what she considered Verity's recklessness.

But Colson Hardwick, noted wastrel and the Marquess of Ware's famously disinherited second son, had strode into her front parlor, sat down on the settee, and announced that she was the most astoundingly competent female he had ever met.

Not *among* the most astoundingly competent females.

Not *one of* the most astoundingly competent females.

The most astoundingly competent female.

She had the category all to herself.

At the declaration she had felt a variety of emotions—flattered, surprised, intrigued, amazed—but the one that had struck her the strongest was alarm. She had been alarmed by the glint of appreciation shimmering in his extraordinary teal eyes, and an unprecedented panic seized her limbs as she contemplated the consequences of his respect.

It seemed, in that moment, to bode strange and wonderful things.

And then the task itself: to giggle girlishly.

To be fair, that was not the entire extent of the assignment. Hardwicke, explaining that he sought an opportunity to get to know the subject of his investigation better, asked her to distract the man's sister by any means at her disposal. Giggling was only one suggestion as to how she might proceed. It was, of course, up to her to decide.

For her efforts, whatever they turned out to be, he would offer fair compensation.

Obviously, Verity could have fulfilled the request with minimal effort. Among her extensive repertoire of amused responses, she counted eight different types of giggles, including the shocked giggle, the embarrassed giggle, and the "oh, dear, I should not have said *that*" giggle, which was the one she employed most frequently.

Appearing to have unintentionally revealed private information was an excellent way either to elicit a confidence in return or convince a target that she was slightly scattered or not very intelligent. During her years of Twaddling, she had yet to encounter a tactic more effective than allowing the other person to feel superior to her. Intellectually, morally, socially—it made no difference. The results were all reassuringly positive.

It was precisely because she had a tidy assortment of giggles that she found the assignment so insulting. If she were so new to the art of deception that she had cultivated only one or two different kinds, then she would have agreed with his assessment and graciously consented to his offer.

In truth, however, she was just as skilled in misdirection and disguise as Hardwicke. If anything, she had *more* experience, for she had been compelled by the circumstances of her childhood to devise schemes to ensure her own welfare. Deposited on the doorstep of an orphan asylum by her courtesan mother, who could not allow an inconvenient baby to disrupt her comfortable existence, Verity had had no choice but to employ a seemingly endless string of devious plots to overcome the institution's malevolent headmistress.

Miss Wraithe would have gladly consigned every last one of her charges to the shed in the back corner of the garden if she could have just figured out how to squeeze all fifty-six malnourished children into the narrow space.

Or perhaps not, for she had been selling many of the older ones into indentured servitude as soon as they reached a useful age, and she needed the merchandise to be in reasonable working order.

Hardwicke, by contrast, had been raised in luxurious splendor as the second son of the wealthy and prominent Marquess of Ware. Wanting for nothing, he enjoyed every advantage of birth and attended only the best schools in England. The superiority of his education, however, could do little to protect him from the inferiority of his choices, and a few years ago he was cut off by his father for stealing a prized family heirloom to settle his gambling debts.

According to Mr. Twaddle-Thum, who exposed the theft

in a column entitled, "The (Signet) Ring of Truth," the sum total of his gambling debts was equal to the annual income of the ruler of a small principality on the Continent.

Despite these setbacks, Hardwicke appeared to be doing quite nicely for himself. Last week, when she had sneaked into his residence in Millman Street to search it for information about his employer, Verity had been impressed by its cozy elegance. The rooms were not only free of dirt and debris but also orderly. Everything had been returned neatly to its place, indicating the home was looked after by someone who cared for and paid attention to the details.

Although that described the Colson Hardwicke she had come to know, it most definitely did not apply to the man she had written about three years ago.

That man was most assuredly a ne'er-do-well.

Struck by the difference, Verity wondered if he had grown disgusted by his own profligacy or if a Good Samaritan had set him on a different path. Given the limitations of self-awareness, she assumed it was the latter. She also suspected that he worked for someone who was either in the government or had connections within the government. His sense of command during the Altick affair—in which a seemingly insignificant inmate was murdered within the confines of Horsemonger Prison in an attempt to conceal other crimes—signaled a kind of confidence that came only with impunity.

Hardwicke had known he would not be held to account.

Was his current project likewise officially sanctioned?

Verity did not know because, in addition to asking her to perform a trivial task, he had withheld details of the undertaking. The subject of his investigation was merely an "individual" who engaged in the business of "agitation."

Intrigued by these morsels, Verity nevertheless resolved to decline the offer. If he had asked her to do something interesting, such as breaking into a target's lodgings to search through his possessions, she might have overlooked the lack of particulars and accepted.

Or if he had proposed a light dollop of pickpocketing.

She was not fussy, just extremely capable.

Only now she was irritated as well because she had allowed herself to be hoodwinked.

Hardwicke had sought her out at home—something no human being had ever done because he was the first and only person in the world to figure out who she was or where she resided—and lavished her with praise. She had not asked for the compliments; he had offered them freely.

And they had turned her head.

The ring of sincerity in his voice, the warmth in his tone, had been pleasurable to her.

By any measure, Colson Hardwicke was a handsome man. He had vivid blue-green eyes and an endearing cleft in his chin and the sort of pillowy lips that generally caused female hearts to flutter. But it was his admiration for Verity's proficiency that she found compellingly attractive.

What she had failed to perceive in his statement, however, was the way his approbation was constrained by her sex. She had been too flattered by his compliment to realize the most important word was not *astoundingly* but *female*. She was astoundingly competent for a female, which was a subclass of female, which was already a subclass of male.

Her competence, as excessive as it was, did not rise to the level of a man's incompetence.

Of course it did not!

Verity, mortified by the naivete of her error, realized she had been too gratified by his esteem to examine it closely. But that was not the only source of her mistake. Having observed his ability to ratiocinate during the business with Altick, the quick and decisive way he drew conclusions, she had ascribed to him an unnerving intelligence. A man who was clever enough to outwit her three times was too shrewd to fall prey to coarse assumptions.

Alas, she had given him too much credit.

Colson Hardwicke was like every other leaden-eyed male who looked at her and saw a pretty woman with hazel eyes and sharp cheekbones.

It was exactly what Mr. Tipton of Black Prince Road had seen when he'd looked at her mother—formerly Lorraine Price, soon to be La Reina—in Verity's grandfather's shop in Cheapside all those years ago and what Sir Thomas Hogan had admired and the fifth Duke of Kesgrave had desired.

Men liked to think of themselves as complex and unique creatures, so varied and distinct from each other, so specific in their wants and needs, but in the end they were all pretty much the same. Drop a pauper into a slot carved for nobility, and you will observe only the slightest variation in behavior.

Verity knew she should be horrified by the banal simplicity of the male mind, but the truth was she appreciated how much easier it made her work. Predictability equaled manipulability, and although human nature itself generally moved along a narrow track, there was something particularly satisfying about the narrowness of men. As with most things, there were exceptions to the rule, and she had counted Hardwicke among them based on his displays of alarming astuteness.

She perceived now how unduly optimistic she had been in her conclusion.

"A reprise of Miss Gorman would be ideal, I think," Hardwicke said, referring to a character she had adopted to obtain information after Altick had been killed. Hoping to throw the upright Sebastian Holcroft off guard—dubbed Holcroft the Holy by Twaddle, who regarded all morally virtuous persons with cynicism—she had pretended to be the guileless sister of a murder victim. When she had burst in on the unsuspecting gentleman in the middle of his morning eggs, Hardwicke had been present in the room and saw easily through her disguise.

Had she giggled on that occasion?

No, not in the breakfast room, Verity was sure of it.

Swinging the door roughly on its hinges, she had affected only fear and panic at the unexplained disappearance of her brother. Outside the townhouse, on the doorstep, maneuvering past the butler, she had indulged in a breathy "clumsy me" chortle.

But Hardwicke had not witnessed that part of her performance.

"Miss Gorman but frothier, I think," Hardwicke added, oblivious to the offense he continued to give. "As I said, you would only need to convey a general lightheartedness with a few bon mots and giggles. I will take care of the rest."

It was baffling, Verity thought, how someone as perceptive as Hardwicke could also be so blindingly unaware as to believe she would agree to such terms. *He* would take care of the rest of it—as if she were a passenger in a carriage who had no control over the direction of the vehicle or speed at which it traveled.

Why would she ever consent to such a relegation?

Despite his opinion, she was in fact astoundingly competent.

In addition to nimbly picking pockets, she excelled at breaching secured lodgings, reading private correspondence, deciphering secret messages, eliciting indelicate admissions, climbing tall buildings, and disappearing into crevices. She once broke into a cellar at Kew Palace to find a document proving that the extravagant conveyance commissioned for King George's coronation—a gaudy confection known as the Gold State Coach—had cost a staggering nine thousand pounds rather than the widely reported sum of seventy-five hundred. She had to contort her body into a tight V to hide in a tin trunk when a pair of maids tripped down the stairs to find a water pitcher from the King of Spain.

She would like to see Colson Hardwicke accomplish anything half as impressive.

Although she was uninterested in accepting the assignment, she still leaned forward and nodded encouragingly. She was too proficient not to obtain as much information as possible about a subject, even one she had no intention of pursuing.

Was indulging Hardwicke really the best use of her time?

Not especially, no.

The Altick matter, which she had resolved only the day before, had been all consuming, and she had allowed various responsibilities to slip. The *Gazette,* for example. Robert Lark had two articles to write—one about the debate over the authenticity of the marble sculptures Lord Elgin brought back from Greece and another about Sir Humphrey Davy's mine safety lamp—and Mr. Twaddle-Thum had yet to follow up on any one of the dozen notes he had received regarding the Duchess of Kesgrave's latest activities. The steam engine explosion that killed its inventor was widely believed to be an accident, as high-pressure steam was notoriously dangerous, but Her Outrageousness detected something suspicious in the tragedy and returned to the foundry the next morning to examine the site. The following day, a constable visited the home of the company's owner and led a man away in manacles. The identity of the murderer remained unknown to Verity.

Would she have happily put these matters aside if Hardwicke had bothered to entice her with a proposition worthy of her talents?

Well, not happily.

Prodding the Duke of Kesgrave's ego with breathless

accounts of his wife's activities was one of her chief delights. Her half-brother had been married to the overlooked spinster for only a few months, and it still amused Verity to no end that the high stickler had aligned himself with an officious busybody who lodged murder accusations at some of the highest-placed members of society. For years she had been expecting him to wed a dull beauty who enjoyed facile pursuits such as watercolors and embroidery. A Lady Georgina, who thought the term *blancmange* described all foods that happened to be white, or a Lady Victoria, whose dark eyes were cheerfully blank.

Even so, Verity would have begrudgingly adjusted her focus for a short while.

But Hardwicke had not offered something interesting.

Instead, he had tasked her with a duty fit for a soldier on his first day of training and expected her to be flattered by the consideration.

"All that is necessary for my purposes is that I appear to have a sister," he said, further minimizing her proposed contribution. "The man I am investigating—his name is Arnold Fitch—has a sister to whom he is very close, and in an effort to uncover his true motive in joining a secret reformist society, it benefits me to have a sister to whom I am very close as well."

Finally, some detail, Verity thought, filing the name away as she leaned forward and wondered about the identity of the organization. As a journalist who had followed the reform movement for half a decade, she was familiar with most of the groups and found it difficult to believe there was one that was so covert she had never heard of it. Consequently, she asked if the society was associated with the Luddite movement, as several so-called clandestine organizations had formed in recent years to address the turmoil caused by the utilization of machines that could do the work of skilled craftsmen for a fraction of the cost. Robert Lark had written several articles about the unrest roiling the north, for he recognized the intractability of the problem of progress and could identify no easy solution. The gains made by the mechanized loom and cloth-finishing machine could not be reversed and nor should they be, for cheaper goods were an unequivocal good for everyone.

And yet it came at the expense of thousands of workers who were now without employment and unable to feed their families.

It was a poor way for a nation to repay its soldiers returning from war.

Exacerbating the situation was the severe stance the government had taken in response to the destruction wrought by the Luddites, imposing the harshest reprisal possible. Although destroying machinery was no longer punishable by death, the crime still warranted transport to a prisoner colony.

Verity, who could not condone violence as a means to any end, however righteous, nevertheless found herself on occasion in sympathy with the laborers, who were clearly outmatched by a system determined to retain power and suppress dissent. Given the government's stance, she could see few pathways toward change, which Robert Lark lamented in his article on the recent attack on lace making machines in Loughborough. Some quarter must be given or the working men would be driven to more and more extremes, which served no one.

"Not in the strictest sense, no," Hardwicke replied, explaining that the society advocated for the repeal of the Frame-Breaking Act and humane treatment of workers but also for suffrage for all men, the elimination of rotten boroughs, and the end of child labor. "It has been around for more than a decade and is made up of an assortment of like-minded tradesmen, clerks, and schoolteachers. For years they have met once a week to discuss the principles set forth by a reformer they admire. But a few months ago, angered by the slow pace of progress, the men came up with the idea for something they are calling the Burnley Blanketeers. It is a group of Lancashire weavers who will march to London to petition directly to the crown for reforms. The society, coordinating with other groups around the country, plans to collect thousands of signatures to present to the prince regent. You may recall a previous effort to submit petitions to Parliament."

Verity, recognizing the Society of Yarwellian Philosophers from his description, said that she did indeed remember the effort. "The Parliamentary clerks rejected all but a handful for specious reasons such as printed sheets, torn edges, and insulting comments."

"They did, yes," Hardwicke replied. "And it was not a particularly deft response, for all it did was underscore the contempt in which the Tories hold the lower classes. The clever response would have been to accept the petitions and then file them away in a dank cellar under the House of Lords."

"False appeasement is just as contemptuous," Verity said.

Hardwicke smiled faintly. "I said *clever,* not *correct.*"

Verity acknowledged the distinction with a dip of her head and contemplated the new plan. She could not imagine the prime minister would allow a horde of Lancastrians to descend upon the capital with petitions for the prince regent. Long before the men arrived, they would be made to disperse.

That could be the source of Hardwicke's interest, she thought. A government agency might have hired him to infiltrate the group and discover its plans with an eye toward undermining them.

If that was the case, then where did Fitch fit into the scheme?

Probingly, she asked if he was one of the organizers.

"Longstanding members of the society are overseeing the Blanketeers," Hardwicke said.

Familiar with the Society of Yarwellian Philosophers only in the general sense, she knew nothing of its membership and could not say if Fitch met this description. She thought it was likely that he did, however, as disrupting the organization's activities was in the interest of the Home Office. The government had no intention of implementing the changes the reformers sought. Allowing millions of peasants to vote went against everything the ministers believed in, for the uneducated masses would make all sorts of decisions that would adversely affect them, such as overturning the Corn Laws. If the price of grain dropped, then so too would the landowners' income.

Lord Sidmouth could not permit that!

Convinced now that Hardwicke must represent the interests of the home secretary, she asked if his assignment was to spy on the society. "Is that why you have targeted Fitch?"

Hardwicke's lips twitched slightly in a fleeting smile before he announced that he was not at liberty to explain his interest. "But if you are worried that my goal is to impair the efforts of the Blanketeers, do let me put your mind at ease. I have no quarrel with the proposed reforms."

Verity found this difficult to believe and eyed him skeptically. "Even the elimination of rotten boroughs? Does your family not control one in Gloucestershire?"

"Actually, my family controls two," he replied easily. "But even if my father controlled seven like the Duke of Newcastle, I would not endorse a system that confers an inordinate amount of influence on a select few. My family already has too much power."

It was an uncommon position, for the opposite was generally believed to be true, but not wholly surprising for a man in his position. He was, after all, a second son, not an heir, which she pointed out.

"A second son who was disinherited, thanks to you," he said with a cynical twist of his lips.

But Verity shook her head, unwilling to accept blame for the mountain of debt that compelled him to steal a cherished ring from his own sire. All Twaddle had done was reveal the sin, not commit it. "It is not my fault you cannot hold your liquor or recognize a losing hand. Perhaps you were not suited to be a wastrel and should have gone into the clergy like your father wanted."

Now his lips twitched with genuine humor as he said not even his fond parent could imagine him ministering to the sick and dying. "He thought I should be a captain in the Life Guards, like him, and to stride among the enlisted men like a colossus. He perceived the army as primarily a preening opportunity and wore his cuirass and plumed helmet even to bed. But that does not signify—and nor is it fodder for your next column. Now will you accept the assignment? You will be well compensated for your time, I assure you."

Although money was the least of her concerns, she could not help but wonder how much he had in mind. No doubt it was a princely sum *for a woman*. "It is an intriguing opportunity, to be sure. But you have yet to say why you are interested in Fitch."

"And I will not," he said bluntly. "It is not something I am at liberty to discuss."

As she herself possessed dozens of secrets she would never share, Verity allowed it was a reasonable position. Nevertheless, his refusal presented yet another problem. "In that case, I must decline. I cannot enter into a situation of which I am not cognizant of all the details. It is a professional decision, you understand, and not personal."

But it was a stupid thing to say—not personal.

Overtly stating the obvious had the paradoxical effect of implying the opposite.

Otherwise, what need was there to mention it?

Verity resisted the urge to frown in annoyance and kept her features smooth. She refused to follow one tactical mistake with another.

Hardwicke, either unaware of her slip or too much of a professional to draw attention to it, expressed his regret and asked if there was anything he could do to change her mind. "You strike me as too practical not to be amenable to negotiation. What if I gave you permission to write about my father's career in the Life Guards? There is a particularly diverting episode involving a rangy mongrel, a musket, and his scarlet tunic that does credit only to the dog."

"It is a tempting offer," she said, only somewhat satirically, for she had never given the Marquess of Ware much consideration other than as the father of a profligate. That he was a peacock she knew well from casual observation, and the only reason she had thought to search for the signet ring at all was he was famous for wearing the gaudy ornamentation. When it had ceased to appear on his finger, rumors began to circulate and it felt incumbent to Twaddle to either prove or disprove the theory that the son had swiped it to pay off the moneylenders. Now that she knew Hardwicke, however, she found she was more curious about his upbringing and wondered if stories about the man who had raised him would shed further light on his personality. "But I still have to pass."

Rising to his feet, Hardwicke assured her he understood. "I will not pretend I am not disappointed in your decision. You are so very impressive, Miss Lark."

Several snide remarks flitted through Verity's mind at the

seemingly effusive praise, which she now recognized as only moderate acclaim, but she kept her expression impassive as she replied, "I am confident you will have no trouble finding someone to play the part of your sister."

She did not add: because it does not require someone impressive.

Instead, she said, "Your Mr. Fitch will be completely taken in."

"I think so, yes," Hardwicke said amiably, which further annoyed Verity, for it underscored the insulting nature of the offer. If all the role required was a female of the right age and disposition, then a woman with her skill and experience was too qualified.

It was like hiring a Royal Ascot winner to pull a hackney coach.

With this unfavorable comparison in mind, she led him out to the hallway and asked if the villain they apprehended the day before was still in the custody of the authorities. "Or has he been absolved by his employer?"

Although it was a deliberately provoking question, Hardwicke replied mildly, "He is still in custody. The coverage of the incident in today's *London Daily Gazette* has made clemency, had Eldon desired to grant it, impossible. But I am sure you know that."

Verity, who harbored doubts about the Lord Chancellor's integrity, did not in fact know that and was relieved to hear that the articles had served their purpose.

"Judging by the tense, heart-pounding account Mr. Marcus provided for the issue, I assume he is suffering no lasting ill effects from his brief captivity?" he asked.

"Apparently, Mrs. Marcus is quite irate that he allowed himself to be taken hostage. She had feared this precise thing would happen when he accepted the position with the paper and he called her a widgeon for even suggesting something so implausible," Verity replied with a hint of amusement. "So now Freddie has agreed to hire a former military man to train the entire staff in measures to fight off an attacker. It is as yet unclear whether the delivery boys will also participate in the training. Freddie does not think it is necessary because they are rarely in the office, but Mrs. Marcus, who considers herself a substitute for their absent mothers, thinks that makes them even more vulnerable to the actions of bad people."

Hardwicke allowed that it was a reasonable argument as they reached the front door and asked if Mr. Lark was going to take part in the lessons.

Although Verity had not been specifically identified as Robert Lark in Hardwicke's presence either yesterday or any time previous to the armed confrontation in the newspaper office, she did not doubt he knew the truth about the reporter's identity. The fact that he had managed to track her down to her home on Bethel Street strongly indicated that he knew all her secrets. Consequently, when she assured him that Mr. Lark did not require further training, as he already counted pugilism, fencing, and several ancient methods of self-defense among his skills, she thought for sure he understood she was talking about herself.

His response—that he was relieved to hear it—seemed to confirm her supposition.

Opening the door, Verity thanked him for his offer in a tone that was far more sanguine than she felt. It was on the tip of her tongue to call it *thoughtful,* but she feared it would be too revealing. Even if she did not imbue the word with all the sarcasm she felt, Hardwicke knew her well enough to wonder at the display of excess civility.

"Thank you, Miss Lark, for hearing me out," he returned politely.

"Of course," she murmured, although it was not as though

she had much choice. Once he had lavishly praised her competence, she would have listened to anything he said— and been disappointed regardless.

As cynical as she was, it appeared she still harbored some undue optimism.

Obviously, that would have to be stamped out posthaste.

Reminded of her foolishness, she tartly bid him good day, closed the door with a sharp bite, and returned to Robert Lark's office to finish an article on Sir Humphrey's invention.

Chapter Two

❧❧❧

Sunday, May 24
4:34 p.m.

Although the meaning of the term *astoundingly competent* might change depending on the varied experiences and perceptions of the person employing it, *astoundingly efficient* had only the one connotation. That was because productivity could be objectively measured, and Verity, crossing the last item off her list of things to do for the day, knew that the description unequivocally applied to her.

Starting her day an hour later than her usual six, she had nevertheless managed to complete not only Robert Lark's article on the safety lamp for the next day but also a strong first draft of his story on the Parthenon marbles, which was not due until Thursday. Moreover, she wrote two columns for Twaddle. The first described Her Outrageousness's apprehension of the steam engine inventor's murderer in fawning detail; the second speculated about a certain Almack's patroness's fascination with Drury Lane's production of *The Country Wife*. Her ladyship had seen the play three times in two weeks, and the most likely explanation was she had developed a tendre for the leading man. The prospect that she had acquired a taste for Restoration comedy was far less plausible, but Twaddle duly allowed for the possibility.

Having finished the two stories, Verity then drew up a list of topics for future exploration. Despite the Duchess of Kesgrave's seemingly infinite ability to find murder victims wherever she looked, including in the burned-out hulls of unfortunate steam engine explosions, her uninterrupted success could not last indefinitely and it behooved Twaddle to have other stories at the ready to fill the space between corpses. Gathering material about her grace was not particularly difficult, for Verity employed a network of spies who eagerly reported stories in exchange for coin. The more challenging part was molding benign information into salacious gossip. Usually, a hint of awe accomplished the goal: *And the amount of sugar Her Outrageousness sprinkles on each one of her rout cakes! Why, 'tis twice what we put in an entire pot of tea.*

The list was good, containing half a dozen ideas, a few of which she could not help teasing out further in her head as she jotted them down. Apparently, the duchess was excessively fond of pineapple and insisted it be included in every dish presented to her. The poor chef's ingenuity had been stretched as thin as week-old broth—at least according to the report she had gotten from Mags, who had befriended one of the stable boys at Kesgrave House. It sounded slightly off to her, the notion that a former spinster had the temerity to make such an outlandish and specific demand, but Twaddle had a source who swore it was true and that was all he required.

To round out the list, Verity also dashed off a few ideas that had nothing to do with her brother's wife. A bumptious turnip had lately arrived to the capital from the provinces and was making a perfect cake of himself with ridiculous wagers and other acts of audacious stupidity. She had yet to compose a sneering ode to the young noble's profligacy, preferring to see the depths to which he would sink before bestowing her attention, but she had taken note of Viscount Ripley. It was impossible not to, as his lordship sent weekly dispatches to the gossip in care of the *Gazette*, and she planned to edify Twaddle's readership—the Twaddleship—at some point with a catalog of the scapegrace's antics ranked from least offensive to most appalling.

Drawing a line through the last to-do entry, she leaned back in her chair and sighed contentedly. It was not even five o'clock yet and already she had completed her work for the day. That meant she could do whatever she wanted in the remaining hours before dinner.

Verity had no obligations.

She was free.

'Twas a wonderful feeling.

For several minutes, she sat there, in the front parlor, enjoying the keen sense of satisfaction as she watched her neighbor disembark from her carriage with a small puppy in her arms. After applying several enthusiastic licks to Mrs. Elkin's chin, the rambunctious beast burst from her arms and raced down the block toward the busier street at the end of the road. The woman stared in horror as her groom and maid dashed after it. After a tense few minutes, the pair returned with the dog in tow and they all disappeared into the house.

"Tragedy averted," she murmured with amusement as she put down her quill, which she belatedly realized she was still holding.

It felt a little strange, sitting at the table in the middle of the day without any assignments to complete, and she wondered if the pendulum clock by the door had always been so loud. Each tick echoed throughout the silent room like a rooster crowing at daybreak.

Tick.

Tick.

Well, yes, it had always been that loud, for its sonorousness was why it had been placed near the entry: to make it difficult for anyone listening at the door to hear the conversation of the occupants within. Although the servants knew their employer engaged in the masculine occupation of newspaper reporting under the guise of being her own brother, they knew nothing about Mr. Twaddle-Thum.

With the gossip's tendency to infuriate his subjects, Verity thought it was better if she kept that identity a secret.

As she remained in her seat contemplating the swath of late afternoon before her, the noise from the clock seemed to intensify, its rhythmic tap resonating with an increasing hollowness she found unsettling.

Tick.

Tick.

It was only because the experience of having nothing to do was so unfamiliar, she thought, and took another look at her list just to make sure she had not neglected something.

Of course she had not.

Each item was on its own line and consisted of only a few words. She would have to be either very inattentive or half blind to miss an entry.

Perhaps her unease was really a nagging sensation that she had not accomplished her tasks well enough. She had felt certain her article on Elgin's marbles properly represented both sides of the argument, but perhaps she had not given Richard Payne Knight's case against authenticity enough attention. As several other prominent artists were convinced they were real, she was inclined personally to dismiss it, and it was possible that opinion had seeped into the story. That was one of several reasons she gave all her stories to Delphine—to check for prejudices.

Convinced that she must have done Knight a disservice, she drew an asterisk next to the article on her list and pulled the story from the small stack of papers at her elbow.

Monday, May 25
  1:04 p.m.

Although Delphine routinely invited Verity to help her in the garden, she knew her friend was profoundly uninterested in agriculture and had no patience for the slow process of cultivation. Even weeding, which wrought immediate results, failed to overcome her indifference because of its inherent futility: Spend an hour clearing the plot on Sunday, and by Wednesday tentative green shoots were already sprouting.

It was disheartening in a way that felt almost nihilistic.

As far as Verity was concerned, soil should simply decide which kind of plants it wanted to support with its nutrients and then support only those. None of this "a good garden may have some weeds" nonsense!

Her friend's attitude amused Delphine, who enjoyed being the sole caretaker of the garden. After so many years in the orphan asylum, where nothing was actually her own, not even the pillow on which she laid her head every night, for she was frequently required to share it with an unexpected new arrival, she relished the sense of ownership. These six beds—planted with potatoes, onions, parsnips, carrots—were hers alone, and although Cook sometimes complained about her yield, she never attempted to take over.

The solitary aspect of raising crops also appealed to Delphine after her extended tenure at Fortescue's. Despite the rambling size of the crumbling monstrosity, all the children were herded into the same four rooms to make supervising them easier for the headmistress, and there was an ever-present tumult in the crush of bodies.

Whatever faint trill of happiness one managed to eke out in the commotion was overwhelmed by the clamor of misery.

And there *had been* laughter, stolen moments of levity under threadbare blankets after bedtime, when Verity would relate some diabolical prank she and Freddie had carried out against the treacherous Wraithe to wonderfully horrifying results.

(That the despicable gorgon never discovered who was behind the seemingly endless stream of tricks, gags, and capers that bedeviled her was in keeping with her erratic management style, which appeared incapable of accounting for obvious factors. Otherwise, why was she always taken aback by new arrivals at the asylum? Wretched souls were left on its steps with such regularity, the wooden door had begun to splinter from all the knocking.)

Even after seven years in Bethel Street, Delphine still delighted in the lovely novelty of being alone, especially in her garden, which was calm and peaceful despite the din of the city around her. In asking Verity to join her, she was merely extending a social courtesy and the only reason she did it was she knew the other woman would refuse.

And she had—for years.

Not two weeks ago, Delphine had barely finished issuing the invitation before Verity declined with an impatient wave of her hand.

And now Verity was there, in her garden, holding a scythe.

A scythe?

"Good God, Verity, put that down!" Delphine ordered, rising to her feet as she stared at her friend, who was wearing a jonquil morning dress with a decorative rosette border. The frock was speckled with the ink stains that marred all of the reporter's writing gowns, but it was still too lovely for gardening. If she was determined to muddy her clothes, the least she could have done was put on one of a dozen dull-colored outfits for Twaddling. "We are not reaping wheat."

"Yes, I know that," Verity snapped peevishly, "for I am not a complete greenhorn. Wheat is for fields, and this is a vegetable garden. But surely there is something here I can cut down? What about the squirrels? You are always complaining about the squirrels."

Equal parts amused and horrified, Delphine reached out and gingerly removed the tool from the other woman's hand. "I complain about them because they are cunning little creatures, and while they are too quick to be caught in the sweep of a scythe, I am not. So let's just put this back in the shed, where it cannot hurt anyone, shall we?"

Verity made no reply to this remark, which was highly insulting given her skill at fencing and sword fighting. In an illustrious career spanning almost a decade, she had never sliced a single thing she was not aiming for—which her friend very well knew.

Returning from the shed, Delphine grasped an implement with a long handle and a thick, pointed head that vaguely resembled a hammer. "Do not get me wrong. I appreciate your enthusiasm and am grateful for your help. There is a lot of weeding to be done before I can plant the second round of potatoes."

"Ah, yes, I see," Verity said, accepting the tool with little enthusiasm as she reminded herself she did not have to be there. Having finished everything on her list of tasks to perform—twice!—she was free to fill her time in any way she desired. She could read a book, stroll around the square, visit Bond Street to purchase a black-colored cravat for a new dandy character she had in mind, place an ad in the newspaper for the footman she had been thinking of hiring, review the household accounts to see if she could afford a third servant, rearrange the books in Robert's office, bring toys to the orphans at Fortescue's, call on the newspaper office, take a nap.

The options were endless.

At any given moment, there were two dozen things that Verity Lark could do regardless of the length of her list. But none of them appealed to her. Just thinking about performing the tasks made her feel annoyed, as if she were already bored, and she had come outside because Delphine found gardening deeply absorbing.

Verity wanted to be absorbed, too.

Whenever her mind was free to roam, it wandered back to Hardwicke and his offensive proposal. Turning it down was her only option, she knew that. Giggling on cue was for actresses and women like her mother, who flattered the egos of insecure men to further their own ambitions. If he had treated her like an equal, not as an underling, she would have considered it. But the terms he offered were untenable.

And yet now she wondered if she could have handled the matter differently.

For two days, she had reviewed the exchange in her head, examining it from various perspectives, and it seemed as though she could have played her hand more astutely. Just because Hardwicke refused to share the details of his assignment did not mean the details were unavailable by other means. Uncovering secrets was her raison d'être. It was the first thing she thought of as she climbed out of bed in the morning.

Well, the second.

The actual first was the expression on the Wraithe's face when she was deposed at Fortescue's—the look of utter blankness slowly overcome with dawning horror as she realized her comfortable feather bed would now be riven with nails.

But next, as Verity was slipping into her dressing gown, she assessed the things she did not know and planned to discover.

There was no reason why she could not have used her skills to satisfy her curiosity about Fitch. Agreeing to Hardwicke's offer did not mean accepting his conditions. She could have at least made an attempt to find out what game Hardwicke was playing—possibly, so she could beat him at it.

So far, the advantage had been all his.

Three times Hardwicke had outwitted her, which was maddening, and by turning down his proposal, she had denied herself the opportunity to even the score.

Verity, her grip tight around the wooden handle, applied herself to the weeds, scraping at the roots and tugging the stems free. It was tedious work, dull and repetitive and even slightly perilous, she thought, as the sharp edge of one of the plants grazed her palm. Yowling softly in pain, she raised her hand and noted a few droplets of blood. As she sucked on the wound, she saw Delphine watching her, her light blue eyes both amused and perplexed.

"Why are you out here?" she asked.

Verity, lowering her hand to her side, replied, "To enjoy the fine spring weather."

It was in fact a beastly day, with cooler than expected temperatures and a daunting thickness to the air that threatened rain.

Impassively, her demeanor matching her friend's, Delphine advised her to run inside to fetch her bonnet. "You do not want to get freckles from the sun."

"As tormented as I am by spots that appear a few days before my monthly, I have so far evaded the scourge of freckles," Verity said with a pleasant smile before raising the weeder again and driving it into the soil. She dug up another three plants, engaging in a protracted tug-of-war with the last one, which ended in a triumphant grunt as she finally dislodged it. She tossed it on the ground and gave it a hearty stamp.

When she looked up, she discovered Delphine still staring at her.

"In all seriousness, though, why are you out here tearing up my vegetable garden?" she asked. "Have those potatoes wronged you in some way? Were they difficult to digest? Did they wake you in the middle of the night with a stomach ache? Do they work for a rival newspaper? They must have done something truly horrendous for you to abuse them in this way."

Verity drove the weeder into the soil so that it stood up on its own and leaned back on her heels. "It is just that this is so boring. I do not know how you stand it."

"So you have said many times before," Delphine replied calmly. "That is why I am confused you are doing it now."

Grunting again, Verity rubbed the cut on her palm, which stung slightly, and admitted with petulant annoyance that she needed an activity. "I have finished my list of tasks for the day and am looking for something else to do. I thought I might find gardening engrossing. But it is deadly dull. I would happily pay someone to do it for me."

Amused, Delphine reminded her that she already did pay someone. "Me."

Verity frowned, for that was categorically not true. "I have offered you money, and you have flat out refused to accept it."

"Because I am compensated via room and board," Delphine replied.

"No, you plan the weekly menu with Cook and help Robert with his articles in exchange for room and board,"

Verity pointed out. "The gardening you do for free, which is madness. At the very least, you should permit me to compensate you for the vegetables you supply. Potatoes fetch three shillings per quarter-hundredweight at Covent Garden."

"Now you are trying to distract me with a familiar quarrel," Delphine said with a trace of impatience. "It will not work. What is the matter?"

Feeling ridiculous, Verity shifted her position so that she was sitting on the gravel, and Delphine flinched at the mistreatment of the lovely dress. "It is Hardwicke. I am teasing myself about his visit. I told you what he said, did I not?"

With a firm nod, Delphine replied, "That you are astonishingly competent."

"Astoundingly competent," Verity corrected.

Delphine's eyes sparkled with amusement as she conceded the very great difference between the terms with grave understanding. "No doubt it is something only the excessively competent can appreciate."

Acknowledging her friend's gentle mockery, Verity insisted it was not a matter of distinction but of accuracy, which was important but not the main issue. "The main issue is his dismissive attitude toward me and my supposed competence. What purpose does either serve if all I am good for is a well-timed giggle? And then to be told to mind my own business! I am incensed by it all over again."

"Are you?" Delphine asked with sincere curiosity. "Or have you yet to stop being incensed by it?"

A smile flitted across Verity's face as she conceded it was the latter. "I would have no cause to seethe over the offer if he had not praised me so lavishly. But to raise my expectations and then to dash them so callously! It was fiendish. And what makes it so much worse is he has no idea. He left here thinking he had paid me the highest compliment possible. I think that is the most infuriating thing!"

Delphine pressed her lips together sympathetically and confessed she was surprised by her friend's sensible response to the situation. "I would have thought you would have run out of the house ten paces behind Hardwicke and followed him around London until you knew every detail of the assignment."

Verity, muttering angrily under her breath, admitted that she was surprised, too.

"Or discover more information about this Mr. Fitch at the very least," Delphine added.

"It is out of character for me, is it not?" Verity asked as a pensive note entered her voice. "When was the last time I just shrugged my shoulders and looked in the other direction? I think *that* is the source of my restlessness. I have been fighting my true nature for days now because the thing is, I do want to follow him. But I have been resisting the impulse because I did not want to give the exchange even that much importance. I have been trying to convince myself that it did not bother me enough to merit one more moment of my time. It was done! But I have been angry about it this whole time, and you are right: I *should* do something to address it rather than seethe silently and abuse your potato plants."

Verity darted to her feet as Delphine insisted that was not what she had said. "I was applauding your restraint. I thought it was a good thing!" she exclaimed as she took two steps to follow her friend into the house, then halted abruptly, turned, and picked up the weeder. "Here! Dig up the weeds! And the potatoes! I do not mind at all."

But Verity, fully committed now to a course of action, thanked her for the offer but insisted the squirrels would enjoy destroying the plants more.

Chapter Three

❦

Tuesday, May 26
9:58 a.m.

Although it was possible to find the clandestine headquarters of a covert group of Yarwellian philosophers without the assistance of a vast network of spies, having access to one greatly simplified the process, which Verity appreciated to the fullest. All she had to do to discover the location was dash off notes to several of her most industrious associates and wait for their replies to arrive.

It was a credit to Twaddle and his ability to oversee a complex coalition of scrappers, street rats, shopkeepers, servants, vendors, and unaffiliated entrepreneurs that she received three responses within a half hour of each other. The secret to retaining excellent informants, of course, compensating them fairly for their time and effort, but it also helped to treat them with dignity and respect. It was no small thing to say please and thank you.

With an address in hand, Verity proceeded to consider the best way to gain information about Fitch and consequently Hardwicke's interest in Fitch. She started by visiting the building, a one-story edifice constructed of worn brown stone with square windows on a narrow lane slightly north of the river. It housed a sewing concern that employed seventeen tailors and seamstresses working three or four to a room from nine in the morning to six in the evening with occasional visits from their employer to collect the garments.

The society's headquarters were in the cellar, and the challenge was how to evade two dozen industrious workers on her way to the basement.

By being a nuisance, she thought. If she was someone they did not want to deal with, they would treat her with careless impatience.

Naturally, Dudley Tiffin sprang to mind. The scion of the H. Tiffin and Son dynasty: Official Bug Destroyers to His Majesty and the Royal Family was certainly an irritant. Nobody liked hearing they had a pest problem, and Dudley himself was something of the kind. He agreed with all your demurrals and denials and yet somehow made you feel as though the next wave of the Black Death was fomenting in your walls.

He was always granted access in the end.

That was true, yes, but if the dilapidated state of the building was an indication of anything, it was the owner's general disregard for the comfort of his tenants. The windows were cracked, their casements worn away, and some of the bricks in the facade had fallen off. Peering into one of the rooms, Verity watched a rat scurry across the floor.

Clearly, the edifice was already overrun by vermin and nobody cared.

In light of its near ruinous condition, Verity decided her first attempt would be as a carpenter sent by the landlord to assess its structural integrity. Even the most miserly owner worried about his property toppling around his tenants' ears, for it made collecting rents particularly difficult. There was always a chance, of course, that the owner himself was among the occupants she had spied through the window, but she categorized the risk as low. There was a level of filth that one typically imposed only on people with no recourse.

To that end, she donned worn trousers that were patched in several places and a clerical hat that had been run over several times by a team of horses. Mr. Stone also carried a durable leather bag that contained the various tools of his trade, including a ruler that he waved around furiously as he pointed to all the potentially disastrous deficiencies of a room.

Rarely had Mr. Stone encountered an edifice that was not in imminent danger of collapse. Did he perhaps speak with an unsettling urgency that he would do well to temper with his more elegant clients?

Of a certainty, yes.

His demeanor *did* have a tendency to put them off.

But he valued life so highly and the thought of anyone's bones being crushed by a weakened support beam, especially a small child's, upset him dearly.

Mr. Stone spoke with his customary fervor now as he rapped on the front door. "Hello! Hello! I am here to make an inspection on behalf of the owner. Please answer because I know ye can hear me. This door is too thin to muffle my voice. In fact, it is too thin to take all this knocking. In a moment it will splinter and then where will ye be? Hello?"

The door opened abruptly, and Verity, who was about to bang it again, pulled her fist back sharply. She drew her brows together in an expression of concern, although it was unlikely the man noticed because he only came up to Mr. Stone's whiskered chin. Modest in height, he was evenly proportioned, with a slim neck, narrow chest, and a dot of a nose. He had a length of string hanging from his thinning hair, and she placed his age at near or approaching fifty.

"Yer all right!" Verity said with a measure of relief. "I thought since ye didn't answer that ye might have fallen through the floorboards and broken ye leg. Come on, then, let's make sure that doesn't happen. Don't worry. Even if the wood is rotted through, most of the boards will support yer weight. It's jest a matter of keeping yer eye out as yer walking around."

As with most people who encountered the gloomy fatalism of Mr. Stone, the man regarded her with a mix of confusion and annoyance. Before he could reply, she continued. "I am Timothy Stone, here to inspect the rooms at the owner's behest. I am tasked with finding out what's unsound and making a list. I have several more properties to look at today so if we could begin right away..."

Trailing off, Verity turned her shoulder and slipped past him. She entered a long hallway with pockmarked walls, which she immediately recorded in her daybook. As she made her notation, the man ran his hands through his hair, dislodging the thread, and swore he knew nothing about an inspection. Mr. Mawburn had not mentioned it when he visited the day before to collect rent.

Verity opened her satchel, felt around, and found the level, which she held out to the man with a request that he help her gauge the evenness of the floorboards. He stared at the implement with distaste and growled that he had his own work to do. Then he bounded down the hallway and disappeared into the second room on the right. Although she wanted to go directly to the society's headquarters in the cellar, she could not risk raising suspicions and comprehensively inspected the ground floor. Its inhabitants, like the man who had answered the door, were too busy with their work to pay attention to her and she moved around them gingerly to cause as little interruption as possible. Even so, she put on a convincing performance, muttering *interesting* and *aha!* under her breath at regular intervals.

Finishing the first room, she moved on to the one next door. Nobody looked up as she entered, not even the man who had answered her knock. Aware of the pointlessness of the pantomime, she spent less time recording figures and marveling over the instability of the floorboards. She wrote down a few numbers, scribbled a note about mold on the windowsill, and thanked everyone for their time.

Surely *now* she could head to the cellar?

It was a little strange, she thought, returning to the corridor, that none of the occupants were concerned about the secret society hatching its schemes in the cellar. It seemed the sort of thing one would want to hide from prying eyes.

Unless they had nothing to do with it or were so consumed by their own obligations, they did not have time to even wonder what was happening belowstairs.

That struck Verity as entirely reasonable. The organization had formed more than ten years ago and had spent much of that decade debating the philosophical texts of Preston Yarwell. Its plan to petition the prince regent via marching Lancashire weavers was the first thing it had ever done to draw attention.

The question, of course, was, whose interests did Hardwicke represent?

Opening the door that led downstairs, she heard voices waft up the spiral staircase. They were low, not quite murmuring, and she caught a few words: stack ... many ... lemon ... donkey. Cautiously, she climbed down until she reached the curve, where she could hear the conversation more clearly. There were two of them, and they were talking about handbills.

"—better take some more," the first speaker said. "Everywhere I go, people are interested. They want to hear what he has to say. The event is going to be a success. I can feel it in my bones."

The other speaker counseled caution. "It is still two weeks away. We don't want to get ahead of ourselves. But here, take another stack just in case you need it. You have been giving out more notices than anyone else. If the mass meeting *is* a success, then it will be thanks in part to you, Mr. Fitch."

Fitch was there!

What a stroke of luck!

Desiring to get a look not only at Hardwicke's target but also the printed material under discussion, she returned silently to the top of the staircase and walked down the steps as she would normally, her footfalls on the wood treads alerting them to her presence before she came into sight. Arriving at the bottom, she found a bare stone room illuminated by a trio of candles sharing a table with bundles of papers and bottles of ink. Underneath the table were buckets and more sheets. To its right was a printing press with a wood frame indicating it was not a modern contraption like the Stanhope in the *Gazette* office. Perhaps it was a cast-off. Standing next to it, his hands black with ink, was a stout man in shirtsleeves, his blond hair tied back with a ribbon. The other fellow had a rough-seeming air about him, his whiskers thick and his light brown locks untamed. In contrast, his features were sharp and narrow beneath the bushy beard, and although he was not excessively tall, he had a resolute presence that was aided by the girth of his stomach.

Which one was Fitch?

Both men turned to look at her as soon as she rounded the bend in the staircase, and she waved her ruler at them reassuringly. "I'm inspecting the building for structural weakness on behalf of the owner. Ye don't have to worry that the walls are going to crumble around ye. By my estimation that will not happen for a good several years. The cracks in the foundation are mild as yet. And ye are probably safer in the cellar, as ye have nowhere to fall in the collapse. Anyway, do not mind me. I will just take some measurements and be on my way."

"Fine, fine," said the blond-haired man curtly. "Just be quick about it!"

"I always am," Verity murmured, walking to the far end of the room to give them the appearance of privacy to resume their conversation. It was sparse on this side as well, with a lone chair indicating that meetings themselves were held somewhere else, most likely in one of the rooms upstairs when the workers were absent, and a bookshelf stuffed haphazardly with ledgers. The latter was sandwiched between a cabinet and the safe.

As the two men voiced their hopes for the upcoming mass meeting, she pretended to record meaningful observations. Slowly, she made her way back to the other side, near the printing press, and as neither man seemed particularly interested in her movements as she drew closer to the table, she made the audacious decision to look through the stacks of handbills. They announced an event in support of reform featuring Christopher "Persuader" Crowley. The famous orator was known for his ability to win people to the cause by convincing them that only a few small alterations in governance were required to greatly improve their situations. Most notably, he was neither a Radical nor a revolutionary. He would never support insurrection or the actions of the Luddites. He believed nonviolence was the only way to effect change, and his willingness to speak on behalf of the Society of Yarwellian Philosophers seemed to affirm the peacefulness of the Burnley Blanketeers.

"Excuse me!" said the blond man harshly. "There is nothing structural about this table."

"Now, Mr. Lemon, don't be rude," chided the man with the whiskers. "Here, take one. The meeting is to gather signatures for petitions that will be presented to the prince regent himself. We are the foundation of a movement that will grow to be thousands strong. I hope you will consider joining us."

Lemon shook his head. "I see now why you go through handbills so quickly. You foist them on anyone who shows the slightest interest. They are not free to print, you know. Each one costs the society money we do not have."

Fitch waved his concerns aside. "The coffers are filled. I have seen it myself! Mr. Anderson has convinced a few toffs to support our cause, and I collect money every time I speak at a tavern. There are coins enough for printing!"

But Lemon disagreed, insisting the money was not theirs simply to do with as they wanted. "Those funds are pledged to the Blanketeers," he said waspishly, then turned to Verity and asked if she was finished yet. "You seem to be done and I have work to do and you are distracting me and the idea that Mawburn cares about the condition of this building is risible. He has not spent a penny on it in the nine years that I have been printing in this cellar."

Filing this exchange away, for it contained several interesting pieces of information, Verity said that she was in fact done and left. Once outside the building, she positioned herself across the street, off to the left, and waited for Fitch to leave so she could follow him home.

Wednesday, May 27
   2:21 p.m.

. . .

Although the best way to avoid being trampled by a pair of bays in the middle of Pimlico Road was not to stand in the middle of Pimlico Road, sometimes it was simply unavoidable. Nothing fostered a sense of intimacy between two people than a harrowing brush with death, and as Verity watched the carriage careen toward her, she screamed in fear, hopeful Miss Fitch would dash into the road to rescue her.

There was plenty of time for it.

Despite the tenor of her terror, Verity was in no real danger of being run over. The horses were not only traveling at a sedate pace but were also a goodly distance away. If Miss Fitch did not respond with appropriate urgency to save her, then Verity would still have plenty of time to dart out of the way.

But she was fairly confident Miss Fitch would act. Having observed her for the better part of twenty-four hours, Verity knew the young lady had a kind heart. She had watched her give apples to the urchins who roamed the nearby square and gently bundle an injured chick into a handkerchief and carry it into the Walpole Street residence where she and her brother kept rooms.

Surely, an old woman with a cane could expect equal consideration.

And to be certain, Verity looked very old indeed, with her rounded shoulders, trembling limbs, unsteady gait, liver spots, and wrinkles that had been applied with a glue-like formulation.

Assuming the disguise of Mrs. Ernst took two hours but was well worth the effort, for few things were less threatening than an elderly woman on the verge of collapse. In this, Verity's height helped her for it made supporting her weight even more arduous. Her cane was dauntingly thin and appeared ready to snap at any moment.

Verity gripped the knob tightly now as her cry rent the

air, and she noted the carriage was still twenty or so seconds away. She would stand there quaking for another count of ten, then throw herself to the side, narrowly avoiding destruction.

The image of her frail frame splayed on the gray muck, her arm bent at a worrying angle, would effectively stir Miss Fitch to pity.

Either outcome would serve her purpose, although Verity preferred the former simply because it was the cleaner option. Scrubbing clay sludge out of one's clothes was always such a bother.

Miss Fitch kindly obliged her by letting out a shrill screech and running into the street. She grabbed Verity's free hand in her own and tugged her mercilessly to the side. The cane dropped to the ground and snapped under the wheel of the clattering carriage as its driver yelled, "Stay clear, you stupid old hag!"

Verity sank dramatically to the ground as Miss Fitch shouted, "Rude man!" Then she squatted on the pavement next to her and asked if she had been harmed in the kerfuffle. "Does anything hurt?"

"I don't think so," Verity replied in Mrs. Ernst's weak and reedy trill. "But it is hard to tell, my heart is racing so fast. I can't catch my breath. I don't understand what happened. The carriage came out of nowhere. If not for your quick thinking, I would be dead. You saved my life."

"Nonsense," Miss Fitch said matter-of-factly. "The driver would have swerved to miss you, I am sure of it. Can you stand?"

Mrs. Ernst shook her head with as much vigor as she was capable, which was to say with hardly any at all, and insisted she would be detritus on the road if not for her timely intervention. "I do not know how to thank you. Please let me compensate you. I have some shillings in my purse. Would two shillings be enough?"

Miss Fitch colored at the suggestion and insisted that no reward was necessary. "But do let's try to stand. I do not want to leave you until I know you are all right."

Now Verity grasped the other woman's hand with trembling fingers. "Do not leave me, please. I am all befuddled and ... and ... shaky. Anxious. If you won't let me compensate you, at least allow me to buy you something like ... like ... tea and a bun at Mead's Bun House. That was where I was going. It is a little treat I give myself on occasion," she offered hopefully, then let out a sigh filled with exaggerated dejection. "What am I thinking? Of course you do not wish to waste your time with a stupid old hag like me. You are young and pretty and have so many other wonderful things to do."

"Oh, but I would adore a treat," Miss Fitch said enthusiastically. "I have not been to Mead's despite being in the city for more than a month and living so near. I mostly confine myself to the square, taking the air every morning as I watch people stroll by."

Well, that was interesting, Verity thought. According to other tenants in the building, Fitch had lived there twice as long. That meant her brother had come to London without her. Filing the tidbit away, she suggested they rectify the oversight at once. Then she indulged in a mild coughing fit that caused her to topple to the side. She waved off Miss Fitch's concern and then tottered to her feet, lamenting the loss of her cane.

Miss Fitch held out her arm and slowly guided her to Mead's, which was only one block away. The enticing scent of freshly baked Chelsea buns greeted them the moment they stepped inside, and Verity's stomach rumbled in anticipation. What she had said was true: She sometimes called on the famous establishment as a treat for her and Delphine, and she resolved to return after parting ways with Miss Fitch to purchase some buns for her friend and the servants.

As they settled into their seats with their tea and buns, Verity realized Miss Fitch was not quite as young as she had originally appeared. Her skin was dewy and her eyes a sharp blue, but there were fine lines around her mouth, and Verity judged her to be nearing thirty-five like herself.

"Is this your first visit to London?" she asked.

Miss Fitch said yes. "Well, for any length of time, that is. I have passed through twice before with the troupe."

Although Verity was fascinated by this disclosure, she kept her tone light and vaguely indifferent as she repeated, "The troupe?"

A shadow darted across Miss Fitch's face as she narrowed her eyes for a second before flitting her gaze around the room. She swept it left and right as she leaned forward and whispered, "I am an actress."

Then she giggled.

It was a merry sound, giddy and loose, and she raised her hand to her lips as if to cut it off at the source.

"I shouldn't say that out loud because I am performing right now in a ... in a ... *capacity* that is very different from what I am accustomed to. There is no audience, you see, at least none that *knows* it's the audience," she added with an embarrassed chortle. "And it has been like a *physical* ache. It is like lying, isn't it, to pretend to be something you're not? And I am sure you can say that is acting all over, but it is a different type of lie when the audience know they are watching a performance. Nobody knows about this perfor-mance, and you must promise not to tell anyone. My employer would be very cross with me if he found out."

As Miss Fitch's revelation depended on knowledge that even Verity in her privileged position did not possess, she readily swore that she would not mention a word about it to anyone. She had an idea, however, and suspected the role was as Fitch's sister.

Why he felt the need for a sibling was the curious thing.

She recalled what Hardwicke had said about Fitch's deep and abiding bond with his sister, forged in the tragic crucible of their childhood—a bond that Hardwicke had planned to exploit by claiming a similar connection with his own sister.

But Fitch was already exploiting it.

Possessing a sincere love for one's family was generally an endearing trait, and she wondered if his motivation was that straightforward. He was a solid man, dauntingly fierce in his whiskers despite his friendliness, and she could understand how a sister might soften his affect.

Ah, but it also disguised it as well, she thought, recalling her own use of Robert Lark. It changed the cast of things and put the attention elsewhere.

Could that be the actress's value?

If that was the case, what was Fitch trying to hide?

The counterfeit Miss Fitch—CounterFitch, in Twaddle's parlance—thanked Mrs. Ernst for her discretion and said again what a relief it was to be able to be her true self even if it was for only a few minutes. "I am not used to hiding my light under a bushel, you see, and at the risk of appearing immodest, I must inform you that I have played my current part to perfection! Amanda is a delicate creature, scarred by tragedy but strengthened by her brother's love. She would defend him fiercely against any threat that rose up to challenge him. Not since Ophelia at the Royal Theatre in York have I so thoroughly embodied a character. The pathos as I handed out flowers: 'There's rue for you and here's some for me.' Mr. Burnside of the *York Observer* called me 'the archetype of regret and despair.' If he could have seen Amanda overcoming her anxiety to serve tea to her brother's new associates, a group of rough-and-ready men who barely grunted thank you before devouring the muffins she had painstakingly prepared, he would have written a glowing review even more enthusiastic than the last."

Ordinarily a woman of Mrs. Ernst's class and breeding would be horrified by these musings—blithely living in sin with a man without fear of damnation!—but she had neatly dodged death thanks to the other woman's intervention and she did not have the heart to quibble over her immorality. After explaining why she would graciously accept the actress's depravity without comment, she complimented her on her wonderful notices and claimed to understand why she missed having an audience. "Applause must be difficult to go without."

"It is, very!" she said.

"All the more because your ... um ... brother's associates sound terrifying," Verity observed.

The other woman shuddered dramatically and said they were ruffians. "To a man. They have no appreciation for the arts. All they care about is money and how to raise more of it. It is so crushingly dull."

Duly sympathetic, Verity tilted slightly forward and said some men had no appreciation of the finer things. "I hope you are being appropriately compensated for your ordeal, both in the company you are being forced to keep and the lack of an admiring audience."

"Although no amount of money can make up for the lack of an admiring audience, I am being compensated well enough. It is not a princely amount," she said, darting her eyes left and right before mentioning the sum of three shillings. "That is per week, which is more than I would make performing, plus it includes room and board. *And* I have been promised a bonus at the end of the run."

"That is generous," Verity murmured, deeply curious about the exact amount of the payment. She could not ask outright, for that was too rude even for Mrs. Ernst, whose advanced age allowed her certain liberties. It would be a modest figure, for a man of Fitch's stature could not be swimming in coins.

Taking another bite of her bun, the actress nodded and chewed. Then she said, "I wouldn't have even considered the role if the company's next play wasn't *The Deeds of the Barber,* which does not have a single good female part. There are only three in total and the one I am most suited for is called Miss Gold Digger, who is exactly as she sounds. And it is not the greed I object to. I think a woman should do whatever she has to, to attain security for herself in a world that offers few opportunities. If that means being comedically driven in your desire to marry well, especially at Miss Gold Digger's age, for she is not in the first blush of youth, then that's fine with me. But the playwright should make some effort at nuance. It is not as though he has written a morality play or even a farce. I would not object to being Miss Gold Digger if the men were called Mr. Aimwell or Squire Sullen as in *The Beaux' Stratagem.* *The Deeds of the Barber* is just poorly written. Mr. Button's other play was equally as atrocious. Mr. Culver in the *Newcastle Daily Advertiser* called *Lord Deftly's Decision* 'a dull drizzle.' It has been like that a lot recently—lackluster roles I am not interested in playing. There are so many wonderful parts for a woman my age. Just imagine me leaping across the stage as the swashbuckling Ann Bonny in *How She Won the Seas.* I can wield a cutlass as well as any pirate. Learning to fight properly was part of my training. I know how to use all the weapons. Ask me anything—about a gun or a sword, anything—and I will tell you the proper way to hold it."

With Mrs. Ernst's age and inclinations, she preferred *Everyman* to tales of female buccaneers (sordid things!) and she spent several minutes lauding the lessons it taught about how men should live their lives and meet their deaths. Then she turned to more practical matters and asked how many more weeks Miss Fitch had left on her contract. "I can tell you are eager to return to a theater."

"It is not a contract," the actress rushed to clarify. "Only an agreement. And I do not know how much longer it will take."

"It?" Verity asked, dipping her head into the teacup. "What is 'it'?"

But her companion raised her shoulders sharply and swore she did not know. "My employer has not shared with me the purpose of our stay. All I know is my own part in the piece, which is as a gracious peg-puff, and I have carried it off brilliantly."

Verity did not have to affect the muddled confusion of an old lady as she repeated the term *peg-puff*. "It sounds dreadful. I hope it does not hurt."

Miss CounterFitch laughed and insisted it was painless. "It just means to be polite and mature. My employer did not want his sister to be a silly young thing."

"No Ophelia in other words," Verity said.

"Gracious no!" she vehemently agreed. "Amanda neither gives flowers nor receives them, and she certainly does not drown herself in brooks. That said, if the part called for it, I would make a very affecting corpse, so sweet and peaceful as I lay in my coffin, arms crossed gently against my chest. Mr. Burnside called my performance in the funeral scene 'heart-rending.' The secret is small gestures, like how the hair falls or the bodice of the dress is arranged. You see, a performance should have subtlety, not bound around the stage shouting, 'I want gold! Give me your gold, rich man whom I seek to marry!'"

Mrs. Ernst owned herself fascinated by these insights and swore she would never watch a play in the same way again.

Something about these words recalled Miss CounterFitch to her duty and her cheeks darkened with color as she dropped the remaining quarter of the bun onto its plate. "I have been horribly indiscreet. I am so desperate for appreciation I have broken my word to my employer. Please do not tell anyone. Please! My wages would be forfeit, and I would have no hope of earning the bonus. Do promise me you will keep my secret. If you want to reward me for saving your life, please say nothing about our conversation to anyone."

Given the tenor of Mr. Burnside's approbation, Verity did not doubt that the actress could feign convincing distress. Even so, she believed it was genuine. Miss CounterFitch had lapsed briefly and now regretted the transgression. "Do not tease yourself, my dear," she said comfortingly. "I won't tell a soul. Indeed, there is no one for me to tell even if I were so inclined. My husband and two of my children are dead. My surviving son moved to Ireland a decade ago. I am all alone and am grateful for the conversation. Now do drink your tea before it gets cold. And perhaps you will do me the favor of having another bun? I am still unsteady from almost being crushed by a carriage and could use the company for a little longer."

Miss CounterFitch pressed her lips together as if to refuse, then smiled tentatively and agreed.

Chapter Four

Wednesday, May 27
5:12 p.m.

Although Delphine cherished an instinctive horror of Twaddling, with its late-night forays, its rubbish heap searches, and its tedious surveillance of targets as they trudge through the errands of their day in hopes of discovering some useful scrap of information, she genuinely enjoyed one aspect: calling on Addison's.

The coffeehouse, located in Neal Street, rarely drew a large crowd, for it possessed none of the academic rigor of Nando's in Fleet Street nor the artistic allure of Old Slaughter's in St. Martin's Lane. It was a dignified establishment, a little threadbare from use, with rickety chairs and scarred tables, which endeared it to Delphine, who considered its lack of broad appeal to be its main appeal. If one wanted a quiet spot where one could hear oneself think, then one could do no better than Addison's.

She was also engrossed enough in the family business to appreciate a venue that provided access to so much information. Every coffeehouse supplied its patrons with a sweeping array of newspapers, but only Addison's reach extended deep into the provinces. There were limits, of course, and it did not have every daily from the more rural towns in the farthermost counties. If, for example, a rapacious London gossip wanted to know more about a theater performance in Portgower, she would have to make the arduous two-week-long journey up to Scotland to discover the details. Perhaps, if she was lucky, a coffeehouse in Edinburgh would have the desired chronicle and she could spare herself the last two hundred miles.

But York was large enough and close enough to be included in Addison's collection.

"Found it!" Delphine cried out, her finger resting about a quarter way down the middle column. "A review of *Hamlet* at the York Theatre Royal by Roger Burnside from March thirteenth."

Verity, who had been searching February editions of the *York Observer,* ceased her perusal and looked up at her friend. "Fitch hired her in late March, then."

"Maryanne Copley," Delphine clarified, as her eyes skimmed the article and she absorbed its contents. "She made a convincing if stilted Ophelia, according to Mr. Burnside, who reports she did her best work in the funeral scene, to which her stiffness was best suited. That is not quite the unalloyed praise she reported to Mrs. Ernst."

"No, it is not," Verity said, reading the review over her friend's shoulder. "I wonder if Fitch's offer was refused by other, more talented actresses."

Delphine allowed that it was possible but also suggested that his options might have been limited. "He was offering minimal compensation—barely more than what a scullion earns—and maximum risk. I do not think many women would be willing to leave everything that was secure and familiar to travel to London with a virtual stranger, putting themselves in his power and exposing themselves to all sorts of mistreatment. Miss Copley is either very brave or very foolish. If the compensation were greater, I could see more women being tempted."

"There is the bonus at the end," Verity reminded her. "That would be a significant inducement."

"Yes," Delphine agreed. "But to what end and how is it defined? Considering how little he is paying her from week to week, I cannot help but wonder if he plans to cheat her by never achieving his goal."

Verity, who had had the same thought, admitted that she had been unable to get Miss CounterFitch to identify her employer's objective. "She insisted she had already said too much and swore she could not reveal one more word. Then we discussed the roles she longs to play—Medea, Lady MacBeth, Ann Bonny—and took our leave of each other."

Delphine, noting it was a pity that Verity had been unable to convince the target to reveal more, suggested that perhaps next time she should throw herself into the river. "If you are truly bedraggled by almost dying, she will be more frank with you."

As her friend had made several provoking remarks of this nature in the past eight hours, Verity knew there was no point in trying to reason with her. Delphine was determined to take exception to her methods. Instead, she pointed out the impracticalities of her proposal: Even if Miss Copley had been inclined to jump into the water to save a stranger, a development that was in no way guaranteed given the ungodly state of the Thames and the varying level of swimming abilities among the lower classes, she would emerge from the ordeal sodden and shivering. "Rather than enjoy a soothing coze with me over tea and buns, she would have run off immediately to her home to bathe."

"Verity!" Delphine growled.

Instantly contrite, Verity apologized for teasing and swore she did it only because her friend was worrying herself over nothing. "My life was never in danger. The carriage was moving slowly, and I had plenty of time to get out of harm's way on my own if Miss Copley ignored my cries. And say what you will about my approach, it was an effective introduction and I learned more than I had expected."

Far from appeased, Delphine muttered under her breath.

"Let us assume Miss Copley was the third or fourth actress he tried to hire," Verity said, returning to the matter at hand. "That means he had begun devising his scheme in late February or early March. What was going on in the north about that time? There was the attack on an ironworks near Tockwith. The factory agent was injured, I believe."

"He was killed but that was earlier," Delphine replied thoughtfully. "It was December or January, was it not? They called it the Christmas Uprising."

"Of course, yes, you are right," Verity said, collecting the newspapers in a neat pile to return to the attendant. "Two hundred men attacked the ironworks to steal weapons and then they were going to march to York with their demands, gathering other insurrectionists on their way. But they never left the factory because the militia was there to meet them. The *Gazette* carried several articles about it. I believe the leaders of the uprising were hanged."

Delphine said that was what she remembered, too.

"Very well, then, let us get issues from late December and see what details we do not recall," Verity announced as she rose to her feet, gathering the stack in her arms. She carried it to the counter and exchanged the dailies for a new assortment.

Reports of the Christmas Uprising were thorough and grim: On December 24, a mob consisting of more than two hundred ironworkers, stockingers, and quarrymen descended on the Catterton Ironworks in expectation of finding the foundry quiet on the eve of Christmas. Arriving after midnight, they were met in the courtyard by the factory agent, who told them to return to their homes. They refused —"on an unholy cry," as the *York Observer* described it—and charged, trampling the agent, who managed to get off one shot before being crushed underfoot. The men, savoring their victory, turned their fury toward the factory doors, which they rammed with collective force as the 15th Regiment of Light Dragoons began to shoot. Trapped against the door, they fell one after the other, some succumbing to musket fire while the vast majority scattered into the night.

By the time it was over, eight insurrectionists were dead and twenty-nine injured. The leaders of the uprising were summarily rounded up, tried for their crimes, and put to death. They were George Wingfield, Fergus Linley, and Barnabas Ibbs. Several other significant members in the movement—Hermann Vane, Russel Horne, Evan Pocock—had evaded apprehension and a reward was offered for their return. Dozens of other men were sought by the authorities for involvement.

The only reason the death toll was not greater, according to the local magistrate quoted in an *Observer* article, was a patriot working on behalf of the government bravely stepped forward to warn officials of what was about to unfold. Without the help of this secret informer, the army would have been unable to thwart the mob of violent insurrectionists. The men would have succeeded in arming themselves and attacking hundreds of innocent women and children on their march to York.

Dozens of innocent lives would have been lost!

Countering the magistrate's report were accounts from villagers, who swore the insurgents were primarily peaceful men who had been spurred by an agitator, who some later suspected of supplying information to the army, as he was seen by the father-in-law of an insurrectionist talking to one of the general's liveried footmen the day *after* the man was arrested at the ironworks.

"Well, they would say that, wouldn't they?" Delphine noted sadly. "Nine men dead—on Christmas Eve, no less—and they do not want to accept that the men they have lived among and known their whole lives could be capable of so much violence. What a tragic waste of life."

Verity nodded, and reaching the end of the article, considered Fitch in light of the new information. Why the elaborate ruse of a sister?

To enhance his disguise, she thought.

If he was an insurrectionist from the north hoping to stir up trouble and mayhem in the south, then changing his appearance would be essential. He could not simply stride into the capital as Mr. Vane or Mr. Pocock. He would need to alter his identity in as many ways as possible. If the authorities were looking for an only child or a man with just brothers, then he would have a sister.

And the whiskers on his narrow face, she realized now. They hid the gauntness of his cheeks, which was at odds with the fullness of his belly. Mr. Fitch possessed a well-rounded paunch, which gave him more of a jolly air. That was fake too, she realized. He wore padding to thicken his waist.

So which escaped leader was he: Vane, Horne, or Pocock?

The one without a sister, she presumed.

But how did Verity find out that information?

The simplest way was for Robert Lark to send a letter to the editor of the *York Observer.* It would most likely yield results but would take at least a fortnight.

She did not want to wait that long.

Delphine, seeming to read her thoughts, said, "I suppose you had better start following Mr. Fitch around to figure out who he really is and if he is trying to start an uprising in London."

Verity was already sifting through her collection of disguises to find the right one for surveilling a possibly violent insurrectionist.

Friday, May 29
  3:45 p.m.

Having created scores of fictional characters and two fictitious reporters, Verity knew herself to be an expert deceiver. Her dressing room held every conceivable item of clothing, from trousers, breeches, and stockings in a variety of fabrics and textures to mob caps, bonnets, and turbans in a dizzying array of colors. Her vanity contained dozens of powders, rouges, and dyes to vary her appearance, and she was adept at darkening her eyes or sharpening her cheeks. It was all sleight of hand and came down in the end to expectation: People saw what they expected to see.

Except Colson Hardwicke.

He saw everything.

Catching sight of a collier several paces behind him on William Road, he had noticed that the man's shoes bore a striking resemblance to the ones worn by the hack driver he had observed the morning before and the fruit seller earlier in the day.

He had been right, of course.

Verity did favor one particular pair of shoes for surveillance work because they were the most comfortable set she owned. Regardless of how long she stood in them, they never pinched at the toes or rubbed at the heels.

Nevertheless, it behooved her to wear a greater variety, and as she followed Fitch along Bessemer Road, she lamented the discomfort of her most recent purchase. A blister was forming on her smallest toe, she was certain.

Damn Hardwicke and his eagle eye.

Fitch paused at the corner to allow a carriage to pass and then darted into the street, dodging a coach and two men on horseback as he crossed to the other side. Verity waited for traffic to lighten, then trotted across the street, her eyes never losing sight of her quarry.

Following Fitch was easy because the man never appeared to be in a rush. Although he always had a destination in mind, he seemed to stroll with an aimless wonder, as if curious what he might find at the end of his ramble.

Verity assumed this was also part of his disguise. A man with a price on his head would be inclined toward nervousness, fearing discovery at any moment, his neck always craning this way and that to see who was watching him, his arms jangling with anxiety.

Fitch displayed none of that.

Although he seemed oblivious to his surroundings, appearing almost to hum with indifference as he sauntered along the pavement, Verity knew he was cognizant of everything around him. After two days of scrutiny, she recognized the effort required to affect apathy. She saw it in the moments when he tensed his shoulders like a snake coiling to strike. It was fleeting, a response he could not control but could easily overcome, and the next instant he was relaxed.

He was most definitely a wanted man, Verity thought.

Even if he had not displayed these brief episodes of excessive alertness, she would have recognized him as an insurrectionist, for he spoke so articulately about the cause. Daily, he visited the taverns and inns where poor and working men gathered to drink and pleaded passionately for the sort of practical reforms the government had deemed radical. He delivered what Verity had come to think of as his table speech because, as he spoke, he slowly mounted a table in the middle of the room. He began modestly, standing in a corner, and moved to the center of the floor and then raised himself higher as he spoke, first to a chair, then to the table.

He always started with a series of questions. His voice imbued with genuine curiosity, he would ask, "Is it radical to take care of your family? Feeding your children—is that radical? Dressing your children—is that radical? Providing your children with a place to lay their heads at the end of the day —are we truly going to allow them to call *that* radical?"

Here, Fitch stopped to allow his audience, which typically began with the few men in his immediate vicinity and then grew to include the whole room as the other drinkers fell silent. After three breaths, he answered his own queries. "I say no, it is not. I say it is the least radical thing you could do. Caring for your family is at the heart of what it means to be an Englishman, and yet they seek to take that away from us. They seek to make it a crime to feed your children, dress your children, provide for your children. In contrast, the reform movement seeks only to alter the system slightly."

Heads would nod, hesitantly at first and then with increasing conviction, as he mounted the chair. "The reform movement seeks reasonable changes. Do you think you should have a say in how our government governs? If so, then you, my friend, are a radical. Do you think that rotten boroughs are unfair and should be eliminated? If so, then you, my friend, are a radical. Do you think treating workers with inhumanity and indecency is wrong? If so, then you, my friend, are a radical. That is all that it means. Government should be fair. Think that and—aha!—you are a radical."

Now a few patrons would call out their support, and emboldened by their enthusiasm, Fitch would climb onto the table, his defense of the movement vigorous and strong. "The powerful men who rule this country would have us believe that these requests are extreme. How dare we, common men who toil in their factories and till their soil, desire something better for our children? How dare we ask for the right to vote? How dare we consider ourselves worthy to cast a ballot to help decide the great issues of our day? They tell us not to worry. They pat us on our heads and tell us to go to bed, treating us like children. But what is the one thing we as Englishmen know above all others?"

Another pause.

At this point, the room was usually so quiet you could hear the barmaid pouring beer behind the counter.

Only when Fitch was satisfied with the pervasiveness of the silence would he supply the answer. "Take care of the children. Englishmen know above all else that our most sacred responsibility is to take care of the children. But they have not taken care of us. They have betrayed us at every turn: driving up the cost of bread with their tariffs, getting rid of the income tax to allow the national debt to spiral. Now we are saying enough. That is all the radical movement is: thousands of men saying *enough* at the same time. And that is what scares the ruling class. To them all our voices speaking at once is an act of violence. Is it? I do not think so. But I will leave it to each and every one of you to find your own response. Because I know you are not children. You are men!"

This last statement always elicited a hearty cheer, and Fitch would wait until it subsided before saying his final piece. Generally, the interval lasted just a few seconds, but on one occasion it extended well into a third minute. Then he would invite everyone to come hear the Persuader himself,

Christopher Crowley, on June fifth 5 at seven at night in the field behind St. Dunstan's in Clerkenwell.

But only if their answer aligned with his!

"If you think crying mercy to the endless oppressions of the state is indeed violence, then do not come," he would add. "You would not feel comfortable among our cohort. If you do agree, then let Mr. Crowley explain the objectives of our movement and how they will be achieved. Add your name to the petition and learn how the Burnley Blanketeers will march across England and march across Yorkshire and march across London and march into the future!"

Although this was the official end to his speech, it was always followed by requests for more information and Fitch was swarmed with men asking how they could help.

The answer was always the same: learn more about the cause, attend the mass meeting, donate money, sign the petition. Heeding the call, the patrons promised to attend and handed over whatever few coins they had to help the Blanketeers reach their goal.

Verity had seen Fitch make the speech five times in three days. He was relentless in his drive to drum up support for the reform movement. It was not surprising given that he was willing to risk apprehension and execution to promote the cause.

Arriving at the Anchor and Whale now, Fitch fetched a beer from the barmaid and settled at a table in the corner. He drank silently for several minutes, studying the patrons with quiet intensity. Then, when he felt he had a solid sense of his audience, he initiated conversation with the men at the table next to him. Then he gradually increased his volume as he warmed to his subject.

As it was a practiced presentation, little changed from performance to performance, and Verity felt as though she could set her watch by it. She could predict the number of seconds in the first rhetorical pause to a hairsbreadth.

And go: I say no, it is not.

"I say no, it is not," Fitch continued as if responding to her prompt.

While she listened to his speech, Verity thought about Hardwicke and wondered if he suspected Fitch of being one of the three leaders of the Christmas Uprising still at large. The amount on offer for their capture was not insignificant, and the disowned son of the Marquess of Ware would eagerly accept the hefty reward as a supplement to the income he managed to scrape together from various unsavory sources.

Whatever the question, money was almost always the answer.

Now that she had the information, Verity considered what she should do with it.

Swoop in and claim the bounty for herself?

That option had definite appeal, to be sure.

Hardwicke had outmaneuvered her on no less than three occasions, and it would feel good to outwit him for once. How very cross he would be to realize she had beaten him at his own game—a game he did not even know she was playing.

Verity smiled, imagining his fury.

Sorry, but that is what you get for asking me to perform a task below my skill level.

On the table, Fitch was finishing his speech, inviting the tavern's patrons to attend the mass meeting at which Christopher "Persuader" Crowley was speaking, and drawing his last deep breath before ending on a high note.

Only he did not inhale deeply.

Taking a shallow breath, he stumbled over the second *march* and tread quickly over the last clause of his climactic sentence. Then he lowered his head and scampered off the table.

Struck by his sudden unease, Verity turned sharply to the door to see who had entered. Expecting to find a Runner or a magistrate standing on the threshold, she was startled to note the only newcomer was an older man with gently rounded shoulders and a cane. Although he could technically be a justice, for many of them were far along in years, his clothes were too shabby. There was a tear in the right arm of his coat, and stains marred his trousers.

Slowly, seemingly uninterested in the proceedings, he made his way to the nearest table and sat down. It was not difficult to find a seat because the majority of patrons had gathered around Fitch to either ask him questions or laud his oration. The old man raised his hand to the barmaid, indicated that he would like an ale, retrieved the *Times* from his pocket and gave every appearance of being engrossed in the news.

But it was a ploy.

His head was down but his eyes were up and they were trained on the crowd surrounding Fitch. He did not turn the page a single time as he kept his gaze steady.

Ordinarily inclined to stay as long as necessary, soaking up every bit of attention and coin, Fitch slipped out of the tavern after only fifteen minutes. He did it discreetly, drawing his admirers closer and closer to the door so that he did not formally take his leave of anyone. Even with these efforts, it was impossible to miss, and Verity watched the old man watch Fitch step outside. Long after Fitch was gone, the old man's focus did not waver, and it was only when his cane was accidentally knocked over by another patron that he looked away. Then he returned to the *Times* and actually read the front page as he sipped his drink.

Verity, baffled by his lack of urgency, remained in her own seat rather than follow Fitch to his next destination. She was more interested in understanding the old man's behavior than hearing the table speech yet another time.

Clearly, the old man recognized Fitch.

There could be no doubt about that, given the intensity of his stare and how his demeanor changed after he left. Fitch, in turn, had recognized him as well. The slight stumble in his words and his eagerness to leave were clear indications that he knew the man and had no desire to linger in his presence.

What Verity was less certain of was whether Fitch realized he had been recognized. The newcomer had hidden his interest well, focusing on his own movements as he hobbled to the nearest table and seeming to notice nothing about his surroundings in the effort. And then he tilted his head down almost immediately to read the newspaper. Fitch, presented with the other man's bald pate, might have rejoiced in this stroke of luck and left the tavern believing he had evaded disaster by a hair.

It was, Verity thought, a credible sequence of events.

And yet the old man's performance had been too studied, his determination not to show any interest too assiduous. For it to be truly convincing, he should have at least glanced up to see what all the bother was about. It was a small thing but enough to make her think Fitch knew the truth. He would have noticed, as well, that the patron had refrained from following him. That could mean only one of two things: that he already knew where Fitch lived or he did not need to know where Fitch lived.

Both prospects would be unsettling to an insurrectionist with a price on his head, especially one who continued to engage in radical activities. There was no published schedule of Fitch's tavern visits, but anyone willing to put in a little elbow grease could easily find him—as demonstrated by the elderly man's appearance.

Although Verity liked this theory for several reasons, she

could not quite reconcile the man's lack of urgency with a bounty of seventy-five pounds at stake. If his goal was to collect the reward, then why would he risk alerting his quarry to the fact that he had been discovered? His best play would have been to arrive with the authorities in tow so they could take him into custody immediately. Coming to the tavern to confirm his suspicion first was tantamount to yelling, "Run!"

By the time the old man finished his beer, Fitch would be halfway to Brighton.

But that prospect did not worry him, which made her question the accuracy of the obvious conclusion.

Consequently, she sought another explanation.

What if they were both insurrectionists?

According to the report she had read in the *York Observer,* dozens of participants in the uprising had evaded the authorities. Staying in the area would make them easier to find, so a significant number of them had probably scattered to the surrounding shires. Presumably, some of those fugitives had made their way to London, and as they were former conspirators, it was not outrageous to imagine they would have a protocol in place for communicating silently with each other in public. Perhaps sitting down at a table and taking out a newspaper was a message.

It was an intriguing idea.

If that was the case, then the man with the cane might also be one of the escaped organizers: Vane, Horne, or Pocock. Capturing two highly sought after leaders of the Christmas Uprising would be worth a considerable amount of money, and as Verity waited for the man to finish his drink and proceed to his next destination, she imagined the look of mystification and aggravation on Hardwicke's face as she sauntered forward to collect both bounties.

. . .

Saturday, May 30
  9:41 a.m.

Verity's assumption that Smith—the man with the cane—was an insurrectionist from up north was reaffirmed by the state of the boarding house where he had taken rooms. Situated on a gloomy road adjacent to Saffron Hill, one of the worst rookeries in London, it leaned subtly to the left, like a wife trying to glimpse a notecard her husband was reading, and was missing more than a quarter of its roof tiles. The windows looked leaky, the stairs felt creaky, and she genuinely feared as she stepped onto the landing that the floorboards would collapse under her weight.

Grimly, she thought that anyone who lodged in its cold, damp quarters deserved to be compensated for the displeasure rather than the more traditional arrangement. That Smith had decided to remain there rather than seek out a less dilapidated establishment spoke to the limitation of his options. He could not afford anything better.

Or perhaps he thought the crooked structure was an ideal hiding place.

Certainly, nobody who could avoid its wretchedness would even glance at it once, let alone examine it for something of interest.

As if the threat of the edifice crumbling beneath one's feet were not daunting enough, it was overseen by a harridan who squawked at her tenants and squeezed them for every last coin. While climbing through a window that opened onto the kitchens, Verity listened to Mrs. Buglehorn berate a boarder for stealing cutlery. Aghast at the charge, the man insisted he was only using the knife to cut his kippers, which he had paid full price for despite their being slightly off.

"Ye paid fer the kippers, all right," she sneered in return, "but not fer utensils. Ye can use yer hands if ye are too parsi-monious to pay for basic amenities. Trying to skint me! I've seen yer kind before, mister, oh, yes, I have. Want everything handed to ye on a silver platter!"

The man's response, offered tepidly with a mixture of outrage and shame, was to swear he had never sought to get anything for free in his entire life.

"Oi, that is what ye all say," Mrs. Buglehorn said before tutting disapprovingly. "The tea is included in the price of ye breakfast, but the teacup is not."

Arriving on the second-floor landing, Verity could not make out his reply.

Yesterday, after following Smith to his lodgings, she had entered the building a few paces behind him to inquire about a room. From her perch in the hallway, she heard Smith tell the landlady that he would not require breakfast the next day because he had something important to do and would be gone by eight. Mrs. Buglehorn received this news of his appointment snappishly and reminded her tenant that it cost extra not to purchase the morning meal from the establish-ment—to compensate her for the lost income.

"I could have rented yer room to someone who ate all me breakfasts," she had said, justifying the policy. "And the room ye have, room twelve, is the finest one in me whole house. I could have charged twice as much if I was a less generous soul. Remember that, Mr. Smith!"

Confounded by either the extra charge or the revelation that the ramshackle pile of decaying wood and rotted joints had anything that could be described as *fine,* Smith stam-mered a reply. Verity, deciding she had enough information to plan her next move, slipped silently out the front door and returned the next morning to search Mr. Smith's rooms. She waited until after nine on the off chance that he had been delayed slightly in leaving for his appointment and upon entering the boarding house was greeted by Mrs. Buglehorn's ardent dissatisfaction with her lodger. Verity was grateful for the grumbling because the noise covered the squeaks of the floorboards.

Room twelve was on the third floor, in the back of the building, tucked next to the staircase. As a precaution, Verity pressed her ear against the door, confident that the wood was so thin she would be able to hear a mouse scurrying back to its hole.

It was silent.

Quickly, before another boarder could notice her interest, she picked the lock and entered the room. It was a narrow space, with a window to the right overlooking a garden, and a fireplace to the left. In the middle was a crush of furniture—settee, table, cupboard, ottoman, writing desk—and she imagined the challenge of navigating to the other side in the dark. One's knees would inevitably suffer in the crossing.

And this is Mrs. Buglehorn's best room, she thought in cynical amusement as she skirted around a chair to examine the writing desk. No doubt that designation was bestowed frequently and with all necessary convenience.

The desk was sparse, with only a single drawer that was empty and a blotter that had not been changed in several years. Covered in thick splotches of ink, it offered no insights, and she turned her attention to the cupboard, which was equally without interest. Moving next to the sofa, she ran her fingers around the edges of the cushion to make sure nothing noteworthy had fallen in between. Although she did not expect to find a signed confession or anything likewise incriminating, she knew it did no harm to check.

She had found more important documents in less likely places.

Alas, the room was bereft of useful information, and she decided to proceed to the next one. As there was only one door, to the right of the fireplace, she assumed it led to the bedchamber. It was slightly ajar, and Verity pushed it, stopping suddenly as the hinges squeaked loudly. She paused a moment as the clamor faded from her ears, opened the door just another two inches, and slipped between the narrow slot. Mr. Smith was still in his bed, a knife protruding from his chest.

And standing over him was Colson Hardwicke.

Chapter Five

✽

Saturday, May 30
9:52 a.m.

Verity was not surprised at all.

Shocked, yes, because the scene was so grisly, the way the blood soaked the sheets under and around the victim, whose eyes were closed as if still asleep before starting the day, his arms folded peacefully across his chest. But he was already dressed, his torso sheathed in a black coat, its fabric just as frayed as the tattered brown one he had worn the day before, his white shirt stained by a bright red darkening to rust. His state indicated he had begun his morning in the regular fashion, rising in anticipation of his early appointment, and then someone had stolen into his room and summarily ended it.

Scarcely nine o'clock and his day was over.

His life was over, Verity corrected herself.

And that was startling.

The fact that Mr. Smith had gotten himself murdered only a short while before was astounding in every way.

But Hardwicke being there?

That was almost to be expected.

He had the disconcerting ability to show up at the most inconvenient time, and rather than rail against this appalling habit, Verity chose to accept it. Whatever wretched, weird, or wonderful thing was going on in the world, Colson Hardwicke would be its first witness.

So be it.

He, however, had not made peace with her own strange ubiquity and gaped with stunned incredulity. If he had any concern that she might think he was responsible for Mr. Smith's regrettable condition, he revealed none of it as he stared at her.

Blinking innocently, as if his confusion were the bewildering thing, not her presence, Verity said, "It would be more productive, my lord, if you shared your initial thoughts regarding Smith's murder rather than goggle at me. You will note, I hope, that I have paid you the compliment of assuming you did not do it—and not only because you do not have a speck of blood on your clothes—and trust you will extend the same courtesy to me. It benefits neither of us to waste time with baseless accusations."

Hardwicke insisted he was neither gaping nor forming suspicions. "Rather, I am trying to figure out how you arrived here—and I do not mean what manner of conveyance you used."

"But is it not obvious?" she asked provokingly.

"No, Miss Gorman, it is not," he replied, demonstrating that even in his astonishment he still had the presence of mind to employ one of her noms de guerre.

She pressed her lips together to smother the smile that rose to her lips, for it was dreadfully cruel to Mr. Smith to draw any amusement from the situation. Nevertheless, her response lacked a certain sobriety. "I accepted the assignment."

"It is customary to inform the offering party of a change of mind," he replied.

Verity shook her head and apologized for wording her response poorly. "I meant I accepted the challenge."

"I did not challenge you," he said stiffly.

"Oh, but did you not?" she murmured.

He might have issued another denial but for the sudden pounding on the door. They heard three hard knocks and then Mrs. Buglehorn calling out to Smith that she knew he was in there. "Ye said ye would be gone by eight and it's after nine now and ye never left. I know yer game! Yer not the first boarder to lie to get out of paying for me breakfasts. I have kippers and tomatoes, which I can give ye for half the regular price because they were served first to the man in room seven, who did not finish them. I can refund the additional charge if ye insist, but I have to warn ye there's a fee for making me charge unnecessary fees 'cause I have to enter it into me book, don't I?"

When this reasonable proposal received no response, the landlady thumped the door harder and yelled, "Mr. Smith! Mr. Smith! I know you are in there! Answer me! If I have to break down this door to get a response, then I'll have to charge a forced entry fee, which is twice as much as the posting fee, which ye owe me for the letter ye left on the mail tray last night. Mr. Smith! *Mr. Smith!* Open the door!"

Having no desire to be caught in the company of a murdered stranger, Verity darted to the window to see if it offered a possible escape option. They were three floors up, which meant it was too far to the ground, but the building next door was one story lower and it was only a solid jump away.

A solid jump usually meant getting a good running start but if she—

"Here!" Hardwicke said, tugging on her arm and drawing her to the wardrobe that leaned against the opposite wall. Its condition was as decrepit as the building, with huge gouges and a crack down the side, but it was large and commodious. They would both fit inside easily.

Verity climbed into the cabinet as the volume of Mrs. Buglehorn's calls increased. The landlady was inside the outer room now, slamming the front door shut behind her, and Verity waited for her to announce that there was a door-closing fee.

The wardrobe swayed sharply to the left as Hardwicke climbed in beside her, dropping back to the floor with a resounding thud that was drowned out by Mrs. Buglehorn's shouts.

"Mr. Smith, Mr. Smith," she called in her shrieky trill. "Ye breakfast is getting cold and if ye make me warm it up for ye, then I have to charge you more. Coal ain't dropped in me hearth for free!"

Hardwicke settled his weight on the opposite side so that the closet would not shift back and pulled the doors closed. It was pitch-black for a moment, and Verity, unable to see her own hand in front of her face, could make out nothing of Hardwicke's form. But within a few seconds, her eyes adjusted to the dark and she could detect his outline. A thin shard of light entered through the crack, providing enough illumination for her to make out the finger he raised to his lips.

Good God, he was exhorting her to remain silent!

Would the insults never stop?

This rickety wardrobe was hardly the first one Mr. Twad-dle-Thum had employed as a hiding spot.

Indeed, rickety wardrobes were his natural milieu as were

creaky cupboards and timeworn trunks. Half of Twaddling was heaving oneself into pieces of inhospitable furniture and holding one's breath until it was safe to emerge. She had once spent two and a quarter hours curled up in a crate with several dozen pairs of shoes to prove that Lord Barlow planned to escape to the Continent without settling his gambling debts.

Was it easy?

Of course not, no.

At five feet eleven inches, she was too tall to fit comfortably in the vast majority of containers she was compelled by circumstance to occupy, and yet she was grateful for the height for it made everything possible. If she had resembled her mother in shape rather than just in her face, then she would never have been able to convincingly present herself as a man. Only her tall stature made the gambit plausible, for there was nothing more masculine than being looked up to—literally—by one's fellows.

It was not even her first time sharing a wardrobe, as she and Freddie had often had to jump into the first available cabinet when tormenting the Wraithe. There they would be, trapped together in a narrow space with nothing to do but wait, and yet somehow she had managed not to chatter her friend's ear off.

Amazing!

Despite her years of experience—decades, in fact—she was willing to concede there was something different about being in a wardrobe with Hardwicke.

It was the lack of familiarity, she supposed.

Although they had worked together to disarm a man who had held Freddie and several members of the *Gazette* staff hostage, he was essentially a stranger. What little she knew about him Twaddle had gleaned from hiding in his laundry pile: He was a thief and a wastrel. Given the comfort with which he resided, he appeared to have come up in the world in the years since he stole his father's ring. But Verity could not discern how he made his money and found him highly untrustworthy.

There had been a moment, fleeting but intense, when she had felt drawn to him, fascinated by his teal-colored eyes and alarming astuteness.

Struck by it, she had succumbed to an odd kind of terror.

Fortunately, he had revealed the true quality of his esteem in the very next breath and the sense of panic eased.

It did not return now as she shifted slightly in the confined space, her shoulder tilting forward so that it did not linger against his. But she did feel a disconcerting awareness, an inexplicable awkwardness in knowing the heat she felt was emanating from his body.

Now that was truly fascinating.

Verity had no opportunity to wonder about it because the landlady stomped into the bedroom, threatening to levy yet another surcharge on Mr. Smith—for performing the service of waking him up.

"It will cost ye two farth—"

Gasping, Mrs. Buglehorn broke off in the middle of her thought as she caught sight of her boarder's murdered body. She stood there silently for several heartbeats, and Verity tried to imagine the swirl of horror churning in the other woman's breast as she beheld the ghoulish spectacle of the carcass, for it was very ghoulish indeed, the way the knife protruded, so violent and brutal, and the blood soaking everything with its sticky redness, like foul syrup that spilled everywhere.

Seeing the corpse, she would immediately think of the killer.

Was it one of her boarders?

Were they still lurking about?

Verity pictured the landlady drawing her shoulders in with fright and was not surprised to hear the other woman let out a shrill cry.

But then Mrs. Buglehorn spoke, her tone heavy with profound exasperation, and Verity realized she was not scared, merely irritated. "Dear gawd, not another one!" she said, clucking her tongue loudly. Her muttered annoyance could be heard as she clomped out of the room. "Ruined the sheets, didn't he? Selfish bounder. What would it have cost him to drop onto the floor? He was dying anyway. Made no difference to him where he drew his last breath."

Verity, waiting to hear the clap of the front door, felt an absurd urge to giggle. It was not funny—no, not at all, the pile of corpses amassing at the Portpool Lane address—and yet the prospect of the avaricious Mrs. Buglehorn finding a seemingly endless trail of dead boarders from whom she could extract no fees for the inconvenience of their death amused her hugely.

Her demeanor revealed no humor when she climbed out of the wardrobe and turned to address Hardwicke. "We should depart immediately before she returns."

Hardwicke agreed.

Neither one of them moved a muscle.

"As she seems familiar with the situation, I am sure she has a standard protocol in place," Verity added. "That suggests to me she will be back momentarily."

Nodding lightly, he agreed it was a reasonable conclusion.

And still he made no effort to leave.

He did, however, wave his hand in a gracious arc and said, "Ladies first."

No, Verity thought, she was not a peagoose to fall for that old trick. The moment she crossed the threshold, he would examine the room for information about Smith's fate. If he wanted to search for clues, he would have to do it in her company.

Vexingly, that development applied to her as well, and she considered the intractable problem from varying points of view before settling on a proposal. "As neither one of us is inclined to leave the other alone with the evidence, I suggest we each search half of the room and share what we find."

To this equitable plan Hardwicke made a vehement complaint, insisting that the matter did not concern Verity. "There is no reason for you to be here. I offered you the assignment that would justify your presence and you refused. And do not say, Miss Gorman, that you accepted my challenge. I issued no challenge."

"You threw down the gauntlet," she said, abiding by his request. "I picked it up."

Having complied with the letter of the law, not the spirit, Verity knew she had earned his annoyed glare. Nevertheless, they did not have all morning to linger over his surliness. "Any minute now Mrs. Buglehorn is going to realize she forgot to charge her boarder a dying-on-the-premises fee and dash back up here to collect it from one of his pockets. It is in our best interest to be gone before then."

Hardwicke was too much of a seasoned campaigner to quibble with her observation when he knew it to be true. The clientele who rented rooms at the tumbledown establishment were far from comfortably set, but there was no telling what cherished items they might keep with them when they traveled.

A father's ring.

A mother's locket.

Whatever funds they needed to complete their journey.

"Very well, then," he said. "You take the right side of the room starting at the doorway and I will take the left."

As Verity had been about to make the very same proposal

except swapping the assignments to give herself the better half, she knew it was far from fair. There was little of interest on the side of the room that contained the bed save the corpse itself, and although she did feel a slight reluctance at the prospect of braving all that blood to rifle through a dead man's pockets, her larger concern was it was not a rich source of information. If there were relevant details to be found, they were more likely to be concealed among his belongings.

Consequently, she suggested they divide the room by items: She would examine the valise and the pile of clothes folded on the table; he would examine the traveling case, the wardrobe, the cane, and the two pairs of shoes lined up against the wall. "That gives you four things to search compared to my meager two," she added generously.

Although they both knew the wardrobe was empty, having so recently occupied it themselves, he did not complain, instead noting that he would also take the bed.

Verity agreed to the amendment with a brisk nod. She had intentionally left the bed out of her proposal to provide Hardwicke with a bargaining chip. It was important for a man of his ilk to feel as though he had retained some measure of control in the negotiation, and she was disinclined to examine the corpse.

Did that make her squeamish?

Well very, she was squeamish.

As it was her first time standing over a slain human being, she thought she was allowed a little latitude in her response.

"And do please recall we are sharing anything we find," she added.

He assured her he needed no reminder. "I intend to be every bit as open and forthcoming as you, Miss Gorman."

It was a taunt.

Obviously, they were both going to hoard whatever evidence they found, and as she watched him bend over Mr.

Smith, she wondered if she had miscalculated by refusing the bed. The knife could be an important piece of evidence, its quality and origin confirming pertinent information about the murderer. And the depths to which it was inserted into the chest cavity—that would be an indication of the killer's strength. If it went very deep, then perhaps they were looking for a large, powerful man.

Ah, but Smith was old and frail enough to require a cane. One did not need to be a behemoth to subdue an elderly man whose bones were probably as weak as twigs.

Opening the valise, she wondered if she had been maneuvered into refusing the corpse. Hardwicke probably assumed she would automatically reject whatever proposal he made, for that was precisely the tactic he had employed in front of the *London Daily Gazette* to ensure he got the assignment he wanted.

Damn her queasiness, she thought without heat.

(And here she paused to stare in wonder at the Duchess of Kesgrave's eagerness to examine decapitated cadavers. Her brother's wife was just as ghoulish and outrageous as Mr. Twaddle-Thum's reports suggested.)

Despite this reassessment, she still believed there was more to be learned from the contents of the valise, a supposition that was almost immediately confirmed when she unfolded a clipping from the *York Observer.* Tucked into the Bible like a marker to hold its place, it was one of the articles she and Delphine had read at the Addison. It reported the offer of a reward for the apprehension of the three organizers of the Christmas Uprising who were still at large.

The story's presence among the dead man's possessions revealed several pertinent facts: that he was from the north, that he knew about the insurrection, that he was aware of the bounties. What it did not clarify was how these three things intersected with each other, and the possibilities that had occurred to her yesterday in the tavern still seemed viable. An insurrectionist himself, Smith could have come to London in search of a fellow conspirator to provide him with material support or an opportunity to rejoin the effort. It was just as likely, however, that he had come to the capital to turn in Fitch and collect the reward.

But if the first theory was accurate and he *was* one of the leaders with a bounty on his head, then why drive a knife through his heart? There was no money to be made on a dead fugitive. The only way to collect the seventy-five pounds was to bring Smith to the magistrate's office. If the killer did not care about the generous sum at stake, then it was more than likely there was no generous sum at stake.

By that measure, Smith was not an insurrectionist.

Fitch was.

Verity was all but certain of it. His defense of the cause was too passionate to be a new or passing fancy. That factor combined with the others—he was from the north, pretended to have a sister, and recognized Smith yesterday— persuasively made the case. He was experienced and in hiding, and the way his demeanor had altered the moment he caught sight of Smith revealed his familiarity with the other man. Perhaps they had a prior acquaintance or maybe they both hailed from the same small town.

Either way, it was undeniable.

Made aware of his vulnerability, a development against which he had to be always on his guard, Fitch would have known to act swiftly. Smith's meeting that morning might have been with the very law authorities the fugitive hoped to evade.

It could not have been very difficult to murder Smith. Mrs. Buglehorn presented no obstacle, as Verity and Hardwicke had both proven, and the victim was old. Overcoming him would have required little.

But how had Fitch known where to find Smith? Had he loitered outside the tavern to follow the man to his lodgings?

Verity could not believe it.

Surely, she would have noticed her original target following her new quarry.

She was far too skilled a Twaddler to miss such an obvious development.

But if her speculation was correct, then Fitch was a hunted man with a significant bounty on his head who remained at large six months later. His abilities would also be well honed.

Or she was wrong altogether and the two men were allies meeting up in London and the murderer was someone else entirely.

It was a conundrum, she allowed, slipping the article into her pocket. Then she held up the Bible as she turned slightly and announced that the victim seemed to be a devout man. If she was not going to hold to their agreement to share information, then the least she could do was give the appearance of holding to their agreement to share information. "It is a well-thumbed copy and the only book he traveled with."

Hardwicke, whose left hand was in the pocket of Smith's torn tailcoat, nodded. Verity waited for him to make an equally facile observation about their victim, but he said nothing.

Wretched man!

She felt certain he also had discovered something pertinent, only he did not feel compelled to make a show of cooperation.

Aside from the newspaper clipping, the valise held sundry items of travel such as tooth powder, a handkerchief, a comb, a thin strip of soap, a pair of threadbare gloves made of thick leather, a wallet with seven shillings, and the copy of the *Times* he had appeared to be reading the day before. The clothes folded neatly on the table likewise yielded few insights. The fabric was coarse and frayed, with uneven stitching that indicated it had been made by an inexpert seamstress.

His wife, perhaps, or a daughter.

The shabbiness of the garments reaffirmed her belief that Smith was not a wealthy man, and the visit to London had probably cost him a great deal. He would have made the effort only for something truly worthwhile.

Seventy-five pounds struck her as an excellent reason to endure the expense of travel.

Refolding the clothes, she looked over to the bed and noted that Hardwicke was now holding one of Smith's hands. He seemed particularly engrossed by his fingernails, and she had to concede she had been well and truly played. The corpse was the only thing in the room he had wanted to examine.

Advantage Hardwick, she thought petulantly.

Deeply curious to inspect the victim herself, she could not bring herself to peer over his shoulder. It was too humiliating. Instead, she opened the traveling case, as he was clearly uninterested in its contents, and reminded herself that she knew Fitch's sister was a fraud.

That advantage was hers.

Larger than the valise, the second bag was actually quite sparse, containing only Smith's nightclothes, a well-stained handkerchief with the monogram BIH, and a pair of spectacles with a cracked left lens. As she removed them from the case to make sure she did not overlook something vital, she silently apologized to Her Outrageousness for failing to comprehend the investigative necessity of a well-scrutinized cadaver. In all of Twaddle's gleeful reports, her interest had been presented as morbid curiosity, as if she studied the sallow, cold skin of her murder victims to satisfy an innate inquisitiveness that was as inappropriate as it was gruesome.

Now, from this side of the room, she perceived it differently, and wondered if she could use something from her own experience in a column.

Not share specific details, of course.

That would be absurd.

But Verity could revisit the duchess's career from the perspective of her new understanding, perhaps by drawing up a list of the ten most pertinent pieces of information the investigator had discovered by examining a dead body.

Reusing old material in a new way was a diabolical stroke.

Would Freddie be appalled or impressed?

Contemplating his reaction to the events of her morning, she smiled lightly and began to return everything to the bag. Then she raised her head and saw Hardwicke was straightening his back.

"We should go," he said briskly. "It has been almost five minutes, and I think you are correct in your understanding of the proprietress. She will be back presently to rifle through Smith's belongings. I am surprised that she left without selecting a few choice items for herself and can only assume she will return with a satchel large enough to hold all his possessions."

As Verity suspected the same thing, she closed the case, rose to her feet, and strode through the apartment, deftly navigating the crush of furniture in the parlor. At the door, she pressed her ear against the wood to listen for creaking floorboards. Hearing none, she opened the door slightly, confirmed that neither Mrs. Buglehorn nor her boarders were nearby and stepped into the corridor. Hardwicke was only one pace behind and he followed her down the stairs with unnerving silence. Every wretched tread her foot landed on groaned in protest, and yet he did not make a single noise.

It was maddening.

Her movements slowed as she turned onto the last flight, and standing on the bottom step, she peered around the corner for a sign of the landlady.

Nothing.

With Hardwicke at her heels, she crossed to the opposite hallway, which led to the front door. They were a few feet from the threshold when she heard the familiar sound of Mrs. Buglehorn levying a fee.

"It's a sixpence to enter the auction," she squawked impatiently. "And it ain't me fault if ye don't win, Jimmy. Bid higher! Last time ye lost out to McMurtry and he found a guinea at the bottom of the man's bag. This stiff had two bags, one large enough to fit a small child. Just imagine what's inside."

By all that was holy, the woman was conducting an auction for her murdered boarder's belongings!

It was the single most audacious thing Verity had ever witnessed in her life, and she could not decide if she was more horrified or fascinated. London, she knew, was a brutal place, but this flagrant disregard for Mr. Smith's humanity was beyond anything she imagined happening in even its worst rookeries.

Mrs. Buglehorn was a marvel, she thought.

A marvel and a monster all in one.

Hardwicke, seemingly unmoved by the shocking display, suggested they leave through the back door, and as they squeezed between the building and the overgrown shrubbery, Verity heard the bidding begin at a bob.

Saturday, May 30
   12:55 p.m.

. . .

Although Verity had known Delphine would not receive news of Mr. Smith's murder with calm equanimity, she did not expect to be bound to a chair, denied sustenance, and commanded to sit still until Freddie arrived.

"For goodness' sake, I did not *bind* you to the chair," Delphine said through clenched teeth when the charge was lodged against her an hour later. "I gave you a handkerchief and asked you to wipe the dust from your hands before you dirtied the upholstery."

"And then you said that if I got up from this chair before Freddie arrived, you would pack your belongings and move in with Lucy's family," Verity replied. "You know how much I cherish your company and could not allow such a tragedy to befall me, so I stayed in the chair. You bound me with your words as tightly as with ropes."

Delphine, rolling her eyes at this extravagant display, ordered her friend to stop being ridiculous. "And I did not deny you sustenance."

"I said that I was hungry after such an eventful morning, and when I asked if I could have an apple, you snapped, 'Go fetch it yourself.' But I couldn't because I was bound to the chair by fear and affection."

"Well, I am here now, so you may fetch whatever you like from the kitchens," Freddie said, sitting down on the settee, which was adjacent.

But Delphine shook her head and pulled the cord to summon Lucy. "I apologize, Verity, for making you suffer"— she glanced at the large standing clock next to the parlor door —"a whole forty-three and a half minutes without food. It must have been torture. I will rectify that as soon as possible. But now that Freddie is here, I would like to discuss the peril to which you are exposing yourself with increasing regularity. You have always been rash, but in recent weeks you have grown utterly reckless. I fear it cannot end well."

Verity, who knew when she was being mocked, managed to say nothing in response to this provoking comment. Her rumbling tummy, however, registered a well-timed complaint.

Freddie, lifting his chin curiously as he crossed his leg, asked what Twaddle had been up to now.

"But that is the thing that is so troubling to me," Delphine replied earnestly. "She was not Twaddling. She was Veritying."

"Veritying?" he repeated, his brows drawn in confusion, for although his friend had spoken the term with an assurance that implied familiarity, none of them had ever heard it before.

"She is chagrined by Colson Hardwicke's lack of admiration for her ingenuity and determined to show him that she is cleverer than he by discovering the truth about Arnold Fitch first," Delphine explained. "Engaging in a dangerous activity that has nothing to do with either Mr. Twaddle-Thum or Robert Lark simply to prove a point. Veritying."

"That is absurd," Verity replied. "The point is to bring an insurrectionist to justice and maybe earn seventy-five pounds to supplement the footman I am thinking of hiring. If Hardwicke also happens to appear ill-equipped to handle his own assignment at the end of the escapade, that is merely an unintended consequence."

"I must say, this is very troubling indeed," Freddie announced as he rose to his feet to pace about the room. "If Verity is going to risk life and limb in the effort to gather secret information, then it should be for Mr. Twaddle-Thum's column. Every advertiser in the city wants to be on the same page as one of his dispatches. We could do much better than a onetime payment of seventy-five pounds."

Delphine growled with frustration as she raised her hands as though in surrender, muttering, "You're as bad as she," while Verity insisted that she neither desired nor needed

Hardwicke's admiration. What she objected to was his lack of respect for her abilities.

"Asking me to giggle like a green miss fresh from the schoolroom!" she scoffed in disgust. "Even an empty-headed Incomparable like Miss Petworth or her sycophantic friend Miss Colbert could do it to his satisfaction."

Freddie paused in his progress across the room to look at her with surprise. "But you always say it's the 'when,' not the 'what' because doing anything on command is the challenging part. I specifically recall being lectured on this very topic while we were hiding under the Wraithe's bed and you told me to sneeze."

Verity corrected this account, insisting that she told him *not* to sneeze, for any noise would have revealed their location. "But it was dusty and your nose kept itching, so I explained the importance of being able to control one's physical reactions at all times."

No, he said, she was describing a different occasion—when they hid under the sofa in the headmistress's study, which further exasperated their friend.

"Do stop bickering over trivialities!" Delphine snapped.

"Bickering?" Freddie echoed blankly.

"Trivialities?" Verity said in wonder. "Twaddle has built his entire career on the distinction between a bed and a sofa."

Delphine snarled at the two of them as a knock sounded at the door, heralding the arrival of tea, and she sent Lucy away with a sharp, "Not right now, thank you!"

Highly amused, Verity laughed and said, "See? Denied sustenance!"

Delphine tossed herself onto the settee and dropped her head into her hands. Verity, immediately regretful, sat down beside her and laid a comforting arm around her shoulder. "I am beastly for teasing you when you are so genuinely upset. I am sorry, my dear. It is only that I really do think you are making too big a deal of this corpse thing. My life was never in peril. And also, I am so very peckish."

Freddie, regaining his seat, swore that he was not trying to upset her either. "I understand your concern, but clucking over Verity like a mother hen is not going to solve anything either. We simply have to trust that she can take care of herself—as she has been doing for decades. And us, as well. I, for one, would have never made it out of Fortescue's with my spirit intact if she had not been there to distract the Wraithe at all the right moments. Now I think it would be prudent if we turned our attention to the corpse. Who is the victim and are we certain there is not some aspect to the mystery that would interest Twaddle's readers?"

Sighing deeply, Delphine acknowledged the futility of her position and announced that she would fetch the tray herself. She returned a few minutes later with a pot of tea, an assortment of biscuits, and an apple, which Verity bit into with enthusiasm.

"All right, then," Delphine said calmly. "Tell us about the corpse."

Briskly, Verity explained how she had arrived at Smith's lodgings after he had been killed. It was a simple tale, surprisingly straightforward given Fitch's attempts to make the matter appear more complicated with his fake whiskers and false sister, and when she finished her explanation, Freddie suggested she contact the Home Office and be done with it.

"There is no use running in circles about it unless you think you can prove that Hardwicke was involved in the Christmas Uprising," he added. "The Twaddleship adores a good Lord Colson story."

Taken aback by the suggestion, Verity said, "The Home Office?"

"Well, it oversees matters of domestic security, does it not?" Freddie asked, as if stating the obvious. "Ending the social unrest that has plagued the north since the advent of textile machines, which has only grown worse since the end of the war. Sidmouth eagerly employs the Frame-Breaking Act. If Fitch is one of the leaders of the insurrection, as you believe, then the home secretary will take care of it. Bring it to Mark Kingsley, the under-secretary who handles the Luddite threat for Sidmouth. You might even get the reward."

Delphine hailed the solution as refreshingly practical and asked if there was not some angle by which Robert Lark might be convinced to report the story. "The apprehension of a dangerous fugitive is an exciting subject, especially one who went to the extreme of hiring a woman to pose as his sister. Lark would be the only reporter who knows all the details, giving the *Gazette* access to exclusive information. That could be as lucrative as a column about Lord Colson."

"Yes, of course, Delph!" Freddie said eagerly. "Lark must write it! And you did say Fitch murdered Smith to keep his secret, did you not? That adds an extra dash of salaciousness."

Verity pressed her lips together as she considered the proposal, then she shook her head thoughtfully and said, "I am not sure who killed Smith. I think it was Fitch for the reasons I have given."

"That is precisely the point of referring the matter to the Home Office," Freddie asserted. "It has the resources to find out the answer *and* if they convict Fitch as a leader of the Christmas Uprising, then it does not matter if they cannot prove he murdered Smith. Justice will be served regardless."

"And you will still have the satisfaction of beating Hardwicke at his own game," Delphine added in a low, cajoling tone. "Think of his vexation when he discovers the mystery has already been solved. *That* will teach him to ask you to giggle."

Freddie, who had nodded firmly in agreement, drew his

brows together and said, "I still do not understand how that is an insult. It sounds as though he trusted her expertise."

Delphine rolled her eyes again and said it was precisely the compliment he thought it. "But Verity will Verity."

Uncertain if she approved of this new usage of her name —it was all right for Twaddle, who did in fact Twaddle— Verity considered the advantages of the proposal. She conceded that investigating Fitch had been allowed to take up far more time than she had anticipated. Yes, she had been restless in the wake of his insult, unable to focus on a new project because she was so annoyed, but that was several days ago now and the irritation had waned. Seeing the astonishment on his face as she strode into Smith's bedroom had gone a long way toward soothing her ego, and there were other things that demanded her attention.

And by "other things," of course, she meant Her Outrageousness.

Having reported on the duchess's latest investigation, she owed it to the Twaddleship to provide an interesting postscript on the fate of the killer and the future of Huzza's wondrous invention.

Turning the matter over to the Home Secretary would allow her to return her focus to the duchess's exploits, which was without question a benefit.

Furthermore, Delphine's comments regarding Robert Lark's interest in the story were on the mark. Although he and the paper generally supported the changes proposed by the reform movement, for too many, power *was* consolidated in the hands of the wealthy, the notion that an escaped insurrectionist was brazenly preaching his ideas in the middle of London was genuinely shocking, and the readers of the *London Daily Gazette* would be duly aghast to know the Home Office was so inept in its dealings that it had failed to apprehend a man it deemed dangerous on its own doorstep.

Satisfied with these two advantages, Verity considered the drawbacks and acknowledged that it was simply less rewarding to hand off her problems to someone else to solve. Seeing things through was deeply gratifying, mostly because she enjoyed the sense of finality that came with it but also because she liked directing events herself.

Retaining control was the only way to ensure she got the outcome she required, and allowing a functionary to handle the matter meant risking a displeasing result. It did not help that the man who oversaw the agency, Lord Sidmouth, had failed to impress her with either his acumen or his politics during his long career in the government, which included a three-year tenure as prime minister.

He struck her as weak in his abilities and draconian in his outlook.

Sidmouth's many shortcomings were not especially relevant, Verity reminded herself, as she would be dealing with Kingsley, as Freddie suggested. Underlings and deputies were frequently more efficient and capable than their employers.

Freddie, accepting a cup of tea from Delphine, suggested that he could submit the information to ensure the reward was paid as promised. "It could raise all sorts of awkward questions if the government tried to transfer the funds to Robert Lark."

It was a practical point, which Verity appreciated, and yet she found she could not agree with the suggestion. She might be willing to allow the Home Office to handle the affair going forward, but she adamantly refused to permit the information to be conveyed via courier. She would call on the department and relate the details herself.

Chapter Six

❦

S aturday, May 30
3:19 p.m.

Although Verity did not count a tavern keeper among the assortment of identities she assumed regularly in the course of Twaddling, she did have an exhausted waterman who enjoyed a glass or two after a long day of plying his trade on the river. He would plunk himself into a chair, sigh heavily, and complain vociferously to the patrons nearest him about the ache that throbbed in his bones after twelve hours of rowing. Gregarious and in search of commiseration, he sought similar confidences, urging others in the tavern to grumble about their own difficult occupations.

Unhappy men, especially ones who had consumed several pints of ale, tended to be obligingly indiscreet.

Swathed now in Bertie Bett's pea green coat and existential weariness, Verity approached one of a dozen industrious-looking clerks in the large office in Whitehall and asked if she could speak with Mr. Kingsley.

Curtly, his eyes focused on the bottle of black ink as he dipped his quill, the clerk said no. "The under-secretary is not in the office at the moment, and even if he were, he does not take meetings with the public. Good day."

Although one would expect nothing less from a high-ranking member of the government, Verity rounded her shoulders as if deeply disappointed and requested a meeting with one of Mr. Kingsley's subordinates. Bertie's weedy baritone reflected his diminished expectations.

His pen scratching the parchment as he signed his name at the bottom of the document, the clerk refused again. "The under-secretary's subordinates also do not take meetings with the public. I would advise you to send a letter to his office and wait up to a month for a response."

Verity inhaled sharply, as if horrified by his proposal. "A month! But London might be engulfed in flames by then, sir. The way he was talking in my tavern last night, so persuasive. Mr. Kingsley must be alerted to the problem long before a month is up!"

The clerk dropped his quill onto the desk and stared up at her, his brown eyes gleaming balefully. "London in flames? What rambling nonsense is this?"

"It is not nonsense," Verity said, withdrawing the *York Observer* article from the pocket of her coat and holding it aloft with slightly trembling hands. "He was in my tavern last night, this man, advocating for violent revolution."

As she did not know which insurrection leader Fitch was, she refrained from mentioning a particular name, but the intentional vagueness seemed in keeping with her apprehension.

Impatient, the clerk snatched the newspaper clipping from

her fingers and read the first line, his lip curled in a sneer. His expression changed, however, as his eyes moved down the page, and by the time he had reached the bottom his face was blank.

Deliberately blank, Verity amended.

The clerk returned the quill to its stand, slipped the document he had been working on into a folder and then rose to his feet. "Please, Mr. ... uh, I do not believe I got your name?"

"Betts," Verity supplied.

"Yes, Mr. Betts," he said with a firm nod. "And you work in a tavern?"

"I own a tavern," she corrected. "Near Blackfriars, in Carter Lane. It's popular with watermen and gets a decent crowd in the evening. It's a goodly distance from here, but if you manage to make your way over one day, the first pint is on me."

He received this generous offer with a stiff smile and gestured to his chair. "Please, Mr. Betts, take a seat. I will just ... I will return momentarily. Please, just make yourself comfortable," he said, taking a half step toward the hallway, then pivoting sharply and grabbing the folder from his desk. "I will just ... Please wait here."

Clutching the file to his chest, he strode out of the office.

Verity watched him disappear around the corner, amused by his lack of trust. The document on which he had been working could not have been so important that he had to hide its contents from a tavern keeper from Blackfriars. She doubted even Mr. Twaddle-Thum would be interested in some dry clerical account.

He would have looked, of course.

A closed folder on the desk of a senior clerk in the Home Office—it was almost a moral obligation for the notorious gossip to sneak a peek.

Poking through the drawers, however, was too brazen even for her. The room contained two long tables at which a dozen clerks toiled silently. Their heads were tilted adamantly down now, but at any moment one of them could look up.

When they did, Verity did not want them to find her reading private government files.

Delphine would be very cross indeed if she managed to get herself arrested for treason in the course of Veritying. (Damn. Now she was using the new coinage!)

Leaning back in the chair, she admired the room, which was large and elegant, with wainscoting halfway up the wall and decorative coving at the top. An intricate chandelier hung from the center of the ceiling, adding an air of formality to the space, and she supposed dignitaries of varying importance were brought to the room to wait for their meetings to begin.

Verity herself did not have to wait long, for the clerk returned only a few minutes later, the file held in one arm as he waved her forward. "Come, Mr. Betts, the under-secretary will see you now. Please come with me."

Heaving a sigh of relief, Verity darted to her feet and straightened the collar on her coat. "Thank you, sir, for arranging the meeting. I am so grateful. I do not want any trouble, I promise you. I'm just the owner of a modest tavern who wants to ensure peace and prosperity for himself and his fellows. I do not want to be a bother."

Mr. Kingsley's office was a short distance away, and after turning right down a bustling hallway, she found herself on its threshold. The clerk announced her presence, then waited for her to enter before closing the door. Alone with the under-secretary, Verity opened her mouth to make her prepared speech about Mr. Fitch and her belief that he was one of the fugitive leaders of the Christmas Uprising. She had no intention of mentioning the reward money in her initial burst of words. She would work up to it slowly.

But Kingsley did not give her a chance to speak.

Rising from his chair, he walked around his desk and crossed the floor in five evenly paced strides. He stopped an inch away from her, his dark head rising only to her shoulder, and craned his neck until he was looking her in the eye. "Mr. Betts, if you say one word about what you know to anyone, I will have your tavern shut down."

Verity did not have to feign astonishment.

"It would not be difficult," he continued. "Just a small issue with your land tax, outstanding for ... what is it ... years, and, lo, it is my tavern now. It is near Blackfriars, I understand."

Kingsley spoke slowly, clearly, his voice low to heighten the menace in his words, and he looked at her with a sort of benign indifference that was meant to be intimidating for its sincere lack of care.

Verity was not intimidated.

Perhaps if she actually owned a tavern that did brisk business in the evenings with watermen, she would be trembling in terror. The land tax was collected by a local man, not a government official, and it was easy to imagine someone like Kingsley bringing the full force of his office to bear on the commissioner, who would agree to say whatever he was instructed. Years of monies could disappear in a stroke.

But even if she were the proprietor of an establishment in Blackfriars, she could not conceive of responding to his threat with anything but confusion.

His reply was bewildering.

She had come to the Home Office alleging to know the whereabouts of a notorious insurrectionist for whom half the law authorities in England were scouring the countryside, and the under-secretary's reaction was to overwhelm her into silence.

It defied sense.

He had his reasons, of course.

A man did not rise to Kingsley's level of success without being clever or prudent in his decision-making. He would not issue a decree without evaluating it from every angle to determine how it would either help or hinder him.

So how did scaring off a tavern owner from Blackfriars help him now?

Verity could not accept the obvious answer: that Kingsley had been directly involved in the Christmas Uprising, and the apprehension of the fugitive risked revealing his complicity. Nor could she believe that he secretly supported the reform movement and did not wish to see the cause weakened by the capture of one of its most effective orators.

Sidmouth was famously hostile to radicals and had overseen the execution of fourteen Luddites on a single day. He would not make the facile mistake of employing a man who did not share his outlook. He was too skillful a player—a veteran politician, a former prime minister—not to know intimately the opinions of all his deputies.

Kingsley's position could not be doubted.

That meant he was motivated by something else.

Glory?

Was he warning her off so that they could demonstrate the efficacy of his office and claim sole credit for the arrest? Did he hope to burnish his reputation or impress his employer or garner favorable reports in the broadsheets?

It was a more likely explanation, Verity allowed, and yet still unpersuasive. A tavern keeper from Blackfriars had no standing. The under-secretary would not be required to share credit with a publican or even acknowledge his existence. It was his office that had offered the reward that elicited the information that led to the capture so in every way that mattered it was Kingsley's doing.

Furthermore, he had no reason to apply a heavy hand. All he had to do to make Betts toddle off was throw a few coins at him. He did not even have to pay the full bounty. (He should, of course, because Betts had fulfilled his end of the contract, but an argument could always be made that he fell short by not delivering the actual fugitive to the authorities.)

Something far stranger was going on, and Verity wondered if she had overlooked a meaningful detail in the article she had given the clerk. Her focus had been solely on the escaped insurrectionists—Vane, Horne, Pocock—and she had not mentioned a name because she did not have one. But that vagueness left the subject of their conversation open to interpretation, and it was possible they were discussing an entirely different matter than the one she thought.

Now that was interesting.

Kingsley, satisfied with her silence because it implied fear and compliance, congratulated her on not being stupid. "That is very good for you. Now Mr. Newton will show you out, and do not let me see you here again. If I do, your tavern will be forfeit," he added as he raised a dismissive hand. Then he turned on his heels and strode back to his desk.

The industrious clerk darted into the room and grabbed her elbow, which earned a nod of approval from his employer. Tightening his grip, Newton told her not to tarry and tugged her toward the hallway. Although he didn't toss her out of the building like an ape-drunk customer who could not settle his bill, he did give her a hard shove and warned her not to return.

Fascinated, Verity watched him stomp back inside.

Goodness, yes, something very odd was happening, and as she watched the clerk disappear into the lobby, she could only marvel at Kingsley's stunning lack of shrewdness. He was a political creature, after all, and should know that behaving in an unexpected way drew more attention to his actions, not less. Instead of walking away with a few guineas jingling cheerfully in his pocket, Bertie Betts was now wondering what was in the article that unsettled the under-secretary.

That Kingsley had been unsettled, Verity did not doubt.

It was the only thing that explained his immoderate reaction.

If he had retained possession of his faculties, he never would have revealed his hand by threatening a concerned citizen who was merely doing his civic duty.

What, then, had undermined his ability to think clearly?

Something in the article—which she no longer had because she had given the clipping to the clerk.

Yes, but she had read it enough times to know what it contained in a general sense and closed her eyes to picture the item. Before listing the names of the fugitives or explaining the reward, it reviewed the events directly preceding the uprising, including a mention of the informer who ensured that the army would be at the factory at the appointed time.

Startled, Verity opened her eyes, spun on her heels, and came within a hairbreadth of colliding into Colson Hardwicke. She lurched left, ramming her chin to her chest as her entire body tensed with recognition and mumbling an apology that received no reply. Hardwicke, seemingly unaware of the incident, continued toward the building, which he entered with purposeful strides.

Well, well, well.

Saturday, May 30
  4:04 p.m.

Verity seized a hat.

She did not reach out haphazardly and snatch it from the head of the passerby closest to her on the pavement.

Obviously not, no, for she was neither a thief nor a cad.

Verity retrieved several shillings from her pocket, tossed them at the startled man, and *then* snatched his hat from the top of his head.

And she called out thank you as she hurried toward the building.

Thieves and cads did not observe the niceties.

Glancing at the chapeau before slipping it on, she noted it was in the chimney style with a narrow brim and slim band. It was also in pristine condition, which did not quite match the state of her pea green coat, which was thin in patches and strewn with stains.

Damn Bertie for not taking better care of his possessions!

It was, after all, the only coat he owned.

His mother would be mortified.

Verity was slightly out of breath by the time she crossed the threshold, but it was from excitement, not exertion. It was an incredible stroke of good luck that she had caught sight of Hardwicke at all. If Kingsley had kept her waiting just a few minutes longer or had been even more curt in his treatment, she would have missed him entirely.

Now she would see whom he knew in the Home Office.

She had surmised a connection of some significance from their very first meeting, when he displayed no anxiety about being found in Mrs. Norton's bedchamber with an assassin. His claim to have received a medal from Wellington himself furthered her suspicion that he was not what he seemed. Although his qualifications as a good-for-nothing could not be questioned—Twaddle had confirmed the depths of his dissipation personally—it appeared as though that was not all that he was.

His résumé was slightly more varied.

Just how much more complex she was determined to find out.

Hardwicke passed through the lobby and turned right. Verity, skirting a pair of clerks who were idling in the middle of the floor, darted after him. The hallway was crowded, but his height made him easy to track and she kept half a dozen people between them as she followed. When he mounted a staircase, she paused several feet away and allowed him to get past the bend midway up before ascending the steps herself.

Arriving at the first floor, he continued straight down the corridor, and Verity, identifying the passageway as the one she had recently been propelled through by Newton, tilted her chin downward.

The last thing she needed was to bump into the officious clerk.

Oh, dear, she thought, her concern deepening as Hardwicke turned left. Now he was in Kingsley's hallway, and she slowed her pace as she considered the wisdom of returning to the lion's den so soon after being forcibly ejected from it.

Stopping here would mean losing the opportunity to discover vital information about Hardwicke—and about the situation itself. Whatever strange thing was afoot in the Home Office, Colson Hardwicke was at the center of it, and if she did not continue her pursuit, then she would never find out if Kingsley himself was Hardwicke's contact.

It would be just like Hardwicke to take marching orders from a heavy-handed lout.

Contemplating Kingsley's shortcomings, she determined there was little chance of his recognizing her. For one thing, she was sporting a very fine topper, the sort Mr. Betts could never afford with the limited funds he earned as a tavern keeper. For another, she had spent very little time in his presence, and the under-secretary did not strike her as the sort of man who paid close attention to the flies he swatted.

He would do well, Verity thought, to memorize the faces of the peasants he threatened. No doubt there were hundreds of them.

Having decided the risk was minimal, Verity raced down the hallway to make sure she did not miss an opportunity to discover Hardwicke's destination and turned the corner just in time to see him disappear into an office.

It was not Kingsley's office; she was sure of it.

His had been on the right side and this one was on the left.

How very curious.

Cautiously, she stepped into the hallway and wondered how close she could get without revealing her presence to either Kingsley or Hardwicke. The room he had entered was two ... three ... six doors away and was diagonally across from Kingsley.

It seemed foolhardy to draw quite so near to the under-secretary's office.

Pausing to consider her options, she checked her pockets to see if she had anything she could use as a message. Pretending to hand a note to the wrong person was one of her delivery character's favorite subterfuges.

Alas, no, she had nothing suitable, but the door she was standing next to was slightly ajar and when she peeked in through the narrow opening, the office seemed empty. Swiftly, she darted inside and grabbed the first thing she saw on the table.

A book!

Critique of Pure Reason.

It was not what she had anticipated but would certainly do well enough, she thought, and raised her hand to stop the first clerk who breezed by her. Opening her mouth to speak, she hesitated briefly, uncertain to which she should match her accent: the hat or the coat.

The former, she decided.

It was easier to come down in the world than to rise up.

In a clear, rich baritone, Verity explained that she was supposed to deliver the work to Mr. Johnston and asked him to confirm his office. "It is the third one to the right?"

The clerk shook his head and said that office belonged to the under-secretary.

Startled by the answer, Verity wondered how she had gotten herself turned around. She had just been in the corridor fifteen minutes ago. "Mr. Kingsley?"

"Mr. Grint," he replied. "There are two, aren't there?"

"Right, yes, of course," she said with a knowledgeable air. "And where is Mr. Johnston? Is he the fourth door, then?"

The clerk pursed his lips and admitted he was not familiar with anyone named Johnston. "You have the wrong floor."

"I suppose I do," Verity said, tightening her grip on the book as she digested the fact that there were two under-secretaries. She wished Freddie had mentioned it. "Thank you."

He nodded and continued on his way, and Verity waited until he was out of sight before returning the tome to the office from which she had stolen it. Then she hurried outside to plan her next move.

Saturday, May 30

   4:21 p.m.

Although the *London Daily Gazette* was an excellent newspaper, with accurate reporting and insightful coverage of important events, it reflected a little too much of its publisher's cynical understanding of power. Raised in an orphan asylum overseen by a cruel headmistress who treated her charges with scorn and neglect, Freddie possessed no inherent respect for hierarchy.

He assumed anyone at the top of any order, be it social or governmental, had been corrupted in some way by their position and subjected them all to scrutiny.

Consequently, Verity did not think Robert Lark was the ideal choice to conduct interviews with clerks in the Home Office about the supremely impressive accomplishments of Under-Secretary Grint.

John Pennie of *The Times* was a much more diplomatic choice. Ardent in his admiration for authority, he had never asked a follow-up question that was not more fawning than the original and he frequently interrupted his subjects to compliment them on the elegant clarity of their responses.

Given his toadying manner, Verity was not sure he could accurately be described as a journalist, but as one could express a similar doubt about Mr. Twaddle-Thum, she was determined to be generous with the description.

Adopting Pennie's insouciant pose now, she sauntered into the Home Office building for the third time in two hours and took the stairs to the second floor.

There was no reason to court disaster.

She reached the landing, walked along the wide corridor, and looked into the first room she passed. It was as large as the clerks' office on the first floor, with the same lovely chandelier but with shorter tables. One was empty but the occupants of the other three looked up the moment she entered.

"Greetings, my fine fellows, greetings," she said, ambling unhurriedly into the open space. "If I may beg a few minutes of your time, I would be desperately grateful. My name is John Pennie—that is Pennie with an *ie*, not a *y*, so as not to be confused with the pence—and I am a journalist for *The Times*. I know what you are thinking, Oh, dear, a reporter to make a scandal out of a misstep and embarrass the Home Office. But you have the wrong idea about me. I write only admiring articles. If I do not admire my subject, then I do not write about them. It is as simple as that. Today, my subject is Mr. Grint. Who would like to be the first to relate the under-secretary's supremely impressive accomplishments?"

Although Pennie began every interview asking for supremely impressive accomplishments, there were rarely any accomplishments to relate, let alone supremely impressive ones. This was because he typically chose to profile men whose success was ordained by their birth and all they had to do to rise in their chosen profession was exist.

Daniel Grint, however, was a different kettle of fish.

Of questionable birth—his parents may or may not have been wed—he had risen through the ranks of the enlisted men to become a sergeant in the infantry. After the Battle of Bailén, he was reassigned to the Exploring Office to report on the movement of French troops in Spain, which required him to sneak into enemy territory. He excelled so well in this position, Wellington took notice and recommended him for the Alien Office, which planned and carried out spy missions against Napoleon from its rooms in Crown Street. As the head of the department, Grint oversaw a stable of agents who recruited French Royalists and anti-revolutionists to foil the emperor's efforts in France.

Countless plots and schemes were hatched.

The clerks were delighted to relate as many of these as they knew, and although their accounts were light on details, they were high in drama: There was the attempt to assassinate Napoleon in Paris with an exploding wine barrel filled with gunpowder, which the emperor only just evaded; the recruitment of one of Napoleon's mistresses as a spy for England; the establishment of a false committee that swindled thousands of francs from the French government; the misinformation regarding the imminent retreat of the discouraged British following the Battle of Dresden, which led to a decisive victory for the Allies, with the French suffering heavy losses.

"The Battle of Kulm was Mr. Grint's greatest victory," said the clerk, who introduced himself as Oliver Jones, then begged that his name not be included in the article. It was not appropriate for someone of his standing to openly discuss his employer, even if his remarks were entirely complimentary.

Naturally, Verity agreed, and the other two men in the room identified themselves as Philip Watson and Joseph Cleese. The former blinked at her through thick spectacles.

Cleese, whose ginger curls tumbled into his eyes, nodded. "A significant part of his job was identifying French spies living in London and giving them false information that they would pass along to their commanders. That was how he convinced Napoleon that our army was in disarray and on the verge of retreating."

"He drew up fake dispatches from the general in charge and had his man feed them to a network of French spies," Jones said.

"Not feed them," Watson corrected. "*Sell* them! Grint gave Boney bad information and made money on the prospect."

It was all very impressive, Verity thought, perplexed by how a man of Grint's cunning and subtlety could hold the same position as Kingsley, who possessed neither of these traits. It seemed as though the qualifications for the office veered wildly in a variety of directions. "How did he do that? Persuade the French spies to pay for bad information?"

"A disgraced nobleman, wasn't it?" Cleese asked, with a glance at his colleagues.

"Yes," Watson affirmed. "A younger son who had been

drummed out of the family and was desperate for money any way he could get it."

Jones snickered at the gullibility of the French. "All they saw was a dissolute gambler eager to sell out his country for a few guineas. They never even questioned it."

At the words *dissolute gambler*, it clicked for Verity.

Suddenly, it all made sense.

All of it.

"The Battle of Kulm was 1813, wasn't it?" she asked.

"August, I think," Cleese said, darting a look at his coworkers, who nodded in agreement.

Verity remained with the clerks for another fifteen minutes, listening to enthusiastic accounts of Grint's further exploits and about his transfer to the Home Office after the war ended, but her mind was far, far away.

Chapter Seven

✦✦✦

S*aturday, May 30*
9:32 p.m.

Breaking into Colson Hardwicke's Millman Street address was a significantly more challenging undertaking when he was not altering his daily routine to make it easy for her. Previously, he had sent his staff away for a few days to give the impression that his only servants were a pair of elderly caretakers who fell asleep before the light had fully faded from the sky. They had occupied a second set of rooms, on the ground floor below his, leaving his own accommodations empty and ripe for an invasion he sought to encourage. Catching her with her hand in the top drawer of his desk had amused him greatly.

In fact, the old couple had retired to a cottage on one of the Marquess of Ware's estates over a year ago, and Hardwicke employed a housekeeper, a maid, a cook, and a footman —all of whom were alarmingly alert. Possessing none of the infirmities of age, they heard every twig snap clearly and knew enough to be suspicious of a peddler hawking chapbooks.

To gain access to the establishment, Verity had to pay three children to stage an elaborate argument about a broken carriage, a missing ball, and a stolen toy soldier. Each conspirator was instructed to complain about their particular problem as loudly as possible, and they excelled in this endeavor with such alacrity almost every resident in the road came outside to see what all the fuss was about. Among those curious onlookers were the members of Hardwicke's household, and as the quarrel descended into tears (for which Verity had paid an extra farthing each), she slipped through the open front door and raced up the stairs to Hardwicke's rooms.

Passing quickly through the drawing room, she noted how much more elegant it appeared in the fading light of the day. She had been struck by the refinement last time, noting the condition of his furniture and the care he took with it were not in keeping with his reputation as a scoundrel, and had suspected he had taken employment with even more unsavory elements since her visit to confirm the stolen signet ring.

She understood now, of course, that it had all been a facade to gain the trust of French spies living in London.

How eagerly Mr. Twaddle-Thum had fallen in line, delivering the coup de grâce that ensured his disinheritance. Without her enthusiastic help, it might have taken him months to establish his bona fides as a wastrel in desperate need of funds.

Verity supposed she should be flattered by Hardwicke's faith in her. She had, after all, accomplished everything he had desired in short order. A report by an inferior-quality prattler merely repeating the rumor verbatim would have done little to ensure his immediate expulsion from polite society.

Even so, she was not flattered.

She was incensed to discover how easily she had been bear-led.

Was it some salve to her ego to know she had aided her country in winning the war against Napoleon?

No, not really.

Perhaps if Hardwicke had not succeeded in outmaneuvering her on several other occasions, she would not mind so much. But given that it was part of a larger pattern, it stung quite fiercely indeed.

Leaving the drawing room, she entered the bedchamber, which led to his library.

There, she settled into one of the two armchairs facing the desk. It was precisely where Hardwicke had sat and waited for her on her last visit, and she knew its high, curved back hid her presence from passersby.

Nevertheless, she was taking a risk because the position was exposed. If a servant entered the room with a candle and took one or two steps toward the desk, he would see her sitting there as plain as day. The smarter move would be to place herself behind the curtains, which were already closed and admitted only the faintest glow of the dying embers of the day.

Drapes were always an excellent option for hiding, and Verity genuinely believed half the challenge of Twaddling was recognizing which swaths of fabric were best suited for concealment.

Drapery and bed skirts, yes.

Dressing gowns, absolutely not.

Although the armchair was not ideal, Verity thought the concern was minimal in light of the situation. The hour was late, which meant the staff would be retiring to their quarters soon, and the library was in pristine condition. She could not imagine the maid coming in to straighten up the desk, and even if a few things were slightly out of place, Hardwicke did not seem like the sort of employer who welcomed interference in his private domain. It was difficult for Verity to imagine the servants in the library at all.

The small amount of risk was worth it, she thought, to recreate the scene with their positions reversed. She relished the prospect of his surprise when he discovered her waiting patiently for him.

And that pose of calm was essential to the presentation.

It would never do for Hardwicke to catch her darting from the window to the chair, and stepping out from behind the curtain would not have the same effect.

Verity grew more comfortable with her decision as the minutes passed. The later it grew, the less likely she would be discovered by a servant, and as the clock on the wall inched toward ten o'clock, she felt much of her anxiety ease.

Indeed, boredom began to set in, and she eyed the desk with interest, wondering what sort of strange and fascinating secrets it held. Originally, searching it had struck her as slightly too bold, even for Twaddle, and increasing her peril seemed foolhardy. In retrospect, however, it felt like a wasted opportunity, although she supposed she could always return now that she had a better idea of what to expect. She could not repeat the gambit with the children, for it would never do to copy herself, but there was always another way to cause a commotion. Nobody looked askance at a screaming fishwife, for example, and an irate husband who had just found his—

Voices!

Verity tensed her shoulders and tilted her head to the right, as if that would allow her to hear better.

Was that low rumble Hardwicke?

Having never heard the footman speak, she could not say

for certain, and although she was tempted to pad silently into the next room so she could eavesdrop better, she nevertheless remained in her seat. It was only a matter of time. Sooner or later, Hardwicke would visit the library, and if for some reason he did not, she would reveal her presence in another dramatic, although perhaps slightly less satisfying, fashion. Gaining entry to the home was the hard part; impressing Hardwicke was not.

She was only a woman, with her feeble abilities, so anything she managed to accomplish would astound him.

The conversation grew louder, allowing her to confirm that one of the participants was Hardwicke. A woman was speaking now, her voice carrying in from the bedchamber as she offered to prepare a plate.

"No, Mrs. Waylett, that is not necessary," he replied firmly. "I have already dined. You have had a long enough day. Please turn in with my gratitude."

The housekeeper murmured something low and unintelligible, which made Hardwicke chuckle softly.

"Yes, my thought exactly," he replied before urging his footman to retire as well. "As you know, James, I am perfectly capable of undressing myself, and if I required the services of a valet, then I would secure the services of a valet."

"As you wish, sir," James replied.

The sound of their footsteps carried lightly into the library, and Verity listened as they bid their employer good night and left for their quarters on the ground floor. Silence followed their departure, then a faint creak that could have been a floorboard groaning or a cabinet door opening.

Then more silence.

Although Twaddle had spent half his career concealed in dark crooks biding his time, Verity found this particular wait unendurable in an inexplicable way. At best she could attribute it to a vague worry that Hardwicke knew she was there and was spitefully drawing out the suspense before turning the tables on her.

She realized it was unlikely.

Not impossible, no, because he had been one step ahead of her on several occasions, but still highly unlikely. During their examination of Smith's bedroom that morning, she had given no indication by word or deed that this eventuality was in the offing—and how could she have? Verity herself had had no idea that she would end her day like this, in his library. It was a wholly unanticipated event.

Even so, her agitation increased the longer she sat there, and by the time the clock advanced to ten-thirty, she had to grip the arms of the chair to stop herself from rising. The urge to peek into the drawing room was almost overwhelming, and just as she was about to succumb to it, she heard another squeak.

Movement—finally!

Verity inhaled sharply, as if to hold her breath, and felt her heartbeat tick up.

Any moment now, she thought.

In fact, it was several dozen more moments, as Hardwicke dawdled in the drawing room, performing whatever tasks were necessary before returning to his bedchamber. He would have to extinguish the candles, but that did not take three ... now, *four* ... minutes.

The chandelier, she allowed, would require some maneuvering, but that was the sort of thing a footman would address before leaving for the night—if it was indeed necessary. Aware of Hardwicke's game, Verity suspected he could afford wax candles, which would burn themselves out safely. At this hour, they were probably naught but stubs anyway, guttering in the—

Verity tightened her grip on the armchair as she heard the clear sound of footsteps drawing nearer. The moment had arrived, and even as she opened her mouth to bid him good evening, she half expected him to say, "Hello, Miss Gorman."

He did not!

His steps continued steadily.

Hardwicke was behind her now, the glow from his candle illuminating the room.

Verity, rising to her feet and spinning deftly on one heel, asked with curt curiosity, "What does Mr. Grint have to say about Smith's death?"

He did not react.

Hardwicke's expression did not alter in the slightest. He came to a halt at the sound of her voice, but even that was measured. He did not jerk in amazement or lurch suddenly. If Verity did not know better, she would have thought this appointment had been recorded in his diary: Meet Miss Lark in the library at ten forty-five on the evening of May thirtieth.

She would not pretend his poise was not infuriating. After insulting her so dreadfully in her own front parlor, the least he could do was reveal a smidgeon of surprise.

A wince, perhaps, or a flicker.

Smoothly, he greeted her, bowing slightly and murmuring, "Miss Gorman, what an unexpected delight. To what do I owe the pleasure?"

It was a misstep.

As she had already announced the reason for her visit, he was well aware of the answer. And yet still he had defaulted to an empty courtesy.

Someone needs a second to gather his thoughts.

Pressing her advantage, Verity said, "Although Smith's murder is a troubling development, I have to believe Grint took it in stride, as presumably that sort of thing happened all the time when you worked together in the Alien Office. You are welcome, by the way. I want to say that such underhanded means were not necessary to gain Mr. Twaddle-Thum's assistance, as he is a patriot with a healthy dislike of impertinent French emperors, but I understand your caution. In all honesty, I do not know how he would have responded if you had applied to him or Freddie directly. I suspect they would have both said something about not doing the government's bidding."

There, she thought, now Hardwicke knew everything she knew about his adventures, both past and present. She had considered withholding a detail or two to reveal at a later date but decided it was more gratifying to disclose the extent of his exposure all at once. It was bad enough that she had managed to infiltrate his private domain under the noses of his well-trained staff; that she had done so while in possession of highly secretive information was adding insult to injury.

It went without saying that Verity was happy to heap on as many slights, affronts, and petty jibes as possible.

Hardwicke, seemingly untroubled by these admissions, strolled toward his desk and then stepped around it, which amused Verity to no end. Surely, the daring war hero did not require a large article of furniture to increase his importance. He could intimidate one intrusive female reporter without a generous swath of mahogany.

In this assumption, she was correct, for Hardwicke did not sit down at the desk but instead put down the candleholder and lit the wall sconces before opening one of the drawers. He withdrew a bottle from its depths and held up the golden brown liquid questioningly.

"How civilized," she murmured.

"Well, we are Englishmen," he replied with a hint of humor as he removed the top from the decanter. "And it seemed appropriate that we raise a glass to your resourcefulness. You have an air of enthusiastic discovery about you, and it would be ungracious not to toast to it."

He was ridiculing her, Verity knew, for his description of her demeanor was simply not accurate. If she had displayed any emotion—although in fact she had not—it was restrained satisfaction. But to offer a protest would be to cede ground to him, for the point of their exchange was to affect competing levels of apathy. "Thank you, yes, brandy would be lovely. I trust it is the best Spain has to offer?"

"But we are at peace, Miss Gorman," he said, carrying over two glasses and placing them on the desk. Then he sat down in the armchair beside her and crossed his leg as he turned to face her. "Trade has resumed with France, and we are permitted to enjoy French brandy with a clear conscience."

"A relief, I am certain, after consuming so much with a guilty conscience in the course of your work for the Alien Office," she replied.

Hardwicke drew his brows together and regarded her with a mixture of confusion and humor. "That is true, yes, for my work with the Alien Office involved many late-night rendezvous over illicit libations in squalid taverns, and my appreciation for superior-quality brandy is such that I find it impossible not to enjoy it even in the most inhospitable environment. That being the case, I am at a loss to understand the faint sneer of disapproval in your tone. I was working to defeat Napoleon and ensure an English victory over the French. I think we can agree my objectives were unequivocally good."

He was right, of course.

Hardwicke had risked his life to serve his country, and whatever small pleasure he derived from the experience was inconsequential. Verity knew that and yet could not quite squelch her resentment at how easily he had maneuvered her. Dangling a rumor about a ne'er-do-well second son in such desperate straits he would steal from his own father—the story possessed everything that Twaddle derided: wasted privilege, squandered potential, feckless dissipation. Second sons were so rife for mockery because they straddled the line between expectation and disappointment, which was an exhausting endeavor. It was so easy for them to tip into corruptive cynicism, and Twaddle was there with his quill well inked when they did.

There was, Verity acknowledged, something festeringly cynical about waiting for someone to fail and then gleefully recounting their failure. It lacked, to be sure, the high-minded righteousness of a Robert Lark article reporting on the abuse of children in workhouses. But it was the nature of the beast, was it not, for nobody cared about the goings-on at the fishmonger in Gilbert Lane (although Verity could tell quite a tale about the goings-on at the fishmonger in Gilbert Lane, for never was there such a cheat for selling two-day-old mackerel at one-day-old prices). Members of the *bon ton* cared only about themselves, and they were the ones who regularly subscribed to newspapers. The antics of Quality, however, interested everyone, from the raw-knuckled scullion to the well-heeled banker.

Hardwicke, exploiting these truths to position himself as an easy target for French spies, had merely followed the line of bread crumbs she herself had dropped.

Why, then, was she so annoyed?

Perhaps because he had complained about his abuse at Mr. Twaddle-Thum's hands as recently as last week. He sounded so genuinely aggrieved, as if the wound still stung. That the goal of his grumbling had been to manipulate her further was undeniable, but Verity could not fathom why that would bother her. She had spent the majority of her life manipulating people, and it would be churlish to protest the treatment. Fair was fair, after all.

It came down, then, to her anger over his offer.

Calling her *astounding* and then assigning her a menial task —it was an insurmountable object for her.

Perhaps, Verity allowed, raising the glass to her lips, but there were larger matters at stake. Her ego was also inconsequential.

She took a deep sip of the brandy, noted the complexity of the flavor, and announced that he was correct. "I apologize for implying that I have anything but respect and gratitude for your service to our country," she continued, her tone slightly satirical despite her best attempt at sincerity.

Giving Colson Hardwicke a compliment, it appeared, was just beyond her reach.

If he noticed anything amiss in her response, he did not reveal it as he contemplated her over the rim of his own glass, his eyes curiously intent as they moved across her face. Then his expression sharpened as something seemed to snap into focus. "The olive green coat!"

Even knowing how astute he was, Verity was startled at this ability to fill in a detail retrospectively.

"Yes, of course, the olive green coat with the tear on the left collar," he added with a thoughtful tilt of his head as if seeing something that was not quite there. "The boots caught my attention. There was just something about them, but I did not pause to consider it because I was already late for my meeting with Grint. But that was you, wasn't it?" He shook his head as if bemused. "I must compliment you again, Miss Gorman, on your cleverness. How did you know I would call on the Home Office?"

Verity did not doubt the admiration in his tone. He was genuinely impressed by her ability to figure out his destination, and although she appreciated his regard, she knew how little it was worth.

A breathless giggle.

Thank you but no.

Biding her time, she took another sip of the brandy and pondered how to respond. If she admitted that she had merely stumbled across him in her pursuit of other information, his esteem would lose a little of its luster, which she was reluctant to allow.

Just because she did not value his admiration did not mean she did not want it.

Furthermore, she knew from her years of Twaddling that what looked like omniscience to the outside world was simply the product of hard work and happenstance. Applying that standard to the situation, she had indeed figured out Hardwicke's next step.

As she swallowed the smooth liqueur, she settled on an evasive answer. "Rational deduction and a little bit of luck," she replied modestly. "I knew from our previous interaction that you serve at a superior's command, and given the nature of Fitch's connections, it was most likely someone in the Home Office."

Hardwicke's lips twitched in mirth. "Again, I must marvel at the disapprobation in your tone. Only you could make being gainfully employed sound like a bad thing. Do I need to remind you of all people, Miss Gorman, that I have been disowned by my father? If I want to live in the style to which I have become accustomed, I have to earn my keep somehow."

"You have not," she said, understanding in a flash that his father had been aware of the plan from the very beginning. It was he, after all, who mentioned the missing ring at Lady Marston's ball. "Your inheritance is secure, as is your place among your family. But why haven't you returned to the fold like a proper prodigal? The war has been over for more than a year." No sooner had she asked the question than the answer struck her. "Your unsavory reputation is still useful."

He lifted his shoulders in an elegant shrug. "I worked so hard to create it, it felt disrespectful to just toss it away."

Having constructed many aliases for herself, Verity appreciated the value of a well-established identity. But unlike her, Hardwicke had just the one identity, and she was surprised that he was not eager to reclaim his good name. One word about his wartime deeds murmured in Lady Jersey's ear, and he would be eagerly embraced by the beau monde.

Everyone adored a hero.

Being petted and feted by society was not a terrible fate for a second son.

True, yes, and yet that was the crux of the problem, was it not? Lord Colson was a second son and remained a second son despite his feats of derring-do. Trapped in a system designed to retain power by keeping its wealth consolidated, he was a mostly useless appendage. His only value was as a spare.

No wonder working for the Home Office appealed to him. It was not that it gave him something to do but that it gave him something *meaningful* to do. It provided an alternative to the usual career of dissipation spurred on by boredom and bitterness. The man Twaddle had written about could have very easily been the reality, and the fact Hardwicke had chosen a different path for himself was something Verity respected.

Respecting him, however, made her feel petulant, and she said with more disdain than was appropriate, "You knew he would have assignments for you."

He shrugged again. "Suspected."

An exceedingly minor distinction. "But a reliable bet with all the unrest in the north."

Hardwicke's lips twitched with amusement as he said wryly, "And we both know I am an inveterate gambler."

Indeed, they did not. Gaming was the time-honored

method by which an aristocrat impoverished himself, and Verity could think of no faster route to convincing a French émigré that you were receptive to his offer than to lose your fortune at a hazard table.

Except perhaps at the hands of a faro dealer.

Contemplating Hardwicke now in the golden glow of the wall sconces, the sculpted curves of his cheeks and chin thrown into sharp relief by the candlelight, she wondered how she could have ever subscribed to his profligacy. It was so obviously a hoax, for there was an unrelenting sturdiness about him, a sense of power and control.

It was no mystery, of course, for Verity Lark knew better than anyone in London how simple it was to control perception. People saw what they expected to see, and they expected to see what you told them they would see. In this respect, they were delightfully accommodating, readily concluding a torn coat meant penury or height masculinity.

It was remarkably easy to hide in plain sight.

Fitch knew that. He had hired Miss Copley to play his sister to alter reality just slightly enough to make himself seem unfamiliar. He added the beard and belly to further distort the picture he presented.

It was, Verity thought, a fairly convincing Twaddle.

Recognizing it almost from the beginning, she had failed to understand the nature of his project. She had assumed he was a fugitive insurrectionist evading the authorities while continuing to agitate for change. The possibility that he was an informer had never occurred to her, and if Kingsley had not responded so immoderately to Mr. Betts's benign visit, it still would not have occurred to her.

But the under-secretary had noted the tear in the tavern keeper's coat and drawn his own conclusions. It was a strategic mistake, the sort she did not expect from the Home

Office, but not every candle in the chandelier glimmered with equal brightness.

Hardwicke would never work with such a dolt, which meant his assignment with Grint was not directly related to Kingsley's interest in Fitch. It was too implausible to suppose that both under-secretaries developed an interest in the informer independently of each other. The attention of one probably drew the attention of the other.

Very well, then, Verity thought. Which came first?

She posed the question to Hardwicke point-blank.

If he was taken aback by how much she had figured out about Fitch on her own, his response divulged nothing as he explained that Kingsley had hired Fitch to inform on the Burnley Blanketeers. "Fitch scheduled an appointment to meet with Kingsley in March and offered his services. He had an introduction from General Singer, commanding officer in the Northern District, with whom he worked months prior. It was Fitch who alerted the army to the uprising at the Catterton Ironworks. He came highly recommended, and as word of the Blanketeering movement had yet to reach the Home Office, Sidmouth agreed that it was imperative that we have a man on the inside to report back on their plans."

Aware that he could have evaded this question as well as every other one she posed, Verity appreciated the straightforward response. His willingness to deal honestly with her was the highest compliment he could pay her, certainly topping any effusive praise about her so-called competence. "That sounds reasonable," she said mildly.

And it did.

If intelligence from Fitch was the reason Singer and his army were able to stop the violent throng from securing weapons at the ironworks and marching on York, then the informer had performed his function well. Far more innocent bystanders would have been slain in the Christmas Uprising than one unfortunate factory agent.

Fitch's proficiency did not surprise her. Anyone who was crafty enough to hire a pretend sister to further disguise himself was clever enough to report on an insurrection without getting caught.

Hardwicke, seeming to almost follow her line of thought, agreed that having someone spy on the organization was the correct tack for the Home Office. "The Blanketeering movement seems peaceful, but there is no disadvantage in making sure it stays that way. The problem is Fitch strikes Grint as just a little too wily."

Ah, so that was his game. "Grint asked you to investigate him?"

"Keep an eye on him, rather," he amended with a press of his lips. "Grint does not trust his motives, but he also cannot be seen questioning Kingsley's judgment, as they are rivals for Sidmouth's approbation. He knew it would be an easy thing for the Marquess of Ware's dissolute son to join a reformist society, for he is well known for resenting both his father and the caste system that denied him a share of the familial wealth, so he brought his suspicions to me and asked me to make a determination."

Given the wild machinations the chancellor's office had deployed to squelch rumors of corruption within its ranks, she thought the under-secretary's handling of the matter was cautious and discreet. "And what does he suspect in particular?"

"That Fitch is inciting violence while collecting a salary from the Home Office," Hardwicke replied. "Grint believes the Yarwellians are using the Blanketeers to hide the fact that they are actually fomenting violent revolution. He fears Fitch is using his position to draw more people to the cause under the guise of reporting on it."

Verity acknowledged this concern with a dip of her head. "Fitch *is* a persuasive speaker."

Hardwicke smiled faintly. "As I know you to be a highly intelligent woman, Miss Gorman, I remain baffled why you would refuse payment for work you were determined to do regardless. If you had accepted my offer, you would have been duly compensated for the time you spent listening to Fitch's addresses."

"You must not worry about me," she said reassuringly. "As you noted previously, everything is fodder."

It was a deliberately provoking comment, and Verity waited for Hardwicke to issue a stern prohibition against details of their discussion appearing in one of Mr. Twaddle-Thum's columns. During the Altick affair, every other word out of his mouth had been a threat or a warning against the infamous gossip.

He issued neither now, which confused Verity.

Despite this pointed reminder of her alter ego, he continued to speak frankly, adding that in the six weeks since he himself had joined the Society of Yarwellian Philosophers, he had observed nothing that had led him to draw a conclusion either way. "Fitch speaks passionately in favor of the cause in taverns and public houses, allowing him to gather signatures and funds in support of the Blanketeers. But his success as an orator has also gained him greater access to the original members of the society who are organizing the march. Recruiting Crowley to speak at the mass meeting was his idea, and that has enabled him to sit in on planning meetings. He has his tentacles everywhere: composing handbills with Lemon, updating the ledger with Anderson, counting donations with Dircks. He is either an excellent informer or a brilliant insurgent, or both."

"And that is why you sought conversation with his sister,"

she said. "To approach the problem from another direction, as it were."

"I hoped that either she would say something revealing or Fitch would, in her presence," he replied. "In my experience, people are different in different environments. After you declined my offer, I arranged to meet them by chance at the market near their rooms and wrangled an invitation to tea, which was pleasant but unproductive. Miss Fitch regaled me with tales of their childhood while her brother corrected her remembrances. I learned nothing of value, and if Miss Fitch knows anything of her brother's true intentions, she is too experienced to reveal it."

Verity, rewarding candor with more candor, said, "Miss Copley."

Puzzled by the non sequitur, he drew his brows together. "Excuse me?"

"The woman you met is actually Maryanne Copley, an actress Fitch hired to play the part of his sister while in London," she said.

Hardwicke's jaw dropped. It was not much, only a fraction of an inch, but there was no mistaking the response. He was stunned.

Chapter Eight

S aturday, May 30
   10:48 p.m.

Verity did not giggle.

A joyful chortle rose in her throat, fluttering enticingly, quivering invitingly, and in the silence that followed her astonishing revelation, she could almost hear the sound fill the room. After everything she had done that evening to incite a reaction in Hardwicke, she had finally gotten the one she sought: astonishment.

It was cause for celebration.

Hurrah!

She did not cheer, of course. Acknowledging the accomplishment would only reveal how assiduously she had pursued it. The better response was to affect indifference and imbue the moment with a sort of apologetic confusion, as if to say, "Oh, but I thought everyone knew."

Bemusement frequently trumped amusement.

And even if the rule did not apply in this case, it would not be sportsmanlike to revel in a triumph. It was not Hardwicke's fault that he had been unable to squeeze the truth out of a stifled actress yearning for applause. He did not have Verity's extensive repertoire of personae from which to draw, and even if he did possess his own large assortment of characters, it did not include a frail old woman.

He simply did not have the build, being all tall and sturdy and muscled.

Nobody would ever believe he needed help.

He did have other advantages that Verity lacked. His handsome face, for one thing. No amount of powder or rouge could make her visage half as appealing as his. And his sinewy heft—it could not be achieved with padding. The combination gave him an edge, and if used properly, all the man had to do to discover secret information from a woman would be to blink his absurdly thick eyelashes and say please.

That he had failed to persuade Miss Copley to include him among her admiring public was a significant misstep on his part, and although Verity could provide him with a few helpful pointers to avoid the adverse outcome in the future, she withheld her advice.

Critiquing his performance, however well intentioned, would also be unsporting.

As a consequence, Verity sat silently in her chair and waited for her host to speak.

Hardwicke's expression changed slowly, surprise giving way to bewilderment as he shook his head, as if to clear it of unwanted thoughts, and he said, "Tell me, Miss Gorman, why did you refuse my offer? I have been unable to make sense of it."

It was not the question Verity had anticipated.

Perched languidly in her seat, her fingers lightly holding the glass of brandy, she had been prepared to explain her tactical brilliance with an unstudied insouciance, as if she deposited herself in front of oncoming vehicles every day of the week. With Freddie busy with the newspaper and Delphine generally irritated with the risks her friend took, Verity had few opportunities to discuss the finer points of her practice. So much thought and consideration went into these decisions. And figuring out the best way to approach a target —that was the most satisfying aspect of Twaddling.

She had relished the prospect of detailing her process, which, she conceded, would have allowed her to gloat a little without seeming to gloat at all.

Hardwicke knew that, too, she realized, and had changed the subject to thwart her.

It was a diabolical play and precisely what she would have done if she had been on the other end of the conversation.

Chagrined, she nevertheless assumed the look of apologetic confusion and replied that she had not refused him. "I accepted your challenge, as evidenced by my presence here."

Again, he insisted he had not issued a challenge but rather offered employment. "I was sincere in my admiration for your skill, which your discovery about Miss Fitch—or, rather, Miss Copley—justifies."

"Well, yes, that was the challenge," she said affably. "To overcome the limitations of your admiration."

"But my admiration *has* no limits," he said with unsettling certainty, his teal eyes regarding her with disquieting intensity as he looked at her over the rim of his glass.

Verity flushed.

Not hugely.

'Twas not as though her face was suddenly awash in a glowing bright pink. The heat in her cheeks was minimal, just enough to make her slightly uncomfortable, and she regretted wearing a woolen coat. A silk mix would have been much more suitable. It was the end of May, after all, despite the unseasonable chill that had bedeviled the capital all spring.

Focusing on the details helped.

It reminded her that she was on an assignment and that she had come to Millman Street in search of answers. Despite the brandy, it was not a social call. She was not there to earn Hardwicke's esteem.

In fact, that was exactly why she was there, she reminded herself peevishly.

But not *that* kind of esteem.

The other kind.

She wanted his sincere admiration for her capabilities.

And yet staring into those strange eyes, neither blue nor green and yet incomprehensively both, she found herself craving every kind.

Captivated, she knew it was merely a ruse and realized she had been wrong earlier in her assessment: He did not have to blink or say please.

His fascinating gaze was enough.

Flirting was an acceptable method for extracting information from a target, and although she readily acknowledged its merits, Verity rarely employed the tactic. It felt just a little too much like crossing into her mother's territory, for Lorraine Price had excelled at playing the coquette. She could wield a fan with the deftness of a master swordsman, bringing her adversary to his knees with an elegant flick of her wrist—and laughing while doing so.

La Reina knew how to giggle.

Verity did not blame Hardwicke for using the trick, for she had invaded his sanctum bearing the upper hand, and he had to even the score somehow. It was not his fault that she was struck beyond comprehension by a pair of beguiling eyes and a flattering comment.

Except that, yes, it was precisely his fault, and it disgusted

Verity to realize she had fallen in line just like every other woman against whom he had used the strategy. Unaware that she was so vulnerable to the facile maneuver, she had in some narrow sliver of her mind suspected it. That afternoon in the front parlor when he had made his proposal, she had glimpsed her susceptibility in the sharpness of her disappointment at being judged on a scale of femaleness. The affront was not simply in his offering her an assignment that belittled her abilities; it was also in his offering her an assignment that considered her solely as a member of her sex.

She was twice inferior.

Verity had endured worse insults in her life. Slurs and abuse were daily occurrences at the orphan asylum where she was raised, and any good Twaddle resulted in a generous helping of scorn being heaped on her head. She was not so thin-skinned that pinpricks harmed her, and yet she had responded to Hardwicke's slights as though they were stabs of a dagger. She had scurried away—a lark in flight—rather than hold her ground and make a counter proposal.

That was the panic, she thought now.

She had terminated the conversation abruptly rather than let it continue because she did not want to find herself tempted to accept less than her due from a man whose respect she desired.

If she started on the lower step, she would always stay on the lower step.

Verity had learned that from her mother, who rose to the dizzying height of duchess and yet somehow remained a lightskirt.

Only seconds had passed since Hardwicke had leveled his piercing gaze at her, and as much as she wanted to look away, she kept her eyes solidly forward.

Aversion was weakness.

Recognizing her feelings helped her dispel them, and

although she still felt an alarming quiver, it was no longer overwhelming. Clarity returned and with it the awareness that it was time to end the impasse.

Enough was enough.

"I threw myself in front of an oncoming carriage and allowed Miss Copley to rescue me," she announced. It was a slightly humiliating admission because he had not asked, but she had to say something and knew the ploy was to her credit. It was audacious and creative. "I sported wrinkles and a cane and wore my best mobcap, even though I was outdoors, to hint at my befuddlement."

Hardwicke smiled.

The gesture increased his appeal, humor glittering now in the depths of those compelling eyes, but it also broke the spell. He took a sip of his brandy as if nothing out of the usual had transpired—as indeed for him it had not. Whatever sensation had passed between them was felt only by her.

Mr. Grint's drudge was merely fulfilling the obligations of his assignment.

"I trust you waited for one that was moving at a reassuringly sedate pace," he observed mildly.

"I did, yes," Verity confirmed, grateful for the sensible reply. Kicking up a fuss about her safety would have been yet another stinging affront. "And I made sure it was a far enough distance away that I could save myself should Miss Copley have decided to leave me to my fate."

"You are a remarkable creature, Miss Gorman," he said with an admiring lilt.

Inured to his flattery, she acknowledged his praise with a curt dip of her head and briskly explained what she knew about Fitch's agreement with the actress, including his promise to compensate her generously at the satisfying conclusion of the affair. "I was unable to ascertain, however, when that will be. She claimed not to know herself."

"I expect it is after Crowley's speech," Hardwicke suggested. "Several society members plan to travel around England to grow the support of the Blanketeers. Fitch might be among them. That would make his double dealing harder to detect. Once he is out of London, there would be no way of knowing if he was inciting revolution or merely reporting on it, and Kingsley is just pompous enough never to question the accuracy of the dispatches his own personal spy is submitting."

Verity, liking this theory, observed that the arrangement was ideal for an informant determined to play his government false. "And not staying in one place for long means he would not require a sibling to help conceal his identity. If anyone recognized him from Tockwith, he could simply move on to the next town. But he had to stay in London, did he not, to prove his worth to Kingsley. He had to make sure that everything he reported could be corroborated. That is why the speech is an excellent arbitrary marker: It is a high-profile event that will demonstrate that all his information is accurate."

Hardwicke, agreeing with her conclusion, stared thoughtfully into the rich-colored liquid and said it still did not solve the riddle he had been tasked with deciphering. "Is Fitch an informer or insurrectionist?"

Unable to arrive at the answer herself, Verity shared his vexation and wondered if examining the matter from the point of view of the slain Smith might help. It was, she thought, a rather mundane suggestion, for his corpse had loomed over the conversation and was connected to Fitch in some way. How precisely, was another mystery, but there were a limited number of possibilities and the one she favored was the most obvious: Fitch had killed him to preserve his secret. Arriving from the north, Smith had recognized the informer and threatened to reveal the truth to the authorities.

If her theory was correct, then Fitch's actions in regards to the radical movement were irrelevant because he would go to Newgate for murder.

Hardwicke immediately put an end to this line of reasoning by insisting Fitch could not be the murderer. "Judging by the state of the blood on the sheets and the wound, Smith was killed around eight-thirty—at which time Fitch was sitting in the same room as me, along with fifty-eight other members of the Society of Yarwellian Philosophers. It was the weekly meeting of the membership, which has more than doubled in size in recent weeks as excitement around the Burnley Blanketeers grows. The meeting ends a little before nine, and you may be sure that if he had left for any reason, I would have followed him."

"Oh, I see," Verity murmured, taken aback by the development.

But of course the solution could not be that simple.

The last murder in which she had been embroiled involved dozens of people, weeks of investigation, a roster of suspects, and one imposter.

"Noticeably absent were two original members who had not missed a meeting since I joined the society in mid-April," he added in the same matter-of-fact tone, identifying the men as John Dircks and Rudolph Oxenford. The former was in charge of overseeing donations, and the latter wrote the handbills that Lemon printed. "As their absences were unusual, I made an effort to discover where they were and received conflicting explanations from several other original members. One said Dircks had a stomach ailment, another said Oxenford was sick, and a third said Oxenford's wife had fallen ill and Dircks had gone to fetch a doctor. Based on these answers I wondered if something nefarious was being planned at the top level of the organization that Fitch had failed to report."

Although Verity appreciated the introduction of new suspects, she was at a loss to fathom a motive for killing Smith. If Fitch was the informant, then the Yarwellians had nothing to fear from the elderly man—unless the Home Office had embedded two spies in the society.

Hardwicke was working with Grint in secret.

Perhaps another official in the agency was conducting his own covert operation.

It was possible, Verity thought, and yet it did not explain why seeing Smith would cause Fitch to stumble in his speech. There was something between the two men, a connection, but she could not decide if it was adversarial or convivial. Nor could she figure out what their rivalry or friendship had to do with the larger issue of the society.

"Why would Dircks or Oxenford kill an elderly man like Smith?" she asked.

Hardwicke raised his shoulders as if he did not know the answer but added that the Yarwellian Society had been an insular group for more than a decade. "It has been the same group of ten since the beginning, and then Anderson came up with the idea of delivering petitions directly to the prince regent. Lemon suggested that working men from up north should deliver them and Oxenford proposed a march to draw attention to their cause as well as additional men. The membership suddenly doubled, then tripled, and now there are all these new faces and nobody knows who they really are, only who they say they are, and the idea of the Blanketeers is gaining momentum. The mass meeting is garnering interest, and the government knows who they are. They were a small, obscure group for more than a decade and now they are not."

"And they know what happened at the ironworks in Tockwith," she added, nodding in comprehension. "The government might have already placed a spy in their midst, and they have no idea who it could be. Everyone is suspect."

"Especially Smith, whose behavior was strange," Hardwicke replied. "He appeared a week ago pretending to be a tailor, but he obviously knew nothing about sewing because his forefinger was cut up from pinpricks. He hovered by the cellar door, asking questions about various members, such as where they were from and how long they had been part of the group, and he never came as early as the other workers or stayed as late. It was obvious he had a private agenda, which is why I followed him to his lodgings and resorted to searching his rooms. I wanted to know for whom he worked."

"Did you find out?" Verity asked curiously.

He shook his head. "You saw what I saw, and now I do not know if Smith was spying for another government office or working with Fitch or was just evaluating the society before deciding whether to join. That is why I called on Grint this afternoon. I wanted to alert him to my concerns. If Dircks and Oxenford are murderers, then this is no longer a simple matter of spying on Fitch as he spies on the society."

Struck by how unusually forthcoming Hardwicke was being, Verity first took his candor as a sign of respect. Finally, he was treating her as an equal.

Not as a female equal.

An *equal* equal.

He knew who she was—London's most tenacious gossip, the *Gazette*'s most determined reporter—and trusted her anyway.

But as he continued to share what he knew, she realized it had nothing to do with trust. It was about expedience. She had unwittingly presented him with an opportunity that he was eager to exploit.

He needed Mr. Twaddle-Thum or Robert Lark to pursue the story because he could not—not in any official capacity.

"You're Grint's man," she said flatly, her tone revealing none of her annoyance at having supplied him with the ideal solution to his quandary. No wonder he had not appeared shocked by her presence in his library; he had been too busy figuring out how he could use her.

It was irksome indeed.

And yet Verity could not deny it redounded to her benefit. Founding members of the Society of Yarwellian Philosophers stabbing an elderly man to death was precisely the sort of story Robert Lark would relish writing and Freddie would delight in publishing.

There was probably an angle for Twaddle to compose an adjacent piece.

What *was* Her Outrageousness's opinion of the reform movement?

Even if she had never made an overt statement about the Luddites or the Christmas Uprising, conclusions could be drawn from various other means. The duchess was a voracious reader, for example, and might have read a book about the treatment of serfs in eighteenth century Russia. Information could be extrapolated from there.

But truly, though, why *had* the duchess never commented on the reform movement? What was she hiding? What was she so cautious not to say?

It was a specious premise for an article, Verity knew, and yet she tucked it away for later as she struggled to smother the keen irritation she felt at being outmaneuvered again. Surliness would get her nowhere.

"And everyone knows you're Grint's man," she said, teasing out his game. "If you are responsible for apprehending either Dircks or Oxenford, then Kingsley will realize you had been spying on his man. That would not reflect well on Grint, who would appear to have been trying to gain an advantage over a rival."

She thought this decipherment of Hardwicke's motives

was a particularly astute bit of ratiocination, but he did not look impressed.

"Not *everyone* knows I'm Grint's man," he corrected with a hint of a smile. "If they did, then I would be terrible at my job. But Sidmouth knows and he would understand at once what it means if I were involved. Grint warned me off and told me to leave the matter to the magistrate. I proposed another option."

Verity tightened her grip on the glass as a new, horrifying thought struck her, and she was appalled it had not occurred to her the moment she had discovered Hardwicke's connection to the Home Office.

He was Grint's man.

"Grint knows nothing of you," Hardwicke rushed to assure her, either noticing her distress or following the obvious line of thought. "I have never mentioned Mr. Twaddle-Thum or Robert Lark in any of our conversations. He is aware of Mr. Reade from the Grimston affair, but only to the extent that he was chosen as a target for violence by a man whose faculties had been degraded by fear and anxiety. He has no reason to suspect the existence of a Miss Gorman."

Although he was as adept at lying as she, Verity believed him. "Thank you."

"I owe Grint my allegiance but not to the extent that it supersedes other loyalties," he explained. "I did not tell him anything about my work for Seb until after it was resolved. I did not consider it any of his business even when I suspected the chancellor's office was in some way involved."

He spoke smoothly, calmly, and yet she detected an underlying intensity to his tone that was almost as disquieting as his gaze.

It was time to leave.

Indeed, yes, beyond time.

Verity took a final sip of the brandy, then laid the glass on the desk. "That is reassuring. I will keep it in mind as I conduct my murder investigation," she said, not quite able to smother her amusement at these words.

Who did she think she was—the Duchess of Kesgrave?

Next, she would be eating rout cakes and demanding pineapple at every meal.

"I will also be sure to leave your name out of it," she added as she rose to her feet.

"You misunderstand me," Hardwicke said, standing as well. "I am not gifting you with Smith's murder as I would a pair of earrings."

"I should hope not, for earrings are a terrible present," she said archly. "They have an alarming tendency to get caught on things and fall out, leaving incriminating evidence everywhere. A much better present would be a spyglass, as my last one was crushed in the Great Squirrel Stampede of 1815."

Although he appeared tempted to ask more about this tragic event, he shook his head firmly and announced that she would not succeed in distracting him. "At no point did I say that the mystery of Smith's death was yours to solve. I will be investigating as well."

"Oh, I see, another challenge," she said with a knowing nod. "Very well, I accept!"

"Now you are being deliberately vexing," he muttered, clearly both disgruntled and amused. "I meant that you would be the one to report the identity of the murderer to the magistrate as Robert Lark or one of your dozen aliases, not that you would solve the murder by yourself."

Verity came to an abrupt halt in the hallway. "My dozen aliases?" she repeated as if deeply perplexed by the notion. "Am I a governess telling fairy stories in the garden to small children? Lord Colson, I have scores of aliases, and any number of them will be happy to alert the Runners as soon as it is appropriate. Naturally, they will also be happy to perform the same service for you in the unlikely event that you find proof first."

"I did not issue a challenge," he said sternly.

She tutted disapprovingly. "You cannot change your mind now that you are intimidated. That is not how challenges work."

"Miss Gorman," he growled.

But Verity would have none of it and thanking him for his hospitality—"Your brandy is very fine indeed"—she left.

Sunday, May 31
  9:45 a.m.

Although Verity had never lodged a false accusation at a murder suspect in an effort to discover where he was at the time of the attack, she had used the device to figure out which kitchen maid sold the recipe for Lord Bredbury's famous banana tart to the *London Tribune*. Vital to its successful execution was identifying the Runner most likely to yield to the shrill cries of an irate fishwife, for there was no point in ostentatiously laying a charge if there was no official present to witness it. After watching the six viable candidates interact with the public for a half hour, Verity settled on Vernon Knowles. His timidity made him particularly well suited for the assignment, and he passed the foot test—that was, he apologized to Verity when she stepped on *his* foot.

Taking advantage of his misplaced remorse, she squeezed out a few teardrops and begged him to help her. A grave injustice had been done!

Knowles followed Verity now as she marched along the pavement, her arms raised indignantly as she screeched about her apple cart being maliciously overturned by a reprobate in a dark coat. "Jest minding me own business, I wuz, jest me and me cart and me customer arguing over 'ow much 'e wuz gonna pay me for a dozen apples. He says one farthing, and I says absolutely not. I ain't no daft Milton to take 'alf of what it's worth, no, I ain't. And then out of nowheres comes *this* daft Milton flying straight at me with no concern at all for me 'ealth and safety. I is lucky to be alive, I is."

Everything about Verity was thick: her bosom, her waist, her accent. Under the bulky folds of her petticoats and short gown, several inches of padding expanded her form in every direction, and a voluminous kerchief wrapped around her shoulders hid the slim column of her neck. Her hair, in wild disarray despite the best efforts of her black bonnet to contain it, fell into her face, obscuring the thinness of her features.

Ewella McTawdry, whose apple cart was sometimes a flower stall and occasionally a fish counter depending on the requirements of the situation, had no patience for her fellow man and saw injustice and iniquity everywhere she looked.

Nothing was an accident, no, sir!

Every misfortune that had befallen the hapless woman since she was old enough to walk had been deliberately arranged by one evil actor or another, and she raised her considerable voice to make sure everyone in Cherry Road knew how horribly she had been mistreated.

"I yells at 'im, don't I? I yells at him that me cart is right there and 'e's gonna knock it over. But what does 'e care? It's not 'is cart, is it?" Verity seethed in Mrs. McTawdry's rumbling growl. The poor woman was always up in arms about something, and her useless children were no help, griping constantly about their sore feet or cold hands.

The miscreants had no idea what it was like to truly suffer!

"Knocks it right over, doesn't 'e, like it were made of

paper," she continued with a darting glance at Knowles, who was several inches shorter than she and had to run to keep up with her long strides. "And 'e runs away! Scampers off like I don't 'ave eyes in me 'ead. I sees where he goes. I followed him all the way back to his 'ouse."

Knowles, slightly out of breath from the challenge of staying abreast with her, observed that from her description of the incident, it sounded as though it was just an accident.

"Jest an accident!" Verity repeated in her most piercing shrill. "Jest an accident! A daft Milton destroys me livelihood and it's jest an accident! I suppose it'll be jest an accident when me and me children starve?"

"No, ma'am," he replied as they turned the corner.

Dircks, who was one of the two founders whom Hardwicke suspected of murdering Smith, lived in Burgston Road. Before fetching the Runner, she had confirmed that he was in residence, but that had been more than an hour ago. He could be anywhere by now.

Nevertheless, Verity located the address and began to knock decisively on the door. *Bam! Bam! Bam!*

Knowles flinched with each resounding thwack and wondered if perhaps a more moderate approach might yield better results, citing the well-worn aphorism about flies and honey. "We do not want to frighten the inhabitants. There might be children inside."

Appalled by the suggestion, Verity tightened her fist and thumped even harder as she complained about already having more flies than she could handle. "Ye know what catches the most flies? Rotten apples!"

Knowles's muttered response was drowned out by her pounding.

The door opened suddenly and a glowering man stood on the threshold. As tall as Verity, he wore his ginger hair long, brushing his shoulders, and he straightened his spectacles as he thanked his callers to stop assaulting his door.

"Oi, so that's 'ow it goes, does it? Ye allowed to assault me cart, but I can't assaults yer door," Verity said in Mrs. McTawdry's pugnacious rumble. "Ye see how unfair it is! Arrest 'im!"

Dircks goggled in amazement, then said, "I beg your pardon!"

"Too late, innit?" Verity said. "And too little! Arrest 'im at once, I says!"

Knowles, taking a hesitant step forward, introduced himself and explained the situation as he understood it. Upon learning that he was supposed to have knocked over Mrs. McTawdry's apple cart in Great Newport Street, Dircks insisted it was impossible. "I have been here, at my home, for the past two hours."

"Not today!" Verity spat.

Knowles looked at her in surprise. "Not today?"

"'Course not! I 'ad to clean up all my apples, didn't I? I 'ad to make sure none of them got stolen and me cart neither," she said angrily. "Do ye think I'm a toff who can stand to lose all 'er apples and 'er cart? 'Twere yesterday morning, likes I said."

Dircks, rightly deciding that Mrs. McTawdry was not inclined to listen to reason, addressed his comment to Knowles. "I could not have harmed this woman's cart because I was nowhere near Great Newport Street yesterday morning."

"Liar! I knows it were ye," Verity screeched. "I saws ye with me own eyes, didn't I? Ye knocked over me apple cart and scurried away like the rat ye are."

Despite this inducement, Dircks remained calm and informed the Runner that he had no idea what the woman was going on about. "As I said, I was not in Great Newport yesterday morning and if I had accidently turned over an apple cart, I would have stayed to help right matters, not run off."

"Aye, but 'e would say that, wouldn't 'e?" Verity asked pugnaciously. "Very noble! But what proof does 'e 'ave? I saws him with me own eyes. Ye not telling me I don't knows what I saws."

Sighing with exasperation, Dircks asked Knowles to wait a moment and disappeared back into his house. An untrusting soul, Mrs. McTawdry complained that the culprit was getting away. "Ye jest going to stand there and let 'im escape?"

The Runner did not think this query deserved the dignity of a reply and stood silently on the doorstep while his companion grumbled. Dircks returned momentarily with another man in tow, whom he introduced as an associate who could verify his account.

It was Oxenford.

Verity, who had not anticipated such a convenient turn, hid her delight with a sneer as the second founder, older than his associate by a dozen years at fifty or so, testified that Dircks had been with him at the time. "And neither one of us was in Great Newport Street yesterday morning."

Naturally, Verity decried this attempt to trick her. "They 'atched it together, didn't they, jest now, while we was waiting. They think I'm a daft Milton to believe a blatant lie. But I knows what I saws. Mebbe his friend were there too. I dunno. I only saws the other one."

"It is not a trick," Oxenford replied tartly. "Mr. Dircks was with me, and I was not near Covent Garden. I trust that is the end of it."

"I bet you do," Verity cried, placing her hands on her considerable hips. "I don't knows ye from Adam, and yet I'm supposed to take yer word for it. I don't think so, ye liar. Yer both trying to trick me, and I won't stands for it. Do ye business, Mr. Knowles, and arrest them!"

The Runner tugged the edge of his hat down farther over his ears, almost if to hide under its brim, and said with exhaustion, "If you would just provide me with the name of one person who could vouch for your whereabouts yesterday morning—"

"At eight-thirty!" Verity interjected.

Knowles sighed. "Yes, that's right, at eight-thirty. If you would just give me that information, then we will be on our way."

"And don't be bringing out one of yer fine servants to speak for ye," Verity added with asperity. "I'm not gonna trust anyone who takes money from ye."

It was, of course, an inane comment—Dircks did not employ any servants, fine or otherwise—and Oxenford muttered under his breath about asinine conversations that never ended. Then he exhorted his friend to just tell her already to make her go away.

Dircks's brow furrowed as he looked at his associate. "Do you really think I should? It seems like too big of a risk. If word were to get out, we would—"

"Oh, for God's sake, just tell her anything to get this harridan off your doorstep!" Oxenford snapped. "We have more important things to do."

"Ye see," Verity cried, tugging on Knowles's sleeve. "They be conspiring together."

The Runner, insisting he did not see, nevertheless leaned forward, as their conduct was just secretive enough to raise his suspicions.

At the end of his tether, Oxenford said, "Mr. Dircks and I were at 12 White Grove Lane yesterday. We arrived for our meeting at eight-thirty and did not leave until forty-five minutes later. Now I trust *that* is the end of it!"

He did not wait for a reply, slamming the door in their face.

"Well, I like that! The manners on some people! Even if them two weren't the ones that knocked over me apple cart, they are the kind of men who *would* knock over me apple cart," she said, huffy with insult. Then she pressed her lips together as she stared up at the building and said, "I could have sworn the reprobate went into this house. But I suppose it could have been *that* house." Verity pointed to one of the buildings across the street. In truth, they all looked vaguely similar, with their worn bricks and dark roofs, which made her growing conviction that she had confused the houses entirely plausible.

"Or was it that house?" she wondered, pointing now to the neighbor on the left.

Knowles, however, did not care, and as Verity called after him to interrogate the resident of the squat building next door, he simply shook his head and kept walking.

Chapter Nine

❧❧❧

S *unday, May 31*
12:52 p.m.

Standing in front of 12 White Grove Lane, Verity felt certain she was in the wrong place. This building, with its molded brick cornice, segmental arches framing the windows, and wooden doorframe with Doric rusticated pilasters, was clearly the elegant abode of a well-to-do merchant. Although the reform movement could count among its adherents men of wealth and power—the Earl Gray, for instance, had long subscribed to its principles and Lord Althorph had spoken in Parliament in defense of liberalism—it drew little support from cits. Prosperous business owners in general had no use for reformers, whose objectives directly threatened to reduce their profits.

In destroying stocking frames, the Luddites and their ilk were not seeking to halt progress so much as to call attention to the callousness of factory owners, who did not consider their workers human beings so much as expensive machinery. Efficient knitting contraptions were not only cheaper to operate but also required less coddling. They did not stop in the middle of a twelve-hour shift to complain about stiff fingers.

It was possible that the residence belonged to a banker, for they also lived in spacious homes with Grecian columns. Verity doubted it, however, based on the neighborhood. This portion of Marylebone was emphatically a merchant district.

What business could Oxenford and Dircks have here?

The answer was none, she thought, as she looked again at the number to confirm she was in the correct place: twelve.

Yes, that was the one Oxenford had provided.

What game was he playing, she wondered, unable to conceive of any dealings the founder of the Society of Yarwellian Philosophers could have with the inhabitant of such an elegant establishment.

Had he fobbed her off with a lie, rattling off the first address that occurred to him?

She allowed it was likely.

Both Oxenford and Dircks had been eager to dispense with the shrill Mrs. McTawdry and would have said anything to send her on her way. In that respect, it was a successful maneuver, for she and the Runner had toddled off obligingly.

But if it was merely a lie to get them to leave, then it was an unintentionally revealing one, for why on earth would 12 White Grove Lane be on his mind at all, let alone the first thing he would think of when pressed for an address?

There was a connection—of that, she was certain—but she could not fathom the nature of the association. If the occupant was not an ally of the cause, then perhaps he was a target of it. Oxenford might have been watching the home to figure out the best way for the Yarwellians to undermine its owner.

Unable to properly comprehend the situation without additional information, including the identity of the merchant and whether he had actually met with the founders, Verity considered how to find out what she needed to know. Shedding Mrs. Tawdry's stained petticoats, she had dressed in a plain wool suit, which suited many of her characters. A capable clerk would do nicely, she thought, one who was following up on his employer's business. Even if Oxenford had not called on the residence yesterday, claiming that he had would elicit useful intelligence.

Decisively, she tugged on the bottom edge of her coat to ensure the smooth line that Phineas Langley-Upton insisted upon and approached the door. She noted the unusual design of the knocker, which consisted of two birds clutching the metal loop within their beaks, and wondered at its significance. Then she grasped it firmly and banged twice.

The door swept open almost immediately, revealing a butler in pristine black. His expression was blank as he greeted her with off-putting coolness. He was neither impressed with the caller nor inclined to be welcoming.

No matter!

Phineas Langley-Upton frequently dealt with curt servants, and adopting an air of expectation, Verity introduced herself as Mr. Oxenford's representative. Then she apologized for the potentially egregious faux pas of arriving early for the appointment.

That was the trouble with capable clerks—always a little too eager to please.

Rushing to explain, she said, "It is a horrible habit of mine and I know it is the height of rudeness to appear before one's presence is expected, but I have so much to do today and more often than not it is no bother at all. The other person is frequently as impatient as I am to get the business settled. But if it *is* a bother, you must not worry about me. I can take a turn around the block, which I need to do anyway to make sure my day is sufficiently active—the more exercise I take, the better I think—and come back at the appointed time. Whichever is most suitable to your needs."

Naturally, the butler furrowed his brow, first in confusion, then in annoyance, at this needlessly informative greeting, which was as confident as it was inappropriate. Langley-Upton's brash assurance always elicited this sort of response, and rather than inform the talkative upstart that he was not expected, he asked the caller to repeat his name.

A look of consternation washed over Verity's features as she displayed her first hint of uncertainty, and tittering self-consciously, she said, "Oh, dear, have I gotten the wrong house again?" She tilted back to examine the exterior of the residence and confirm the house number. "I could have sworn that this was twelve."

Stiffly, the butler replied that she had the correct address. "But we are not expecting a Mr. Upton today."

"I am sure you are not, for I am Mr. *Langley*-Upton," she said with pointed emphasis, as if her full name made a difference.

Of course it did not, and the butler announced that the house was not expecting a Mr. Langley-Upton either. "It appears there has been a mistake. Please take it up with your superior."

Mystified, Verity drew her own brows together and wondered at the source of the problem. "I supposed Mr. Oxenford could have given me the wrong address, but that would be strange because he is so very meticulous. As I am sure you know, he oversees an organization with a large membership, which requires a keen attention to detail. It is possible he switched the numbers by mistake. Is there a twenty-one in this street?"

Although these thoughts could be of little interest to the

butler, he remained in the doorway and replied, "There is not. The numbering ends at nineteen."

Shaking her head at the conundrum, Verity murmured, "How very odd. And you are certain Mr. Oxenford and Mr. Dircks did not call here yesterday morning? Is that what you are telling me—that I am in the completely wrong place and you have never heard of either of my employers and my afternoon has been wasted and somewhere in London there is an extremely important gentleman waiting on me to call and he is pacing up and down his drawing room because I am now several minutes late despite being a few minutes early? Is that truly what you are telling me? Because I must inform you, my good man, that that is an utter catastrophe for me. I will be turned off without notice for failing to discharge my duty."

Mr. Langley-Upton's onslaught of words expressed with escalating agitation had the desired effect and the butler ordered the clerk to get ahold of himself. "I said nothing of the kind! Mr. Blasingame did have a meeting with Mr. Oxenford and Mr. Dircks yesterday. They arrived promptly at eight-thirty, conducted their business in the study, and left the house about an hour later. You have the right location. *That* is not the problem."

Verity recognized the name at once.

Blasingame was one of the most successful hosiery firms in the country. The company had a manufactory near Hatton Gardens in Holborn, where it produced silk stockings with cotton feet. They sold for seven shilling and sixpence per pair, which was more than Verity could afford. She bought Cosway stockings for five shillings from a shop at 45 Bucklesbury.

Was it the same Blasingame?

Judging by the wealth on display on the home's lovely exterior, she could only assume it was. But that was even more puzzling, for not only was the occupant of 12 White Grove Lane an exceedingly wealthy merchant but also one who employed the very machinery the members of the society railed against. What could the original Yarwellians and a hosiery nabob have in common other than strong feelings about stocking frames? And yet even then, there could be very little overlap, for the former sought to destroy the knitting machines and the latter wanted to exploit them.

The meeting, such as it was, could have only been acrimonious, with the men standing on opposite sides of the issue. But she could not imagine why Blasingame would entertain the topic at all. He had nothing to gain by negotiating with radicals and reformers—unless Oxenford and Dircks were somehow capable of ensuring his protection from Luddites and insurrectionists.

Was that their scheme—to squeeze the wealthy factory owner?

It struck Verity as a perilous way to garner funds for the Blanketeers. Blasingame had all the money and power on his side and could easily charge the members with extortion. With the mass meeting only a week away, it seemed like a foolish risk.

Hoping to learn more about the meeting, she increased her agitation and pulled from her pocket the freshly laundered handkerchief Mr. Langley-Upton always had on his person. Although she swore she was relieved to hear her employers had in fact met with Mr. Blasingame as she had been informed, her manner belied it. Dabbing her forehead with the pristine square, she professed her relief a second and third time. "You had me scared for a minute, insisting that I was in the wrong place. I had begun to worry about feeding my family. I have three children, you see, all angels, and it would break my heart if they had to go to the workhouse. But that is neither here nor there," she added fervently, folding the cloth before returning it to her pocket. Her manner had finally begun to calm.

The butler, taking her composure as an indication the conversation had reached its natural conclusion, nodded stiffly and opened his mouth to bid her good day.

Before he could speak, however, Verity announced that she was ready for her appointment. "And please convey to Mr. Blasingame my sincerest apologies for creating so much confusion. I would hate for my shortcomings to be held against my employers, who are passionate men who believe in their mission to better the lives of all Englishmen. That is the only reason they caused Mr. Blasingame so much dismay yesterday. They cannot help themselves, and I am not surprised Mr. Blasingame lost his temper. Discord and acrimony seem to follow Mr. Oxenford and Mr. Dircks wherever they go."

Affronted on his employer's behalf, the butler insisted with a cool sneer that his master had not been upset by anything or behaved immoderately. "He had a most cordial meeting. Now I must bid you good day, as I will not be conveying anything to Mr. Blasingame on your behalf, since you do not have an appointment with him."

A most cordial meeting, was it?

Verity was enthralled.

Although it was futile, she made one last attempt to cross the threshold. Mr. Langley-Upton was a devoted campaigner and always wanted to believe he had tried everything before abandoning the field. "Oh, I see, that must be because I am confused again. The appointment is probably with his secretary, so he and I can review the agreements arrived at yesterday. Yes, that makes a lot more sense, doesn't it? Why would the owner of the finest hosiery concern in the country want to meet with a minor clerk from a reform society? If you will just convey my apologies to Mr. Blasingame's *secretary* for all the confusion I have caused and tell him I am here. And do please explain why I am late. I would hate for him to think I do not care enough about our appointment to arrive in a timely fashion. You might also want to mention that I was, in fact, early."

But the butler could do none of these things, for the same issues applied to this directive as to the previous one—specifically, that Mr. Langley-Upton did not have an appointment with Mr. Blasingame's secretary.

Verity, owning herself completely flummoxed by the development, asked if there was someone in the home with whom she could speak.

Anyone at all, really, as she was not fastidious.

"It is just so that I am able to report honestly to my employers that I had a productive meeting at number 12 White Grove Lane. It does not have to be one of the upstairs servants. Perhaps a kitchen maid who has an opinion about rotten boroughs?"

His patience at an end, the butler offered a starched refusal and slammed the door. At its sharp snap, Verity called out, "I shall just count this exchange as my appointment, then, shall I?"

Naturally, silence greeted this absurd proposal, and as she stared at the firmly shut door, she realized the birds on the knocker were weavers.

How suitable for the home of a hosiery purveyor.

Contemplating the identity of the owner, she marveled yet again at the strangeness of the situation: Blasingame having business with members of the Society of Yarwellian Philosophers.

'Twas confounding.

And, she realized to her dismay, consuming.

There she was, having attained the exact confirmation she had come there to achieve, and her mind was fixed on an entirely different mystery.

Think about Mr. Smith!

But it was a struggle to keep her focus on the victim when something far more interesting had captured her attention, and she had to force herself to consider what it meant for her two best suspects—indeed, her only suspects—to have alibis.

Unassailable alibis, she thought irritably.

Did that mean they had nothing to do with the murder?

Not necessarily, no.

As founders of the organization, Oxenford and Dircks might hold considerable sway over an ever-growing membership that was passionate about the cause and eager to fulfill its mission. If they raised their suspicions about Smith with one of their followers, then perhaps that member had decided to act on an unspoken command.

Or even a spoken one, Verity thought.

Recalling what Hardwicke had said about the increasing level of alarm and anxiety among the organization as the mass meeting drew closer, she knew it was possible. So much of the society's future depended on the success of Crowley's speech. Gathering signatures helped them raise money, generating enthusiasm, which in turn helped them gather more signatures and raise additional funds—all of which advanced the movement. Even if the prince regent did not receive their petitions graciously, the march to London would create lots of interest. The newspapers would be unable to ignore such attention-getting goings-on, which meant Parliament would have to take note.

If the Blanketeering action proceeded as planned, then change might actually be within reach.

And that was why the whole society was on high alert.

Any one of its members could have noticed Smith hovering by the cellar door with his mangled forefinger and arrived at his own conclusion.

The prospect of almost sixty suspects disheartened Verity, who did not have the first idea of how to winnow the list.

That was not entirely true, no.

Obviously, she would start by establishing the alibi of each member.

But the thought of conducting one-on-one interviews with almost five dozen men, devising schemes and donning disguises, exhausted her.

And that was just to find out the information.

She would have to devise more schemes and don more disguises to confirm it.

How many days would it take?

How many *weeks*?

Surely, there was a better way to conduct the investigation, but even as she turned her mind toward concocting one, her thoughts kept wandering to Blasingame and his appointment with Oxenford and Dircks.

It was simply the more interesting riddle.

Sunday, May 31
  6:03 p.m.

Obviously, Verity was always going to don the clothes of a Bow Street Runner and knock on the door of John Dircks. Despite what she told herself during the journey back to Bethel Street or Delphine over tea upon her return, she had known in her bones the inevitability of the moment. She denied it as a matter of form and out of respect to poor Mr. Smith, whose brutal slaying was somehow not absorbing enough to hold her attention. But it would take a stronger woman than she to resist the mystery.

There was simply no innocent explanation for why the purveyor of hosiery would agree to meet with the founders of a radical reform society. If their game was not extortion, then perhaps it was blackmail. Or maybe the connection was personal, such as one of the members was Blasingame's illegitimate son from an illicit relationship and seeking a generous payment in exchange for his silence.

No, not a payment.

Ownership of the stocking manufactory.

Either Blasingame surrendered the deed to his company or Oxenford would ruin him so utterly no one would ever want to buy a stocking bearing his name again.

It was an outlandish story, even for Twaddle, and yet it made more sense to Verity than the notion that the three men had actual business to discuss.

Even Delphine, whose underwhelming response to shocking developments sometimes frustrated her friend, admitted the association was extremely odd. She did not, to be clear, subscribe to the bastard son theory, but agreed that the matter warranted further investigation.

To that end, Verity had assumed her Runner garb, which consisted of black trousers, worn boots, and a dark blue coat, and returned to Dircks's home to question him. Although Oxenford had been the more forthcoming one of the two, Mrs. McTawdry had identified Dircks as the villain who overturned her apple cart. That meant she had to keep her focus on him.

As far as the Runners knew, Oxenford was blameless.

Assuming an aggressive pose, Verity knocked on the door with the side of her fist and then called out as if she had been waiting for several minutes. "Are you in there, Dircks? Come on out. I don't have all day! Dircks!"

She continued to pound even though she heard the shuffle of footsteps approaching and when Dircks opened the door with a scowl, her hand was midway in the air. As she let it drop to her side, she pressed her shoulder against the jamb so that he could not easily shut the door.

"You took your time, didn't you?" Verity asked, her deepened voice rumbling with impatience. Although she rarely impersonated a Runner, preferring to keep her distance from legal authorities, she nevertheless had Tommy Greenwood, with his five children, interfering mother-in-law, and war injury that never quite healed, at the ready. She shifted her weight to the other leg now, as if it hurt to stand in any one position for more than a few seconds. "I know a malingerer when I see one. Well, it won't make a difference. Fast or slow, I will get you there before nightfall."

"I was in the back of the house eating dinner with my family," Dircks replied crossly, his long ginger hair pulled back in a queue. "And I will not go anywhere with you until I know what this is about. State your business."

"Well, I like that, don't I, you're giving me orders!" Verity said snidely. "That is not the way this works, Mr. Dircks. You are under arrest for the wanton destruction of Mrs. McTawdry's apple cart. Come along, then."

Dircks took a step backward, deeper into his home. "That is ridiculous. I had nothing to do with that damned woman's apple cart! I told the other one that."

"You told the other one—whose name, for the record, is Vernon Knowles—that you were attending a meeting at the time of the incident," she said, pulling a small daybook out of her pocket and opening to the appropriate page. "At 12 White Grove Lane. Is that not correct?"

"*I* didn't tell him that," he clarified. "My associate did. But it is true. At the time that abominable woman's cart was being knocked over, I was in a meeting at 12 White Grove Lane, which means I couldn't have had anything to do with it. I trust we are done."

Verity shook her head as she jotted down a brief notation in her daybook. "As I have just added another charge against you, I would say we are definitely not done."

More shocked than alarmed, Dircks glared at him. "Add a charge? But I have done nothing wrong! And there cannot be 'another charge' when there is no first charge!"

"Defamation," Verity said.

Dircks repeated the word silently, genuinely baffled by the term, and when he spoke a few seconds later it was with utter confusion. "What?"

"I added defamation, for slandering your victim," she explained.

"Have you *met* Mrs. McTawdry?" he asked.

"A lovely woman," Verity replied. "A voice like a sylvan glade."

Naturally, Dircks knew this to be false and he narrowed his eyes threateningly. "I do not know what game you are playing, but I will have no more of it. I did not touch that woman's apple cart, I have given evidence to prove it, and I will not waste anymore of my time talking about it!"

"I have a weak hip from the war, so I can't play games— just ask my children, who are always trying to draw me into hide-and-seek—your evidence is nonsense, and if anyone's time is being wasted here, it is mine," Verity replied, testy with impatience. "Now let's go. If you're going to be difficult, I'll have to restrain you."

Dircks took another step back, indicating that he would be difficult indeed, and swore his evidence was not nonsense. "I was where I said I was."

"At 12 White Grove Lane," she repeated flatly.

"Yes!"

Verity smirked. "The home of Charles Blasingame, owner of Blasingame's Fine Silk Stockings."

"Exactly!"

Slipping the daybook under her arm, she retrieved a leaflet she had gotten from Fitch during her visit to the society's headquarters, unfolded it, and held it up for his inspection. "Is this not yours, Mr. Dircks?"

He barely glanced at it before disavowing all knowledge of it. "I have never seen that piece of paper in my life," he insisted, which was, Verity allowed, technically accurate. Unless he printed the handbills himself, he could not have beheld every single one.

"You are a member of the society that published it," she pressed. "You are a Yarwellian philosopher, is that not correct? And as such you subscribe to the principles of Mr. Yarwell, who advocated for the humane treatment of workers. What business could you have with a man like Blasingame, who employs machinery in his factory at the expense of the skilled craftsmen he summarily dismissed?"

"I am not a ... a ... what did you call it ... a Jarwellate," he said with unconvincing vigor. "I am a schoolteacher and devoted to the welfare of my students. I would never join a society that ... that ... sought to upset the gross power imbalance ... that is, argued for the fair treatment of ... er, that society."

"Mr. Dircks," Verity said with a morose shake of her head, more saddened than angry at his ineffective attempt at denial. "If that is the best you can do, then I will have to add another defamation charge, for impugning the intelligence of a Runner because you must think I am a simpleton to believe that nonsense."

A belligerent look swept across Dircks's face, only to be replaced a moment later by fear and then resignation. His eyes tilted down and he admitted that yes, he was a member of the Society of Yarwellian Philosophers. "But we are a peaceful group that meets to discuss the ideas put forth by the great Preston Yarwell, so I can't imagine what that has to do with this conversation."

"But I think you can, Mr. Dircks," she said. "The principles of your organization directly conflict with the way Mr. Blasingame runs his factory. You can have no business with a man like that."

Dircks insisted that he did have business with him but refused to explain its nature, which compelled Verity to introduce new evidence. "Not according to Blasingame. I spoke to his butler myself and he says nobody matching your description or Mr. Oxenford's had ever visited the home, let alone at eight-thirty in the morning when he is typically still abed. Now let's go. It's growing late and I promised my wife I would be home in time for dinner."

"He is lying. The butler is a liar!" Dircks cried, then cursed under his breath when he saw Verity make another notation in her daybook. "Devil it, man, that is not defamation. It is the truth. I was at 12 White Grove Lane, from eight-thirty onward. I met with Blasingame. Ask me what the house looked like. The front door is red and has a knocker with two birds. The entryway has marble. The study has dark wood furniture."

Mindful of Greenwood's injury, Verity shifted her weight again and noted that she, too, could describe the front door. "But that doesn't mean I had tea with Mr. Blasingame."

"But the entryway! The study!"

"What was it again? Marble. And dark wood for the study?" she asked scornfully. "Such precise descriptions. They do not seem made up at all."

Incensed by her dismissal, he snarled, "I was there, I tell you, I was there!"

"All right, then," Verity said with a sigh. "What did you discuss?"

Dircks stiffened. "Well, that I can't tell you."

Verity pulled a pair of handcuffs from her pocket.

"Sabotage!" he shouted frantically, his disquiet at the prospect of being carted off to a dank cell beneath the Brown

Bear fraying his nerves entirely. Rigid and unmoving, he allowed the word to hang in the air between them for a moment, then, struggling to regain his composure, sought to clarify his answer. "No, no. That is, we talked about Blasingame making a generous donation to our workers' fund, which goes to skilled craftsmen who have lost their jobs because of machinery, and in exchange we would focus our protests on other manufactories."

Well, well, Verity thought, their conversation was far more interesting than the sensational tale of woe she had devised. "But, Mr. Dircks, you just finished telling me that the Society of Yarwellian Philosophers is a peaceful group that only meets to discuss ideas. What protests are Mr. Blasingame worried about and what form do they take?"

"We *are* peaceful, I swear!" he said, beads of sweat beginning to form now at his temple.

"But in recent months the composition of our group has begun to change as new members join, and some of them might not be as committed to the principles of Yarwellian peace. They might be in favor of a more uncompromising response, but we would never allow that! Still, if they were to take action on their own ... well, then, there is nothing I can do about that!"

"You said *we,* Mr. Dircks," Verity reminded him pointedly. "*We* would focus our protests on other manufactories—those were your exact words."

Aware of his unintended revelation, Mr. Dircks tried to assert that he had merely misspoken, using the wrong pronoun. He should have said *they*! Obviously, that would not fly, and although he made a halfhearted attempt to claim the agreement with Blasingame consisted of the society printing up handbills disparaging his main competitor, Cosway, he ultimately conceded the action was a little more aggressive.

"Just so we are clear regarding your alibi during the time

Mrs. McTawdry's apple cart was destroyed: You're saying you could not have done it because you were in White Grove Lane with Mr. Blasingame agreeing to destroy the equipment in the Cosway factory in exchange for money?" Verity said. "That is what you want me to put down in the official record?"

"I don't want you to put it anywhere!" he snarled.

"No, you would not," Verity noted calmly, almost unable to believe the information she had managed to elicit. Her instincts had been correct. Deciphering the mystery of Dircks's meeting with the hosiery manufacturer was far more interesting than figuring out the identity of a murderer.

Poor Mr. Smith!

She stepped away from the door jamb, said she had no further questions, and thanked Mr. Dircks for his time.

"Is this finally the end of that woman's absurd charge?" he asked cautiously. "Or will yet another Runner come pounding on my door tomorrow?"

"It is, yes," she replied.

Visibly relieved, Dircks allowed his entire body to slacken.

Chapter Ten

❧❧❧

S*unday, May 31*
   8:12 p.m.

Mindful of how Freddie responded to her last missive asking him to call on Bethel Street at his leisure, Verity made a point of stating with unequivocal clarity that nothing serious, worrisome, or even concerning had happened. All was well with herself *and* Delphine (well, there was a small mishap with the gardening shears but nothing a soaking in vinegar and a cotton bandage could not fix), and she merely sought his opinion in figuring out a course of action.

Then she added that truly nothing was the matter and that she was not trying to bamboozle him with false assertions. "You must not feel any need to dash over. I am fine. Delphine is fine. The squirrels are fine. Lucy is fine. (Cook is cross about having to use the last of the vinegar for medicinal purposes rather than the piccalilli she had planned to make with the onions that are on the verge of turning.) We look forward to seeing you soon—but not too soon!"

Despite these soothing reassurances, Freddie appeared within the hour.

Verity watched him enter the front parlor, her lips twisted in chagrin, and announced that she was deeply insulted by his lack of faith in her. "I said nothing is amiss, and so nothing is amiss. You did not need to run over here as if Delphine has impaled herself on the scissors."

As he was more of an honorary member of the household than a guest, he did not stand on ceremony, removing his hat and placing it on the sideboard. Then he sat down at the table next to Verity, who was enjoying a glass of port after dinner. "I know Delphine is fine because she sent a note along with yours telling me that she had barely scraped her knuckle and you insisted on wrapping her hand up like a mummy."

"Not her whole hand, just her thumb," Verity corrected, selecting a Shrewsbury cake from the plate. "And if it is not to nurse Delphine back to health, why did you come here so quickly?"

"You expressly sought my opinion," he replied.

It was a simple comment and yet so portentously stated.

"As I do all the time," she said.

But even as she issued the comment, Freddie was shaking his head and firmly denying it. "No, you never do. You frequently ask for it offhandedly when I am already around and are torn between Twaddling as the Turnip or Archie Jones. And you sometimes seek it just to be provoking. Last week, for example. You asked me if you should climb into the second-story window of Mrs. Ralston's townhouse or the third story."

"I am sure that is not right," Verity countered. "Unless there is a sturdy tree nearby, there is no way to climb through a second-story window. I would climb in through the ground floor and then sneak *up* to the second floor."

"Yes, that is why it was provoking," he said, drawing the plate of cakes toward him.

As Verity considered her response to this comment, Delphine poked her head in to see if Freddie had arrived yet. "Ah, there you are!" she said with pleased delight. "It certainly took you long enough."

"Long enough?" Verity echoed in confusion. "I sent the note not even a full hour ago. Lucy has been back for only fifteen minutes."

Striding across the room, Delphine nodded with satisfaction. "Precisely. I expected him to return with her. After all, you expressly sought his opinion. When was the last time she did that?" she asked, turning to Freddie for confirmation. "1809? 1810?"

"September 21, 1808," he replied soberly.

"Ah, yes, of course, the first Twaddle-Thum column," Delphine said. "She was not sure what tone she should take and asked you to read four different versions to help her figure it out. You advised arch knowingness. A wise choice. It has worked well for her."

Freddie accepted this praise with a humble nod. "Thank you."

As Delphine assured him he was most welcome, Verity protested their abuse, convinced they were having a laugh at her expense. She sought Delphine's opinion—expressly!—on a daily basis.

"Do you, though?" her friend murmured.

"But that is neither here nor there," Freddie said, passing the dwindling assortment of Shrewsbury cakes to Delphine as she sat down. "Do tell us what your quandary is, for we are eager to offer our opinions."

"Oh, but not me," Delphine replied, demurely insisting

that she would never intrude on her friend's moment. Then she giggled and admitted that *now* she was having a laugh at Verity's expense. "But do go on, darling, and tell us what is worrying you. No more teasing, I promise."

Smothering an inclination to argue further, for she knew she was often more uncertain than they gave her credit for, Verity recounted that afternoon's discovery.

"It is news, obviously it is, and the *Gazette* must publish it at once," Freddie said vehemently. "The leaders of a radical reform society conspiring with the wealthy maker of silk stockings to destroy the equipment of his main competitor is shocking!"

"It *is* a scandal," Delphine agreed. "The only question is, who should write about it: Robert Lark or Mr. Twaddle-Thum?"

"I should think Lark, as the reform movement has been constantly in the news since the Christmas Uprising, and Robert has already registered his disapproval of the Frame-Breaking Act," Freddie said.

"But Verity does not have proof unless she wants to return to Mr. Blasingame's residence and convince him to confirm Dircks's story," Delphine pointed out. "I do not doubt that she could do it, but I am not sure if the effort is necessary. It is enough for Twaddle to make vague hints and insinuations."

Before Freddie could provide his counterpoint, which he was prepared to do as soon as he swallowed his cake, Verity said that she had already decided to report the story as Mr. Twaddle-Thum, for precisely the reasons Delphine had outlined as well as to protect her sources. "I do not want anyone to think Robert Lark has an informer among the Runners. He has a more pristine reputation than Twaddle, about whom people already suspect all sorts of dastardly things, including being a Runner himself, according to a report in the *Brighton Herald*. But I did not ask Freddie here to discuss what to do about Blasingame. That is all sorted. Smith is the problem."

"Smith?" Delphine said, furrowing her brow. "The murder victim?"

Verity nodded. "Noticeably absent from their own weekly meeting, Dircks and Oxenford were my two best suspects. Having eliminated them, however, I am left with the rest of the membership of the Society of Yarwellian Philosophers. Hardwicke says about sixty men have attended the most recent meetings. That is a large suspects pool and, as I am daunted by it, I was hoping you and Freddie might be able to propose a way to bring that number down."

"Ah, so you want to scheme with us," Delphine said with a meaningful glance at Freddie. "To be fair, you scheme with us fairly regularly."

"Naturally, I do," Verity replied, uncertain of the distinction but happy to abide by it. "You are both devious and clever and have a different perspective than I do."

Freddie, his mind already sifting through the predicament, said the first thing she should do was get an accurate count of the suspects. "You do not actually have sixty, do you, because you can eliminate the members who were present at the meeting. You have to look only at the members who were not there, which will be substantially fewer. I would hazard no more than a dozen."

"That is right," Delphine said, tilting slightly forward in her chair in her enthusiasm. "The true number of suspects is only a fraction of the membership, which you would have realized, Verity, if you had not been so daunted. And since they belong to the same organization, I think it is safe to assume they have several commonalities. It should be possible to find a disguise who could relate to many, if not all, of them. That will simplify the process greatly."

"Precisely," Freddie said. "Mr. Potts, whose wife went missing on the eve of their wedding anniversary, might work."

"Mr. Potts is an excellent suggestion," Delphine said. "I was thinking perhaps that Shaw the grocer might be looking to hire a new assistant."

"Shaw is a brilliant idea," replied Freddie. "Much better than sad old Mr. Potts. Because he would want to know if his prospective worker was a member of a secret reform society. The real challenge, of course, is finding out who was absent from the meeting. I suppose it is too much to hope that a secret society keeps an attendance list."

Delphine agreed with this assessment, noting that she would expect the furtive organization to be light on records in general. "But they have been collecting money for the Blanketeers, have they not? You mentioned, Verity, that Fitch was particularly good at soliciting contributions. They would have to track those funds in some way, wouldn't they? In a ledger, most likely. If they are meticulous—and I should think they would have to be with the amount of money at stake— it's possible they do keep attendance lists."

Verity had been so focused first on Fitch and then on Smith and ultimately on Blasingame, she had not thought much about the inner workings of the society. But Delphine's point was well taken. There had been a bookshelf haphazardly stuffed with ledgers in the basement with the printing press.

As she contemplated how to access the cellar again, Freddie said, "You know what would make compiling a list of suspects even easier? If there was a disinherited second son of a marquess who was actually at the meeting yesterday who was willing to work with Verity to identify the murderer. Then she could simply ask him for the names of the absent members."

Delphine, hailing his plan as highly practical, noted that

there was one large obstacle he had failed to consider. "Verity's ego. She is too stubborn to ask for Hardwicke's help because she thinks they are in competition with each other."

"We *are* in competition," Verity replied calmly, aware that her friend was being deliberately provoking. "He believes he holds the upper hand in our association, which obligates me to prove that he does not. If I go to him seeking his help, it will only validate his assumption. Identifying a murderer cannot be so difficult. The Duchess of Kesgrave does it once a week."

"Yes, and I am sure the secret to her success is refusing to accept her husband's assistance," Delphine replied satirically.

The idea that there was any parallel to be drawn between the Duke of Kesgrave's relationship with his wife and Verity's with Hardwicke was an unmatched absurdity, and she smiled thinly to smother the ardent objection that rose to her lips. She was too clever to fall into the trap of issuing an overly strong reply. Such protests never convinced anyone and frequently wound up revealing more than they concealed.

Consequently, Verity observed that Mr. Shaw of Shaw and Sons was indeed looking for an assistant to help with stocking, thank you very much for the suggestion. Then she rang for Lucy to refresh the plate of Shrewsbury cakes and asked her friends if they had any items for the children at Fortescue's. It had been several weeks since her last visit to the orphan asylum and in the interim she had acquired several toys she planned to deliver that week. Delphine replied that she had knitted a few blankets, Freddie said he had printed two dozen spelling primers, and the subject of Hardwicke was irrevocably dropped if not entirely forgotten.

From the London Daily Gazette
  Monday, June 1

. . .

Twaddle Tales
by Mr. Twaddle-Thum

Why, yes, darlings, I do pop into your home every few days and vow you will be stunned by my latest on-dit, and I would not be aghast if by now you tilt toward ennui. If you roll your eyes at my giddy promises and dab gently at your lips with the serviette and prepare yourself to be underwhelmed, I take no offense at all.

Trust me, my loves, I understand.

Sometimes even I doubt myself, for it all seems to defy reality, the way I can keep discovering information that is wildly shocking. Surely, at some point I will uncover a secret of middling interest that causes you to shrug and turn the page to Mr. Proscenium's review of *The Double Disappointment*.

But not today!

Indeed not, for I have stumbled upon a development so inconceivable you will accuse me of making up fairy stories. I am not, I swear, for that goes against every principle I hold dear, but as true as that is, I will begin this report with an obliging familiarity: Once upon a time there was a hosiery king who ruled the land of Stocking with a silken hand. He was beloved by most, though not by all, for some of his subjects found the price of his goods simply too dear for their coffers. Although they wanted the best-quality product, they settled for slightly inferior and counted themselves fortunate to live in a realm blessed with abundance and choice.

But the king did not like this!

No, he did not, for as much as he craved the love of his people, he desired their money more, and so he conspired with the rebels who bedeviled his kingdom. Holding his gold crown aloft, he offered it to the first member of the Society of Anti-Monarchist Weavers brave enough to raise an army to attack Sir Woolen's fiefdom.

And, lo, his challenge was accepted!

Ah, but of course it was, for the bejeweled prize glinted with dazzling beauty.

'Twas ever thus, that men of principle bow to rapacity, which they adorn in the lustrous satin of justification, listing all the mouths they will feed with the filthy lucre.

Did the scheme prosper? Did the rival fall?

I cannot say!

I swear, I am not being coy.

The outcome is unknown because the battle rages on—in our mythical kingdom of hosiery most fair and perhaps in our own somewhat less idyllic land.

Why, yes, *now* I am being coy, for I am like you, merely a spectator, and spectators do not lodge accusations at powerful men who might take a pet at having their devious schemes exposed. We must watch and wait.

So that is what I will be doing with a freshly brewed pot of tea and possibly a few of Her Outrageousness's beloved rout cakes at hand.

And the moment something changes, I will pop back to apprise you.

Until then—adieu, my darlings.

Monday, June 1
   11:54 a.m.

Publishing the item by Mr. Twaddle-Thum was such a reliable way to draw Colson Hardwicke to Bethel Street, it might as well have been an engraved invitation. That he did not appear until well after breakfast was an unexpected development, for Verity had been so sure he would arrive first thing in the morning she had lingered over her eggs to present a picture of blithe indifference. She had planned to return his frown with a blank expression, taken aback by the interruption to her meal but happy to offer her hospitality.

By the time he darkened her doorstep a little before noon, she had been pacing the front parlor for almost an hour. She knew he had read the story and perceived its meaning. He was too clever not to recognize Blasingame and the Society of Yarwellian Philosophers. The identities of the particular members might have eluded him but not the broad strokes, and the fact that he did not immediately charge into her home to berate her for withholding the discovery meant that he knew that she knew how much it would irk him.

He was intentionally denying her the pleasure of relishing her triumph.

Naturally, she would never be so uncouth as to gloat openly. That sort of brazen glee was for constables and children. But a certain air of satisfaction, however well contained, would be impossible to miss. Avoiding the scene entirely was a facile maneuver worthy of Verity's disgust, and yet she could not begrudge him it. With his understanding of female competence, highly limited whether it was astounding or not, he could only have found it galling to realize she had outmatched him. He was the one who proposed Dircks and Oxenford as potential suspects and then she invalidated his theory by proving they were part of a larger conspiracy.

And informed him of it in the most public way possible.

Comprehending his motive, she was nevertheless disappointed by his failure to appear. She had been relying on the visit as an opportunity to solicit a list of society members who were not present at the Saturday meeting. To be sure, she had sworn to her friends that she would not go to Hardwicke asking for his help, but she had said nothing about his coming to her. Despite Delphine's claims about the generous size of Verity's ego, it was still small enough to slip through a loophole.

But it would not work if Hardwicke refused to call, and it was this frustration that had her pacing the front parlor from eleven o'clock onward. Delphine, who had been knitting quietly in the window, enjoying a rare burst of sunshine, announced that she could not work under these conditions. Standing abruptly, the half-finished blanket in a soothing, gentle blue bundle in her arms, she said her friend was emitting waves of agitation. "It is like the surf pounding the shore, I swear it is."

That had been ten minutes ago now, and when Verity heard the door open, she assumed it was Delphine returning to fetch something she had forgotten—a stitch marker or a needle. Pivoting on her heel, she opened her mouth to apologize for running the other woman off and to promise to calm her agitation.

Then abruptly shut it when she saw that it was Hardwicke.

She did not have to affect surprise.

Having arrived at a reasonable explanation for his absence, she was genuinely taken aback by his sudden appearance and asked with unaffected candor, "What are you doing here?"

He smiled faintly as he sauntered into the room, his steps unhurried as he crossed the floor to where she stood near the window. "Yes, what interest could I have in Miss Gorman on this day of all days? What could she have possibly done to garner my attention? Certainly not uncover a plot by the founders of the Society of Yarwellian Philosophers to do the destructive bidding of Cosway's primary competitor,

Blasingame, for that is of minor achievement and not worthy of my notice."

Verity felt an absurd impulse to simper.

It was the admiration in his voice, she thought, for he seemed almost to be gloating himself, as if her accomplishment were his. She could not fathom the respect and basked in his glow for several moments before realizing it was another maneuver. Outmatched indeed by a mere female, he had no choice but to salvage whatever he could from the situation. Ignoring her indefinitely was unfeasible because, ultimately, he needed to know everything she did. Grint would expect a full report. Denied the smug pleasure of the high road, he had no choice but to co-opt her success.

Although she would have preferred he deal honestly with her, Verity did not protest or demure. She simply dipped her head in acknowledgment of the praise—most definitely not a simper—and asked if he would like some tea. "I was just about to order a fresh pot."

"So you mentioned," he said softly, his lips twitching slightly.

Amusement glinted in his teal gaze, and Verity was struck yet again by the beguiling strangeness of his eyes—one color, then two colors, then one again. Tempted by the distraction but refusing to succumb, she said coolly, "Did I? I do not recall that."

"Mr. Twaddle-Thum did," he reminded her. "In his column."

"Ah, yes, the flourish at the end," she said with a knowledgeable lilt. "I am always a little uncertain how to draw an item to a close. One does not want to be too abrupt or too loquacious. Please take a seat and I will go fetch the tea. It won't take a minute."

In fact, it took four, but the last one was only because Verity required a moment to organize her thoughts. Hardwicke's cheerful demeanor unsettled her, and she could not decide what it meant for achieving her objective. Did his good humor make him more or less likely to give her the list of names?

Returning to the parlor, she found him sitting on the settee, flipping through the book on gardening that was on the marble slab table. "We have a problem with the squirrels eating our plants, and Delphine is determined to rout them. She has tried almost every method known to mankind to no avail," she explained as she laid the tray down, bewildered by her own unprecedented impulse to make banal drawing room conversation.

Was she anxious?

She thought perhaps so.

"The Great Squirrel Stampede of 1815," Hardwicke murmured as he closed the book. "Has Miss Drayton tried chilis? The hotter the better, in my experience. Squirrels hate the spiciness. I find drying it out, seeds and all, and making a fine powder to sprinkle over the soil keeps them away."

Even knowing his wastrel pose was merely a facade, Verity was nevertheless startled to receive helpful gardening advice from the Marquess of Ware's wastrel son. "I will tell her that, thank you," she said, lifting the teapot to pour. "Tensions have increased in recent weeks, and Freddie and I have begun to fear open warfare."

"That is to be avoided at all costs," Hardwicke said fervently as he received the cup. "My brothers and I spent a summer locked in a battle royale with the rats in our gardens at Winslow Hall, and we were soundly trounced. I even have the scar to prove it. I had the bright idea of catching the rats and putting a bell around their necks to scare away their fellow vermin. You can tell I was six years old because the jingling sound terrified me. I associated it with ghosts. When the bell did not work, I singed their fur because I thought the burned smell of their own kind was properly horrifying. That bore disappointing results as well, and I burned myself in the effort. My mother was livid."

Verity, who did not know what to make of this glimpse into his childhood, found herself curiously reluctant to change the subject. She wanted to hear more stories about six-year-old Colson but could not bring herself to ask. Instead, she said, "For openly defying a prohibition against playing with fire?"

"For engaging in what she believed amounted to the torture of a small animal," he clarified. "My mother has a fondness for all creatures and a particularly soft heart. It would drive my father mad how she would shoo away the cats in the barn when they were chasing a mouse because that was why they were there in the first place. They were literally called mousers."

Oh, dear, Verity thought, now she was even more intrigued. A gentle mother who rescued small rodents from predators—the kindhearted woman must have been distraught at Hardwicke's expulsion from society. Even if she had known it was in service to a heroic mission, she would have felt some measure of pain watching her son weather the scorn of his peers.

No doubt she detested Mr. Twaddle-Thum for exposing him to it.

Good God, Verity, it is no business of yours what the Marchioness of Ware thinks of the *Gazette*'s infamous gossip, she told herself, appalled by where her mind had been allowed to wander.

Evidently arriving at a similar conclusion, Hardwicke returned the conversation to the topic at hand, chiding her for creating utter chaos within the Yarwellian society. "Every member is now convinced every other member is a spy, and I have just spent the past hour swearing on holy books and various scraps of paper that it is not I. Thank you very much, Miss Gorman, for making a difficult assignment an absolute misery."

"As much as I would like to take the credit, especially for something that has increased your discomfort, I cannot accept it in this case," she said modestly, her fingers gripping the delicate porcelain handle. "That credit goes to Dircks and Oxenford for having such devious minds. I do not know them well enough to judge the truthfulness of their claim that the money was to go directly to weavers turned off from the factories, but I do find it difficult to respect either man's sense of honor."

"It is beside the point now, as you have scuttled their plan," Hardwicke said after taking a sip of tea. "And in a spectacular fashion. Mr. Twaddle-Thum might disguise the particulars of his accounts in allegory, but the code is so simplistic even a small child could figure it out."

"Be careful, Hardwicke," she said gently. "I would hate to see a report of your contempt for Twaddle's readership appear in a column for Twaddle's readership."

"Oh, but my contempt is not for his *readership*," he said with meaningful emphasis. "But that is not why I bring it up. It is only to request that next time you expose a scandal related to my assignment you warn me in advance."

Verity's heart hitched at the prospect of the situation repeating.

That meant their association would continue.

Irritated by her response, she reminded Hardwicke that she did not work for him.

An odd fierceness entered his eyes, but his tone remained amiable as he said, "You do not, no, and I perceive now why you refused my offer. You do not work for anyone, do you?"

And yet he posed the question with a mixture of censure and approbation, as if he himself could not figure out how he felt, and the fact of his indecision flustered Verity. She preferred things to be clear and simple. With that in mind, she calmly replied that his observation was accurate. "I work *with* Freddie and Delphine."

"Noted," he said softly.

Silence followed this comment.

It was, Verity found, as disconcerting as his uncertainty, but she refused to introduce a new topic. Hardwicke had called on her to discuss the business between them, and she did not believe chastising her for her column was the extent of it. He had something else on his mind, and she would sit there, sipping her tea, until he was ready to share it.

After what felt like a very long moment but was actually quite brief, he said, "I suppose the revelations in your article mean that you have ruled out Dircks and Oxenford as the killers. Presumably, they were meeting with Blasingame at the time of the murder."

"They were, yes," she said amiably. "It seems whoever plunged the knife into Mr. Smith's chest also stabbed them in the back."

"An unintended consequence, I am sure," he said, dipping his nose into the teacup. "May I ask how you discovered the truth?"

"Of course you may ask," she replied, very tempted indeed to introduce him to Mrs. McTawdry, whose grotesqueness she thought he would admire. Nevertheless, a fulsome answer was not in keeping with the tenor of the conversation and she politely declined to explain. "My methods must remain secret lest they lose their effectiveness."

"I am certain that is not true, Miss Gorman," he said. "Your ingenuity seems boundless, and that is why I have decided to accept *your* challenge."

Having instigated the game, she knew its rules well and acknowledged the claim with cool assurance, owning herself relieved to hear it. Then she leaned back in her chair and waited to find out to which of her challenges he was referring, for she had issued so many.

Hardwicke, his movements unhurried, finished the last of his tea, returned the cup to its saucer, and pulled a slip of paper from his pocket. He laid it on the table between them and slid it across the surface.

Verity unfolded the sheet.

It was a list of names.

Amazed to be simply handed the very thing she had invited him there to cajole, she said, "These are the members of the Society of Yarwellian Philosophers who were absent from the meeting on Saturday morning."

"They are," he confirmed.

"The list of suspects in Smith's murder," she added needlessly, almost as if he did not comprehend the significance of what he was giving her.

"Yes," he said.

Verity resisted the urge to shake her head in refusal, for she knew it had to be another tactic or trick, and she did not want to walk blindly into a trap. It both angered and annoyed her that she could not discern the move or intuit the larger play. Hardwicke was, as Delphine had observed, irritatingly astute, and she feared he saw the board in ways she could not. But holding herself still to avoid a snare was cowardice.

Pressing the paper tightly between her thumb and forefingers, she read through the names, as if any of them would be familiar. Then she said, "This is helpful. Thank you."

"You are welcome," he replied.

The room once again fell silent, and although she had refused to fill it with chatter earlier, she now cast about for something to say—anything that was not the one thing on the tip of her tongue.

She would not ask why.

But even as she swore to withstand her overwhelming curiosity, she realized there was nothing to be gained by denying herself information. If Hardwicke was once again outflanking her by giving her the list, then it behooved her to do all she could to comprehend the maneuver.

With that in mind, she said, "Which challenge in particular are you accepting?"

It was, she realized, the one question he himself had failed to ask, which was why for all his vexing shrewdness he did not seem to understand her.

Ah, but he did not seek to understand her, did he?

That was the difference between them, for the thing she desired more than anything else was clarity. She sought to comprehend his motives so she could anticipate his next move. It was the only way to assess an opponent.

"To permit you to find Smith's killer without my assistance," he said succinctly.

Although she could not say what she had expected to hear, it was not this reply bathed in condescension. "How very generous you are, my lord. Your permission means everything to me."

But even as she sneered, he shook his head and said, "Well, that was bloody patronizing, wasn't it? I must apologize, Miss Gorman, for that was not the way I meant it to sound. The challenge is for me not to interfere. I know you do not require my permission or approval or help or indeed anything from me. And frankly I am not in the position to give it right now because Grint has become increasingly convinced that Fitch is inciting violence and unrest. He is unsettled by Smith's murder, certain that Fitch had something to do with it, and angry to discover that the sister is an imposter because neither he nor I suspected anything was amiss in that quarter."

Pleased not so much by his words but the way he delivered them with sincere disgust at himself, she resolved to be gracious. "You had some suspicions about this sister, which is why you wanted to hire me."

"Merely to distract her," he said, refusing her kindness. "So you can see I have enough to keep me occupied and I am grateful to leave the murder in your capable hands. I will admit that I doubted your proficiency, and that was habit on my part. I am not accustomed to interacting with competent women. But the impressive speed with which you ruled out Dircks and Oxenford settled the matter. All I ask is that you eliminate suspects in a slightly less spectacular fashion. It would be better for Grint's disposition—which is really to say better for me—if he did not read a thinly veiled exposé on a delicate subject every morning."

"On that score, I am delighted to put your Mr. Grint's mind at ease, for Twaddle publishes dispatches twice a week and remains resolute in that number despite his editor's attempt to squeeze a third one out of him," Verity replied, unwilling to make a more meaningful promise. It was impossible to know from what seemingly minor detail might spring the next nine days' wonder and she would not limit herself.

Hardwicke, recognizing the evasion, noted that her response was not quite the reassurance he sought.

Verity lifted her shoulders delicately in an apathetic shrug. "How very disappointing for you."

"But it is, Miss Gorman, it is," he said, rising to his feet. "Now, since you appear to have everything in hand, I shall leave you to it. I am certain you do not require help from anyone, but if you want my assistance, I hope you will not hesitate to ask for it. The mass meeting is on Friday, and I expect Grint's anxiety to lessen after that. He is worried it will turn into a riot at Fitch's instigation now that the society is roiled by controversy. He sees in the scandal a lack of strong leadership."

"Is his understanding correct?" she asked, standing as well.

"The dozen original members are showing a united front, refusing to acknowledge there was a meeting with Blasingame, let alone revealing who was in attendance. They insist it is all a misinformation campaign on the part of the government to sow dissension in advance of Crowley's pivotal speech. Some of the newer members are calling for Anderson's immediate resignation because they see him as the leader, and others are demanding a vote. All of them are eyeing each other with suspicion. And now I have to return for yet another loyalty oath and possibly a test of my fealty. As I said, it is chaos. Thank you for that, Miss Gorman."

Verity accepted his gratitude, as facetious as it was, and noted that it was a shame he could not dispel their concern about a misinformation campaign by announcing he knew from personal experience that Mr. Twaddle-Thum did not take his marching orders from anyone, including the English government. A smile hovering over his lips, he said this afternoon did not strike him as an opportune time to remind any of his fellow Yarwellian philosophers of his connection to the infamous gossip.

Then he urged her to tell Delphine about using chilis and left.

Chapter Eleven

❧

Monday, June 1
6:11 p.m.

Delphine held aloft a slip of paper and said she had another one near Spitalfields Market.

Verity, her head bent over a map of London spread out on the dining table in the front parlor, drew her fingers along the main thoroughfare in the district and asked which street.

"Bell Lane," her friend replied. "I believe that makes four in total."

"It does, yes," Verity confirmed. "Four in Spitalfields, three in Saffron Hill, two in Clerkenwell, one near Covent Garden, and one in St. Giles."

"That is not so bad," Delphine said, leaning over the map herself to get a better sense of the ground Verity would have to cover to interview all eleven suspects. They had acquired the addresses with relative ease, alerting Twaddle's network and waiting for the information to be sent to the *Gazette* office, then delivered to Bethel Street by Freddie. It had taken only six hours.

"I do not think I will need more than three days to interview the whole lot. Confirming their alibis, however, will most likely take longer," Verity added, unable to smother the sigh that rose to her lips. By any measure, eleven suspects was a vast improvement over sixty, but she was still less than enthusiastic about the task at hand. Although she delighted in mocking Her Outrageousness for her investigative prowess, she had to concede that the undertaking was far more impressive than she had given it credit. The painstaking examination of clues required a patience Verity lacked.

"Maybe some of the fellows can help with that," Delphine suggested. "I know we usually rely on them just to pass along information, but they are clever lads and capable of more. If they prove successful, I thought I would talk to Freddie about apprenticing some of them."

"That is an excellent idea," Verity said, vexed that she had not thought of it herself. "Mags in particular would be well suited."

Pleased, Delphine considered the map again and asked if she would start with the four around Spitalfields in the morning. "Since they are conveniently clustered."

Verity glanced at the standing clock by the entrance, noted it was only a little after six, and said there was plenty of daylight remaining for her to begin now.

"Is that really necessary?" Delphine asked, leaning back in the chair as she darted a glance outside. It was true that the sun would not set for almost three hours, but it was a rainy June day and they were comfortably ensconced in the parlor. Cook was roasting a chicken and planned to serve it at seven. "I do not mean to sound harsh, but poor Mr. Smith will not be any more dead if you wait until tomorrow."

Acknowledging the truth of the statement, Verity nevertheless rose to her feet and raised her arms above her head to stretch. She had been sitting at the table for more than two hours and her muscles were stiff. "It is more a matter of my forging determinedly ahead despite a marked reluctance. 'If it were done when 'tis done, then 'twere well / It were done quickly,' as they say."

"Yes," Delphine agreed mildly, "when they are committing regicide, not conducting interviews. I do wish you would pick your Shakespeare quotes with more discretion."

But that was not meant to be, at least not at that moment, and as Verity crossed the floor to the doorway, she tossed off other well-known lines that had nothing to do with the situation: "Once more unto the breach, dear friends, once more"; "Cry 'havoc' and let slip the dogs of war"; "Methought I was enamored of an ass."

Laughing, Delphine called after, "Oh, but, darling, *you* are the ass."

Monday, June 1
  7:43 p.m.

The greengrocer was a mistake.

The moment the words were out of Verity's mouth—the prospect of employment, the possibility of hope—she perceived the wretchedness of the approach. She could think of few things crueler than offering the false promise of work to a downtrodden and beleaguered man.

What had she been thinking?

Only of expedience, she realized now, which was appallingly shortsighted.

Changing tack, she apologized to John Winthrop for misspeaking. The position that she had described as empty was in fact filled by Mr. Shaw's son, Jimmy, who had been missing since Saturday, which meant the position was currently empty.

But it was only a temporary condition!

"I am explaining myself baldly," Verity said in the apprehension-filled whine of a distressed father, her fingers desperately clutching the brim of her hat. "I am sorry. It is just that I am so worried. The boy turned fifteen only last week and now he is gone. He was last seen near here, around the corner. Were you here on Saturday morning, around eight-thirty? Did you see Jimmy? Did you see my boy?"

Although more details might be required before giving a definitive response, such as the color of Jimmy's hair or his height or his general appearance, Mr. Winthrop said no.

At this sharp reply, Shaw pressed his right fist against his lips as if to hold in a cry and then he asked the other man how he could be sure. "This is a bustling street, with the market so close. See how many people are about now, and this is a Monday evening. It would have been bustling on Saturday morning. Please give it proper thought. Jimmy has blond hair like his mum. And he is as tall as me. Taller! He is growing like a weed. Did you see someone like that on Saturday at eight-thirty?"

Winthrop was a reed of a man, slender and tall, with hollowed cheekbones, a firm mouth, and hard eyes. And yet his voice was kind when he told the distraught father that he had not seen his son.

Verity shuddered and asked how he could be so certain. "To not have a trace of doubt in your voice!"

Despite being pressed, Winthrop replied in that same gentle tone that he had not been there on Saturday morning. "I was working at the smithy on Floral Street. I have been every day for a week. One of the men burned his hand something fierce and I've been helping out. Look, I am sorry about your boy. I really am. Maybe Mrs. Hunt can help. She's my neighbor and keeps an eye out. See, she is watching us right now," he said, hailing the woman with a raised hand. "You should ask her. And good luck, sir. I hope you find him soon."

"Yes, thank you," Verity said, bowing slightly forward as she put the hat back on her head. "Thank you very much."

Winthrop nodded in turn and told her again to talk to Mrs. Hunt.

Obviously, a frantic father could not refuse any avenue of inquiry and Verity trotted over to Mrs. Hunt, who was standing on her doorstep watching her approach with a cantankerous expression, as if already annoyed by the stranger.

It was, Verity thought, a fair enough reaction given that she was in fact wasting the woman's time with her questions. But with Mr. Winthrop hovering nearby, she was compelled to follow through on her story before seeking out her next suspect, Chester Filkins, and apologizing for interrupting Mrs. Hunt's day, she launched into a description of her dear, sweet, lost Jimmy.

Monday, June 1
  10:02 p.m.

"See, and *that* is when the horse clopped me on me head," Mr. Davidge explained excitedly, his arms flapping at his side like the wings of a rooster despite the bucket he was holding in one hand. It was filled halfway with peat, which threatened to spill out as the container bobbed to the left, then right. "That is why me pappy always said to never get on the wrong side of me horse 'cause he'll clop me in me head. In me eye! And cor blimey, does it hurt! I says to meself, Never mind the black eye, Sam, me boy, ye can still go to your meeting—because I had an important meeting with the men to get to—but the second I took a step me head ached so badly I could barely hold it up. So I went home and lay down on me bed for a few hours. It looks better now. You should have seen it on Saturday when it happened. It swelled right up. Me wife screamed when she saw me. 'What did ye do to yerself, Sammy?' she said. So I told her the story, and she just shook her head, disgusted with me because she knows me old pappy had warned me about horses. Anyway, I'm sorry about yer son. How old did ye say he was?"

The abrupt change in conversation startled Verity, for Mr. Davidge had been speaking for almost ten minutes without pause, relating in minute detail every aspect of the mishap that led to the horrible bruise on his face, starting with the pebble in his shoe, which he knew he should have ignored. 'Twas only a minor annoyance and now he was practically blind in one eye.

But it would heal!

He was convinced of that.

It would just take some time.

"Fifteen," Verity replied. "Jimmy is fifteen."

Davidge nodded knowledgeably and announced that he had sons of his own, eighteen and twenty-one, and although they were good boys who treated their ma with respect, they still sometimes acted as though they knew everything in the world. "Bleeding infuriating being told how to empty a cistern by a pup who can barely fasten his own shirt. He'll come back. I bet he's just taken a meander. Boys will do that."

Convinced young Jimmy was off exploring life on his own —young pups were always rife for adventure—he recalled fondly the time he himself had left home for more than a month to see the Highlands. "Did not get farther than Roys-ton, did I?" he added with a self-conscious laugh.

Familiar with his verbosity, Verity announced that she had to keep looking before he could launch into a lengthy description of the town. It had taken her only a few minutes to discover his whereabouts during the time of the murder, and she had been trying to extricate herself from the conversation ever since. She would have to confirm his account, of course, but the discoloring of the bruise was consistent with an injury that was two days old. She was inclined to believe Davidge was innocent.

It was the same conclusion she had drawn about the three other suspects she had interviewed that evening. Although their stories might not withstand scrutiny, on the surface they were persuasive, and Verity was grateful that she could begin to cross men off her list. Already she had drawn a line through Winthrop's name, as a brief stop at the smithy in Floral Street had confirmed that he was indeed working there in his relative's absence. Next, she would task Mags with corroborating Filkins's claim to be at the apothecary seeking treatment for his infant daughter's stomach ailment, and Mr. Parker with confirming Broom's claim to have still been abed.

All in all, it had been a productive first outing, and she was ready to cry quits. The prospect of sinking into a soft chair with a plate of roast chicken was highly appealing.

"Thank you for your time, Mr. Davidge," Verity added firmly, slightly terrified the man would insist on providing helpful advice on the best way to conduct the search for the missing Jimmy. "Not everyone I've spoken to has been as generous as you. And good luck with your eye. I'm sure it will heal up right and tight."

Davidge nodded gratefully and raised his right hand to wave goodbye, forgetting the peat and knocking himself on the jaw with the bucket.

· · ·

Tuesday, June 2
  1:30 p.m.

Having successfully elicited useful information from nine previous suspects using the ploy of Mr. Shaw's missing son, Verity was frustrated by Dylan Morton's refusal to respond coherently to her questions. All he did was offer a series of growled invectives before snarling, "Go away!"

The last was issued at the top of his lungs, drawing the attention of his fellow patrons in the lightly populated tavern where he sat staring morosely into a tankard of ale. As a weaver formerly employed in Blasingame's manufactory before being replaced by a knitting machine, he had taken the news of the society's double-dealing extremely hard. According to his wife, a patient woman with tired eyes, he had spent all his waking hours wallowing in disappointment at the Spotted Donkey.

Although his inebriation had made it clear conversation would be difficult, Verity nevertheless tried several times to discover his location at the time of the murder. He was, alas, utterly indifferent to poor Jimmy's fate and even implied that the father was a fool for even trying to look for him. "Ruddy idiot, stupid blighter," he grumbled.

Conceding the futility after the fourth try, Verity made a point of asking the men at the other tables if they had seen Jimmy on Saturday and then slunk out of the tavern with despondent shoulders when none of them could offer her hope.

Obviously, a new tack was in order. Having been so thoroughly rebuffed, Mr. Shaw could not make a second attempt, and she needed to approach Morton before he began drinking for the day, presumably first thing in the morning.

Verity had a few ideas but was too disgruntled to consider

them at the moment. The failure to elicit the information from Morton irritated her, yes, but she was more annoyed at having the steady progress she had been making abruptly halted. The drunken weaver was her penultimate suspect, and now that she knew she had to Twaddle after him again tomorrow, she felt little enthusiasm for seeking out the last name on the list. She could change course and focus on confirming alibis, but she had assigned that duty to her informants and it seemed at once churlish and wasteful to repeat or preempt their work.

Already, she had eliminated three suspects.

Steady progress indeed.

And yet as gratifying as it was to tear through the list, Verity wondered what she would do if all eleven men proved innocent.

Look for more suspects, she supposed, and it was precisely that notion that worried her because it sounded so tedious. If interviewing men to discover their alibis was tiresome, then finding the men to interview to discover their alibi would be deadly.

But there was still Morton, drowning his sorrows in the taproom, she thought in an effort to cheer herself up. The intensity of his disillusionment, which was beyond anything the other members had displayed, would make sense in the context of Smith's murder. It would be horrifying indeed to discover you had taken a life to protect an organization whose own founders were determined to undermine.

Verity was still thinking about Morton as she entered the house in Bethel Street, and placing her hat on the table in the narrow entryway, she decided she wanted to do something entirely different with her afternoon. She had all those toys to give the children at Fortescue's, and their happy smiles would be a welcome change from the boredom of a murder investigation. And Mrs. Chaffey, the matron who oversaw the asylum, was a sensible woman with whom she enjoyed talking. She would deliver the playthings, visit with the children, enjoy a cup of tea, and then resume her investigation.

Satisfied with the plan, she donned a simple walking dress in a once-vibrant cerulean that had long since faded to a much duller shade. She selected a bonnet, likewise plain, and sought out Delphine to collect the blankets. She found her in the kitchens with Cook planning the menus for the week, and although Delphine was disappointed she had not had the time to finish a fifth blanket, she darted upstairs to fetch the other four.

A half hour later, Verity disembarked in front of Fortescue's Asylum for Pauper Children. The path leading to the edifice, like everything else about the orphanage in which she was raised, was crumbling and decrepit, with cracked bricks overgrown with weeds. The pavers were so uneven, it was easier to walk on the grass, which was also untended, and Verity crossed the lawn in wide, easy strides. That the building continued to stand at all was a testament to its dogged contrariness. Large and rambling, with sections added in haste as the former convent's needs expanded and changed, it should have collapsed a hundred times over from neglect. Like the children it sheltered, it was unloved and neglected, and seeing it now, its aged stones seemingly exhausted from the effort to remain upright, she felt a familiar sense of kinship. As a child shunted from one cold room to another, she had been grateful for its dreary grayness and air of hopelessness, for it matched her misery. Had the building been a place of light and beauty, all gracious hallways and elegant rooms, she would have felt mocked indeed by her home.

That would have been intolerable.

Approaching the front door now, its wood freshly painted in a deep forest green—a comforting color that was not needlessly cheerful—she thought yet again about how much had changed since she and Freddie had routed the Wraithe and forced out the corrupt board of supervisors. Fortescue's would never be a joyful place, for there was just too much sadness in orphaned and abandoned children, but it was a kind place and sometimes even a happy one.

A bell jingled as Verity crossed the threshold, its tingle alerting the residents to a newcomer, and she was greeted with a cheerful hello from a brown-haired young woman named Julia, who helped look after the children. She had been hired about six months ago and seemed to have settled well into the position.

"And of course you have more presents," Julia observed with an amused shake of her head. "No wonder you are their favorite visitor. You never arrive empty-handed, and they know it."

"It is just small things," Verity said, as she followed her down the corridor to the drawing room that looked onto the lawn and the road beyond. "Some toy soldiers, a jumping rope, a few dolls, blocks for stacking, playing cards. And books, of course. I would never dare call without an assortment of fairy tales and wild adventures."

"You are too good to them," Julia said approvingly.

It was a platitude Verity heard often. Perceived as a woman of modest means who had the luxury of spending her time in any way she saw fit, she was constantly lauded for choosing to devote any of it to beleaguered children. No one who worked at Fortescue's now knew she was a former resident. The name Lark was nowhere in the records because she had bestowed it on herself.

"It is impossible to be too good to an orphan," she said.

Although the observation was meant as a gentle rebuke, Julia assumed Verity was merely being modest and smiled at her fondly. Then she warned her that the roof had sprung multiple leaks with the persistently wet weather and to tread carefully on the top floor. "It is so slippery! We are always dodging drips. I swear the whole wretched thing is about to cave in at any minute."

The head matron, as if summoned by these dispiriting words, appeared to assure Verity with earnest confidence that the roof was fine. "The leaks are a problem, and Julia is right in that it is like there is a light drizzle on the third story. I have to caution the children against running, for they are constantly darting here and there and the floor is quite slippery when wet. But I assure you the roof is not in danger of falling in—as I have told you repeatedly, Julia."

Julia lowered her gaze again. "Yes, ma'am."

"I understand her concern," Mrs. Chaffey added generously, "because it does feel biblical when it storms and the water seems to stream down. Like we are in the story of Noah's Ark and are about to be drowned with the rest of humanity. But that is not at all the case. Miss Carter, would you be a dear and fetch tea for me and Miss Lark?"

"Happily," Julia said, dipping into a brief curtsy before dashing out of the room.

"The roof really isn't that bad," Mrs. Chaffey said as she gestured to one of the chairs. "Do not get me wrong: It is a significant problem that needs to be addressed, but it is not a catastrophe, at least not yet. Remembering to change the buckets regularly seems to be the worst of it at the moment. I have someone visiting later in the week to assess the problem so I can figure out how to proceed. I am reluctant to inform the board of supervisors because our patroness has already been so generous with us and I am hopeful of getting the money another way."

Verity, sitting down in the worn chair, with its flattened cushion, lamented her lack of deep pockets. "If I could hand you a thick stack of notes to fix the roofs, I would do it in a heartbeat."

But Mrs. Chaffey shook her head and insisted that Verity gave something more valuable than money: warmth. "As generous as the supervisors are—and they are very generous, which I do not discount—they do this work out of a sense of good Christian charity. It is a noble impulse but cold. I am grateful to you for coming here every so often and showing the children true affection. And I see you brought toys again. Good."

"As well as some blankets from Delphine and primers from Freddie," Verity replied.

"Lovely," Mrs. Chaffey said before inquiring about their health. After ascertaining they were both well, she asked about Verity's brother, Mr. Lark, whose newspaper articles brought about the downfall of the previous regime and led to Mrs. Chaffey's current position. Although she had met Robert only once, the matron had formed an enduring impression of him as a tenacious reporter with a heart of gold. She never failed to send him her best wishes and hope that he would pay them a call.

As always, Verity gushed over how busy her brother was, expressed his own disappointment at not being able to visit more (*more,* as if he visited at all!), and gave a general overview of his current preoccupation. "I think the next story he will publish will be about the reform movement."

Mrs. Chaffey nodded with approval as Julia returned with the tray and laid it on the table nearest their guest. The teacups clattered in their saucers as the surface tilted to the left because of a pair of wobbly legs. "And that is why the roofs are not really an emergency despite being an emergency," the headmistress said with weary amusement. "Everything in this stately old building is broken in little ways and large. As soon as we fix the roof, we will need to repair the windows, for so many of the sills are rotted away, and then the floors."

Despite this litany of problems, the matron's demeanor remained sanguine, and Verity was grateful yet again that the supervisors had hired her. She was, to borrow Hardwicke's term, astoundingly competent.

Nothing daunted Mrs. Chaffey.

"So you see, even if you had that thick stack of notes, it would still be a drop in the bucket," the other woman continued. "We need half a dozen Lady Petershams. I have some hope of our getting a significant donation from Mrs. Gaitskill. As you may recall, she and her daughter visit regularly to spend time with the children."

Verity nodded. "Miss Gaitskill gives art lessons."

"That is right," Mrs. Chaffey confirmed. "She does not have much talent for drawing herself but is enthusiastic and has an eye for color. The children enjoy her instruction. Mrs. Gaitskill's father died last week. He was a very wealthy man and left his daughter comfortably set. I think she might decide to share some of her inheritance with us. I am certain Miss Gaitskill will make an effort to convince her, for she is very happy spending time with us."

Familiar with Mr. Dugmore's death, Verity made only a vague reply and took another sip of her tea. The deceased patriarch had done little to draw Twaddle's attention, and the most she could say about him was that he was a careful man who knew the value of a well-negotiated deal. But his youngest grandson was the pesky dandy who had done so much to draw Twaddle's attention.

After they finished their tea, Mrs. Chaffey escorted her to the second floor, where the children were engaged in their studies. Although they were busy, their teachers were happy to allow them to take a break to say hello to their visitor, and Verity handed out the toys to gleeful cries of delight. A small tussle broke out between two girls who both wanted to play with the jumping rope, and Mrs. Chaffey expertly stepped in to calm their nerves and convince them to take turns.

Verity, impressed as always by her deft handling, thought again that the head matron was a marvel, and taking her leave a little more than an hour later, she clasped the other woman's hand gratefully.

"You seemed to have every troubling matter firmly under control, even the blasted roof, but please do not hesitate to contact me, Robert, or Freddie if there is anything we could do," she said, tying the silk ribbons under her chin. "We are eager to help."

"I know it," replied Mrs. Chaffey with a reassuring smile, "and appreciate it."

Her spirit greatly restored by the visit, Verity said goodbye, straightened her bonnet, and reached for the handle. Opening the door, she stepped outside, a brisk breeze brushing her cheek as she first noted, then recognized a pair of figures standing a dozen feet away from her on the lawn.

It was her brother.

Her mother's son.

Damien Matlock.

The Duke of Kesgrave.

Oh, dear.

Chapter Twelve

T*uesday, June 2*
3 p.m.

Verity did not freeze.

Her arms, her legs, her hands, her head, her eyes—every single part of her body remained in motion, continuing forward, one foot in front of the other, as she proceeded down the broken path.

Her stride was smooth and confident.

Her expression was cool and impassive.

Her eyes stared ahead as if fascinated by the traffic on Austrel Street.

She oozed outward calm, and anyone looking at her would assume she was in the midst of an unremarkable day. Having accomplished one errand, she was now off to see to another: the milliner, perhaps, or the fishmonger.

All was well.

Everything was ordinary.

Do not linger, for there is nothing to see here.

Oh, but inside ...

Inside her chest, there were whirlwinds twirling, whirlpools swirling, and great vortices churning with unbearable pressure, for it was the one thing she had sworn never to do, the one promise she had made to herself, the only pledge she had taken and never veered from despite great inducement to the opposite: to get close to her brother.

It was utterly bewildering, his presence at Fortescue's, the way he had suddenly appeared, like Banquo at the banquet, an inexplicable figure, so ghostly and strange. In all her imaginings, she had never pictured him there, in the shadow of that crumbling old pile of stones she used to call home.

She could not fathom why he was there now.

And the figure standing beside him—that was the duchess, surely.

Verity had noted only an elegant pink dress and a lovely bonnet before recognizing the even features of her brother and smoothly glancing away to focus on the horizon.

But of course it was she.

Who else could it be?

Married two months, the pair lived in each other's pocket, the duke dutifully following behind his wife as she sought out mystery after mystery. He had even accompanied her to a steam engine foundry in Bloomsbury at the ungodly hour of six.

Besotted fool.

And yet she could not deny the ripple of pleasure she felt at her brother being a besotted fool for *this* woman, this plain spinster with an interesting mind and an inexplicable audacity who failed to draw the attention of a single suitor during her six seasons. Verity had been so certain he would wed one of the two dozen or so Incomparables he had escorted during his decade in London and had chortled at the prospect of the endless years of tedium he would spend leg-shackled to an empty-headed beauty.

She had found it impossible not to feel smug.

All that wealth and privilege, the freedom and resources to do whatever he wanted, and he would make the same boring choice as every nobleman before him.

He was nothing special, her brother.

And then he had married Beatrice Hyde-Clare.

It pleased Verity.

She had not known it was possible to want good things for a stranger.

As it was the two of them together, both the Duke and Duchess of Kesgrave, Verity's thoughts naturally turned to murder. Why else would they be there except to investigate a suspicious death, and at once her mind sifted through the things she knew about Fortescue's. In short order, she had reviewed the children, attendants, servants, and supervisors, and could come up with nothing of note except Mrs. Gaitskill's recently deceased father.

Roger Dugmore, who was typical of the sort of ruthless businessman who rose to wealth on the backs of people less powerful than he, had died less than a week ago in a fall. He had tripped while trying to climb out of bed in the morning, which was not an altogether unexpected development given that he was well over eighty and suffered from various ailments. His family had treated the matter lightly, withdrawing from social events but attending to other pursuits, as evidenced by Mrs. Gaitskill and her daughter continuing their work at the asylum. His grandson Lord Ripley had also persisted in his lessons at Gentleman Jackson's salon, a decision he had defended in his weekly note to the *Gazette*'s offices apprising the staff of his schedule.

But there was nothing suspicious about Dugmore's death.

At least, not at first glance.

Could Her Outrageousness have noticed an irregularity?

It was possible, Verity allowed, for that was precisely what happened with the explosion of Peter Huzza's new steam carriage. She had perceived something awry in the destruction wrought by the blast and proceeded to investigate. A few days later she arranged for the apprehension of the culprit.

That was true, yes, but the duchess had been present at the demonstration of the *Bright Benny* steam engine. She had witnessed the explosion firsthand, a happenstance that did not apply to Dugmore's accident.

How, then, could her suspicions be raised?

His obituary, as far as Verity could remember, was unexceptional, offering the usual accolades and providing a sundry list of accomplishments.

It contained nothing to raise one's eyebrow.

And yet Her Outrageousness still managed to detect a suspicious peculiarity in the slim two paragraphs in the *Morning Courier.*

Or not, Verity thought, reminding herself that her grace was not magical. There was another explanation for her presence, and it was slightly more logical. Fortescue's was an asylum for orphans and Miss Hyde-Clare was an orphan married to a man of obscene wealth. Desiring to help others in a similar situation, she could be there to inspect the institution with an eye toward making a donation. Alternatively, she might be inspecting how orphanages were generally run in anticipation of setting up her own.

There were several options available to her, and with the amount of money now at her disposal, she could finance all of them.

And she would need some other interest to occupy her, would she not?

A new bride could not spend *all* her time chasing killers.

Examining the information available to her to arrive at

this conclusion had the beneficial effect of calming Verity's racing heart. The tumult thundering inside her chest quieted to a dull roar as she realized that nothing in fact had happened. It had felt like so much in that moment of recognition, a cataclysmic event with far-reaching repercussions, as if the universe had been irrevocably altered.

It seemed so silly in retrospect, and Verity smiled as she imagined telling the story to Freddie and Delphine. She had kept her composure, holding firm to her resolution never to panic, and yet the way her mind had spun a tempest in a teapot testified to her loss of poise. Fear was all in the head.

As she approached the end of the path, she slowed her footsteps and wondered how much time had passed. It could hardly be more than a minute, and yet that was more than enough for the pair to have disappeared inside. Giving in to an irresistible compulsion, she turned around and saw the two figures still on the lawn.

It struck her as odd, for the lawn at Fortescue's was not the opportune location for a discussion about anything—except the building itself. If Her Outrageous was actually considering giving money to the asylum, then the condition of the edifice would interest her.

More like horrify her, Verity thought in amusement, imagining the duchess swiveling her silk-clad shoulders in the opposite direction. Nothing about the structure suggested care or kindness. It was a picture of pure Gothic desolation. Looking at it now under the gray sky of a wet spring, she was almost surprised not to hear an ominous clap of thunder.

If the duchess was seeking a new challenge in the wake of the distressingly easy murders she had taken to solving, she could do no better than Fortescue's.

Unable to contain her curiosity, Verity held off on hailing a hackney and waited to see if they decided to go in. She was no longer unnerved by the proximity, for the space of two dozen yards afforded her enough distance to disappear even if the couple turned sharply and marched toward the road.

As she waited, she began to compose the item.

Naturally, Twaddle could not stumble across his favorite subject in such an unlikely place and not write a few paragraphs about it for his devoted readers. They were eager for details about Her Outrageousness, consuming banal reports about her favorite food (rout cakes) and most expensive item in her trousseau (diamond-encrusted bandeau) with unrestrained enthusiasm. Verity's account did not even have to provide certainty. It was enough to present the situation as insufficiently known and construct the article around a series of questions.

She ran through them now as the first flurry occurred to her: What was the Duchess of Kesgrave doing at Fortescue's Asylum for Pauper Children? Was she hoping to alleviate the suffering of the children by making a significant donation? An orphan herself, did she feel a kinship to the woebegone waifs in its care? Did their sad little faces remind her of her own childhood? Was that why she lingered so long on the lawn in front? Did the prospect of entering the gloomy building cause her to—

Verity's mind went stunningly blank as she watched her top-lofty brother tug his wife into his arms, lower his head, and kiss her.

Out in the open.

In the middle of the day.

And it was not a brief thing, a quick peck or a fleeting caress.

It was passionate and long, ardent, and sincere, and Verity darted her eyes away, then turned her body toward the road, mortified at the intrusion. It did not matter that the Duke and Duchess of Kesgrave were out in the open and it was the middle of the day. She was spying on a deeply private moment, and it felt wretched.

Damn the Twaddleship, she thought. It was none of their business.

It was none of *hers*.

Rigid with determination, she raised her hand and deftly summoned a cab. She directed the driver to Bethel Street, climbed into the vehicle, and settled on the bench as her mind whirled.

The questions would go.

Verity would not fill three breathy paragraphs with speculative queries regarding the duchess's thoughts and actions. She would not propose her own answers or devise coy responses. She would simply report the facts as she knew them: Her Outrageousness was spotted at Fortescue's Asylum for Pauper Children on Tuesday afternoon.

She would keep it sparse and spare.

And the Gaitskills, she thought.

She would mention them, too, for they were related to nobility and on the fringe of society. Their good works deserved attention. Acts of charity were to be encouraged—that was, she decided, Mr. Twaddle-Thum's official position.

Verity could indeed squeeze a tidy little item out of those simple facts, and if including Viscount Ripley's aunt and cousin while continuing to ignore his antics tweaked the ego of the shameless provincial, well, then, that was just an unexpected benefit.

Wednesday, June 3
 9:24 a.m.

. . .

Rage suffused Dylan Morton's face so thoroughly even the tips of his ears turned bright red and he kicked the door with his booted foot, making a thunderous sound that caused the Turnip to flinch and take a cautious step back.

Verity, in the guise of her favorite character, a rustic hayseed lately arrived to the metropolis to pursue his dream of becoming a journalist, apologized profusely for the misunderstanding. "I did not mean ... you *must* believe ... I would never—"

"It wasn't no 'misunderstanding,'" Morton interrupted with a sneer. "You accused me of entering into a devil's bargain with Blasingame. How dare you!"

Grappling for coherence, the Turnip fumbled through a reply, stuttering incoherently, which he often did even when he was not so frightened for his well-being. Although he had been in the city for almost three months, he had yet to shake the dirt of rural Lancashire off his shoes. "N-no, not ... not me. It w-w-was Mr. Lark. He w-works for the *London Daily Gazette*. He sent me here to ask you—"

"Accuse me!" Morton seethed.

"—if you ... you h-had anything to d-do with the pact ... er, arrangement," Verity continued in the Turnip's halting stammer, her shoulders pulled toward her chest to make her slim frame appear even more narrow. It was difficult to appear small and vulnerable when you almost topped six feet. Morton's fury helped, for it made him less attentive to both his surroundings and his words. The angrier he was, the more honest he would be.

Morton clenched his fist and waved it menacingly in the air before him. Then he dropped it uselessly to his side and kicked the door again.

Despite this frightening display, the Turnip raised his chin bravely and said before he lost his gumption, "You were absent from the society's meeting on Saturday, and nobody knows where you were and your name has been mentioned as you used to work in the factory and I ... uh, we ... er, Mr. Lark wants to—"

"Who's mentioned my name?" Morton asked.

The Turnip shook his head violently and replied, "I can't say."

"Tell me!" the weaver demanded, thwacking the door with his boot again.

"I can't," the Turnip screeched. "Mr. Lark did not tell me. He only said that nobody knew where you were and that there were whispers and I should find out or ... or ... I could pack up my things and return to Whiston Cross. You won't do that to me, will you, Mr. Morton? Please, *please* do not make me go home to Whiston Cross. Please! My pa will make me work on the farm again, and Lizzie Runcorn expects me to marry her, and she has such a tiny, little nose. It's like it's not there at all. *Please!* I am begging you."

As humiliating as this speech was, the Turnip had delivered worse, for he was always on the verge of having to slink home with his tail between his legs. It was a combination of his lack of town bronze and the difficulty of the tasks assigned to him. Any reporter with a few years' experience would know that sending a greenhorn like Joseph Pope to ascertain if a man of Morton's disposition had participated in the decision to ally with Blasingame conspiracy was folly.

"Oh, for God's sake, you weevil, have a little self-respect!" Morton snarled.

The Turnip hung his head in shame. "Y-yes, Mr. Morton, of ... of course, but if you could just give me something to tell Mr. Lark?"

Disgust supplanted anger as Morton muttered under his breath that he should let Pope return to Whiston Cross, and Verity knew she had him. The Turnip was now a fly to be swatted so that he could continue to nurse his resentment in peace.

"It is no business of yours or Lark's or anyone, but I was with my sister on Saturday," Morton said matter-of-factly. "She went into labor on Friday and still hadn't delivered by morning, so I went to her house to keep my brother-in-law company while he waited. My nephew was born around noon."

Verity, displaying the Turnip's visible relief at this information, fervently thanked him, offered her congratulations on the birth, confirmed that the new mother was well despite the length of her ordeal, and flinched as the door slammed behind him.

Wednesday, June 3
    2:11 p.m.

"And that's when the bucket fell from the shelf, see, knocking over the chair that was keeping the floorboard in place, causing him to trip and land smack at me feet," the shop owner said, a broad grin on his face as he recounted how he had apprehended the thief who had tried to steal a loaf of bread from his establishment. "And I pulled him up by the scruffs until he was standing in front of me and I said, 'See, that's the Lord working in his mysterious way.' Then I put him in the chair—the one that had fallen over, the one that keeps the floorboard from popping out—and I made him sit there for the whole day. Twelve hours! I did not let him get up once. And, boyee, let me tell you, he was squirming like mad by the time he left."

As Clemmon Miller was the last suspect whose alibi Verity had to confirm, she received this news with disappointment. She did not, to be sure, wish for any member of the Yarwellian society to be guilty of murder, but if one of them was responsible for the stabbing death of William Smith, then it would have been most convenient if the killer was among the eleven men who had missed the meeting.

"You are certain the bread thief was Clemmon Miller?" she asked.

Nodding his head vehemently, the baker said he could not be more certain if his own son stole it. "I've known Clem his whole life. He used to come in here as a boy and knock over my baskets. He's a rascal. I don't even think he wants the bread. He just likes riling me up! I told his ma to send him to the colonies before he winds up on a transport ship. He will end up no good."

Despite this gloomy prediction, Miller had yet to descend into full depravity, Verity thought as she removed him from contention.

That left her with no suspects.

Smith's murderer was either not a member of the society or only loosely connected to the organization. Both possibilities required Verity to begin her investigation from scratch, starting, she supposed, with the victim himself. If she wanted to know his enemies, she would first have to get to know him.

It was a daunting prospect.

Even if his possessions had not been sold off by a rapacious landlady, the luggage she had searched in his room had yielded little of interest. The most useful thing she had dug up was the newspaper clipping about Fitch, and that revealed nothing that could not be found at Addison's. Unless Smith had concealed documents in the walls or floorboards, he had brought nothing revealing with him to London.

That left her with few options.

Verity was certainly not going to hire a coach and embark

on a multiday journey to York. The effort would require time and money and have little hope of prospering.

She could send a note.

Or hire a lawyer in the area to ask some questions on her behalf.

Regardless of how she decided to proceed, she would do it with little enthusiasm.

Again, she thought how dull murder solving was. She could not conceive why the Duchess of Kesgrave, with the endless options now available to her, would decide to spend so much of her time indulging in such a boring occupation. Indeed, *that* should be the subject of Twaddle's next column. He should compose a list of all the more interesting things Her Outrageousness could be doing rather than conducting tedious interviews with suspects.

"I believe that is all I need," she said to the owner, thanking him for his time.

"And you say this is about a job?" he replied, his brow furrowed in confusion. "You're making sure he is suitable for a position?"

Verity, who had not known about Miller's penchant for devilry or thievery when she introduced herself as an agent for a foundry, said that it was. "I represent the Brookdale Ironworks. He applied to work with sand molds for pouring and setting cast iron."

"Hard work," the baker said with a note of approval. "That doesn't sound like Clem at all."

No, Verity could see that it did not, and thanking the man once again for his time, she promised to keep that in mind. Then she left the shop to figure out the next step in the alarmingly tiresome investigation into Smith's murder.

Thursday, June 4

3:17 p.m.

Delphine spent so much of her time pleading with Verity to be more cautious in her pursuits that it felt strange to urge recklessness. Not a rash sort of recklessness, of course, or a hasty kind and certainly not the jump-on-the-footboard-and-careen-down-the-streets-of-London-while-holding-on-to-the-underside-of-a-carriage variety.

No, Delphine was advocating for a thoughtful recklessness in which her friend reviewed the missives from her informants, decided which ones had merit, and left the front parlor to find out if the claims were accurate.

That last item on the list was key—leaving the front parlor.

Verity had done very little of that in the past four and twenty hours.

As far as Delphine knew, her friend had left the room only twice and, on both occasions, she had scurried back as quickly as possible, seemingly afraid that an indoor windstorm or some other freakish event might disrupt her carefully splayed papers in her absence. Verity was sitting at the table reviewing her notes when Delphine went up to bed the night before, and she was sitting at the table reviewing her notes when Delphine came down in the morning. In between, she had taken a nap on the settee.

A short nap, by the looks of it, Delphine thought, noting the smudges of exhaustion under her friend's eyes. "If you will not go outside for some fresh air, then at least consider changing your focus for a little while. I am certain it will help you think. What about the thick packet of missives Freddie delivered this morning? You have not even glanced at them. Are you not a little curious about what your spies have discovered?"

"Yes, of course, always," Verity replied, flitting her eyes briefly upward before tilting them down again to scribble another note on a slip of paper. Then she held it in front of her and considered where it should go. It was a question about Smith's family, so it belonged in the Lancashire pile.

Having no obvious suspects, she had decided to approach the problem like one of Robert Lark's newspaper articles. He always began by drawing up two lists: things he knew, things he did not know. Sometimes those categories would divide into smaller sets.

In the case of Smith's murder, those smaller sets broke into tinier groups.

Verity had fourteen different lists before her, and that did not include the master list keeping track of all the other lists.

Although she understood how it looked to Delphine—a chaotic scattering of scraps and nonsense—there was order in the chaos. Everything was precisely where it belonged, and seeing the whole, she knew what she needed to do.

Gather more information.

Among her lists was a directory of people to interview.

There was so much she still did not know—for example, where he planned to go on the morning of his murder. She felt confident he had arranged to meet with someone, and that someone could be the killer.

Delphine, worried by the distracted response, sat down at the table and dismissed her friend's chiding admonition to be careful of her papers. "I have not upset a thing, darling," she said soothingly as she looked for a clear swath of wood to lay down the package from Freddie. Moving a few sheets ever so gently to the side, she created a space and tugged at the ribbon. "Even if you are not interested in what has your network so excited, I am. I bet it has something to do with the duchess's visit to the orphan asylum on Tuesday. Your supposition that she and the duke were inspecting it with an eye toward making a donation makes sense but is inordinately sensible for Twaddle. Are you sure there could not be some element of a mystery attached?"

Verity, her attention focused on the many unknown aspects of the Smith affair, pursed her lips as she considered the landlady at the rooming house for the dozenth time that day. She made such an excellent villain: greedy, venal, cruel.

And yet Hardwicke and she had been present when Mrs. Buglehorn discovered the body. Patently, she had nothing to do with it.

Unless she suspected they were hiding in the wardrobe.

Impossible.

Still, Mrs. Buglehorn was on the interview list.

Distractedly, she reminded Delphine of the kiss she had witnessed. "I think it is extremely unlikely they would indulge in such libidinous behavior if they had murder on their minds."

"Well, they *are* newlyweds," Delphine replied as she slipped off the ribbon and removed the paper binding the notes together. "And as such are prone to spontaneous displays of affection. I would not be surprised by anything."

Verity conceded the point and promised to look into the matter as soon as she figured out who killed Smith. "I will finish organizing my thoughts, then I will conduct interviews and identify the murderer, and *then* I will return to Fortescue's to ask Mrs. Chaffey some gently probing questions, I promise," she added, then sighed and looked up, her expression weary but amused. "You are allowed to be interested in the duchess's interest in the place where you grew up without the pretext of a murder. It is entirely natural, and I am certain Mrs. Chaffey will understand. You can come with me yourself. I am sure you will have finished the blanket by then."

Delphine, unfolding the missive on the top of the stack,

confidently noted that the blanket in question was already finished. "I think we should call on Mrs. Chaffey today. She will be delighted to have two visits from you in one week. We can see how the roofs are faring *and* find out about the duchess. I am sure you can take a short break from your investigation. There is no rush."

Verity turned her head away abruptly and said, "Hardwicke is relying on me."

About this revealing statement, Delphine had many thoughts, but they all flew out of her head when she read the note from Parker. Emitting a squealing laugh, she held the square of paper up and said, "Ha!"

Verity paused and echoed her friend. "Ha?"

Fluttering the sheet in the air, Delphine said, "Ha, ha, ha!"

"I think you are the one who needs to take some air," Verity said gently. "You are incoherent."

But Delphine just shook her head and said "ha!" yet again, causing her friend to snatch the missive from her hand. Verity read the note, darted to her feet, and ran across the room. Laughing as she watched her friend dash into the hallway, Delphine called, "Would not indulge libidinous behavior while investigating a murder, you said? Extremely unlikely, you insisted?"

Resisting the urge to cackle, Delphine leaned back in her chair and extracted the next note from the pile.

Chapter Thirteen

*T*hursday, June 4
5:59 p.m.

Verity waited until Viscount Ripley had turned onto Ryder Street before trying to gain his attention with a murmured *psst*. He shook his head slightly, as if to evade a fly near his ear, and continued walking. Drawing closer to him, she made a second attempt, the breathy syllable louder and more insistent. Now his lordship raised his hand, determined to swat the annoying little beast, and waving it in the air, thwacked Verity on the cheek. As she yelped, "Ouch!" in a deep, masculine voice, he gasped in mortification and exclaimed, "I am sorry! I did not see you there."

"No, no. It was all my fault," she insisted. "I was standing too close to you. You see, I was trying to get your attention without making a big fuss about it because that's what *he* instructed me to do."

It was a puzzling explanation, and his lordship was duly

perplexed. But only for a moment. Then comprehension swept across his features. As he opened his mouth to speak, Verity pressed a finger to her lips and said, "Shh!" Then she looked around as if to make sure no one was watching and gestured with a tilt of her head that he should follow her to an empty doorway.

"What is happening?" he said. "I do not understand."

"*He* sent me to make initial contact with you regarding a recent shocking event," Verity explained in a conspiratorial whisper. The melodramatic intrigue was excessively done and a little silly, but she knew it would appeal to the viscount, for he himself was excessively done and a little silly. During his month in London, he had earned a reputation for foppishness and frivolity, rarely appearing in public in anything other than chin-high shirt points and brightly patterned waistcoats.

His style today was not as ruthlessly perfect, with his shirt points possessing a faintly exhausted air, as if they had grown weary of standing up so straight. His sandy hair, always impeccably styled in the Bedford crop, appeared as though it had been patted into place by impatient hands. Only his brown eyes looked sharp.

"*He* knows what has occurred under your watchful gaze," Verity continued in the same vague manner, "and seeks your assistance in compiling an account. It is a sensitive matter and he understands if you must refuse. If you do, he asks only that you tell no one about this exchange."

Although Verity rarely approached a target so directly, his lordship's assiduous courtship of her attention all but demanded the tactic. From the moment Ripley arrived to London from an obscure district in the country, he had resolutely set himself up as a dasher, aping the ways of dandies and Corinthians alike, dressing brightly and gambling wildly. He seemed at once desperate for people to look at him and determined to give them a disgust of him when they did.

He was young—only two and twenty—and foolish and would eventually develop a more sophisticated understanding of popularity, but for now being mentioned by the country's most scurrilous gossip in one of his columns was as high as the aspiring Pink could soar.

As he contemplated the achievement of the dearly sought goal, Ripley's eyes glowed with excitement and his lips parted with eagerness.

And then the light flickered out.

The viscount threw his arm against his forehead and wailed. "I cannot! I renounce Twaddle and all that he stands for! I will never read another word he writes as long as I live!"

Although Verity had had no reason to anticipate a passionate disavowal, she was nevertheless unsurprised to receive one. The rarefied existence enjoyed by Quality made them capricious creatures, and she would never expect its members to hold the same opinion from moment to moment, let alone day to day. It was the reason Twaddle preferred to interview kitchen staff and footmen. They were constant in their resentments.

Thanking him for his time, Verity promised to convey his refusal to her employer and never to bother him again.

Aghast, Ripley stared at her. "But don't you want to know *why* I have renounced Mr. Twaddle-Thum?"

In truth, Verity was more than a little curious because the reversal was so striking. Revealing her interest, however, would make satisfying it less likely so she said she would never dream of imposing on a renunciation. "That is a private matter between a man and his conscience," she said soberly.

This courteous demurral was all the invitation the viscount required to bitterly air his grievance against Mr. Twaddle-Thum. "It is all his fault! Every awful thing that has happened in the past week! If he had just made one small mention of my exploits, then all of this could have been avoided. But he refused to acknowledge me and I was driven to a fateful act that has destroyed my aunt. It is so unfair! If only he had written about my ladybird race. It was so elegant, so well-conceived. I taught two dozen ladybirds to race. I trained them for hours! I spent an entire day looking for the best tree to hold the contest. It was an excellent lark, and yet not a single word from Twaddle. It makes no sense. The man hates me! And now to seek *my* attention after I ruined my family seeking *his*. No, my renunciation stands! Tell him I will have nothing more to do with him."

Although the intriguing reply raised more questions than it answered, Verity readily recognized the guilt at the heart of his anguish and wondered how he was at fault for his aunt's fate. As he was not the one who harmed his grandfather, it was odd that he felt responsible for the one who did.

Had he aided the duchess in her investigation?

If he had provided the piece of evidence that proved his relative's guilt, then that might explain his turmoil. It was a reasonable conclusion, and she made a note to explore it further when questioning the servants about the investigation.

"I will tell him precisely that," Verity said soothingly. "He will never bother you again. Of that you may be certain."

As reassuring as these words were, they unsettled his lordship further and he apologized for using such a strident tone. "Please do not tell him *precisely* that, for I have no wish to give offense. You may convey a general air of dissatisfaction."

"Of course, my lord," Verity said. "I am confident that *he* has no wish to cause you further distress and I offer my apologies on his behalf for any actions his lack of attention has forced you to take. If I may speculate, I believe he was giving you time to adjust to London. Life here is very different from the country."

The viscount allowed that this explanation was possible.

"It had not occurred to me, but it is true that all my decisions have not been stellar. I stand by the ladybirds! That was inspired. But sneaking into my grandfather's room every day to read letters from my mother and summoning the duchess were perhaps not my finest moments," he added softly, as if to himself. Then he raised his chin slightly, meeting her gaze, and announced that he was softening his stance against Mr. Twaddle-Thum. "You may thank him for his consideration. I remain firm in my renunciation but have a new level of understanding. Now if you will allow me to return to my solitary walk."

"Of a certainty, my lord," Verity murmured.

Ripley took three purposeful steps away, paused, and looked back. Then he said with seemingly genuine regret, "I am sorry it could not have been different."

Piecing together an incomplete picture based on his few incoherent statements, Verity imagined he was indeed sorry. If by "summoning the duchess" he meant he had invited her to investigate the death of his grandfather, which had been widely understood to be an accident before Her Outrageousness's interference, then he was directly responsible for his aunt's disgrace.

What Verity was at a loss to comprehend was how letters from the viscount's mother contributed to his guilt. He said they were hidden in his grandfather's room. If he was searching through the deceased's private papers, perhaps he had stumbled across something that raised his suspicions, which led him to contact the duchess.

It was a plausible theory, Verity thought, leaving the doorway as his lordship turned the corner. The first order of business was discovering what it was he had found hiding amid his mother's letters, and as she contemplated which disguise to assume to gain entry to the house, a thought struck her so forcibly, she halted in her tracks.

The letter!

Yes, yes, of course!

It had been in front of her nose the whole time and yet she had missed it. Mrs. Buglehorn had been blatant about it, literally shouting that she would not mail it until Smith paid the posting fee.

Verity did not doubt that the landlady still had it. Mrs. Buglehorn was too calculating not to consider the last words of a dead man to be of value. Within an hour of her boarder's death—well, rather, within an hour of the conclusion of the auction of her dead boarder's possessions—she had probably sent a note to the family offering the posthumous letter in exchange for a delivery fee and dispersal fee and storage fee.

Oh, yes, Mrs. Buglehorn would not fail to exploit such a rich opportunity.

Although part of Verity wanted to dash over to Portpool Lane to fetch the missive at once, she knew nothing would be served by acting rashly. She needed to settle on an identity, and it was already after six in the evening. Mrs. Buglehorn would be busy preparing dinner for her residents, and Verity herself was more tired than she had realized after spending the night in the parlor. She had passed the majority of it at the table, with a brief nap on the settee, which was not conducive to slumber.

Smith's letter could wait till the morning, she thought, and as she turned onto Jermyn, she conceded that Delphine's assertion had been correct: Switching her focus *had* helped clear her mind.

Friday, June 5
10:05 a.m.

. . .

Verity found Mrs. Buglehorn on the third floor of her rooming house banging loudly on a tenant's door and yelling that he was late with that week's payment. All monies were due by nine a.m. on Friday, and as it was now several minutes after ten, he owed an eight percent late fee *and* a six percent very late fee. If she had to come up there a second time, there would be an exertion surcharge in addition to the fee for excessive lateness, which was twenty-two percent.

"Do not make me tell you what happens after that," she shouted.

The door swung open to reveal a young man in his shirt-sleeves, his hair in wild disarray and two days' growth on his chin. He blinked his bleary eyes with a blank unseeingness, and Verity wondered how much alcohol he had consumed not just the evening before but the whole week.

Noting his lack of comprehension, Mrs. Buglehorn said she was waiting for her money. "If ye can't find it, I can take a look meself."

Verity did not doubt the landlady was exceptionally skilled at finding shillings concealed in the private compartments of her tenants' belongings.

The man muttered that he had the rent and shuffled off to find it. Mrs. Buglehorn tapped her foot in the doorway, calling out the extra farthings owed due to his delinquency. When she had the coins in hand, she thanked him sweetly and reminded him that breakfast was served only to ten-thirty. Then she turned to bound down the stairs, giving Verity her first look at the harridan who all but charged her residents for the air they breathed. Her appearance was startling, for she had a large birthmark high on her right cheek. The color of port wine, the splotch encompassed a portion of her eye and extended to the base of her ear.

Mrs. Buglehorn, whose height was considerable, especially when she stood on the top step, scowled down at Verity and said that potential boarders were instructed to wait for her in the blue parlor. "It says so right on the front door. I have a mind not to rent to ye at all, breaking rules before ye even paid me a pence," she muttered irritably.

Verity assured her that she was not a potential boarder.

"Are ye not?" the landlady said, narrowing her eyes. "Well, I run a respectable establishment and do not allow male callers. Off with ye!"

"Nor am I a caller," Verity replied smoothly, introducing herself as a constable as she tipped her hat higher on her crown. "I am here to discuss a serious matter that is not appropriate for the stairwell. Let us have our talk in the ... I believe you called it the blue parlor?"

Mrs. Buglehorn inhaled sharply as if to argue against the suggestion, but the only sound she made was a disgruntled harumph.

Verity waited for the other woman to pass her in the corridor and then followed her to the parlor, which was a small square room with two hard chairs, the stench of rotting garbage, and a set of filthy windows facing the street. It was difficult to picture any prospective tenant enjoying its comforts and deciding to see more.

Puzzlingly, it was painted red—unless "blue" described the mood of the space, not the color.

"People are pustules and pimples! They complain about everything," she said, launching into a refutation before she even heard the charge against her. "I know me rights! I can charge whatever I want. The bill is posted right there. All the prices and the fees and the surcharges. I ain't doing anything I shouldn't."

To that end, she was correct.

Written in faded ink on a square of paper, its edges tattered and yellowed, was a list detailing the cost of each room in the house with the schedule for additional charges.

As the sheet was so small and the information so great, the words were written in letters so tiny they looked like squiggly lines from even one foot away.

Praising the woman on her integrity, Verity observed that her guests no doubt appreciated knowing precisely where they stood. "I am calling about another matter. It is regarding William Smith."

Mrs. Buglehorn scrunched her nose as if trying to recall the name. "Who?"

"His family is accusing you of murdering him to steal his possessions. Tell me, Mrs. Buglehorn, do many of your tenants die of knife wounds in their chests?" Verity asked coolly. Assuming the landlady had contacted the addressee of Smith's last letter was a risky gambit but one she felt certain would prevail.

"I can't believe what I am hearing!" Mrs. Buglehorn said on a laugh. "Kill Smith for his possessions? What he owned wasn't worth more than two pounds, five shillings and a couple of pence. It wouldn't be worth the cost of scrubbing the sheets."

Although Verity thought the landlady would gladly expend the labor and lye in exchange for a mere farthing, she did not belabor the point. "I find it curious that you know the precise value of his possessions."

Mrs. Buglehorn jerked her head backward and objected to the implication. "I did not sell them off and anyone that said I did is a liar! Bring them here and I will call them a liar to their face!"

"If that is true, where are his possessions?" Verity asked. "If that is true, why did you send a letter to his family offering to sell them Smith's last communication? Admit it! You killed your own tenant and then tried to squeeze every last coin out of him! Only a murderess would hold a dead man's letter for ransom!"

At the mention of the letter, the landlady's face lost some of its color, confirming Verity's suspicion. "It was for monies owed! That's all, I swear! Smith died before paying me for the week's rent, and I asked for money to settle his bill fair and square. If they thought I was holding the letter hostage, then that was their misunderstanding. I am sure I was clear about it being only in exchange for his last week's rent."

Verity regarded her with a gimlet eye. "And his possessions?"

"I had no choice! The bedclothes were ruined by the blood," she insisted, her manner slightly frantic now as she seemed to realize her own peril. "There was so much of it! It seeped into the mattress, making it useless, and it even got onto the curtains. I had to replace the sheets and the blankets, and that costs money. It is only fair that Smith contributed to the expense."

Verity could not altogether deny this claim. Under the strange peacefulness of the scene—the folded arms, the closed eyes—pulsed the murderous frenzy of the act itself. Blood *had* spewed freely. But that did not justify stripping a dead man of his valuables.

"Wait here!" the landlady said, darting out of the small room and turning right. Verity watched as she disappeared into the back of the house and returned thirty seconds later with an envelope held aloft. "Here! You take it!" She shoved the letter into Verity's hand. "Give it to the family. Tell them I am sorry. I swear I did not mean to hold the letter hostage. I just wanted the rent. That's all I said. They gave my words a most evil meaning. They're in mourning. I understand! I should have been more careful."

Slipping the envelope into her pocket, Verity allowed that it was possible that the family had misjudged the situation. "But you did yourself no favor sending that letter, especially after dispensing with his possessions as you saw fit. That would not appear to be the actions of an innocent woman. Maybe you *are* innocent. But right now, you are my only suspect."

It was an invitation to Mrs. Buglehorn to suggest other possible culprits, and she was not shy in accepting. Closing the door to the tiny room so that nobody would overhear, she went through the house lodger by lodger explaining why each one was most likely a murderer. Then she turned her attention to the bookbinder who lived next door, the three shop-keepers with stores on the road, and the workers who performed various services for her, including the collier, the milkmaid, the chimney sweep, the privy cleaner, the seam-stress who brought the new tablecloth she did not recall ordering, and a rag-and-bone man who refused to believe she had no cast-off scraps he could resell.

Portpool Lane
  Clerkenwell, London
  Friday, May 29, 1816

Dear Betty,

It is late, I am tired, so I will be brief.

My doubts are gone, and I am now prepared to say that the man who goes by the name of Arnold Fitch is the traitor we know as Tyrone Thorpe. Your brother was right to raise the alarm.

. . .

Much about Thorpe is different. He wears whiskers, which change the shape of his face and make it appear thicker. He has gained some weight. And in this incarnation he has a sister, which Thorpe did not. Even with these differences, I am certain it is the man who encouraged Barney to attack the ironworks. He speaks with the same passion and authority.

I have confirmed it two ways. First, I spoke at length to the woman who calls herself Amanda Fitch in the park on Tuesday morning, and although she gave consistent answers to all my questions about her childhood despite my many attempts to confuse her, I can't believe they are related. She has a Leeds accent, and as you know, he is from Tockwith, near York. It's a small distinction but a telling one. Next, I visited a tavern where Thorpe was speaking. Although I have watched him come and go for several days in my guise as a tailor, this was the first time I let him see me. I pretended to be completely unaware of him, so he does not know that I know that he recognized me as the man who saw him talking to General Singer's liveried footman after the uprising.

I will tell Silas Anderson in the morning. He is an original member of the Society of Yarwellian Philosophers with whom I have had several conversations in the past week. He also believes I am just a tailor, but I know he will listen to me and be incensed when he learns the truth. He thinks Thorpe is one of us and has put as much faith in him as our son-in-law did. If he continues to trust him, then he will end up hanging from the gibbet just as our dear Barney did.

. . .

As always, I send my love to you and sweet Priscilla and little Charlie. I cannot believe he took his first steps and I was not there to see it. How beside himself with pride Barney would have been to watch his son walk. I am gutted to think about it.

William Smith

Friday, June 5
  12:41 p.m.

Verity sat with the letter for almost an hour.

On the settee in the parlor, away from the orderly jumble of notes on the table, she drew her knees against her chest and stared out the window as she contemplated the information contained in Smith's brief missive to his wife. Two things were clear to her now: Smith was the man cited in the *Observer* article revealing the army's use of a secret informant, and his son-in-law was one of the three men hanged within days of the Christmas Uprising. That he bore a deep hatred for Fitch neé Thorpe was not surprising, given the part the other man had played in Barnabas Ibbs's capture by government troops, nor was his desire to see him exposed before he could betray the cause again.

It was also readily apparent that William Smith greatly underestimated the precarity of his situation. He thought he had been so clever, pretending to be a tailor when he obviously could not sew, revealing his presence to Fitch while affecting obliviousness, and slyly interrogating Miss Copley. Knowing how difficult it was to conduct a covert operation, Verity could only assume his interview of the actress was heavy-handed. As a man of a particular age, he probably began the conversation by offering her a compliment—observing, for example, how pretty she was—and then saying something like, "I have a daughter just about your age. She loves taking walks in the park. Do you love taking walks in the park? Were there lots of parks where you grew up? Where did you grow up?"

His description of her answers as consistent implied that he repeated himself in his attempts to confuse her, and Verity had little doubt that in the end the only one he confused was himself. Miss Copley was sure to have figured out his game. She was too clever and complicit not to suspect something when a strange man pressed her on her childhood, and she might have followed him back to his lodgings to see what she could learn about him. Then later, when she told her employer about the exchange, she could provide useful details. Fitch might have recognized the threat from Miss Copley's description, or perhaps it was only when he saw him in the tavern that he recalled their conversation in the wake of the uprising.

Regardless, it did not matter what Fitch thought because he was with the Yarwellians while Smith was being stabbed, and if there was one thing Verity did not doubt about the whole intrigue, it was Hardwicke's evidence. If he identified the time of the murder as around eight-thirty, then the murder was around eight-thirty.

But if the man who had the strongest motive was not the killer, then who was?

The woman with the strongest motive, she thought.

Although Verity had been toying with this idea for fifty-two minutes, she was no more comfortable with it now than when it first struck her. Her unease was not at the notion that the murder was too violent for the actress. She absolutely believed that given the right circumstance, Miss Copley could wield a knife with brutality and accuracy. She had mentioned during their conversation that she had learned how to use a sword and a dagger as part of her theatrical training.

No, what struck Verity was the brutality of the murder in respect to the circumstance. Miss Copley was only an actress hired to assume a role and as such had little to lose if the deception were revealed. In theory, her reputation could suffer if her recent living situation became known, but the damage would be minor in light of her profession, for few women who trod the boards were considered respectable. Whose good opinion would she actually lose?

Nobody she cared about, Verity thought. The scandal in London would not reach the ears of her family in Leeds—that was, if she even had family to hear it.

The notion that a woman of Miss Copley's character driving a dagger into the chest of an elderly man to stave off a threat that did not really exist was insanity.

And yet there had been a hint of theatricality in the way the corpse was arranged on the bed, its arms folded gently across its chest. The composition closely matched the description Miss Copley had given of Ophelia's peaceful repose during the burial scene.

It was a most specious piece of evidence, and Verity felt foolish considering it.

But she also felt foolish rejecting it.

And that was why she had been sitting on the settee, her knees pressed against her chest, for almost an hour.

Searching for a plausible motive, she could fathom only money.

Great heaps of it was always worth killing over.

But surely nothing on that scale was at stake.

Fitch was paying her three shillings a week, which was a good salary for an actress but not nearly enough to justify murder. He had promised her a bonus at the end of her tenure, and although Miss Copley had not mentioned the figure, Verity assumed it was in line with the compensation already on offer, such as a month's worth.

Again, Verity could not believe Miss Copley would stab a man to death for a dozen shillings.

Could she believe it for a dozen pounds?

Well, yes, she thought.

For that amount of money—the equivalent of a scullion's salary for three years—she could believe it of the vast majority of Londoners.

But there was no way Fitch could have offered that much. At most, the Home Office would be paying its informant ten or twelve shillings per week. Even if he gave every farthing of his compensation to Miss Copley, it still would not be enough to confer significant wealth.

That left Verity without a motive for Miss Copley, and without a motive she could not validate her suspicions. Every attempt to consider the actress without a motive made her feel like the veriest peagoose, working so hard to fit a square into a circular slot when the real culprit was out in the world moving with impunity.

Part of that effort was the seamstress Mrs. Buglehorn included in her list of tradesmen who had tromped through her boarding house and all made much better suspects than she. The landlady mentioned a new tablecloth that she did not recall ordering, and Verity, in her infinite wisdom, kept wondering if the seamstress was Miss Copley.

Yes, she thought, tightening her grip around her legs.

And then: no.

For Verity, the only thing more unbearable than indecision was inaction, and so she loosened her arms, slid her feet onto the floor, and ran upstairs to figure out how to make a dark-red stain for her cheek.

Chapter Fourteen

*F*riday, *June 5*
3:37 *p.m.*

Verity knew her theory had merit when she saw the flash of recognition in Miss Copley's eyes as she beheld a reasonable facsimile of Mrs. Buglehorn. The glare of impatience with which she had answered the door in response to a series of annoyingly persistent knocks was briefly supplanted by comprehension. The scowl returned so quickly that Verity thought she might have imagined it in her eagerness to find Smith's murderer.

"May I help you?" Miss Copley asked in a blandly uninterested tone.

Attempting to mimic the landlady's whine, which was higher than her natural register, Verity announced that *she* was there to help *her*. "And I will charge ye a very reasonable fee, see if I don't. I defy ye to find a better deal in all of Lunnon."

It was far easier for Verity to imitate Mrs. Buglehorn's appearance than her voice. The landlady's height, though not as considerable as her own, lent a good deal of believability to her impersonation, as did the birthmark high up on her cheek. Re-creating it had required more effort than she had expected, and it was only after mixing various amounts of rouge, pomade, paint, and port wine that she arrived at the ideal formulation. The splotch looked wholly natural unless one pressed their nose against Verity's cheek.

She was reasonably confident the actress would not.

Like most people, she would note various traits that indicated a particular person. The birthmark, the slovenly apron, the height, the hair secured with twine—these factors were enough to imply Verity was who she said she was. Miss Copley's interaction with Mrs. Buglehorn could not have been so extensive that she noticed more specific details. She would have worried more about the landlady being able to recognize *her*.

Miss Copley's forehead furrowed in a look of confusion that might have been sincere or part of her performance. "I'm sorry. What is the fee for?"

"Solving yer problem," Verity explained.

Although the actress had to suspect by now what the difficulty was, she still professed not to understand. "I do not have a problem in need of solving. Good day to you, ma'am."

Verity placed her foot in the corner of the door before Miss Copley could shut it and confidently said, "Oi, but ye do. I am ye problem. As I said, me fee is reasonable, but if ye want to negotiate it, I can do that, too. I am a respectable businesswoman, I am, so I do charge a fee for negotiating the fee. Do ye want to discuss it here in the hallway or should I come in?"

Miss Copley crossed her arms across her chest as she

leaned against the door jamb. "I am happy to discuss it right here."

"Bold as brass, ye are," Verity said, opening her eyes wide in admiration. "Most people would consider murder to be a private matter. But not ye. I like that."

Miss Copley let out a lighthearted chuckle. "Murder? I have no idea what you are talking about. I believe you have the wrong address."

The laugh sounded sincere, which impressed Verity. Even if the actress had perfected the skill of producing various emotions on demand, affecting amusement in the face of a genuine threat was an entirely different beast. "I must warn ye, Miss Fitch, I also charge an argument fee."

"Well, I charge an annoyance fee," Miss Copley said with the same cheerful expression, seemingly untroubled by the fact that Mrs. Buglehorn knew her name. That was most likely because the rapacious landlady in fact did not know her name. "And it rises exponentially the more annoyed I get."

Verity volunteered to deduct Miss Fitch's surcharge from total monies due. "Before I show ye my evidence, I jest want to confirm yer comfortable chatting about it in the hallway."

Although Miss Copley's demeanor did not alter at the mention of proof, she opened the door wide and gestured for her caller to enter. "Well, this will certainly be entertaining. Do come in. I don't want to give the neighbors a free show."

The first thing Verity noticed when she entered the room was the luggage lined up neatly against the wall opposite the door. It was not much: a valise and a portmanteau. "I got here just in time," she observed in Mrs. Buglehorn's most querulous tone. "Traveling, I see. I hope yer going somewhere exciting."

"Not especially," Miss Copley replied as she strode to the fireplace and lifted a pot of tea off the grate. "Just the seaside

—for the summer, I think. Would you like something to drink? I do my best problem solving over a spot of tea."

Obviously, no, Verity would not be partaking in any refreshment in the home of a killer. But she agreed as she surveyed the furniture for anything that could be used as a weapon and noted the surfaces were clean. Almost everything had been packed up.

Miss Copley, placing the pot on a tray, apologized for not being able to offer her sugar. "But it is just as well, as I would have to charge you a sweetener fee and you would have wound up owing me more money than you think I owe you. Now please have a seat and tell me about this evidence you seem to think you have."

Her ability to maintain a sanguine appearance impressed Verity, who attributed it partly to her training as a thespian, partly to her assumption that she could buy Mrs. Buglehorn's silence. Anyone with even a passing familiarity with the land-lady would rightly conclude she was a practical woman at heart. Rather than embroil herself with the authorities, she would take whatever amount she could get from the bargain and consider it well earned.

Even so, Verity approached the table with a cautious eye. Never the reckless wretch Delphine frequently thought her, she had a dagger in her bootie and another in the slit under the apron on the left side. She knew Miss Copley could like-wise be armed—tending to the tea would certainly allow her the opportunity to slip something into a pocket—but she was confident her years of training would give her the advantage should the actress decide to attack.

Nothing about the table struck her as concerning. It was old and worn, its unadorned wood scarred from years of abuse, and Verity, considering the two chairs available to her, chose the one nearer the wall. It seemed extremely unlikely that someone would sneak up behind her with a garrote, but there was no harm in making sure. The chair creaked as she sat down, the seat tilting backward as it accommodated her weight.

Miss Copley added a second cup to the tray and lifted the salver. As she crossed the room she owned herself fascinated by how Mrs. Buglehorn could have evidence of something that never happened. "I am all ears," she said, lowering into the chair as she placed the tea on the table, which tipped toward her with such ferocity the cups clattered, then away from her as she grasped the edge, raised her arms, and heaved the wildly uneven table toward Verity.

It landed with a hard thump against her chest, knocking the air out of her lungs and pinning her to the seat as the boiling-hot liquid ran off the edge, scalding first her arm, then leg. She lurched forward with her shoulders, dislodging the heavy weight as she stretched her arm down to grasp her knife, which her fingers just skimmed as the table wobbled back toward her. Then her head jerked back, her neck wrenching painfully as Miss Copley yanked her hair, and Verity lurched her body to the right. The chair toppled over, slamming into her back before rolling off, the burn on her arm throbbing as it thwacked against the floor. Gritting her teeth at the pain, she pawed frantically at the folds of the apron, desperate to find her knife, when suddenly a new agony tore through her.

Not a burn.

Worse than a burn.

In her shoulder.

She smelled the blood before she felt it trickling down her arm.

A stab wound in her shoulder.

It hurt like bloody hell.

"I can do this all day," Miss Copley said, a silver dagger held lightly in her grasp, its point red with blood. Her tone was calm, her expression composed, and Verity readily believed it. "There are dozens of places I can cut you that will hurt terribly but won't kill you. But I would much rather not, Mrs. Buglehorn, because I was on my way out and that would just delay my departure. If you will agree to stop fighting, I will agree to stop stabbing you. Does that sound reasonable?"

Verity nodded.

Struggling further would get her nowhere, not with Miss Copley wielding a knife and her own defenses hindered by pain. The best way forward was to agree to a cessation in hostilities and use the interruption to figure out another tactic. She thought it was safe to take the time because her attacker had voiced a reluctance to kill her.

The words could have just been for show, Verity acknowledged, as she shifted positions, drawing her legs up, but she could not imagine why Miss Copley would make the effort. If she wanted to stab her to death like she had Smith, then she would just stab her to death.

Or had she taunted him with games first?

Her shoulder screamed in protest as she tilted into a sitting position, then she herself shrieked when Miss Copley tugged her arm to bring her to her feet. The cry—so shrill she sounded more like Mrs. Buglehorn than Mrs. Buglehorn herself—echoed through the room, and Verity wondered if the neighbors could hear.

Was that how she got out of this predicament? Rescued by the curmudgeon next door who wanted them to keep down the noise?

If that was the best she could do, she would accept it gratefully.

She was happy to yell for her life if that was what it took.

Her head swimming in pain, she did not realize Miss Copley was tying her to the chair until the actress explained why she was tying her to the chair.

"I have no wish you to harm you further," she murmured as she concentrated on knotting the twine around Verity's ankles. "We are both women of the world doing the best we can with what little we have. I do not begrudge your trying to gouge me. I *thought* you had seen me sneak back into the house after I delivered the tablecloth, but when you didn't call after me or try to stop me, I decided I only imagined it because I was so nervous. You must know I did not *want* to harm the old man. I just wanted to frighten him so he would leave us alone, but he kept arguing with me, insisting I did not understand what was at stake. *He* did not understand. I am an actress whose best roles are behind her. I need the bonus that was promised to me. All of that is to say it would have been much better for everyone if you had not followed me home. But here we are!"

Verity heard these words but as if at a remove, like a rumble of thunder in the distance. It was an effect of the pain, she thought, its intensity dulling everything but its own pulsing ache—but it was also the softness of Miss Copley's voice. It was almost as though she were talking to herself.

Leaning back on her heels, the actress examined her handiwork. Satisfied, she turned her attention to binding Verity's arms, tugging them behind the back of the chair to secure. Continuing in the same low tone, she told Verity she was doing her a favor. "I know you can't appreciate it yet, but you will when you return to your home in a day or two. Clerkenwell will be in shambles tonight."

Verity, hearing this comment through the anguished haze, repeated the statement in her head several times before the words themselves registered as a coherent thought.

Having done that, however, they failed to make sense.

Clerkenwell in shambles?

Something more was going on, Verity thought, determined to overcome the pain.

It is just physical. Just flesh and blood, skin and bone. Nothing compared to shivering in bed in a gloomy old convent wishing someone loved you.

"What—" Verity began, then immediately stopped when she realized the register was too low for Mrs. Buglehorn. She tried again. "What do ye mean?"

Miss Copley, wrapping the twine around Verity's wrists, explained that there would be a riot that night. "A lot of people will get hurt. That's why you're better off here."

Verity shook her head, confused. "I don't understand."

"Crowley's speech tonight? You've seen the handbills, I'm sure. They're everywhere," the actress replied.

"But it's a peaceful event. It's to collect signatures on petitions to be submitted to the prince regent. Crowley is just going to be talking about the reform movement and why the Burnley Blanketeers need support," Verity said, confident that what she said was true. The Persuader would never have agreed to participate if there was the possibility of violence. Then, fearing she sounded too informed for a rapacious landlady who soaked her boarders, she added, "That's what it says on the handbills."

"Maybe so," Miss Copley agreed mildly, "but that's not what the home secretary thinks. He expects the men to be armed, and maybe they will be. It is impossible to know."

Verity felt her entire body grow cold as understanding slashed through her, and she looked again at the luggage against the wall.

A valise and a portmanteau.

Fitch was already gone.

He had lied to Kingsley about the event and then disappeared.

But why would he do such a thing? What did he stand to gain by convincing the Home Office that another insurrection was about to take place?

It proved his usefulness, she thought. Kingsley was paying him a regular salary to report on the Yarwellian Society, and Fitch probably wanted him to feel as though he was getting a good return on his investment. If he reported that nothing more noteworthy was in the offing than a peaceful meeting, then his employer might lose interest.

Repellent to the core, it was certainly one way to ensure an income.

But *was* he trying to ensure an income?

He was already gone, she reminded herself, and the actress he hired to play his sister was on her way out the door.

They were at the end of a scheme, not in the middle.

Crowley's speech was the final scene.

And Miss Copley was determined to get her bonus. She had killed to ensure it.

It was about money, and yet Verity still could not fathom where the riches would come from.

Find the pot of gold, Verity told herself, and work backward from there.

The only viable prospect she could identify was the contributions the society had collected for the Blanketeers. Given the level of enthusiasm for the march she had seen in various taverns and barrooms across London, she imagined the sum was rather significant by now. If the members of the organization were either arrested as insurrectionists or deemed fugitives, then all those lovely donations would be forfeit to the government.

But not if nobody could find them.

And of course they would not because Fitch will have absconded with the funds before the Home Office even had a chance to look for it.

This whole thing was about money, Verity thought in disgust. All the scheming and the double-dealing and the fawning and the fake-sister-hiring boiled down to just another greedy man stuffing his pockets with as many coins as possible. He did not care whom he hurt in the satiation of his voracity. Sending armed troops into a peaceful crowd to break up what they believed was an insurgency would end with dozens of people dead.

It would be a massacre.

"There you go," Miss Copley said, pulling the knot. "Now you just sit tight and wait for someone to come by. It will most likely be the landlord seeking his last week's rent. I expect he will be cross about the mess, and you may tell him for me that the table is a menace. It is constantly spilling my tea. If you are worried about the gash in your shoulder, don't be. It's actually quite shallow and the loss of blood will be minimal. Just make sure not to get an infection. Those can be the very devil."

Verity remained silent. She could not conceive what an appropriate reply would be in the situation and furthermore had no interest in delaying the actress's departure. She could not free herself from the restraints and stop the Home Office from making an egregious mistake until she was gone.

Miss Copley, rising to her feet, surveyed the room with a thoughtful look and nodded at intervals as though running through a list of items in her mind. "Yes, yes, I have everything," she said as she picked up her luggage. The two pieces were heavier than she would have liked, and she regretted that she could not summon someone to assist her. "Your unexpected arrival has thrown my whole leave-taking off. I was going to enjoy a cup of tea before I began my journey, then seek help with my portmanteau."

Smothering the snide response that rose to her lips, Verity watched as the other woman heaved the two cases across the floor. Her progress was slow, and arriving at the door, she slid the handles of the valise up her right arm to the bend of the elbow. With her free hand, she opened the latch and pushed the portmanteau into the hallway. She grunted, her face red with exertion, and Verity hid a smile as she imagined the actress attempting the three flights of stairs.

It was a long way to the street.

Miss Copley, either distracted by the challenge before her or genuinely indifferent to the ordeal behind her, offered no final word. She shut the door without even a parting glance. She might as well have been quitting an empty room.

Verity waited to hear the click of the lock, then got to work.

Friday, June 5
    4:18 p.m.

Although Miss Copley's training as a thespian had equipped her with several skills that would aid her in her pursuit of a life of crime, the ability to effectively secure a prisoner with ropes was not among them. While binding Verity's wrist, she failed to make sure they were pressed against each other and did not think to wind the twine through the spokes of the chair's back. Consequently, there was enough slack in the restraints for Verity to free herself within ten minutes. It required another two to untie her ankles and a further three to dress her wound with strips from her apron. Miss Copley's assessment had been accurate in that the laceration was not so deep as to endanger her life, but it was long and jagged and continued to bleed. Her burns were mild by comparison, and the throbbing had begun to subside.

Fifteen minutes after her captor left the room, Verity followed her down the steps, mildly surprised not to stumble across her still grappling with her heavy luggage.

No doubt she had managed to get help in the end.

Verity hoped that was the case because it would make finding her easier if Fitch managed to evade capture or refused to provide her direction. Whomever Miss Copley hired was likely to live in the neighborhood. If necessary, Verity would return in the morning to start asking questions.

Now, however, she needed to get to Hardwicke's residence as swiftly as possible, for he would be able to use his connections to stop the massacre. He would inform Grint, who would either confront his fellow under-secretary over his terrible judgment in informants or go straight to Lord Sidmouth.

Verity knew she looked a fright—bloody dress, unruly hair, filthy apron, a bizarre stain the color of wine on her upper cheek that had smeared to her chin—and was not surprised when procuring a hack became its own small ordeal. In the end, she held up a crown, which was an outrageous fare for the short distance, and waited for its glinting brilliance to capture a driver's attention.

Arriving in Millman Street, she was reminded again of her wretched appearance when the footman gasped in dismay and insisted she had the wrong address. "The workhouse is on Pullman Street. Go down the road to Bitters Lane, turn left, then make the first right."

With a calm she was far from feeling, Verity announced that she was there to see Lord Colson. "Please inform him that Miss Gorman awaits his pleasure."

She expected to be rebuffed again, for the bandage had begun to leak and red droplets of blood trickled down her arm, but the footman stiffened in surprise and said, "*The* Miss Gorman?"

It was a strange reply, and she answered it with a slight hesitation. "Well, um, yes."

"I have orders to admit you whenever you call," he explained with a note of bewilderment he was unable to suppress, for he could not believe there was anything about this horrifying creature from the depths of the dirtiest rookery that would appeal to his elegant employer. "But my lord is not at home at the moment."

Having anticipated this very development, Verity was nevertheless unprepared for it and swore in frustration. Then she reined it in, for emotion would only muddle her thoughts. She needed information to devise a plan. If he was not to return shortly, then she would have to go fetch him. "When do you expect him?"

The footman stared at her blankly for several seconds, seemingly incapable of answering what was a fairly standard question from a caller. Finally, he said, "We do not expect him! That is, we expect him at any moment! He should have returned by now."

Verity bit back the snarl of irritation that rose in her throat and ordered herself to think clearly. Hardwicke's wandering off to who knew where was an asinine complication she could not handle right now, not with the minutes ticking away, and yet she forced herself to examine it coolly. From the servant's demeanor, she concluded it was not common for Hardwicke to disappear without a word, and the fact that he was sharing the information with a complete stranger, one who looked as though she had been regurgitated by a witch in an enchanted forest, indicated a high level of concern.

Alarmingly, he thought Miss Gorman could help.

That was not a very auspicious sign.

Determined to be logical, she asked when his lordship had been expected to return.

"Around four in the afternoon, yesterday," he replied.

Damn, she thought again. "He has been missing for more than a day?"

"It is unprecedented," the footman claimed. "Lord Colson

frequently changes his plans but always sends word. We, the staff, have begun to grow concerned. We are not sure what, if anything, to do. I could alert his father, but it seems cruel to needlessly worry him."

"But you are happy to needlessly worry me?" she muttered under her breath, her anxiety ticking up as she tried to fathom what his disappearance could mean. She started with the most obvious explanation: It was related to the Society of Yarwellian Philosophers. If he had been surveilling Fitch, then perhaps the latter discovered his interest and disposed of Hardwicke before he could thwart his plan to steal the Blanketeers' funds.

It was a terrifying notion in light of Mr. Smith's fate, but Hardwicke was not an elderly tradesman from the north—he was the Marquess of Ware's second son. If being a member of the aristocracy served any purpose at all, it was allowing one to be spared the sordid death of an unemployed Yorkshire weaver.

"Well, there is a standing order to admit you, and there is not one to admit his father," the footman said, replying to her query, which had been clearly rhetorical.

Accepting the truth of this, Verity felt her shoulders bend as if bearing a physical weight and she promised to look into it. "I will send word as soon as I know something."

The footman exhaled with relief and thanked her fervently, which did little to increase her confidence that she could halt a massacre, apprehend a villain, and rescue a government agent within the next three hours. The situation was dire indeed when one was the last best hope of a servant.

Dashing back to the road, she flagged down another hack and was on the verge of telling the driver to take her to the Home Office when he snapped, "Watch it with that blood. I see any of it on my cab, I am charging ye three times the fare."

Her appearance!

She would not get through the front door looking like an inmate at Bedlam.

Returning to Bethel Street to change was a bloody stupid waste of time, and yet she knew it was more efficient than going directly to Grint's office only to be turned away.

And that was the entirety of her plan: alert Grint.

He was the former head of England's wartime spy network, Hardwicke's boss, a powerful official in the government, and the loose screw who knew Fitch was up to something havey-cavey but did not have the gumption to openly question it.

Surely, she could leave the whole mess in his capable hands.

Except, of course, *she* could not, for who was she?

Hardwicke had sworn he had made no mention of her or any of her identities to Grint, so presenting herself as Miss Gorman would not have any magical effect. She could not introduce herself as Robert Lark because the situation was far too sensitive to place in the hands of a reporter. Grint would snap shut like a clam. Furthermore, she did not want to use any name that could possibly be traced back to her.

Sending Freddie in her stead would produce the same problems, and even if it did not, she could not bring herself to trust someone else to successfully convey the information. Convincing Grint might be as simple as stating a few salient facts or it might require the marshaling of a hundred little details.

As the hack stopped in front of her house, Verity realized she was looking at the question from the wrong angle. The best person to persuade Grint was someone who was associated with Hardwicke, not her. Obviously, his family members were removed from contention. She did not have either the gall or the wardrobe to impersonate a marquess. She did have several items suitable for a footman, however.

That would do, yes, she thought, recalling the servant's demeanor. He knew just enough about his employer's activities to be concerned.

Entering the house at a dead run, she called for Delphine at the top of her lungs, then darted upstairs to change. She was removing the strip of cloth from her wound when Lucy came in to say that Miss Drayton was visiting the lending library. She halted midsentence and gasped when she saw the gash.

"Good heavens, miss, that must hurt!" she said, scurrying over to take the dirty rag from her mistress's grasp. "I don't even want to know how you did this. It looks like someone cut you on purpose."

"That is good, Lucy," Verity said, torn between impatience and gratitude, "because I don't want to tell you. But there are terrible things afoot and something awful will happen if I don't warn the right people, and to do that I need to change into a footman's livery as quickly as possible. I would appreciate your help."

Accustomed to the strange goings-on of a household that pretended to have one more inhabitant than it actually did, Lucy was nevertheless taken aback by the request—not by its substance but its delivery. There was something like anxiety in Miss Lark's voice, which the maid had never heard before.

"I'll get the clothes," Lucy said as she strode toward the dressing room. "You finish cleaning and dressing the wound. And don't forget to wash that ... that ... clown mark off your face."

Verity thanked her as she dipped a clean cloth into the basin and dabbed gently at the incision, which still stung with surprising ferocity. Gritting her teeth, she wrapped the cut with a fresh strip and turned her attention to the wine-colored stain, which was considerably easier to remove than to affix.

Fifteen minutes later, she was dashing again, this time from the room as Lucy gathered the discarded pile of bloody clothes for scrubbing. As she was bounding down the stairs, a knock sounded on the door and since there was no time to waste with the formalities—that was, summoning Lucy to answer it—she pulled the door open herself, fully prepared to tell whomever it was to call again tomorrow.

The mistress of the house is too busy staving off a massacre to see you now.

But standing there was her brother.

Chapter Fifteen

Friday, *June 5*
5:07 p.m.

It was a shock.

The Duke of Kesgrave on her doorstep was an unfathomable sight, a wild fantasy and a dark nightmare, and all she could think was: Not now, you bloody idiot!

She could not indulge a dramatic family reunion now.

British army troops were about to slaughter innocent men and women.

Get out of my way!

But even as she opened her mouth to announce that the mistress was not at home, she realized he was the solution—to saving Hardwicke, to sparing lives.

The Duke of Kesgrave was a man of influence and power. He knew Lord Sidmouth personally, and his consequence was enough to cow low-level functionaries. Men like Kingsley and Grint would respond without pause to his command.

Turning him away when he could make all the difference was madness.

Forthrightly, she said, "I am Verity Lark, your grace, and I am wearing these clothes because I am on the way to the Home Office to try to persuade Under-Secretary Grint to stop a terrible tragedy from unfolding in the next two hours. I did not expect him to listen to a woman and so assumed this disguise. Your timing is extraordinary and I would be grateful if you would accompany me to Whitehall to clear the way. I believe you will be able to secure an audience more quickly and easily than I."

To say that Verity's heart was racing would be to vastly understate the case. It was pounding, thundering, exploding into a million little pieces only to pull itself together and wrench apart again.

It was so very painful.

She revealed none of it.

A lifetime of controlling her emotions, of overcoming or ignoring her fear, allowed her to wait for his response with an expression of mild interest. She expected him to refuse and braced for it. There she was, a perfect stranger dressed in an absurd costume making outlandish claims.

It did not really matter, she told herself. The only thing the request cost her was a few dozen seconds, perhaps a full minute. His denial would be swift and his contempt absolute, and whatever curiosity or confusion had drawn him to her doorstep would be forgotten in his eagerness to leave it.

The irony of the situation did not escape her. Decades of elaborate scheming and Byzantine plots, and the most effective evasion she had ever employed was the unvarnished truth.

"All right," he said. "We will take my gig."

The pain in her chest increased at his ready agreement.

Dumbfounded, she nodded stiffly and followed him to the

carriage. It was an elegant vehicle, with red-painted molding and cream-colored wool upholstery, and as soon as the horse drew them into the road, she noticed how well sprung it was.

Although Bethel was ordinarily a quiet road, there were several other carriages in the street, and Verity was grateful for the traffic because it gave her something to focus on other than the duke. He was, of course, a skilled driver, light in the grip but firmly in command, and she knew Freddie would envy the sleek Cleveland Bay pulling the carriage. It was far more evenly proportioned than the Yorkshire trotter he had purchased last year.

The rhythmic clomping of the horse's hooves on the cobbles helped calm her nerves, and she listened to it for several minutes before growing aware of the daunting silence. The Duke of Kesgrave had agreed to help based on a very slight understanding of the mission and deserved a more fulsome explanation.

Without preamble, she launched into one.

"A man named Arnold Fitch has been working with Under-Secretary Kingsley in the Home Office to inform on the Society of Yarwellian Philosophers, a once-secret reform organization that is holding a mass meeting in St. Dunston's field in less than two hours. You may have heard of it. Christopher Crowley, the famous orator known as the Persuader, is to speak. It is a peaceful event, but Fitch told Kingsley the men will be armed. Kingsley is sending in troops to put down the insurgency. Fitch lied about it so that he could steal the funds raised by the society in support of a march to London from Burnley. Kinsley's fellow under-secretary, Daniel Grint, found Fitch untrustworthy, so he hired Colson Hardwicke—the Marquess of Ware's son—to keep an eye on Fitch, who went by the name Tyrone Thorpe when he informed on the group that started the Christmas Uprising. I would have given this information to Hardwicke to pass on to Grint, but he has disappeared, which is also concerning."

Hearing herself run through the salient details of the situation, Verity felt an almost irresistible desire to laugh. The story had all the plausibility of a farce, and she half expected him to draw the horse to a stop in the middle of the street and order her from the conveyance.

False informers!

Stolen funds!

Missing lords!

Surely, it was all nonsensical faffle to mock his investigative tendencies.

She imagined describing the scene to Delphine and Freddie and how entertained they would be by the absurdity of it: Verity Lark in a handsome gig with her duke half-brother racing to the Home Office to avert tragedy.

It was a shame Mr. Twaddle-Thum could not repeat a word of it.

Not a single, solitary word.

The thought of her alter ego increased the pressure in her chest, which her amusement had eased to some extent. It was a salutatory reminder of all that stood between them as well as a rebuke, for there was no "between them" of which to be reminded. Despite an accident of birth, they were nothing to each other.

"Who are you?" the duke asked, his tone matter-of-fact as he glanced at her before returning his eyes to the road.

"Verity Lark," she replied simply, giving an answer that she knew was disingenuous. He was not asking for her name but her identity.

"You look just like my mother," he said.

Now her heart squeezed, tightening like a fist, because nobody had ever said those words to her. No comparison had ever been made between her and La Reina, and at once it pleased her to know she bore a connection to the past and annoyed her to realize she did not exist outside of history. Having constructed herself one tale at a time, she tended to think of herself as a sui generis creation.

As the duke pulled the gig abreast of a hack with an eye toward passing it, she contemplated how much she wanted to tell him. She felt keenly the futility of the question, for he already knew everything pertinent. From that one fleeting glance at Fortescue's, he had intuited enough to find her at Bethel Street. It had taken scarcely seventy-two hours.

And now she was sitting beside him in a well-sprung carriage as he maneuvered his horse around a hackney pony.

Despite the unsetting sense of inevitability about their meeting, she knew it was just the result of his extraordinary timing. Arriving at Bethel Street on any other day—or even any other hour of *that* day—he would have found Miss Lark permanently removed to the country with no forwarding address. He would never have seen her again.

Given the speed with which they were approaching the Home Office, she could not regret the decision to make herself known and ask for his help. Colson Hardwicke's life alone was worth any number of painful exchanges with her mother's legitimate offspring.

Thinking on it, she could not even fathom what it mattered if he knew she existed. They were not siblings in any meaningful sense. Their mother was the most successful courtesan of her age with a string of lovers that went back more than a decade and a half. Surely, Verity's existence had been a conceptual reality if not an actual fact.

Or did he truly never wonder?

Considering how easily she was deposited on the steps of Fortescue's, she had always assumed there were others like her.

With all this in mind, she replied honestly. "I look like La Reina because she was my mother as well."

The duke received this confirmation impassively, tightening his grip on the right rein to lead the horse onto Spur Road, and remaining silent just long enough for Verity to think his curiosity was satisfied. Then he said, "Who is your father?"

A reasonable question, it nonetheless surprised Verity, who wondered if he feared the connection was even closer. Did he think his parents had simply tossed away a daughter whose existence in no way furthered their ambitions? Or did he suspect his wicked, recently deceased uncle of additional sins?

"I do not know," she said, which was the truth. If La Reina had told the matrons at Fortescue's his identity, they never shared it with her, and she had not bothered to discover it on her own. The fact was, she was simply uninterested in the man who had sired her, for he could never be as fascinating as her mother. He was just another wealthy, well-born gentleman who had used her for his pleasure in a long line of wealthy, well-born gentlemen. Verity could not imagine anything of distinction.

She kept these thoughts to herself, of course, because they fell outside the purview of the question. Furthermore, they were none of the Duke of Kesgrave's concern.

She did, however, add that she was born in June 1781. "A year before your father wooed La Reina away from the Marquess of Telford," she said.

Obviously, the use of *woo* was a wry taunt, for her mother —*their* mother—was enticed by only wealth and rank. The fifth Duke of Kesgrave could have had the wit of a used kitchen mop and La Reina still would have been charmed.

This information likewise drew no reaction, and Verity found herself annoyed by the studied blankness. Originally grateful for the gig, which allowed her to avoid looking at him directly, she now wished she could see his whole face. She was adept at reading expressions and knew she would be able to glean something from his visage. In one sense, it was no business of hers what he was thinking and feeling. His emotions were his own, and she respected that. But it would help in their dealings at the Home Office if she had some awareness of where she stood in his estimation.

"And your brother?" he asked. "Is she also his mother?"

Oh, dear, Robert, Verity thought, amazed to realize her fictional brother had momentarily slipped her mind. Now she truly regretted she could not look into his eyes, for she could not imagine his having no response to that revelation.

"I have no brother," she said plainly, determined to keep her reply brief and unadorned. But it sounded a little too derisive, as if she were toying with him by denying the obvious. "There are certain limitations imposed on a woman who would seek to set up her own establishment, and inventing a brother resolves many of those issues."

It was, she thought, a reasonable explanation.

If the duke agreed, it was impossible to tell as the gig's left wheel dropped into a deep hole in the road, causing the conveyance to sway. Verity held fast to the edge of the bench to stop herself from brushing shoulders with the duke. A moment later, the carriage, steady again, turned onto King Charles Street.

They were almost there—and with enough time to stop Kingsley from endangering the lives of hundreds. Whether it was too late to save Hardwicke remained to be seen.

The prospect of Hardwicke's death roiled her gut and she swallowed hard, hoping to quell the nausea. It was stupid to be worried about a man who had spent years spying on the French and had not only deduced her true identity but also found her location.

Clearly, he was more than capable of taking care of himself.

"The Robert Lark who wrote articles about Fortescue's Asylum for Pauper Children," the duke said. "Was that you or someone else at the newspaper?"

Of course he knew about the series exposing the Wraithe's corruption. Mrs. Chaffey had never been shy about discussing her venal predecessor. "I am Robert Lark," she said, adding that there were also restrictions imposed on women who sought to pursue careers in journalism.

This explanation warranted a curt nod, which was a curious thing in light of his previous lack of response, but before she could begin to puzzle what it meant, he drew the horse to a stop. They were there. Eagerly, she alighted from the carriage, physically restraining herself from running into the building at top speed. She was in the company of the Duke of Kesgrave, who did not run or trot or dash or dart. He moved at a dignified pace that came from knowing the world would wait for him.

He secured his horse, then gave several coins to a street urchin to keep an eye on his gig. Verity, who was unable to see how much money changed hands, knew from her informants' reports that he paid well. The boy, his fingers closing tight around the tip, nodded solemnly and promised to keep everything flat. "You won't be disappointed, sir."

The duke thanked him, which surprised Verity. She did not expect him to be either thoughtful or kind. Then he walked to the building in long, even strides, and Verity, jogging a little to catch up, noted that Grint's office was on the first floor.

"We will speak to Sidmouth," he said mildly but with a disconcerting confidence, as if he knew for certain that the home secretary was in the building and would agree to meet with him. He walked past the grand staircase and turned left.

The hallway ended in an airy rotunda, all light and marble, and on the far side was a door, which he knocked on briskly before opening.

A clerk standing at a bookshelf looked up as they entered the room, which was large and square, with a long table in the center. Its walls were painted pistache and two elaborate chandeliers hung from the ceiling. Taken aback by the interruption, he dropped the ledger he was holding and immediately apologized for the thump it made on the wood floor.

"Good day," the duke said, greeting the startled clerk. "Please tell Lord Sidmouth that Kesgrave is here to discuss the mass meeting that will be held later today in St. Dunston's field."

The clerk, who had been about to bend over to pick up the book, straightened abruptly, indicating a passing awareness if not a deep comprehension of these words. "Lord Sidmouth is not here."

But Kesgrave had noted his response as well, for it had hardly been subtle, and refused to believe that his lordship was not actively involved in coordinating the government's response to the perceived threat. "If he is not here in this room, I am nevertheless confident he is here in the building. Please tell me where I may find him."

Haltingly, the clerk stammered in a disjointed rush about authority and authorization, grappling to explain in the least offensive way he could that providing the information was outside his purview. His speech trailed off when Kesgrave began to cross the room, and he flinched when the duke, his lithe figure towering over his, bent close as if to issue a threat. All he did, however, was retrieve the ledger from the floor. Handing it to the nervous clerk, he said, "His location."

Verity, observing the maneuver, was struck by how subtly the duke displayed his power, using his stature to convey his importance, not words. He did not have to say anything. His regal bearing spoke volumes.

Responding to it now, the clerk spurted, "On the second floor, the northwest side of the building. He is meeting with Mr. Kingsley and General Jentleson."

Kesgrave thanked him coolly, glanced at Verity, and left the room.

Following him into the hallway, she decided the general's presence in the building was an auspicious sign. If he was in conference with the home secretary that meant they had yet to finalize their plan. The details were still being sorted out.

The duke faultlessly led them to Kingsley's office, demonstrating a daunting familiarity with the building that intrigued Verity, and barely paused to beg permission to enter. Like before, he rapped briskly on the door and then strolled in. Four men were convened around a table, their faces arranged in various expressions of bewilderment as they perceived the Duke of Kesgrave's graceful form striding into the room. Kingsley, his dark brows pulled tight, was already known to Verity, and Sidmouth was immediately recognizable by his tufts of gray hair and aquiline nose. The third gentleman was readily identified as the general by his uniform, leaving only the status of the last man unknown.

Kingsley darted to his feet and protested the intrusion. "This is a private meeting dealing with highly sensitive information, sir. I must ask you to leave."

At the same time, Sidmouth announced that he was delighted to see his grace, but the timing was less than ideal. "As Kingsley mentioned, we are discussing quite a delicate matter that is not suitable for general consumption. May we resume this discussion at a later date? I am at your disposal."

Recognizing Kesgrave belatedly, Kingsley sketched a bow, professed himself delighted to see the duke again, and announced that he was available to meet at any other time, as he and Jentleson had pressing business to discuss. "My clerk will be happy to schedule an appointment at your convenience. I look forward to discovering how I may be of service."

"Gentlemen, I am aware of the topic under discussion," Kesgrave said bluntly, which caused Kingsley to smile with wry amusement at the overstepping duke. "And I am here to inform you that the intelligence you have been given by Fitch is inaccurate and designed to lead you into the very mistake you are planning on making."

Kingsley's expression turned stormy and he immediately scorned this statement by contemptuously calling it ignorant drivel. Then he coughed self-consciously and rushed to soften his stance by insisting that what he meant to say was that his grace's understanding could not be complete, as he was unaware of several unassailable facts. "Mr. Fitch's bona fides are impeccable, and I recruited him myself. If you have any reason to doubt his commitment to the cause of peace, that is merely a testament to how well he has played his part as an agitator. You may take my word for it when I say the British government is fortunate to have a patriot like him on our side."

Kesgrave ignored the under-secretary's ardent defense of his own poor judgment and looked at the man standing behind the general's right shoulder. Identifying him as the lowest ranking person in the room, he asked him to please invite Mr. Grint to join the conversation.

General Jentleson watched his aide rush out of the room to do the duke's bidding with an expression of outrage mixed with annoyance. "I say, your grace, this is highly irregular. I do not doubt that you believe you are helping the situation. Like everyone else in London, I have read about your recent exploits with your wife and know you have helped apprehend several murderers of late. You are to be commended for your expertise, and I for one appreciate your service. But those are trifling domestic affairs and we are speaking now of matters of the state. The security of England is at stake, which is far too important to leave in the hands of an enthusiastic dilettante. I advise you to depart before you embarrass yourself further."

It was a withering insult, belittling and dismissive, with its use of *trifling* and the employment of *wife,* as if the duke were being bear-led up a hill and thought he was traversing a mountain. Verity would not have blamed him for altering his manner, making it even just the slightest bit more conciliatory. He was there, after all, on the word of a stranger—one who claimed kinship in the most shocking way and dressed like a footman and told a wildly fantastical tale about deception and betrayal.

That he believed her at all was baffling; that he agreed to help was an act of madness beyond comprehension. And now he was surrounded by men he knew, peers who shared his exalted position in society. Their derision should be anathema to him, and yet he did not care about it at all.

He was that certain she was right.

Mortified on the duke's behalf, Kingsley looked down while Sidmouth praised his eagerness to assist his government. "It is a laudable impulse."

"If his grace wants to try his hand at governmental affairs, perhaps he should take up his seat in the House of Lords," General Jentleson suggested helpfully.

Oh, dear, Verity thought. Condescension was worse than scorn.

His ego seemingly inured to these attempts to deflate it, Kesgrave again explained that Kingsley had been misled by his informant Fitch, who had gone by the name Thorpe when spying on the leaders of the Christmas Uprising.

Now the under-secretary looked at him sharply. "How do you know that?"

"That information came to me courtesy of Mr. James, who is Colson Hardwicke's footman," the duke explained, gesturing toward Verity.

A voice in the doorway exclaimed, "Hardwicke!"

Verity turned to see Grint, his prominent chin raised, bound into the room with an agitated glare. "Is he here? We had a meeting earlier this afternoon, but he did not show up or send a note, which is very unlike him. I sent a message to his residence and got an unhelpful response saying he did not come home last night. The lack of communication is highly unusual for him, especially when he is on assignment. You there"—he pointed at Verity—"what do you know? Tell me at once!"

But Kingsley stepped forward, scowling fiercely, his dislike of his colleague plainly etched on his face. "What do you mean 'on assignment'? I do not understand why you have been summoned, Grint. Gathering information on the Yarwellians was my operation. It has nothing to do with you or the Marquess of Ware's wastrel son. Good God, he is worse than a dilettante duke, whose motives are at least good," he said hotly, then bowed stiffly to Kesgrave when he realized his anger had led him into indiscretion. "I am sorry, your grace, for speaking so plainly. Your concern for your fellow citizens is admirable and proves you are a man of conscience."

The duke's expression remained impassive through both the insult and the accolades, and whatever reply he might have made was forestalled by Grint offering an apology to Lord Sidmouth for conducting a sub-operation to supplement his fellow under-secretary's efforts without first seeking his permission.

Further incensed by these remarks, Kingsley cried, "*His*

permission! It was my operation you tried to undermine, and look at the calamity you have created. There is a *footman* in my office." Now he apologized to the home secretary for the outrageous scene to which he was being subjected. "I understand now that Mr. Grint saw an opportunity to outflank me, and I should have been more wary of an attempt. This is my fault. I take full responsibility."

To his credit, Grint did not respond to this provocation at all, turning instead to Verity and asking what she knew about Hardwicke's disappearance.

Kingsley sputtered in protest and said, "I cannot believe we are going to stand here listening to a footman talk about things he could barely understand when a revolution is about to begin on our doorstep!"

Jentleson, concurring strongly, added that he had an obligation to act. "If the intelligence I have been given is accurate, then the Yarwellians intend to use this mass meeting as the first step in a full-scale rebellion. They plan to seize the Tower of London and conduct their insurgency from the stronghold. I have two hundred men standing by to quell it, as is my duty, as well as another dozen to seize control of the organization's assets to ensure it can never threaten the peace and prosperity of our great nation ever again. I do this because I have sworn to prevent violence, not embolden it by allowing it to spread."

The plot described by the general sounded so ridiculous Verity wanted to scream, for she could not believe a military man who had fought on the Continent could swallow such swill.

Nevertheless, she kept her tone smooth and calm as she replied, "Then you will be relieved to know, General Jentleson, that the best way to achieve your goal is to do nothing. The information Fitch neé Thorpe gave Lord Kingsley is wrong. The mass meeting of the Society of Yarwellian

Philosophers is a peaceful event. I swear it to you. They are only collecting signatures on their petition, which they plan to present to the regent directly. That is all. Mr. Crowley will speak, they will collect signatures, and the crowd will disperse. It is not an insurrection. None of the men will be armed. But if you send in troops, people will die, and Fitch does not care. He wants you to arrest the leaders of the organization so that he can take the funds they have raised in support of their cause. The Home Office would not know the difference, and none of the members would be in a position to complain. It is a significant amount of money and worth the effort. I swear this is the truth."

Sidmouth, looking from Verity to Grint, said, "This is what Hardwicke discovered?"

Grint hesitated because much of the information in her long speech was new, and she jumped in to say, "Yes! Hardwicke uncovered all of it. And now he is missing. And you must not send the army into St. Dunston's field. It will just end in needless death."

"I cannot believe you are entertaining this folderol," Kingsley seethed. "Fitch is a patriot. You know what he did for us at the ironworks, my lord. If not for his warning, the Christmas Uprising might have turned into a rebellion that consumed the north. We would be in the middle of a civil war right now without his information. You want to save lives? Then put down this insurrection before it starts. Do not allow the spark that will ignite the flame. Regardless of the accuracy of Fitch's information—and I do not for a moment believe he led us astray for reasons I have already explained—the fact of the matter is you do not want the reform movement to gain momentum. Crowley is a persuasive speaker. He will win hundreds to their cause. End the meeting before the reformers grow more powerful. If anyone dares question your decision, you can say with all honesty that you had credible intelligence that it was an armed rebellion."

Repulsed by Kingsley's practical approach and utter lack of morality, Verity glowered at the under-secretary with avid dislike. Grint, equally horrified, said that his proposal was unsupportable for any man of decency and honor to consider.

Sidmouth, however, seemed somewhat swayed by the argument, as he had in general taken a repressive stance on the reform movement. He supported the Frame-Breaking Act, oversaw the execution of fourteen Luddites on a single day, and argued in favor of suspending the writ of habeas corpus. A harsh response now to a threat that could not be disproven would bring him one step closer to the total repression he sought.

Perhaps noting his inclination as well, Kesgrave observed that assuming the editor of the *Morning Chronicle* would not learn the truth about Fitch's information was naïve.

Doubtful, the home secretary wondered how Perry would find out, and the duke replied with a cool stare. Bland as it was, it conveyed a complete thought, and Sidmouth blanched as he realized he had been driven into a corner. The Duke of Kesgrave could not be bullied into silence with threats of prosecution the way a lowly footman could be.

Angrily, Sidmouth turned to Verity and snapped, "Proof! I need proof! I cannot act on the word of a footman alone."

Struck by his fury, Verity realized how poorly she had comprehended the situation. She had been so worried that these men would not believe a word she said that she never spared a thought for what would happen if they did. Kingsley, who had been quick to use intimidation in response to the imagined threat of Bertie Betts, might have resorted to violence. If he feared she would reveal the truth to anyone, she might have been struck unconscious and dragged to the hull of the first convict ship departing for New South Wales.

"Fitch has vacated his rooms," Verity replied, aware of its thinness as evidence. But it was difficult to prove something that would not happen. "If you send someone to check, you will find that he left without alerting his landlord or paying his rent. Why would he give up his lodgings if he intended to remain in London and continue his work with the Home Office? He plans to leave tonight with the funds, which are, as I said before, sizable."

"I will go myself," Grint volunteered.

General Jentleson objected on the grounds that men changed lodgings all the time. It was nonsensical to consider it significant. Then he added with a hint of wonder, "The footman is in league with the Yarwellians! They sent him here to stop us from interceding. They knew Fitch was an informant. *That* is why his rooms are empty! They made him disappear so we would suspect his motives. The duke is merely his dupe."

Grint had little patience for this line of reasoning and said, "Is the fact that the rooms might be empty significant or not? You can't have it both ways."

The general, having no immediate reply to the query, looked to Sidmouth, who was examining Kesgrave with a thoughtful expression, trying, Verity supposed, to figure out what the duke would like him to do.

No, she amended, not *trying* to figure it out, because Kesgrave had made his position clear. What Sidmouth sought to discern was if there was a way he could satisfy the duke without actually ceding to his wishes. Was there a way to allow the army to suppress the meeting in St. Dunstan's field but not suffer adverse consequences for it in the press? She could not fathom one, but she applauded the home secretary for making the effort.

Kesgrave's recent descent into public spiritedness must be exasperating for his lordship, Verity thought wryly, capable, it seemed, in finding some sort of amusement in the wretched situation. Indolent nobles with little interest in matters of the state were infinitely preferable.

The home secretary, seeming to arrive at this same conclusion, sighed so softly Verity wondered if she imagined it and consented to Grint's plan. "Do hurry, please. And take Oscar with you."

"Yes, my lord," Grint said, dashing out of the room with the general's aide at his heels, and Verity watched him leave with a mixture of relief and dread. She was grateful that he would confirm her story, but she also wanted him to stay so they could discuss what was to be done about Hardwicke. The fact that he was missing had gotten lost in the larger discussion about Fitch's machinations, and she worried that time was running out for him as well. The two were related, she was convinced, which meant that apprehending the informant was the first step in finding Hardwicke.

And yet every moment they wasted wrangling and arguing about Fitch's intentions gave him more time to escape.

Except that was not true, Verity reminded herself. He was not going anywhere without the contents of the society's safe, and he would have to wait until the headquarters were empty.

She had at least until the start of the mass meeting to catch him.

It was not a huge amount of time, especially if she had to cool her heels in Whitehall waiting for Grint to return.

Kingsley was no happier with the development than she and grumbled that the consequences for the country would be dire indeed if the wastrel's footman turned out to be wrong—a theme that the general picked up on and amplified. Sidmouth reminded both men that they were just confirming the information, which, as Englishmen, it behooved them to do. But that did not stop them from preparing for the worst-case scenario and he exhorted the general to continue with his arrangements. He wanted the Fifth Battalion and the Royal Fusiliers ready to go.

Somewhat mollified, General Jentleson called for his aide, who had already left with Grint, which he had forgotten, and left the room.

"Well, then, nothing to do but wait," Sidmouth said confidently, gesturing to the chairs at the table. "We might as well make ourselves comfortable. Kingsley, please arrange with Petrie for a pot. Off you go, thank you!"

The look Kingsley darted at Verity as his employer waved him out of his own office to perform the menial service was lethal, and she returned his glare blankly. Then Sidmouth sat down, following his own directive, but the duke waited until she had taken a seat before availing himself of one.

His manners, Verity noted, were impeccable.

While they waited for Kingsley to return with the tea, Sidmouth inquired after the health of the duchess, and ascertaining that she was well, asked how Kesgrave's grandmother fared. The duke gave a polite answer, which the home secretary immediately dismissed, saying he knew the dowager too well to believe she had no complaints. The duke allowed that she might have a few grumbles about the quality of medical care she received from London's best physicians but generally enjoyed good health. Sidmouth owned himself delighted to hear it and asked if he had seen Hartlepool lately, for he had been too busy with his duties to condole him on his recent loss at Epsom. Kesgrave had indeed.

The pair continued on the topic of horseracing for several minutes—Sidmouth was looking forward to Ascot, although he feared the weather might adversely affect the track—then switched to estate management, the challenges of finding a reliable valet, and Archie "Whipster" Tierney's feud with Marshall "Dab Hand" Jones. The home secretary broke off when Kingsley entered with the tray, and Verity, who had heard nothing about the ongoing quarrel between the two members of the Four Horse Club, was disappointed not to learn how their standoff in Tunbridge Wells ended. She would have to Twaddle it out for herself.

Kingsley glared at her petulantly as he sat down at the table and protested yet again at Sidmouth taking the word of a footman over his own under-secretary's.

"On the contrary," Kesgrave said languidly. "He has taken mine."

Kingsley colored at the rebuke, falling silent as he drank his tea, and Sidmouth resumed his conversation with the duke, asking if he planned to attend Lady Diana's come-out ball in a few days. He was determined, Verity thought in amusement, to treat the situation like an afternoon at his club, and when Grint returned a half hour later to confirm her report, he received the news calmly, as if learning the cellar did not have his favorite port. He lamented the development and professed his optimism that the matter would resolve itself satisfactorily through other means.

Kingsley was outraged. He did not care that Grint had spoken to the irate landlord, who had been cheated not only out of the rent for the week but compensation for damages done to the furniture, which, he insisted, was in pristine condition when the tenants took ownership of the rooms.

Sidmouth told his underling to stand down. He would keep the troops at the ready in case violence erupted but would not allow the army to make a preemptive strike, as originally planned. Attacking peaceful people would not look good for either him or the office, and to ensure his orders were followed to the letter, he sent Grint to inform the general. Kingsley felt the demotion keenly and folded his arms across his chest with a surly grimace.

Verity watched Grint leave and contemplated her next step. Visit the society's headquarters to apprehend Fitch as he tried to steal the Blanketeers' funds—well, yes, obviously. She was convinced he was responsible for Hardwicke's disappearance, and the only way to locate him was to press the informant for answers. He was also her best chance of bringing Miss Copley to justice for murdering Smith. Fitch would know where she was to give her the promised bonus. And, of course, he must suffer a consequence of some sort for trying to spur a massacre to stuff his own pockets. There were statutes against inciting violence.

The question was: Should she remind the home secretary of Fitch's plan to abscond with the funds? It struck her as an appropriate courtesy in light of his cooperation, and yet it would hinder her ability to move swiftly. Kingsley would argue while Sidmouth equivocated and called back the general to seek his opinion.

It was already six forty.

If she left right now, she would get there a little after seven.

Embroiling the Home Office would all but guarantee failure.

Verity stepped forward to thank Sidmouth for treating her information with respect, then she directed a churlish scowl at Kingsley and bowed gracefully before the duke. Begging permission to leave, she walked out of the room at a sedate pace and widened her stride as she passed into the hallway. By the time she arrived at the staircase, she was running.

"You will get there faster if you permit me to drive you," a voice said.

Kesgrave, she thought, her shoulders tensing for a moment. It required no great feat of ratiocination to figure out her intentions. She had stated plainly several times her belief that Fitch had harmed Hardwicke, and that she would seek him out in the place where she knew he would be was the natural assumption. Anyone who gave the matter a modicum of thought would arrive at the exact same conclusion.

And yet there was something oddly unsettling about his ability to intuit her thoughts so clearly, as if there were a bond between them. They were siblings in the most pedantic way, to be sure, but in practical terms the happenstance of birth was meaningless. He was nothing to her; she was nothing to him. Verity could not fathom why he wanted to help.

It was perplexing.

It confused her.

It made her question everything she knew about the Duke of Kesgrave.

But she was also grateful for the offer and said yes.

Chapter Sixteen

F *riday, June 5*
  7:14 p.m.

Verity wondered if she should mention her flintlock.
Embarking on a mission with many unknown variables, she
had taken the prudent step of arming herself. The familiar
weight of the gun in her pocket was reassuring, and as she felt
it now, she thought perhaps she should disclose its presence
to the duke—not because she was such an indifferent
marksman that he had cause to worry about a stray bullet,
but so they could include it in their assessment of how to
capture and interrogate Fitch. It could do them the—

"By whom were you raised?" Kesgrave asked.

Her thoughts interrupted by the query, which was as
sudden as it was disconcerting, she cast a sidelong glance at
him and wondered what he expected her to say. La Reina's
success such that she had the funds to ensure her
daughter had a comfortable childhood with a family who

treated her kindly in exchange for a monthly stipend. That she did not think that was a worthy expense and instead chose to dump her on the doorstep of an orphan asylum and walk away revealed everything there was to know about the quality of Lorraine Price's maternal affection.

Determined to conceal the worst of it, for she wanted neither his pity nor his suspicion that she was trying to earn his pity, she said, "In a home for orphans."

To her ears, the word *home* sounded so much more pleasant than *asylum,* with its hint of coziness and warmth, and *orphan* carried none of the excessive despondency of *pauper children.* (It carried, of course, the regular amount of despondency, which could not be avoided given the facts of her childhood.)

"Did she visit you?" he asked.

"No," she said.

The answer was abrupt, but she had nothing to add. To assert that she had never met her mother would be ridiculous, for the woman had delivered her to Fortescue's herself. They had spent some time together, however insignificant or fleeting.

She could say, Verity supposed, that she never *knew* her mother, but that conveyed more sadness than she actually felt. At the end of the day, she was indifferent to the woman who gave birth to her. If she resented La Reina at all, it was for the way she carelessly left her in the care of a cruel headmistress, seemingly incapable of possessing just enough concern for her offspring to make sure the place was overseen by decent people.

And yet for all its brutality, Fortescue's forced her to cultivate valuable resources in order to survive. Verity Lark was a creature of adversity, and she had no idea who she would be if the road to maturity had been even a tiny bit less arduous.

So perhaps she owed her mother that.

Kesgrave, who had received this answer silently, directed his horse to turn left and said after some minutes of thought, "Was it Fortescue's? The home for orphans where you were raised—that is, Fortescue's Asylum for Pauper Children?"

Although Verity had decided with the duke's engagement to Miss Hyde-Clare that he was not quite the leaden-eyed dullard she had supposed him to be, she still had not credited him with a particular intelligence or astuteness. She had simply promoted him from dumb to dim. Now she realized he was actually quite clever. He had ably followed the trail from Robert Lark to Verity Lark to Lorraine Price's daughter.

"It was, yes," she said in a deliberately cool tone to discourage further conversation about her upbringing. The only reason he would care about the deprivations of her childhood was as a way to improve his understanding of La Reina. In that pursuit, she would not oblige. Despite the unsettling revelations of the day, she refused to be the candle by which he saw his mother more clearly.

To preempt the next question, Verity had every intention of changing the subject but she paused for the count of ten heartbeats first. She did not want to appear eager. Avidity implied discomfort.

"We should discuss how we will proceed when we arrive," she said firmly. "Given that Fitch tends to avoid conflict by working in secret and manipulating others into doing distasteful tasks for him, I think it is logical to assume he will not be armed. That said, I believe it is unwise to take anything for granted and am armed with a flintlock. You may be assured that I am skilled with a firearm and will not shoot you by mistake if I am forced to discharge it to apprehend Fitch."

Having mentioned her proficiency only to put his mind at ease, Verity wondered now if she had increased his alarm by raising the specter of an accidental shooting. It might not have occurred to him to worry about it.

But of course it did. She was a stranger and a female one at that. He would naturally assume she was deficient in a wide variety of ways.

The duke, however, responded with only a polite thank you.

Another inscrutable answer, she noted, at once grateful for his disinclination to chatter and frustrated by it. She truly knew nothing of his thoughts.

They turned into Mantle Street, and Verity, observing the dilapidation of the buildings, was struck by a problem she had never before encountered: Their conveyance was too lavish for their surroundings. Not only was the gig beautifully adorned, with its brightly painted dowels, but it was also in pristine condition, and spotting it among the rubble, Fitch would immediately realize something odd was afoot.

A block away from their destination, Verity told him to stop and pay a street urchin to guard his vehicle. "We will walk from here."

Kesgrave complied without comment.

The one-story house was empty when they arrived, the tailors and seamstresses having left at least an hour before, and Verity removed a slim device from her pocket to open the door. Faintly self-conscious under the watchful gaze of the Duke of Kesgrave, she undid the latch on the first try.

He must be flummoxed by the idea that anyone would need to acquire such a skill, she decided wryly, because doors opened for him as a matter of course. He had almost certainly never clambered through a window.

Finished, Verity pressed the door gently, widening the aperture slowly to avoid making the loud squeak she recalled from her last visit. Once they were both inside, she reengaged the lock so as not to raise Fitch's suspicions when he did arrive.

If he had not already arrived, she amended.

The secured door did not indicate anything meaningful because he could have locked it again himself or entered through another egress.

Since it was seven-fifteen, she thought it was likely that he was either already in the building or minutes away. As tempted as he might be to watch the meeting from a distance to make sure events unfolded according to his plan, he would recognize it as folly. Having set his diabolical scheme in motion, he would just have to trust others to carry it out faithfully. His only goal now was to retrieve the money and leave. Then, after events unfolded precisely as he prescribed, he would resume his spying activities for the Home Office in another part of England.

The corridor was dimly lit by the thin reed of light entering through the narrow window over the doorway, and Verity stepped cautiously to avoid creaking floorboards. Behind her, Kesgrave also moved soundlessly, and Verity was taken aback by the display. One simply did not expect a duke to excel at skulking. Leading them to the cellar door, she opened it slowly … slowly … and halted suddenly when she glimpsed a faint glow of illumination flickering around the bend in the spiral staircase.

Fitch was there!

Silently, she closed the door and whispered to the duke that someone was down there. "I can see light. It must be Fitch. We have the advantage. There are two of us, and he is not expecting company. But that does not mean he won't be prepared. I will immobilize him with the flintlock. Stay behind me so you do not get hurt," she added with a daunting amount of authority for such a hushed tone. "Do you understand?"

The duke said yes without quarreling or adding a caveat, which Verity also found startling. She would not expect a man of his standing to tamely submit to the commands of another —it was simply not in the nature of the aristocracy to concede any wisdom but its own—and the fact that he would do so was reassuring in light of their current circumstance. If he did not habitually assume he was correct about everything, then he would follow her directives without questioning their legitimacy. That meant she could trust him to handle himself without endangering either of them further.

Opening the door again, she gently dropped her weight onto the first step and withdrew the flintlock from her pocket. As she lowered to the second, she considered the scene she might find when she reached the last one. The staircase itself was in the bottom left corner of the room, only a foot or so from the table bearing the piles of recently printed handbills. Fitch, if he was still gathering the money from the safe, would most likely have his back toward her. That was simply a matter of probability, as the majority of the room was to the right. In that case, sneaking up behind him would be easy. If he was walking to the stairs with the money in his possession, then it would be harder to gain the advantage because she would have lost the element of surprise.

Even so, she had her weapon and the duke, who, she was certain, would not be a complete hindrance. Like most men of his rank, he had spent decades sparring with Gentleman Jackson and his ilk. All those hours of training had to have some beneficial effect, even if it was minor.

At the turn in the staircase, Verity paused and tilted her head around the curved stone pillar to make sure Fitch was not barreling toward them with his ill-gotten gains.

Indeed, he was not.

All she could see from her perspective was the table next to the printing press. A candle burned low.

She resumed her descent, stopping again when she reached the penultimate step and pressing her back against the right side of the staircase. From that vantage, she inched forward until she was at the edge of the wall. Gingerly, she shifted her left shoulder as she twisted her torso to see more and more of the room, which was gradually revealed to her, its inky depths cast in shadow as the light thrown by the lone candle diminished with distance. In the gloom she saw a figure, a tall man with straight shoulders standing in the middle of the floor, one arm raised before him.

Was that Fitch? she wondered.

It did not look like him. His frame was narrower without the padding he had assumed to change his shape and he seemed taller. Gauging scale in the darkness, however, was difficult, and the cellar had a low ceiling, which would alter his height.

But if it was not Fitch, who else could it possibly be?

Frustrated, she inched forward with increasing boldness. Since he was facing away from the stairs, there was little chance he would notice her.

Except there was a second figure!

As her eyes adjusted to the murkiness, she detected another man, his arm also raised, his hand clasped tightly.

Was he holding something?

Verity leaned further still, her eyes trained on the fist, and thought the object could be a knife. Utterly baffled, she looked again at the first figure, realizing now that he must be a member of the society who had stumbled upon Fitch in the middle of his theft.

Could it be Dircks or Oxenford?

No, the hair was too thick and—

She swallowed a gasp.

Hardwicke!

It was Hardwicke!

Astonished, she pulled back sharply, her injured shoulder smacking the rough stone. Smothering a cry of pain, she turned to the duke, who was one step above her, and spoke softly. "Hardwicke is here. I believe he is facing off against Fitch, who may have a knife. Hardwicke is closer, his back facing the stairs. Fitch is opposite him about four feet away. The room is dark. The candle on that table is the only light."

Before Kesgrave could respond, Fitch broke the silence. "This standoff is stupid. You are risking both our lives. The king's army is coming, I swear! Any moment now they will break down the door and swarm this building and destroy everything they find. And they will steal this money! They have already attacked the mass meeting. Troops fired into the crowd! It was the most horrible thing I've ever seen, and I am not ashamed to admit I ran away. But I came here to make sure the money is safe. It is what Anderson would want. The Yarwellians might be finished, but the dream of the Burnley Blanketeers will live on!"

Hardwicke replied that the British army would never attack a peaceful gathering, and Verity sought to make sense of their conversation. Fitch was playing a fervent Yarwellian and in that role was trying to convince Hardwicke, whom he still thought was just another member of the society, to let him take the money.

Had Hardwicke come across him in the middle of his theft?

If so, how had he known that was his plan and why had he not warned Grint of Fitch's lie, which endangered hundreds of lives?

It was all so confounding!

"But they don't *think* it was a peaceful gathering!" Fitch cried. "That damned clever spy who has been informing on us for weeks must have told his superiors that it was a rebellion. It is almost impossible to believe, I know, but it's the only thing that makes sense! Now do let me pass before the troops arrive to arrest us both. Please!"

"You're the spy. If the Home Office believes the mass meeting was an uprising, you told them," Hardwicke said with a hint of revelation in his voice, as if something that had long confused him finally made sense. "That was your plan all along. You're just stealing the money."

Clearly, Hardwicke had not known what Fitch intended.

So how was he there to thwart him?

Fitch remained in character, vehemently swearing that he had nothing to do with the Home Office. All he wanted was to secure the funds before the army arrived to steal it and make sure it was given to their allies in the north. His tone was urgent, increasingly frantic, and Verity realized he believed soldiers were in fact on their way. Convinced that his scheme had proceeded without a hitch, he thought troops would arrive momentarily and arrest him as a member of the society, thereby destroying his chance to abscond with the funds. As far as he knew, hundreds of pounds were at stake. "You must believe me! Here, the valise is so heavy. Why don't you help me carry the money out? You could relieve me of … I don't know … maybe one fifth of it?"

It was a mark of Fitch's desperation that he was willing to relinquish a full twenty percent of his bounty after the lengths he had gone to secure it. And to introduce his bribe with that tentative air, as if he was willing to go ever higher— he clearly had no idea to whom he was speaking. He genuinely believed Hardwicke was the man his reputation alleged him to be: the Marquess of Ware's dissolute son, whose crippling gaming debts threatened to crush him entirely. *That* Hardwicke would eagerly accept a bribe.

Alas, Fitch was dealing with *this* Hardwicke.

Grint's man.

Hardwicke's reply, however, further obfuscated the difference between perception and reality, as he countered with sixty percent, insisting a valise that heavy would require him to use two hands. "I would have to put down my weapon."

This proposal elicited a seemingly sincere chortle of amusement from Fitch. "You genuinely think I would just hand over sixty percent of the Blanketeers' money to a ne'er-do-well who has never done an honest day's work in his life? I'd sooner take my chances with that crowbar. I will give you a quarter. No more."

"In the spirit of cooperation, as we both believe in reform and improving conditions for our fellow man despite our varying levels of industriousness, I will accept fifty-nine percent," Hardwicke offered graciously.

The exchange revealed two new tidbits that Verity found interesting: Hardwicke was armed with a crowbar, and he was determined to negotiate in tiny increments. Fitch seemingly had the advantage with a knife, but his fighting skills were not honed enough to compensate for the long sweep of the steel shaft. He would have to get close to do damage with the dagger—too close for comfort, apparently. While Fitch waited for the right moment to strike, Hardwicke was clearly stalling for time. If he had been tempted even slightly by the bribe, he would have countered with something reasonable. Instead, he had taken Fitch at his word and assumed the army would arrive at any minute to end their impasse.

Once again, she was struck by how little he appeared to comprehend about the situation. Why was he in the cellar if not to stop Fitch from stealing all the funds? But if he knew about the plan to steal the funds, why had he made no attempt to halt the massacre?

It was bewildering.

Putting her confusion aside, she allowed that Hardwicke's plan was a good one. He would be swept up by the soldiers alongside Fitch, but his connection to Grint would secure his immediate release. Fitch would not be so fortunate. Kingsley could argue for innocence, but in light of the peaceful mass meeting, that would be difficult to prove. That he had intentionally misled the Home Office would be uncontestable to Sidmouth.

Having Fitch in custody would give the authorities an opportunity to question him about Miss Copley's whereabouts. If they cared about the murder of Mr. Smith—and that, Verity allowed, was an open question—Fitch would be able to provide vital information.

The only flaw in Hardwicke's plan was the lack of troops. The army was not on its way. She and Kesgrave, however, could remedy that easily enough.

Fitch, in an audacious move that was unlikely to bear the fruit he hoped, reduced his offer to fifteen percent. Hardwicke duly upped his by six, and Verity tugged on the duke's sleeve to regain his attention and explain her idea. As with every other piece of information she had given him that day, he accepted it stoically. He did not protest that the plan was ridiculous or point out that a single person could not be a whole regiment. He merely nodded and agreed to wait for her signal. Then he crept up the stairs to put himself in position to bound down them again.

Reversing course yet again, Fitch announced that he would give Hardwicke a third, reminded him soldiers were on their way, and described the rough treatment he was likely to suffer at their hands. "Sidmouth will not treat you gently just because your father is a marquess. If anything, he will exploit your notoriety and punish you with extra severity to demonstrate what happens when a man with your privileges dares to go against his own kind. He will create a show, putting you on the dock for treason, and it will end at the gibbet. Do not be a fool over a few coins. Take my offer!"

It was, Verity thought, a persuasive argument that would

most likely have produced results if Hardwicke were the man he pretended to be.

Since he was not, he was able to respond smoothly that everything Fitch said was true. "I wish to avoid the noose at all cost, especially because you are right. My father won't save me and might in fact administer the rope himself. That is why I am willing to be sensible. Give me seventy percent, and I will allow you to pass unmolested."

Led to expect a genuinely reasonable offer by the seeming rationality of Hardwicke's reply, Fitch responded with fury, inhaling so sharply Verity could hear air draw into his lungs all the way across the room. "You ninnyhammer! You imbecilic sapskull! No wonder you can't win even the simplest game of dice," he screeched. "You understand nothing! The *British army* will be here *any minute* and you continue to argue. You do not negotiate by going *up*, you fool. You go *down*. You meet me halfway at the very least, you cork-brained clodpole! Did they teach you nothing in those fancy schools you attended?"

Recognizing his rant as an opportunity, Verity climbed the steps to where the staircase curved and she could see Kesgrave. Fitch was frothing with so much anger, he would not notice that he had failed to notice the sound of boots thumping on the floor upstairs. She nodded at the duke, who began to stamp his feet on the heavy wood tread. Verity, too, pounded on the step to make as much clamor as possible.

She did not think they needed to impersonate an *entire* regiment. Just a small contingent of five or six enthusiastic soldiers.

Kesgrave called out in a fair approximation of General Jentleson's pompous authority, "Search everywhere, men! Leave no stone unturned. You, Picket, take the basement with Clarkson. Go! Go! Go!"

It was a lot of noise for what it was—the officious general yelling, the hollowed wood planks splintering, Verity clumping. She tromped down the stairs, the duke at her heels, in time to see Fitch ram into Hardwicke with his left shoulder, knocking the other man to the ground as he swung his knife in a wild arc. It landed in the dirt, narrowly missing Hardwicke's collarbone as he twisted his torso to the left to evade the sharp weapon. Then Hardwicke raised his legs to lever himself into sitting position as he sought to dislodge Fitch, but his attacker threw all his weight forward to immobilize Hardwicke.

He raised the dagger again and sneered, "You will not escape, you traitor."

Then Fitch cast a glance to the stairwell.

It was only a moment, a narrow slice of a second, but it was enough to give Hardwicke the advantage. He swung the crowbar up, the tip of the metal rod thwacking Fitch on the back of his skull, stunning him. Before the dazed man could regain his wits, Hardwicke heaved him to the side and levered his legs again to stand. Fitch was faster, though, rearing up and pouncing, his head down as he flew through the air and landed on Hardwicke's chest. But Hardwicke, already in motion, met Fitch with equal force, shoving his attacker's body forward, so that the other man continued the roll, tumbling off him as soon as he landed. The somersault propelled him across the floor to the table, which he knocked into with so much power, the candle toppled over.

Briefly, in the hairbreadth before the candle reached the floor, Verity could see the fury on his face, the high red color in his cheeks, the murderous glint in his eyes.

And then the pamphlets ignited.

The flames spread from one sheet to another with breathtaking speed until suddenly an entire stack of tracts was burning. The gloomy room blazed with light, fully illuminating the horror of Hardwicke's deadly struggle as Fitch's knife brushed his neck.

"Go," Kesgrave said with a beseeching urgency that belied his otherwise calm demeanor. "I have this under control."

Verity did not know what he meant.

Clearly, he had nothing under control, for he was standing next to her at the bottom of the staircase and the growing conflagration was two feet away at the table.

And *go*—as in leave this room now?

Did he really think she would scurry away to safety while he fought for his life?

Or *go*—as in resolve that mess over there while I handle this mess over here?

The latter.

Obviously, the latter, she thought, raising her gun, pointing the barrel to the ceiling, and pulling the trigger. The shot echoed off the stone walls as debris rained down and Fitch's eyes sought the source of the sound. Hardwicke, his focus unbroken, clasped his fist around Fitch's wrist with so much pressure, the other man was forced to loosen his grip on the weapon. The dagger thudded to the floor, and Hardwicke, rising to his feet, kicked it toward the back corner, where it could not easily be retrieved.

Fitch also stood, his balance somewhat unsteady as he rose to his full height, words of gratitude spilling out of him as he praised the soldiers on their timely arrival. "Thank God! A few minutes later and he would have escaped with all the money. But I have intervened ... to ... save ... to save ... "

The informant trailed off as he beheld the strange scene before him bereft of uniforms and battalions and generals. All he saw was a liveried footman by the staircase holding a flint-lock in his grasp and an elegant gentleman wearing a bottle-green morning coat stamping on cinders in top boots polished to within an inch of their lives.

Following his gaze, Verity noted that the duke had extinguished the flames by heaping dirt onto them from a pair of large buckets. His assessment of the situation was accurate: He had it under control. Then he used the embers to light a trio of rushlights. The smell of burning fat wafted over the scent of scorched paper.

Fitch, grappling to understand, turned to Kesgrave, whose importance could not be doubted, and said, "I ... are you ... well ... I ... am ... allow me to introduce myself. I am Arnold Fitch, a representative of the regent's government. I work with Mark Kingsley in the Home Office. This is a member of the insurrectionist organization that is headquartered here. His name is Hardwicke and he was trying to steal the society's funds, which are forfeit to the crown. I intercepted him in my capacity as a representative for the government and surrender him now to you to be dealt with as the army or, er, you see fit."

"You are wasting your breath," Hardwicke said as he crossed the room to a chair near the back wall. There, he bent down and picked up something.

Cord, Verity noted.

Accessing its condition, he found the length suitable for his purposes and walked back to Fitch. "The man standing with the gun is my associate, Mr. Gorman, and the man by the table is his associate," he explained.

Although Hardwicke spoke confidently, with an air of satisfaction, as if the affair had unfolded according to his plan, the look he sent Verity was befuddled. Apparently, he knew the Duke of Kesgrave well enough to recognize him when he stood before him in a ramshackle cellar having extinguished flames with buckets of muck. Unable to fathom how such an outcome had come about, he was nevertheless amused that it did. He seemed to be holding back a wide grin.

"Neither man reports to the army," he continued, tugging

Fitch's arms behind his back so that he could bind his wrists. "It would seem by all indications that your scheme has failed —to what extent remains to be seen. We will discover those details when we have a chat with Daniel Grint. He is the man in the Home Office with whom I work, and he never trusted you for a second. I have been watching you for weeks."

Unable to believe his clever plot had unraveled at all, let alone so spectacularly, Fitch struggled against the cord, his shoulders flailing. "You must believe me, sir," he said pleadingly, his face red from exertion. "I do not know who you are or how they have managed to convince you that I am the villain. I can tell from your appearance that you are a discerning man of means, and I fear they have misled you in an attempt to gull you out of hundreds of pounds. This man, the one who dares to tie *me* up, he is Lord Colson Hardwicke. You must know the name, for he is a notorious scoundrel. He has gaming debts up to his eyebrows. Do not be fooled by anything he tells you. Talk to Kingsley. Please! He will tell you everything. And Lord Sidmouth! Everything I've done has been with his approval. I *saved* England from an uprising today. If it were not for me, the streets of London would be overrun right now. You must believe that I speak the truth."

Although Verity could not explain to Hardwicke the complicated tangle of events that led to Kesgrave's presence in the basement at Wood Lane, she could at least clarify for the informant some of the misconceptions under which he continued to operate. "It is no use, Fitch. Lord Sidmouth knows everything and has in fact ordered the army to stand down. Your attempt to instigate a massacre so you can steal the society's funds has failed. My colleague"—she gestured to the duke—"and I told him everything. Your plan has failed, and you will be tried for attempting to incite a riot and as an accessory to William Smith's murder."

Hardwicke, who had intuited much of the scheme from

Fitch's own words, displayed surprise at the last revelation. "You mean the actress did it?"

Sputtering in outrage, Fitch addressed the duke again and insisted that he could not be held responsible for the actions of a deranged female. "I had nothing to do with Smith! She acted on her own. I told her I would handle it and I would have! I had a plan to make it appear as though *he* were the informant, then nobody would believe a word he said. It would have been easy. Everyone suspected everyone else! But she said we have to frighten him. And then she killed him and I began to fear for my own life. I was going to tell Kingsley everything. I swear!"

"Oh, I'm sure," Verity said with a cynical twist of her lips. "That way you wouldn't have to pay her the bonus you promised. Speaking of Miss Copley's compensation: How are you to deliver it? Miss Copley has vacated your rooms in Pimlico, so I assume you agreed to meet at another location?"

A calculating look entered Fitch's eyes as he stopped struggling against the restraints. An informant, he knew the value of information and was trying to figure out what the whereabouts of a murderess could be worth to the Home Office.

If that was the tack he had decided to take, he would have very little success, Verity thought. Smith was too poor and too northern to excite the interest of the local authorities. He was also the father-in-law of a known traitor who had been hanged for his crimes. Even if Smith made a compelling victim, Kingsley would be disinclined to negotiate with Fitch, whose lies had led to his humiliation in front of his superior, Lord Sidmouth, and his rival, Grint, as well as the general who had been prepared to attack a mass meeting on his word.

Nevertheless, Fitch announced that he would speak only to Kingsley. "You will not convince me to say another word," he announced, clamping his jaw shut with a dramatic flourish only to open it a moment later to whine about the tightness of the rope. "Can't you loosen them just a little? My fingers are growing numb."

Although Hardwicke ignored his complaint, he agreed to bring Fitch to the Home Office at once. "I am sure Grint is wondering what happened to me. We had an appointment earlier to discuss the mass meeting. But I was restrained here on the urgings of Dircks, who swore I must be the informant because I was the only one among the membership who had ties to Twaddle-Thum. Anderson was not convinced but agreed it was too risky to chance it with Crowley's speech so near. He tied me to a chair and had someone keep watch over me until the last man left at six for the meeting. I had just managed to work myself free of the ropes when I heard footsteps upstairs. I hid in the corner because I did not want to be bound again and was surprised when I saw it was Fitch. When he opened the safe, I drew the obvious conclusion. I did not realize he had told the Home Office that the mass meeting was an uprising."

As all captors could not be as inept as Miss Copley at tying knots, Verity was unsurprised to hear that it had taken him over an hour to free himself. That he had been trussed up and detained for being the spy, however, was vaguely hilarious to her, and she made no effort to smother the smile that rose to her lips. Hardwicke, seeming to bear no resentment, met her amusement with his own.

In perfect accord, they grinned amiably at each other.

The duke said, "As I assume you have no conveyance, you may take my gig. I will escort Mr. Gorman to his home."

If Hardwicke was intensely curious to know the connection between Verity Lark and the Duke of Kesgrave, he did not reveal it by look or deed. "That is very helpful. Thank you."

Kesgrave nodded.

Verity glanced at the worn leather satchel that had been knocked over in the fight and remained buttoned despite the rough treatment. "What should we do with the money? Put it back in the safe?"

"I think that is a reasonable solution," Hardwicke said, picking the bag up by its handles, carrying it to the safe and briskly returning the funds.

Fitch whimpered as he listened to the coins land in the box with a clatter.

He had been so close!

Perhaps discouraged by his failure, Fitch allowed himself to be led to the duke's gig without complaint and he did not protest when Hardwicke used more rope to bind him to the rail behind the seat. Confident that his prisoner would not escape, Hardwicke turned to Kesgrave and thanked him again for the use of his vehicle. "And for convincing Sidmouth to listen to Mr. Gorman. His lordship can be dismissive of people whom he does not perceive to have social or political consequence."

The duke accepted these remarks with a nod as Hardwicke climbed into the gig. Then he settled onto the bench, adjusted his grip on the reins, bid them good-bye, and directed the horse into the street.

Friday, June 5
  7:43 p.m.

Although Verity firmly refused the duke's escort several times in her head, she compliantly boarded the hack and sat down across from him. Being in the enclosed vehicle with him felt even stranger than being in the gig, and she forced herself to keep her gaze inside the carriage because looking out the window felt cowardly.

Oh, but how ardently she wished to look out the window!

The silence was also discomfiting and she thought about what she could say to break it that would not make the situation more excruciating. She could thank him again, yes. Everything he had done that day had smoothed her path, and she was infinitely grateful for his help. That she had not rammed against her own limitations in her efforts to thwart a massacre was entirely due to him—and she acknowledged that.

Indeed, she had acknowledged that several times already, and at some point sincere gratitude crossed into sycophantic toadying. She did not know where the line was but feared she was perilously close to crossing it.

Alternatively, she could compliment him on his deft handling of the fire. She was genuinely impressed with how he had kept a cool head and neatly resolved a problem that could have had devastating consequences. If he had hesitated for even a few seconds, they might have become trapped in the cellar or escaped to watch the entire row of houses burn to the ground.

But she could not bring herself to say the words, imagining how paltry they would sound coming from a courtesan's daughter dressed in a footman's garb. He did not need her approval for anything, and her bestowing it would only make the lack of need starker.

Verity pressed her lips together, stared at a mushroom-shaped stain on the upholstery across from her, and wondered how close they were to Bethel Street. If she just looked out the window, she could gauge the distance....

No, peeking is cheating.

It had become a test of her endurance.

As the hack jerked roughly over a hole in the road,

Kesgrave tilted his head slightly and said, "Are there others?"

Verity did not know what he meant.

Other what?

Avaricious spies who might manipulate information to enrich themselves?

Why, yes, my lord duke, I suspect there are a great many.

Ne'er-do-well second sons who feigned degeneracy to benefit their country?

She rather thought not.

Courtesan daughters who dressed in the garb—

Oh, I see, yes, she thought, comprehension dawning.

That was precisely what he was asking, and understanding the query, she wished for the first time that she could see inside his head. Did he think there were a great many of them? Did he imagine they gathered around the hearth, an assortment of La Reina's unwanted mongrels, all warm and affable, forming a strange and misbegotten fraternity?

And then there was he on the outside.

The lonely boy in his castle.

"I cannot say," Verity replied. "I have never met another. In theory, I suppose, there could be several others."

Kesgrave acknowledged the truth of this statement with a sober nod but did not say anything more, and Verity marveled again at how little he revealed. His face was blank.

It was always blank.

The carriage swayed as it turned to the left, and Verity told herself it did not matter what he thought. He had unstintingly provided his assistance when he should have by rights walked away. It was a remarkable thing. She had never expected to have any contact at all with her mother's son, and then he performed for her an act of incalculable importance and generosity.

Verity Lark, not given to sentiment, would cherish this one interaction with her brother for the rest of her life.

Even so, she held herself stiffly as they arrived in Bethel Street. She alighted from the hack and accepted his escort to the door coolly. There, she thanked him again for his willingness to help. "I know it was not what you expected when you knocked on my door."

The duke smiled faintly, displaying humor for the first time since she had met him, and admitted he had had no idea what to expect when he knocked. "But I am glad I did. It has been edifying, Miss Lark."

He bowed slightly, bringing their association to an end, and Verity went inside.

Friday, June 5
  10:28 p.m.

Delphine was still fussing when Hardwicke arrived.

Not about the knife wound.

Although she had paled when she unwrapped the dressing and saw how very jagged it was, she did not say a word about it.

But the duke!

Appearing suddenly on their doorstep!

It was already inconceivable to her that he would bother to track down a woman who happened to look vaguely like his mother—

"No, not vaguely," Verity interrupted. "Exactly."

Delphine, who had only ever seen La Reina in a print by Rowlandson depicting her among a coterie of gamblers around the Duchess of Devonshire's hazard table in Piccadilly, found this difficult to believe. Verity had an angular jawline, while Lorraine Price's was gently molded. "And she had rounded cheeks."

Verity, who had not paused in the tumult of the day to consider what it meant for her to look *exactly* like her mother (and nor did she do so now), posited that perhaps to her son a few features looked like the whole. "Sixteen years on, his memory of her is probably more than a little hazy."

"That is possible, I suppose," Delphine allowed as the parlor door opened to admit Freddie, who was eager to discuss the duke's call on the *London Daily Gazette* earlier in the day.

"As I said in my note, it is not a reason to panic," he announced, striding across the floor to the table, where Verity had settled for a meal after Delphine finished changing the bandage on her incision. Having eaten kidney pie, she was now enjoying an assortment of biscuits. "I am sure he will not call on Robert Lark directly but send a note requesting information or he will send an emissary. Even so, I think it is best if we establish a strategy for how to deal with his attention now, before it becomes a problem. Verity's Robert is very convincing—I am sure nobody at the newspaper doubts his authenticity—but it is still too close for comfort. I will purport to be him if it comes to that. But I am sure it will not."

"Oh, my, your note!" Delphine said, reaching into her pocket to withdraw the message, which remained sealed. "Lucy handed it to me at the same time she informed me that Verity had been stabbed, so I completely forgot about it."

Freddie gasped, his expression a compelling mix of concern and anger as he turned to look at Verity, who was calmly swallowing a rolled wafer. He opened his mouth, presumably to chastise her for exposing herself to situations involving sharp objects when Delphine forestalled him.

"We are not taking her to task about that now because our dear Verity stopped a massacre at St. Dunston's field by convincing Lord Sidmouth not to send in troops with the help of her brother, the Duke of Kesgrave, and a knife wound seems minor in comparison to her other astonishing accomplishments for the day," Delphine explained. "We *are* chastising her for it tomorrow at whatever time is most convenient for us. I myself have set aside the nine-to-ten-o'clock hour tomorrow morning."

While Verity scoffed at the notion that her friend would require a full sixty minutes to say in summation, "Stay away from pointy things," Freddie gawked in utter bemusement at the notion that Verity *had spent time with her brother.*

Her brother, whom she had spent half her life observing.

"Start at the beginning," he said. "At the very moment Kesgrave arrived at Bethel Street and knocked on the door."

Naturally Verity could not start there because the narrative actually began in Pimlico, with Miss Copley and the wobbly table, for only that specific set of circumstances could have produced the emotional state that allowed her to meet her brother's gaze forthrightly and request his help.

Delphine, hearing the tale for the second time—well, really the third because she made Verity repeat each and every incredible sentence—knew when to applaud and did so at regular intervals, even darting to her feet when Kesgrave extinguished the fire. Although Freddie did not give the duke a standing ovation, he admitted it was an impressive feat and wondered who at the paper should report the story.

"Not Robert. He is too close to Verity and I do not think we want any connection that could possibly be traced back to her," he said thoughtfully. "Banks wrote an article last month on Kingsley using government funds to pay for his carriage repairs, so he has sources inside the Home Office. I wonder if Hardwicke would consent to an interview. We would not mention him by name, of course, only describing him as someone close to the story who has information."

Verity asserted that Hardwicke was unlikely to consent

under any circumstance, and Delphine, her mind turning to business matters, asked what Twaddle-Thum would do now that a connection with the duke had been established. Although Verity took issue with the use of *connection* to describe her association with Kesgrave, she agreed that ceasing to write about his wife was the least she could do to repay him for his very great service. Despite the smooth practicality of her response, her cheeks flushed with an intense mortification for past transgressions, some of which now felt unbearably petty, and she sought to hide her discomfit by asking on whom Twaddle should focus his attentions next.

"What about that provincial turnip who has been standing on his head to get your attention?" Freddie suggested as he took a filbert biscuit from the plate.

"Viscount Ripley," Delphine said.

Verity shook her head, noting that the young lord had changed his position on fame and notoriety in the wake of his grandfather's murder. To bestow Twaddle's attention now would be cruel. She countered with Mrs. Fawcett, whom the Twaddleship knew as the Leaky Fawcett for her ability to make young misses cry, and Delphine allowed that she was a good target. The society matron had become insufferable since her main rival had been forced from society on account of her husband's crimes.

"She is like a voracious sea creature who has no natural enemy to keep her in check, so she keeps growing larger and larger," Delphine observed with a hint of disgust and then lamented the loss of Her Outrageousness. "She was just the right amount of interesting without being waspish. But it is untenable now. I still cannot believe the duke showed up here! Do you think he will come back? I wonder if we should get new curtains? The room could do with a little sprucing up, do you not agree?"

A knock sounded on the door before Verity could respond

in the negative to all three queries, and Lucy announced the arrival of Lord Colson Hardwicke.

"Wonderful," Verity said, rising to her feet. "Admit him at once. Thank you."

Hardwicke entered, his features drawn from weariness, and Verity recalled that he had spent the night tied to a chair in a cellar. She resolved to ascertain only the pertinent facts from his meeting with Grint and Sidmouth and then allow him to retire. She could wait till tomorrow or the next day to pester him for details.

"Miss Drayton," he said, greeting Delphine affably before turning to Freddie, whom he had last seen in the *Gazette*'s office after the editor had evaded a distraught clerk with a gun. Referencing their previous encounter, he noted that the newspaper editor looked well. "I trust you suffered no ill effects from the harrowing experience."

Freddie, who planned to seek Hardwicke's cooperation for a series of newspaper articles, thanked him for his concern and expressed her own. "And you are well, too, my lord? You are unscathed from your tussle with Fitch? No knife wounds like Verity?"

Nodding amiably as he moved to join them at the table, Hardwicke stopped abruptly, turned to Verity, and glared at her with a mixture of anger and concern. Then he bellowed, "*What?*"

Verity felt something flutter in her stomach at his reaction. It was slight, merely a quiver, but worrying nonetheless. She squelched it. "Miss Copley managed to get in a small slice when I went to confront her about the murder. Her years of theater training have stood her in good stead. But it is so minor even Delphine is not making a to-do about it, and she to-doeses about everything."

"Correction," Delphine said firmly. "I am not making a to-do of it *now*. We have an appointment for that tomorrow at nine a.m. You may want to schedule one for yourself, my lord. I can check her diary for you if that is helpful."

Hardwicke thanked her for the offer and promised to keep it in mind. "For now, I will take the fact that Miss Lark is looking so well as proof that the wound is indeed minor."

Verity refused to allow him to distract her with flirtatious nonsense, for that was all it was—a distraction—but Freddie tilted his head sharply and contemplated her with a thoughtful expression. Ignoring her friend's curiosity, she asked Hardwicke to tell them what had happened at the Home Office. "Most importantly, did the Fifth Battalion and the Royal Fusiliers hold their fire or did General Jentleson find a pretext that justified shooting into a crowd of innocent laborers?"

"Not a single shot was fired," Hardwicke replied. "Crowley spoke, the society gathered signatures, and the crowd dispersed by nine o'clock. The entire event was calm and peaceful."

"That is good," Verity said with palpable relief. She had been reasonably confident the mass meeting was precisely as advertised but one could never be certain.

As Hardwicke sat down at the table, Delphine slid the plate of biscuits toward him and he selected one as he continued. "By the time I arrived, Jentleson was chastened by what had almost happened and Kingsley had been removed from his post. Grint took Fitch into custody and has sent Runners to apprehend Miss Copley at the inn where she was to meet him. Sidmouth is grateful to my footman for informing them of Fitch's scheme and urged me to increase his compensation by a shilling a week. He also commends me for securing the Duke of Kesgrave's patronage because without his support, he would never have listened to my footman. He did not ask me *how* I secured the Duke of Kesgrave's patronage, which was a good thing, as I would be at a loss to answer."

The remark was pointed, and Verity, who had known this moment was inevitable, said only that she was surprised by it as well.

"But that is the thing that is notable," Hardwicke said nonchalantly. "I am not surprised at all. That Kesgrave was in the cellar of the Society of Yarwellian Philosophers stamping out a fire in his top boots was the most inconceivable sight I have ever seen and yet the fact that you arranged it by whatever wild contrivance is not at all shocking. You are remarkable, Miss Lark."

Now the flutter was a flurry, for he was looking at her in such a way—admiration mingled with respect doused with affection—and she did not know what to do with the giddiness that swept through her bones.

Squelch that too, Verity thought.

"He used dirt from the buckets under the table," she said, relieved that none of her anxiety could be heard in her voice. "The duke smothered the worst of the fire with dirt."

"Oh, look, all the biscuits are gone," Delphine said, holding up the plate that had been half full only a minute ago. An incriminating trail of crumbs led directly to her lap, and Verity imagined her friend's pockets were stuffed with pastries. "I shall run down to the kitchens to get more. Freddie, you must come with me because you know how difficult I find carrying a plate *and* opening a door. It won't take long, only five minutes."

Slow to comprehend his friend's sudden descent into helplessness, Freddie nevertheless rose to his feet and agreed to accompany her belowstairs.

Delphine thanked him, then reiterated that they would not be gone long. "It will take us only *five minutes* to refresh the biscuit plate."

As the door clicked shut, Verity was roiled by a host of emotions, each at once valid and invalid: amusement at

Delphine's utter lack of subtlety, apprehension at the thought of being alone with Hardwicke, mortification at her agitation, embarrassment for all four of them (or perhaps all six, for Cook and Lucy would be confused by the friends' insistence that *they* fetch the biscuits), a tremulous fear that she had nothing to fear.

Hardwicke, seeming untroubled by an excess of feeling, reached into his pocket and withdrew two gold coins. He placed them on the table in front of her and announced that Grint was determined to pay her for her excellent work. "Do not worry. He has no idea who you are," he added quickly. "He knows enough to realize you are not my footman, but that is all. He has given me these guineas to compensate you for the time and effort you expended on what he calls the Fitch debacle. It is also, I believe, an investment in the future. He wants to demonstrate that the Home Office is a fair employer should he have further need of your services."

As his strange teal eyes were disconcertingly compelling, especially glinting with humor, she looked down at the coins, grateful for the distraction. She slid the pair to the edge of the table, dropped them into her palm, and slipped them into her pocket. She would give the windfall to Fortescue's. "You may thank Grint for me. It is unlikely that I will accept a future offer from him, but I respect the forethought."

Hardwicke laughed and reminded her that she had not accepted *this* offer. "You refused me and then proceeded to do everything I proposed for free."

"Well, you asked me to giggle," she said flatly.

Disconcerted, he drew his brows together. "Excuse me?"

"In seeking my assistance, you asked me to perform a facile task that was an insult to my skills and abilities," she explained. "As it seemed as though you did not in fact need me, I was obliged to refuse."

"Naturally I did not need you," Hardwicke said with blunt

candor. "I have been engaged in spy work for years and am perfectly capable of distracting a young lady, even one who turns out to be a homicidal actress. I *wanted* you. After the resolution of the Grimston affair, I knew there would be no reason to see you again, so I invented one. You are the most fascinating person I have ever met in my life. I want to scheme with you, Verity. I want to scheme with you for hours, and every time I enter my study now, I hope you are there, in the dark, waiting for me."

Verity could not breathe.

Her heart squeezing, her head pounding, she found it impossible to draw air into her lungs and wondered if this was what it felt like to swoon. Would she collapse in a heap like a ragdoll or a schoolgirl?

That thought alone was enough to restore her composure, and she inhaled sharply.

She was not a simpering miss to dissolve at the first hint of ...

Well, that was the problem, was it not? Verity thought.

She did not know *what* Hardwicke was implying—and that lack of understanding *did* make her feel like an insipid henwit. It was facile to say she could not discern his intentions, but the truth was, she could not. Obviously, it was not a carte blanche. As audacious as Hardwicke was, even he would not have the temerity to sit in an unattached woman's front parlor and offer to set her up as his mistress during the brief absence of her companion. If he did think she would be amenable to the arrangement, then he would have the sense and address to make a considered proposal, and knowing her to be practical-minded, he would come prepared with a list of ways the position would benefit her.

But that was the thing, she realized: He was not prepared.

Hardwicke had not intended to say any of those words when he entered the room, which was why his proposal was so slapdash. It had slipped out by mistake, almost like a confession.

Clearly, the only way to handle the awkwardness was to pretend it had not happened, and yet she could not fathom how to do that.

Should she laugh?

Would a self-conscious giggle paper over the awfulness?

A brisk knock sounded at the door and Delphine entered, holding the plate aloft, Freddie trailing after a few feet behind, and Verity stared, unable to comprehend how five minutes could have passed so swiftly. Hardwicke, unperturbed by her lack of response—no doubt relieved by it— smiled easily and rose to take the biscuits from Delphine, who reported Cook's delight in how well her new recipe for rolled wafers had been received.

"It is, in fact, from Mrs. Newsome next door," Delphine continued cheerfully. "It was a swap. She gave her her mother's recipe for suet pudding. Apparently, the secret is using more molasses, not less."

Hardwicke said that his own cook made an excellent suet pudding, but his orange biscuits were a little dry. "I wonder if we can arrange a recipe swap," he said, the eagerness with which he had grasped onto the mundane conversation convincing Verity he had not meant to declare anything.

He was determined to paper over it, too.

That was good, she told herself.

"I am certain our cook would be amenable to an exchange provided your cook proposed something interesting to trade," Delphine replied reassuringly.

Freddie, noting something of Verity's confusion, brushed her on the shoulder to gain her attention and cocked his eyebrow with concern.

She shook her head, either to assure him everything was fine or to clear her head. To be honest, she could not say which. It was just all so baffling—the wild excitement, the dizzying terror, the frantic panic, and now something like disappointment.

And yet she knew it would never work.

Whatever illicit arrangement Hardwicke had in mind, it would have collided headlong into her sense of self. Accepting his proposal would have nullified a lifetime of distancing herself from her mother's choices, and despite the dozen offers she had rejected over twenty years, she would have wound up where she had begun: La Reina's daughter.

The thought repulsed her.

"Since we are arranging things, Miss Drayton," Hardwicke added pleasantly, "I *would* like to schedule a time to harangue Miss Lark about her stab wound."

"Not harangue," Delphine corrected soberly. "Make a to-do."

Intrigued, Hardwicke asked what the difference was.

"It is a matter of tone, conveying apprehension over her well-being rather than disapproval of her recklessness," Delphine explained as she retrieved Verity's diary from the sideboard. "As I mentioned, I have taken the nine-to-ten slot tomorrow. Then we shall give Verity an hour to compose herself after my gentle scolding and put you down for eleven if that is agreeable to you."

"That is ideal, thank you," Hardwicke continued in that same genial tone, which further confounded Verity. Having made the mortifying misstep of declaring ... something, he should devote his energies to spending less time with her, not more. "And I noticed Miss Lark's wrists are scraped. May I also schedule a time to make a to-do about those?"

It was an absurd question, for her wrists bore only minor lacerations from the rope the murderous actress had tied around them, but Delphine thought it was reasonable and suggested the day after tomorrow. "Say, noon?"

"Very good," Hardwicke said, before asking if there were further rules governing the administering of to-dos. "May I convey my apprehension over Miss Lark's well-being during a drive in Hyde Park? Or is that too much like haranguing?"

Delphine smiled brightly and assured him it was permissible.

"Then let's also schedule an appointment for me to make a to-do about the bruise on Miss Lark's cheek," he said.

There was no bruise on her cheek!

Hardwicke was inventing things out of whole cloth now.

Verity's heart tripped when she contemplated the reason why.

"You mentioned Hyde Park," Delphine said in the smooth tones of a clerk checking his bank ledger for a client. "Presumably, you are thinking of the Fashionable Hour? How does Monday work for you? Are you prepared to commit to that or do you need to consult your own diary?"

Hardwicke, his eyes seeking out Verity's across the table, said with unsettling sobriety that he was prepared to commit to anything.

***

VERITY LARK RETURNS WITH ANOTHER ADVENTURE SOON!

In the meantime, look for the
Duchess of Kesgrave's latest investigation:
A Murderous Tryst.
Available for preorder now.

***

About the Author

Lynn Messina is the author of almost two dozen novels, including the Beatrice Hyde-Clare mysteries, a cozy series set in Regency-era England. Her first novel, *Fashionistas,* has been translated into sixteen languages and was briefly slated to be a movie starring Lindsay Lohan. Her essays have appeared in *Self, American Baby* and the *New York Times* Modern Love column, and she has been a regular contributor to the *Times* parenting blog. She lives in New York City with her sons.

Also by Lynn Messina

Verity Lark Mysteries Series

A Lark's Tale

A Lark's Flight

Beatrice Hyde-Clare Mysteries Series

A Brazen Curiosity

A Scandalous Deception

An Infamous Betrayal

A Nefarious Engagement

A Treacherous Performance

A Sinister Establishment

A Boldly Daring Scheme

A Ghastly Spectacle

A Malevolent Connection

An Ominous Explosion

An Extravagant Duplicity

Love Takes Root Series

Miss Fellingham's Rebellion (Prequel)

The Harlow Hoyden

The Other Harlow Girl

The Fellingham Minx

The Bolingbroke Chit

The Impertinent Miss Templeton

Stand Alones

Prejudice and Pride

The Girls' Guide to Dating Zombies

Savvy Girl

Winner Takes All

Little Vampire Women

Never on a Sundae

Troublemaker

Fashionista (Spanish Edition)

Violet Venom's Rules for Life

Henry and the Incredibly Incorrigible, Inconveniently Smart Human

Welcome to the Bea Hive

FUN STUFF FOR BEATRICE HYDE-CLARE FANS

The Bea Tee

Beatrice's favorite three warships not only in the wrong order but also from the wrong time period. (Take that, maritime tradition *and* historical accuracy!)

The Kesgrave Shirt

A tee bearing the Duke of Kesgrave's favorite warships in the order in which they appeared in the Battle of the Nile

Available in mugs too!

See all the options in Lynn's Store.

Printed in Great Britain
by Amazon

38734137R00189